A VAMPIRE POSSESSED

DEATHLESS NIGHT SERIES #3

L.E. WILSON

EVERBLOOD
PUBLISHING

NOTE FROM THE AUTHOR

This book was previously released as "Blood Obsession" with a different cover.

ALSO BY L.E. WILSON

Deathless Night Series (The Vampires)

A Vampire Bewitched

A Vampire's Vengeance

A Vampire Possessed

A Vampire Betrayed

A Vampire's Submission

A Vampire's Choice

Deathless Night-Into the Dark Series (The Vampires)

Night of the Vampire

Secret of the Vampire

Forsworn by the Vampire

The Kincaid Werewolves (The Werewolves)

Lone Wolf's Claim

A Wolf's Honor

The Alpha's Redemption

A Wolf's Promise

A Wolf's Treasure

The Alpha's Surrender

Southern Dragons (Dragon Shifters & Vampires)

Dance for the Dragon

Burn for the Dragon

Snow Ridge Shifters (Novellas)

A Second Chance on Snow Ridge

A Fake Fiancé on Snow Ridge

Copyright © 2015 by Everblood Publishing

All rights reserved. No part of this publication may be reproduced, distributed, or transmitted in any form or by any means, including photocopying, recording, or other electronic or mechanical methods, without the prior written permission of the publisher, except in the case of brief quotations embodied in critical reviews and certain other noncommercial uses permitted by copyright law. For permission requests, email the publisher, addressed "Attention: Permissions Coordinator," at the address below.

All characters and events in this book are fictitious. Any resemblance to actual persons – living or dead – is purely coincidental.

le@lewilsonauthor.com

ISBN: 978-1-945499-42-5

Print Edition

Publication Date: December 26, 2015

Cover Design by Coffee and Characters

DEDICATION

I would like to dedicate this book to my Mom, who introduced me to my love of books and reading at a very young age, starting with such classics as Charlotte's Web and The Little House books.

When I was a teenager, she handed me a book called Ride The Wind, by Lucia St. Clair Robson. That book introduced me to the world of Romance Novels, and being the romantic that I am, I couldn't get enough. I became a regular at a little bookstore near me where you could trade in old paperbacks and get store credit for new ones. Once a week, I would walk out of there with an armful of Historical Romances.

Now, throughout all of this time, I was a huge paranormal junkie. I watched every show on Bigfoot, UFO's, ghosts...you name it. I also discovered Steven King and Anne Rice. So, imagine how psyched I was when I found...you guessed it...PARANORMAL ROMANCES.

So, thank you, Mom. I couldn't imagine my life without books, and now, I write them! And I've never been happier.

1

Aiden awoke with a jerk and tried to suck in a breath. Fine grain filled his mouth and nose, suffocating him. More came in as he tried to spit it back out, and he panicked. His heart rate rose to a violent staccato as he tried to raise his hands to his face to wipe it off, only to find he couldn't move at all.

What the fuck?

Adrenaline flowed through his tired limbs, flooding them with a sudden spurt of energy. He tried to swing his arms and legs back and forth, but it was so thick it was like pushing against a wall. Determined to find his way out of this wonky situation, he kept wiggling his body around, until little by little, the grain loosened a bit around him.

More adrenaline surged into his muscles with every inch he gained, and a desperate longing to be free stimulated his exceptional strength until he was able to swim through the stuff.

It was kind of like swimming through a mass of thick quicksand, but he kept going, hoping like hell that "up" was actually above his head and he wasn't working his way deeper into the stuff. He needed air. And he needed it now.

The rough granules stuck to his sweat-soaked clothes and skin, but those that didn't stick trickled down the pile every time he raised an arm or a leg, gradually adding up enough so he had some purchase.

It was an exceptionally slow and painful process, but after what seemed like an eternity, he managed to haul himself to the top. As soon as his nose and mouth broke free, he spit the crap out of his mouth the best he could and sucked in a huge lungful of hot, stale tasting air.

Exhausted, he hung out where he was for a bit while he inhaled some much-appreciated oxygen. He didn't really need it to survive, but the habit was so ingrained, he couldn't help but freak out if he didn't have it.

Gathering up some more energy, he pushed with his legs until his entire head was free. He worked an arm out and wiped the grit off his face. Blinking it out of his eyes, he took a look around.

"Bloody hell," he rasped from his dry, aching throat.

He was lucky he'd stopped "swimming" when he had, or he would've smashed his head into the top of the damn metal shipping container he was in.

How in the world had he managed to get in here? And for that matter, where exactly was "here"?

Following the line of the container around to the front, he found a crack where the door must be, and he started kicking and paddling through the grain towards it. He had just enough room to keep his head above the top of the pile.

Keeping a wary distance from the opening until he saw that no sunlight was shining in, he moved closer and stuck his eyeball right up against it. Straining to make out something...anything...that would give him a clue as to where he was, he turned his head this way and that. But all he saw were more shipping containers.

So he was either in a shipyard, or on a ship, and being that he wasn't feeling any movin' or groovin' going on, he would hazard a guess that he wasn't in the middle of the ocean.

Now, how to get out of this bloody thing? There wasn't enough room for him to get a decent amount of momentum going to bust his way out, not fighting through the grain that filled this thing, and not in the weakened state he was in.

Maybe he could find the latch for the door? Bust it open? But at the thought of voluntarily burying himself again to get down to it made him shudder.

Right then. Perhaps not.

He was racking his brain for an alternative plan when he heard the beautiful sound of male voices heading his way. Tilting his head to hear better, he calmed his breathing and listened, trying to make out what they were saying.

After a moment he frowned, pulled back from the door and shook his head. He must have grain in his ears, for he was having a hard time understanding them, even with his supernatural hearing.

Working his way closer to the door again, he pressed his ear right up against it.

He stared at the door in disbelief. Was that...Chinese?

He *was* going daft.

His heart rate accelerated back up to double-time as he pressed his eye back up to the crack: Nothing there but other shipping containers no matter how he strained to see around them.

Okay, mate. Just stay calm. No need to make things worse by having a fit.

He backed away from the door as well as he could and tried to think through this new information logically. Truly, he could be back in Seattle for all he knew. There was a large Chinese population there, and they spoke their native tongue with each other all the time. It didn't mean anything that these humans weren't speaking English. There was no need to get all riled up just yet.

No matter how his instincts were telling him to do exactly that.

The voices of the two males wandered closer, still talking. Aiden leaned in towards the crack again, and this time he could see them as they approached.

In all of his years, why had he never bothered to really learn this language? All he could pick out was a word here and there.

One of them swung his arm up as his voice rose with it, apparently to make an important point in the conversation. His scent wafted through the air and up to the small opening to infuse the air within the container.

The scent of sweat, and spices...and blood.

His gums burned as his fangs burst through, his body eager to feed. His guts felt shriveled and loose, and his stomach nearly about to cave in on itself.

A feral growl rumbled from his parched throat, and his body tensed, preparing to strike.

Crazed with thirst, he snapped into predator mode. Sweat stinging his eyes, they zeroed in on the door as the humans approached it.

A clanking noise resonated loudly throughout the metal container, followed by a low humming sound. The box jerked as the hydraulics underneath it came on, slowly lifting the back end and tilting it forward.

His mouth watered and his throat burned with thirst as his muscles swelled and tightened in preparation for the hunt. The grain started to shift forward as the back end inclined, carrying him with it. He let it take him, not wasting his energy fighting the heavy mass, saving what he had left for taking down his prey.

He needed to feed.

The grain engulfed him completely again just as the doors began to swing open, concealing his presence from the humans. Closing his eyes, he pushed away the fear of being buried again, opening his remaining senses and moving within the grain to keep his body upright. The back end tilted up higher, and he slid out through the opening as the doors swung open wide.

Landing in a graceful crouch on the concrete beneath a waterfall of grain, he wasted no time, launching himself to the side and barely escaping the gritty cascade of granules as it was dumped out of the container.

Following the scent of the humans, he tracked them to the back of the shipping container, where they were waiting for the last of the grain to spill out so they could switch off the lift.

They never even saw him coming. He moved so swiftly and silently, he was nothing but a dark blur in the deepening twilight.

He grabbed one of the humans around the throat. Holding him at arms length with ease, he pulled the other one towards him and sank his fangs deep into his throat, directly into the artery. Sucking down deep swallows of the life-giving liquid, he quickly drained the first male dry and tossed him aside.

The other human's eyes bulged from their sockets as he turned to him, the stench of fear and piss souring his scent right before he became the second course. The man's body quickly joined his friend's on the ground.

As soon as he finished feeding, his knees buckled and he collapsed beside them, his ass hitting the asphalt hard enough to jar his teeth. He gripped his head in his hands as he fought down the guilt that wracked him.

Fuck. Fuck. Fuck.

He hated killing them. He really did. It went completely against his nature. He never killed the innocent. Ever.

He wasn't a bloody monster.

Taking a deep, shuddering breath, he slowly lifted his head, and resigned himself to the fact that he didn't see how it could have been avoided. Although he couldn't remember how he'd gotten to this place, or how long he'd been here, it was obvious he hadn't fed in quite a long time. Really no sense in beating himself up about it.

He stared down at himself. Looked like he hadn't changed his clothes for a while either, for that matter. Of course it was hard to tell with the coating of dust that now covered him.

He slapped at his jeans and removed his hoodie to shake it out, trying to dislodge some of the stuff.

The last thing he remembered was Leeha, the sneaky tart, filling him in on her latest hijinks. She had told him she was sorry, and her blood red eyes had filled with tears.

His hoodie dropped to his lap as the memories came flooding back.

She'd told him about the altar, and the demons that were tied to it, and how she was giving them bodies to possess. Vampire bodies. Vampires who'd been created by Luukas, the same Master vampire who'd created him, because the vamps *she* made weren't strong enough to handle the possession. That in spite of all of her efforts, her creatures were slowly rotting, turning into smelly, grotesque, grey monsters that resembled the demons that possessed them more than the vampires they'd used to be. They only lasted long enough for them to be used for the easier tasks, like guarding her lair and kidnapping unsuspecting witches.

She'd seemed sincerely sorry that he was about to be the next one on that altar.

He looked down at himself in confusion.

But I'm not possessed. I'm still here.

Was he?

Yes! Of course he was! He was looking at himself at this very moment.

Maybe she hadn't been able to go through with it.

As he rolled that thought over in his mind, wondering if it could possibly be true, something within him seemed to sigh sadly.

He stilled, listening, but that strange feeling didn't return again. With a self-conscious chuckle, he gave himself an internal shake and scrubbed his face with his hands.

Get it together, mate.

His hands came away bloody. Scowling at the memories and his unusual lack of decorum during his feeding frenzy (he wasn't normally quite so messy about it), he leaned forward and wiped his hands clean on one of the humans' pant legs, then ripped off a piece to wipe off his face.

Well, he could at least give them a decent burial, and then he'd get back to the business of figuring out where the bloody hell he was. He needed to find a phone at least, and call Nikulas. His best friend was probably worried sick. He should be able to pinpoint the location of the call and come and get him.

Also, a shower and some new clothes would be nice.

2

Grace Moss dropped down behind a parked car before she was seen, ignoring the beep from a passing bus because she was in its lane. Duck walking awkwardly around to the back of it, she peered around the bumper and watched as the three men she'd been following walked up to the entrance of a tall, industrial looking building.

The last one to enter paused briefly on the threshold and took a quick look behind him. He had a small, black duffle bag slung over his shoulder.

She barely stopped herself from squealing with happiness when she spotted it. Until now, she hadn't been able to risk getting close enough to them in the darkness to be able to see if they still had it.

As if he could sense her watching, he frowned suspiciously and gripped the bag tighter to his side. But after another quick scan of the empty street, he turned and followed his friends inside.

Taking off as fast as she could go in her favorite strappy sandals with the wedge heels, she ran to the door and stuck her arm inside right before it closed and locked.

She winced as the heavy steel smashed against her forearm, and stuck her sandaled foot in to share some of the burden. Dammit, that was gonna leave one hell of a bruise.

If she were any kind of a witch worth her salt at all, she'd be able to open that heavy door with nothing but a thought. But unfortunately, she was pretty damn useless as far as witches went. Even her family thought so. Why else would her parents have risked death to bring her here when the new High Priest had taken over? Other than to hide their worthless daughter where no one would find her?

Only she and her mother had made it out. Her father had died the day they'd escaped the coven.

She stayed as she was for a few heartbeats, wanting to be sure no one had noticed that the door hadn't slammed shut. When she didn't hear any alarms being raised, she used her other hand to pry it open just wide enough for her stick her head through and peek inside.

Leaning forward one cautious inch at a time, she squinted into the gloom, then pulled her head out again with a frown. It was pitch black in there. She couldn't see a damn thing. Why the hell didn't she carry a flashlight with her? Just in case?

Oh, wait! She did have a flashlight. On her phone! If she could just get it out of her back pocket...

"Whom are we spying on, poppet?"

The low, masculine voice came from directly next to her right ear. With a surprised screech, she leapt back away from the doorway, colliding solidly against a hard, male body.

She froze at the impact, momentarily shocked at the body heat that now warmed her from her shoulders to her ass. Helplessly she watched as the steel door in front of her slammed shut in with a loud "clunk", effectively locking her out.

Her heart resumed pounding again at the sight, hard and heavy at first, then gradually slowing to its normal rhythm. She shook her fist at the door. "Dammit to hell!"

With a frustrated sigh, she suddenly realized the tall dude behind her was, at this very moment, noisily smelling her hair.

Spinning around to give him a piece of her mind, she was caught off guard for the second time when she found herself eye to eye with a dusty T-shirt that had the saying "I <3 Girls In Wellies" sprawled across the front in bold, blue letters.

Wellies? What the hell were wellies?

Refocusing...again...she craned her head back to let him know exactly how *not* amused she was by his sneaking up on her like that. But as she caught her first up close and personal look at her interloper, the angry words got stuck somewhere in the middle of her throat. And to make matters even more awkward, her mouth hung open for a good five seconds before he reached out and closed it with a gentle finger under her jaw.

Whatever she'd been about to say had gone up in smoke, and she found herself blinking stupidly at the pair of luminescent grey eyes smiling down into hers.

Framed by long, dark lashes, with little creases at the corners, they glimmered from the shadow of his hoodie like beacons of light in the darkness.

Backing up a step, she boldly ran her eyes over all six feet or so of him. Living where she did, it was rare to see a man taller than she was. It was rarer still to see one of his ethnicity (meaning anyone that wasn't Asian) that wasn't a total computer nerd. And this one was most definitely not a computer nerd. He looked more like a model.

She squeezed her eyes shut to make sure she wasn't having some kind of psychological breakdown, but he was still there when she opened them, looking all hot and yummy in his form-fitting jeans, combat boots, and grey hoodie. Having been up close and personal with him, she already knew those dusty clothes covered nothing but lean muscle underneath. His nose was straight, his cheekbones were high, and he had a slight dimple in his chin.

"Who the hell are you?" she blurted out in English.

He smiled, revealing straight, white teeth and small lines that crinkled around his eyes and created attractive crevices in his cheeks. "So sorry, love," he said in a charming British accent. "That was rude of me. I should have introduced myself before scaring the bejesus out of you." He stuck out his hand. "My name is Aiden. Aiden Sinclair."

She stared at his large hand a moment before taking it tentatively with her own.

"Grace."

Instead of shaking her hand, he flipped it over and lifted it to his mouth to press a soft, firm kiss on the middle of her palm with his perfectly sculpted lips.

Her mouth dropped open in surprise for the second time as warm tingles shot up her arm and straight down to her groin at the feel of his lips on her skin, where they morphed into fluttering butterflies.

She tamped those suckers down with sheer force of will, unwilling to let him see how much he affected her. Instead, she raised a skeptical eyebrow at his blatant attempt at flirting. "Really, dude?"

His beautiful eyes narrowed at her knowingly, one side of his mouth curving up into a half smile, but he released her hand.

"So!" He clapped his hands together, rubbing them together in anticipation. "Now that we've been properly introduced, tell me, who are we spying on?"

Her irritation with him returned. "I wasn't spying on anyone."

He quirked an eyebrow.

"Well, not really. I wasn't spying, I was following. Those dudes in there took my Mojo, and I need it back. I was about to sneak in there and get it, before you so rudely scared the hell out of me, causing me to jump back in fright, dislodging my arm and foot from the opening. So now that very large, very thick, very heavy door has closed, and it's locked and I can't get in."

Aiden cocked his head and stuck his hands in the pockets of his hoodie. "Your mojo?"

"Yeah. My Mojo."

He eyed her up and down as boldly as she had him. "You do realize, poppet, that if you're going to be sneaking around and following people, you should really make yourself less conspicuous. And wear stealthier shoes."

She looked down at her jeans and moss green pullover shirt. "What do you mean? I'm dressed like most of the girls do around here."

"That may be." He reached out and picked up a lock of her long, wind-blown mahogany hair, skimming his fingers lightly along the top of her breast as he did so. "But this hair is quite beautiful, and quite distinctive. You should cover it if you're going to be out and about 'not' spying on people."

Grace's pulse raced at his too-brief touch, and she frowned. She never reacted to men like this. Not even disgustingly gorgeous ones. Jerking her head back, she pulled her hair out of his grasp.

"Also," he continued, putting his hand back in his pocket. "You're quite taller, and paler, than most females around here, so you do stand out a bit."

She crossed her arms in front of her chest self-consciously. It was true. Although she was only 5'5", she was a good few inches taller or more than the majority of the women here.

Pushing his hood back, revealing short, messy dark hair, he scratched his head in confusion as he looked around. "By the way, would you be so kind as to tell me exactly *where* we are, poppet?"

It took her a moment to catch up to his change of topic. "You don't know where you are?"

"Not exactly, no. But let me back up. I realize I'm in China; I'm not completely daft. I'm just not certain of the exact location."

She scrunched up her face at him. "How does a person not know where they are? I mean, you know *who* you are, so you don't have amnesia or anything. And you got yourself here, didn't you?"

"Yes, you see, about that...I, uh..." He shrugged and let out a breath, as if to say *what the hell*. "I just kind of woke up here, over by the docks there. And the events leading up to my arrival here are a bit...hazy. And by that I mean I don't remember anything at all."

Grace studied his expression. He sounded sincere, and he certainly was good looking, but there was something about him...something that wasn't quite...right. Something weird. Something that was making her instincts fire off caution signals all over the place. She should lose this guy, and the sooner the better.

Except, he really *was* panty dropping hot. And that was something a girl didn't come across very often in real life.

"Were you drunk?" she asked, her tone conveying her disgust with that type of behavior.

"No. No. I never over imbibe with alcohol."

"Do you remember anything of your life at all? Up until now I mean?"

He gave her a roguish grin. "Oh yes. Quite well."

She wasn't even going to ask what *that* grin was all about.

"It's just the last...um, what day is it?"

"It's Tuesday."

He looked thoughtful for a moment. "Tuesday...of what month?"

"June."

A slightly panicked look crossed his face, but it was gone so fast she wondered if she'd only imagined it.

"Look," she told him. "Do you want to use my phone? Maybe call someone who can come and get you?"

He gave her a hurt look, slapping his chest with the palm of one hand over the vicinity of his heart. A small dust cloud poofed off of his shirt and floated away. "Are you trying to be rid of me already, poppet? And here I thought we were well on our way to becoming fast friends, you and I."

"Yeah, look dude..."

"Besides, you still haven't told me where I am. And what about your mojo?"

She faltered, crossing her arms in front of her and thinking quickly. He had a point there. It *would* be helpful having another person with her. There were three Suits in there that she knew of. He would help even the odds.

"Trust me," he added, dropping his eyes to her chest, pushed up as it was by her arms. "I think I'm just the male to help you get that mojo back."

She tilted her head to the side and returned his look with an *Are you kidding me?* one of her own.

Dropping her arms back down to her sides, she sighed. "Look, dude, do you want to use my phone or not?"

He tore his gaze from her chest with a regretful sigh and smiled. "Yes. That would be helpful. Thank you."

Pulling it out of her back pocket, she handed him her cell. "Take as much time as you need, I have unlimited everything. Oh, and international calling."

She watched him punch in a number from memory (who remembers phone numbers these days?), and the thought crossed her mind that she should probably give him some privacy. But then again, if he was worried about her listening in, he gave no indication of it. And she didn't want him taking off with her phone.

Glancing up at him from under her lashes, she caught him watching her intently. She'd never found herself under such intense scrutiny from a guy before, and she didn't like it. It made her uncomfortable. Glaring at him irritably, she crossed her arms in front of her, only to drop them again when his eyes immediately fell to her cleavage.

She rolled her eyes. Men.

He just grinned.

"Nikulas? Yes, yes, it's me. Would you be so kind as to send a plane to..." He looked at her pointedly.

"Dalian, China," she told him automatically.

His mouth went slack and his brows lifted in surprise. "Dalian. China, yes." He tilted the phone away and looked around at the buildings as excited shouting sounded from the other end of the line.

"Dalian. Really?" he asked her. "It's changed a bit since the last time I was here."

He put the phone back to his mouth. "Yes, I seem to be fine." He paused again. "I have no idea, mate. It's a bit of a mystery to me as well. I woke up in a container full of grain. I'm still shaking it out of my trousers. I'm quite chafed. This stuff is worse than sand." He scowled off into the distance. "Don't laugh, you Estonian bastard."

Grace's lips quirked as she fought back a giggle and failed.

His eyes came back to her as if drawn there by some invisible force. They roved over her smiling features, burning brighter with every second, and then he smiled back at her. "Actually, mate, if you would hold off on that plane a bit. I'll call you when I'm ready to come home. Just ring this number if you need me. The lady who'll answer is Grace."

The smile fell from her face.

What?

"I'll be fine, mate. Yes, I'm sure. I just need to help her out with something. All right. I'll talk to you soon." He clicked off the call and handed her cell back to her.

"Thank you, love."

She automatically reached out to take the phone from him and shoved it back into her jeans pocket.

"Why did you tell him to wait? And what makes you think you're going to be anywhere near my phone, or me for that matter, if your friend decides to call?"

He gave her a roguish grin, and took a step closer. "Because, poppet, I've decided to stay here for a bit and help you get your mojo back."

She opened her mouth to let him know that she could handle things just fine on her own, remembered the locked door and three Suits inside, and snapped it shut again. He hadn't done anything threatening towards her so far, and he certainly appeared to be in good shape. She wondered if he could fight.

"Do you think you can get this door open?"

His grin widened. "Quite!"

The butterflies fluttered as she stepped out of his way. This was either the best or worst idea she'd ever had, but she wasn't so stupid that she would turn down help getting her Mojo back.

Especially when that help was looking at her with sparkling grey eyes, and smelled like the clean outdoors, in spite of the dust covering him.

3

Nikulas Kreek hung up the newly installed phone in his brother's kitchen and set the cordless handset back in its cradle. Unable to contain his excitement, he flashed over to the office where he found his brother gazing out the floor-to-ceiling window at the pre-dawn Seattle skyline. A line of concern briefly crossed his brow to find him there.

It was never a good sign when he got too lost in his head like this.

Ever since they'd rescued him from Leeha's little shop of horrors where he'd spent the past seven years being starved of blood and beaten to within an inch of his immortal life, he'd been struggling to readjust back to his life as Master vampire of their colony. There were still many days when he would fluctuate between sane and not-so-sane, sometimes so badly at times that Keira, his mate, would be the only one who could bring him back to them. Anyone else who had the balls to get near him at those times would be taking their life into their own hands. Only his mate was safe when he was like that, for his instincts wouldn't allow him to hurt her.

He really hoped this wasn't one of those times, because Keira was currently on a coffee run with her sister, Emma.

Hoping for the best, he called out casually, "Hey, bro!"

Nik worried for a moment that he wasn't going to get a response. But then his older brother clasped his hands behind his back and turned to him, a haunted shadow passing over his face before he schooled his features and raised his brows in silent question.

Nik let out a breath of relief and stepped into the room. "Aiden just called." He grinned thinking of his best friend. "I knew he'd manage to get himself away from that bitch, Leeha. He always does. And get this. He's in fucking China."

"China? How did he end up there?" Luukas asked as he strolled back over to his desk and took a seat behind it.

"Don't know. Says he woke up there, and has no recollection of how he got there. And, he said he woke up in a shipping container full of grain."

Luukas nodded. "Makes sense. The grain would protect him from any sunlight that managed to make its way inside." His expression became thoughtful. "We ship grain from Seattle to Dalian, but if he'd made it back to Seattle, why in the world would he send himself off to China?"

Nik shrugged. "Who the fuck knows with Aiden?"

The front door opened, and Keira and her sister Emma, Nik's mate, came giggling into the apartment, each with a cup of fancy coffee in hand.

Although they had the same hazel eyes, that was pretty much where the resemblance between them ended. Whereas Keira was small and curvy with long, dark hair, Emma was slightly taller and more athletically slim, her shoulder length, strawberry-blonde, wavy tresses enabling Nik to spot her a mile away.

Emma gave him a dazzling smile when she spotted them. "Look! We made lattes!" she told him, holding up her cup.

"You're gonna be awake all day now," he scolded her teasingly. "Instead of in bed where you should be, keeping me warm." A glance at the clock behind her had him scowling. "The coffee shop isn't even open yet." He narrowed his eyes. "How exactly did you manage to get those lattes?"

Her smile faltered a bit. "Um, well, Keira thought I should work on my lock spell...to open locks..."

"But don't worry!" Keira broke in. "We're going to go back later this morning and pay for them."

Luukas stood up so fast his chair went toppling over onto the floor. The air turned icy cold as he strode out of the office towards the girls.

Nik watched in amazement as Keira just smiled at him sweetly, love and protectiveness shining from her eyes. His brother's behavior didn't faze her anymore.

Not that it ever had, from what he'd heard.

"NO," Luukas told her forcefully. "You cannot go back out. It's nearly dawn. If something happened..." His breath hitched and he struggled to continue. "If something happened...I wouldn't be able to get to you."

She closed the distance between them, allowing him to wrap her tightly in his arms. His relief to have her against him, where she was safe, was so obvious it was nearly palpable.

"It's ok, don't freak, we left money on the counter. I'm not going anywhere," she reassured him. "We just like to rile up Nikulas."

Nik struck a casual pose, his hands low on his jean-clad hips. "I'm not riled."

Emma scoffed at him. "This from the male who tried to turn himself into a bonfire when I went outside for just a teeny minute."

"And got kidnapped by werewolves in the middle of the day," he added. "Who then sent you right into the arms of Leeha's wannabe zombie vamps, who were *attacking you* when I finally got there." He paled just thinking about it.

She waved her hand in the air, blowing off those minor details. "The wolves didn't know those things were there. They were just playing a joke on you."

"Yeah, so not funny."

"But I'm fine."

He narrowed his eyes at her, but there was really no sense in arguing, when they could be doing things that were so much more fun.

"Come on, woman," he growled at her. "Let's go back to our place, so I can punish you for scaring me like that. And if you're nice to me, I might tell you who just called here." He took her gently by the arm and started heading towards the door. "See you tonight, Luuk. 'Night, Keira."

Emma waved at her sister and brother-in-law happily as he smacked the minx on her hot little ass to get her out the door and into his bed where she belonged.

4

Aiden rubbed his palms on his dusty thighs and approached the door. If this stunning female with the beautiful breasts thought her mojo was in there, then by God, he was going to get them inside and help her find it.

It was the least he could do. She *had* let him use her phone, after all.

Not wanting to give himself away too soon and frighten her off, he gripped the handle tightly and pulled, making the appropriate grunts and faces that a human male would make when straining muscles.

Of course, he wasn't a human male anymore, but he'd been around long enough to fake it pretty well when the occasion warranted.

The metal lock soon began to bend, and with a quick, imperceptible yank, he broke it completely. Pulling the door open wide, he bowed low and grandly gestured for her to precede him inside. Eyeing up her dainty feet in her cute little sandals, he waited for them to move towards the door.

They didn't.

Running his eyes up her shapely legs, over her flared hips, and past those lovely breasts to her lightly freckled face, he raised his eyebrow in question.

Forest green eyes were widened in shock, and her mouth was hanging open again.

"How did you do that?" she asked incredulously.

He straightened up to his full height. Hmmm. Perhaps he could've faked it a mite better. He'd have to distract her with nonsense.

"Are we going in?" he huffed impatiently. "Or did I exert all of that effort for nothing?" Holding the door open with one booted foot, he grasped his opposite shoulder with one hand while he swung his arm in a wide arc. "I think I may have pulled something."

She hesitated a moment, like she wanted to say more, then finally shrugged it off and marched into the building ahead of him.

Aiden let the door slam shut loudly behind them and promptly ran into Grace. She...in her female wisdom...had stopped short just over the threshold. Her heart was pounding loudly, but when no one came running, it slowed back to its normal speed.

When the faint scent of her fear wafted to him, souring her natural yumminess a bit, he took it upon himself to lighten the mood.

"I know it's all dark and romantic and you really want to snog me right now," he whispered loudly, grinning when her spine straightened with indignation. "But it's really going to have to wait, poppet. Your mojo is waiting to be rescued, after all, and I'm certain we can find a more comfortable location to do that than here." The building smelled as new as it looked, and was void of any furniture or decor.

She didn't react to his teasing, at least not that anyone would notice. But his vampire hearing picked up on her accelerated breathing easily, and his nose picked up on a completely new and enticing scent. He barely stopped himself from moaning aloud as his body immediately responded to her siren's call.

Ah, so she wasn't unaffected by the idea he'd suggested.

Interesting.

He took advantage of the moment to look his fill at her flawlessly rounded arse. The tight jeans she was wearing left very little to the imagination, and his cock stirred in anticipation. He held his hands out in front of him, bare inches from her voluptuous behind.

Yes. She would fit perfectly in his palms.

His blood began to burn with a hunger that was quite different than the one he'd woken up with.

"It's too dark. I can't see anything," she snapped, rudely disturbing his daydream.

"Funny. I can see plenty," he whispered back, his eyes never leaving her luscious curves.

She stiffened at his husky tone but otherwise ignored it, and pulled out her cell phone.

Calling for help?

Ah, poppet. No one can help you now. It's much too late for that.

She peeked back over her shoulder. "My cell battery must be dead. Do you have a flashlight or something?"

With a regretful sigh, he released her lovely backside from his hungry gaze, stepped up alongside her, and took her hand. "Come on, love. I've got brilliant night vision. Just hang on to me."

Lacing her fingers through his, she gripped his upper arm with her other hand and cautiously walked forward with him.

He smirked when he felt her subtly feeling his bicep, and flexed it just a bit for her. His grin widened when he heard her sharp intake of breath, and she dropped his hand. He could practically feel her embarrassment at getting caught feeling him up.

He decided to let her off the hook. "So, where exactly are we going?" he asked quietly.

"I'm not sure, but those three dudes brought my Mojo in here, and I need it back."

Aiden stumbled at her casually spoken words, but quickly regained his footing.

"I thought you said you could see," she accused.

"I can," he insisted. He wasn't going to ask, he wasn't. It wasn't any of his business.

"You gave your mojo to three males? *Three*? At the same time?"

"I didn't *give* them my Mojo. They took it."

Aiden pulled up short at her confession. "They *took* it?" he grated out, an unexplainable rage filling him.

"Shhh!" she scolded. "I think I hear something."

He couldn't hear anything but for the loud, angry buzzing in his head that had appeared directly after her startling confession. Forcing himself to calm down and concentrate, he realized she was right. He could hear male voices coming from another hallway to the left. He started walking again, dragging her along with him as he single-mindedly headed for the males who had dared to violate his Grace.

When they got to the turn, a dim light swung on an old chain, illuminating the way. Sort of. Aiden stopped and turned to Grace to tell her to stay where she was and wait for him to check things out, but she released his hand.

Her sandals flapped noisily as she marched purposefully past him and directly towards the voices.

Catching up to her in two easy strides, he put a hand on her shoulder and spun her around. "What the bloody hell are you doing, woman? You can't just barge in there by yourself!"

She shrugged him off and started walking again, faster this time.

"Grace!" he hissed.

"It's ok," she whispered loudly over her shoulder. "I know Tae-bo."

The female had completely lost her wits.

It was really the only reasonable explanation.

He followed closely behind her, letting her take the lead against his better judgment, rather curious as to what she was going to do next.

Striding confidently into the room, she called out, "Where is Mojo?"

When no one immediately answered her, she repeated the question in Mandarin.

Aiden rounded the corner of the doorway to find she had stopped just inside the room. Hands on her hips, she fearlessly faced down the three human males she must have followed here. He nearly laughed aloud at the shocked expressions on their faces. They appeared to think she was as daft as he did.

Their eyes widened even more when he stepped up behind her. He didn't say anything, but stood quietly backing her up. He took advantage of their momentary lack of motor skills to scan the room, automatically checking for exits.

The humans sat facing the door at the head of a large conference table. No other furniture or decor adorned the place as far as he could see. Two windows were boarded shut behind them from the outside. They were the only other way out besides the way they had came in.

"Well?" Grace threw her arms up impatiently. "Where is he?"

He? Mojo was a he?

"Where's...the...bag?" she continued, speaking slowly and clearly. When no one answered, she heaved a great sigh and stomped farther into the room, bending over periodically to look under the table. She started yanking the empty chairs out one by one, checking the seats.

"Dammit. Where is he?" she mumbled to herself. "I know he's in that bag. He has to be."

Aiden let her go, watching with amusement as the humans looked back and forth between each other while she searched the room, unsure of what to do about it.

Finally, she turned back to Aiden. "It's not here," she told him despondently.

He crossed his arms over his chest, keeping an eye on the humans. "What's not here, poppet?"

She gave him an exasperated look. "The bag! Have you not been listening to anything I've told you? They have my Mojo! He's in the bag they brought in here."

Aiden took another quick look around the room until he saw what she was looking for sitting on a built-in shelf. "You mean that bag over there? The one breathing on its own?"

Grace's head whipped around to where he pointed, sidestepping until she was in front of him until she could see where he was pointing.

A black leather shoulder bag sat there, and it seemed to be filled with something other than money by the way it was scooching its way towards the edge all by itself.

"Mojo!" she squealed happily.

She'd barely taken a step in that direction when one of the humans jumped up and grabbed it off of the shelf, shouting something at her in Mandarin Chinese. She shouted back in the same language, ran up to him, and tried to yank the bag from his arms.

The other two males sprang into action then, rushing over to assist their friend. One grabbed onto the bag while the other one pulled at Grace's wrists and tried to force her to release her grip.

Aiden snarled at the sight of the human's hands on her, revealing his fangs. He was about to give her a hand by knocking the male through the wall behind him when a strange, tingling feeling ran up his spine and flooded his limbs. An unusual awareness rose up inside of him, unlike anything his normal heightened vampire senses had felt before.

It was almost as if the feelings didn't belong to him at all, but were someone else's emotions filling his body.

An ominous growl rose up from somewhere within his depths. The men in suits froze as it shook the walls, like rabbits hoping the predator wouldn't see them if they were very, very still.

Grace, however, obviously lacked that self-protective instinct. Instead of cowering in fear, she took full advantage of their shock. With a shout of triumph, she pried the bag away and held her prize up in the air.

Before Aiden had time to ponder where *that* particular sound had come from, the hair rose eerily on the back of his neck.

Someone, or something, was behind him. Distracted as he'd been by all the strange feelings and the growling and such, he hadn't even heard them approaching.

Slowly, he turned around, and found himself face to face with five of his creator's former vampires. The males had all been part of the group that had left Luukas' colony to follow Leeha when she'd been banned from the area. They'd gone north to create their own group of miscreants somewhere in the wilderness of Canada, and they hadn't thought much about them until she'd decided to kidnap and torture Luukas.

Leeha, a female vampire adopted into the colony and illegally changed, had somehow gotten it into her pretty head that she would rule beside the Master vampire when she was old enough. An idea that Luukas had quickly put an end to, so she'd thrown a tantrum and declared that she was leaving.

Luukas had let her go and told her she wasn't allowed back, happy to get her out of his hair without having to resort to violence, although Aiden would bet money he now sincerely regretted that decision.

The vampires entered in a single line, dressed much more casually than the suits at the table. They stared Aiden down as they filed into the room and took up positions around him, effectively blocking him from the door, the only means of escape other than the boarded up windows.

He smiled broadly, happy to see his old friends in spite of their strange behavior. "Hallo, mates! Fancy seeing you here, of all places? Don't tell me the queen booted you out?"

That weird presence stirred deep within him again as they stood shoulder to shoulder, nearly enclosing him within the center of their group, but not quite.

Aiden placed a hand on his chest, willing it away by sheer force of will.

He glanced around again at his old mates, his welcoming smile slowly slipping from his face. Instinctively he knew that the hostile eyes that stared back at him were not the males he once knew. With a sad heart, he realized that they had no idea who he was.

"Ah, bloody hell," he murmured sadly. "She's already gotten to you."

The vamp directly in front of him smirked, then looked around at the others. He seemed to give them some sort of silent signal.

Moving as one, they closed the circle around him, completely cutting him off from his female.

"Aiden?"

He heard the nervous tremor in Grace's voice, and hurried to reassure her.

"It's all right, love. Just keep your knickers on. I'll have us out of here in a jiffy."

He hoped.

Bracing himself for a fight, he took up a defensive stance, feet apart, arms at his sides, ready to bust his way out of there if it came down to it.

One of the males stepped closer, and Aiden turned slightly to meet him head on, holding his ground as the vamp got right up in his face.

"Hey, Steven," Aiden greeted him, deceptively casual. "All right, mate?"

The vamp zeroed in on him, hatred burning from his black eyes. Baring his fangs, his body bowed up at Aiden aggressively.

"Don't play with me...*Waano.*"

Aiden glanced around. Waano must be a new guy, maybe from another colony. Poor sap. Leeha had sucked him in, just like the rest of them.

Even Aiden had never been immune to her...um...charms.

Then he realized he was talking to him.

"Waano?" he asked. "Who the bloody hell is Waano?"

"I thought you wanted nothing to do with this world?" the vamp seethed. "That the beings here, with all of their disgusting physical needs, were below you?" He moved even further into Aiden's personal space, continuing to speak without waiting for an answer. "So what the fuck are you doing here? If you think you're going to be able to stop us, you're in for a rude awakening. You have no power here," he sneered, practically touching noses. "You can't send us back! We're corporeal now. And we fucking like it."

"Fine, ok," Aiden responded, leaning away with his palms up to ward him off. "Stay as you are. I don't give a bloody hoot," he added as an aside. "But I *would* recommend reading up a bit on dental hygiene." He waved his hand in front of his face, trying to dissipate the stench.

Steven grinned an evil grin and blew his bad breath in Aiden's face.

"Who the hell is Waano?" he asked again as soon as he could breathe.

"Knock it the fuck off!" Another one said from behind him. "We can sense you in there, just like we can sense the others who've made it out and been given a body."

Aiden's gut churned at his words. However, right now, he just needed to get to Grace and get them both as far away from these things as he could.

"Hmmm...yes, well...I'm sorry to say, I believe you're mistaken this time around. I'm still me. Still Aiden!" He grinned at them. "Now, if you'll excuse me, I'll just grab my female and," he looked around the shoulders of the one in front of him, searching for and finding her. "We'll be on our way."

As he went to walk through the circle, they tightened it further.

"I don't think so," Steven said. "Leeha is looking for you, Waano."

Aiden rolled his eyes. "Still stuck on this, are we?" He sighed loudly. "Again, I am not this 'Waano' person. Or thing. Or whatever. I am *Aiden*. And, I hate to cut the reunion short, but..." Quick as a lightening strike, he head butted Steven, busting his nose and then tossing him into the arms of his friends. "We really need to go."

Throwing all of his weight forward, he broke through the opening of the circle. Leaping onto the table, he sent papers flying every which way as he ran down the length of it to the window. Hopping down, he grabbed an empty chair and swung it at the glass, shattering through it to the boards behind it. A hard front kick broke the boards in half, opening a good-sized hole.

"STOP HIM!"

The roared order came from behind him. Wasting no time, he reached back and grabbed a startled Grace, who still had a death grab on the bag.

"Out you go, love." Picking her up, he sent her feet first through the busted window and into the night, glad they were on the first floor. She grunted in pain as she hit the pavement, but there was no time to coddle her and her bad choice in shoes.

Tipping an imaginary hat at the human males, he apologized to them for their loss. "Sorry, mates. The lady needs her mojo back."

Diving headfirst through the window just as one of the vamps made a grab for him, he rolled as he landed and came up into a crouch. Throwing Grace over his shoulder, he took off running as fast as he could go, the bag bouncing against the back of his thighs.

5

Grace squeezed her eyes shut, fighting to breathe against the whipping wind as Aiden raced away from the building at a speed that should not be possible.

Not for a human anyway.

As the blood pooled in her head, it brought with it a sudden burst of clarity, and she wondered how she hadn't seen it before.

Holy crap. She was draped over the broad, muscular shoulder of a *vampire*; an annoying, hot, yummy vampire who smelled really, really good, in spite of the dusty grain that still covered him from head to foot.

Right on cue, she sneezed as it blew off his clothes and into her face.

"Bless you!" he shouted over his shoulder without a break in stride.

"Thanks," she squeaked in a high voice as he suddenly left the ground, landing without the slightest break in stride a few seconds later.

She held the black bag in a death grip with both hands, and prayed to any gods who were listening that he wouldn't drop her and her precious package. No sooner had the thought crossed her mind than she lost the feel of him underneath her. She let out a frightened squeal as she waited to go flying through the air, but he only adjusted her on his shoulder and clamped his arm down firmly across the backs of her thighs again, getting a better grip.

Wait. Was that seriously his frickin' hand on her ass?

She scowled at the blur of pavement as it flashed past. If she were able to do more than suck in raspy gulps of air, she'd rip him a new one right now. But as it was, at least she wasn't skidding across the rough pavement. *That* would definitely leave a bruise or fifty at the speed he was going, along with some nice, juicy road rash.

She really needed to learn to appreciate the little things.

Her top half swayed back and forth as he abruptly changed direction without missing a beat. She lifted her head as much as she could and tried to see where they were through her long hair, but it was no use. The stuff was hanging to his calves in a thick curtain, effectively blocking her view, and she couldn't move it out of the way without releasing her grip on the bag.

Unable to do anything for the moment but go along for the ride, her mind wandered back to her recent *ah-ha!* revelation.

Could it be possible that he was really a vampire? She knew about them, of course, though she'd never actually met one. Her mother had talked openly about them in front of her ever since she could remember. She often warned her about them, telling Grace how charming and convincing they could be when there was something they wanted.

More specifically, that they could not be trusted. Not under any circumstances.

Apparently, their old coven used to work quite closely with some that lived in their area to help them protect their shared territory; before the new High Priest took over and her family had attempted to flee to the other side of the ocean.

However, he wasn't anything like she'd imagined as a kid. In retrospect, it seemed kind of silly now, but she'd always pictured vampires as being all dark and creepy, with waxy, white skin, long fingernails and black, slick-backed hair. Like in the old movies.

Not a hard-bodied, olive-skinned, grey-eyed, charismatic Brit that looked like a model and sent off vibes that made her want to rip off his dusty clothes and ride him like a rodeo bull.

When he wasn't creeping her out, that is.

She still couldn't quite put her finger on it, but there was just something...off... about him. And it wasn't the vampire thing. It was more than that, she realized now. Something else that her senses were picking up on, something that urged her to sprint in the opposite direction even as she wanted to curl up in his arms and let him make sweet, sweet love to her.

"Don't play with me...Waano."

The scary dude's voice echoed around in her head.

I thought he'd said his name was Aiden. Who the hell is Waano?

Just when she was certain her ribs weren't going to survive this escape attempt intact, his pace finally eased up and he slowed down to an easy jog.

The dude wasn't even breathing hard.

Looping the bag's short strap over one arm, she placed both palms on his firm ass and straightened her arms, pushing herself up until she could take a deep breath.

He gave her an answering squeeze on her own derriere and she swatted him, eliciting a rakish chuckle from her frisky rescuer.

The smell of the ocean was strong, which meant they were close to the water, but that didn't tell her much. Two thirds of Dalian was surrounded by the East China Sea. And with all of the skyscrapers surrounding them, it wasn't always visible anyway, but it did tell her they were downtown.

He slipped into a narrow alley between buildings, and she dropped her head down again. She pulled the bag close and shoved her face back into the small of his back just in time to avoid either one from being smashed into the side of the building as he whipped around to check that they hadn't been followed.

Aiden chuckled again, "What a bunch of wankers."

Striding to the back of the alley, he hefted Grace easily up and off his shoulder and set her on her feet in front of him.

"Ow! Dammit!" Her left ankle throbbed painfully when she tried to put her weight on it. She must've twisted it when he threw her out the window.

He grabbed her upper arms to steady her. "What's wrong?"

She swatted his hands away. "You broke my ankle!"

"When?" he demanded.

"When you threw me out the window!"

"I wouldn't say I *threw* you, exactly."

She shot him a glare.

"Here, let me see." Crouching down in front of her, he took her foot gently in his hand as she balanced herself with one hand on the top of his head.

Probing the joint until she winced, he carefully set it back down and stood up.

"I don't think it's broken, just sprained."

"No thanks to you," she grumbled.

"I told you you should've worn different shoes," he reprimanded.

She stared up at him in disbelief. "I didn't know when I left the house this morning that I was going to be chasing a bunch of Suits all over town. Or, that I was going to be THROWN OUT OF A WINDOW!"

"Would you rather that I'd left you there with them?"

"Oh, shut up," she huffed at him.

He took the bag from her hand and held it up by his ear, giving it a shake. "So, what's in this all-important bag anyway?"

"Stop jostling it!" She hobbled towards him, trying to take the bag back as he held it above his head.

"But what is it?"

"I *told* you. My Mojo. Give it to me!"

He gave her a skeptical look, but lowered the bag until she could grab it from his hand.

"Give me that." Setting it carefully on the ground, she eased herself down onto her butt next to it and carefully unzipped the zipper. A little bit scared of what she might find, she tentatively opened it up and peeked inside.

"Mojo!" she squealed excitedly a second later. Thank the gods he was all right!

Reaching into the bag, she slowly and carefully cupped her hands around her beloved Mojo, wincing slightly as he huffed and bristled.

Seemed he was still a bit shaken up from the bouncy ride.

She ignored his spiky quills and lifted him up in front of her to show the vampire, her smile lighting up her face.

He stared at her for so long her smile began to slip. "What?" she asked.

He blinked a few times and looked from her to the small creature in her hands, and then back at her, his blank features not giving anything away.

Finally, he lifted an eyebrow. "That is what I risked life and limb for? A rat with prickles stuck in its bum? A boot brush?"

She cradled her pet to her chest, attempting to calm him. "He is NOT a boot brush!" she scolded. "He's a hedgehog, you dork. He's my pet, and my friend," she added. Cooing to him softly, she smoothed down his spiky quills.

"You have a porcupine for a friend?"

She glared up at him while she tried to decide if he really had never seen a hedgehog (though she didn't see how that was possible), or if he was just yanking her chain. "He's not a porcupine. He's a hedgehog."

His face screwed up in confusion. "But, why ever would you want that thing? You can't even snuggle with him without getting jabbed. What good is it? Does it even do any tricks?"

Mojo wiggled his nose at her, happy to be with her again now that he had calmed down enough to realize who she was, and she touched it with her own. "Don't listen to him, Mojo. He's just a stupid vampire."

Rubbing her nose with Mojo's again, she suddenly shivered. She hadn't really noticed how chilly it had gotten until just now. Looks like it was going to be a long, cold, painful walk home.

At least until the vampire went away and she could fix her ankle.

Caught up as she was in her reunion with her beloved pet, it took her a moment before she sensed the tension hanging in the air. Glancing up, she found Aiden had become eerily still, his normally animated expression completely closed off.

"What did you just call me?" he asked softly.

Uh oh.

Well, she saw no reason to lie now. "A stupid vampire."

His expression didn't change. "Why would you call me that?"

Dropping her eyes, she sighed as she carefully pet Mojo. He was right. That had been a mean thing to say.

Looking directly at him, she grudgingly apologized. "I'm sorry. I shouldn't have said that," she told him with as much sincerity as she could muster. "You're not stupid. I'm sure you're very intelligent. You probably have multiple college degrees."

Shaking his head, he said, "No, I meant the 'vampire' part."

Now it was her turn to be confused. "Because that's what you are, aren't you?"

He just cocked his head at her and didn't answer.

She rolled her eyes. "Come on, dude. No human could run the way you just did."

"Maybe I'm just extremely fast and agile."

"Yeah, ok," she scoffed. Then another thought came to her. "Or are you a shifter?" She paused. "A werewolf? Shit. Are you a werewolf?!"

That seemed to snap him out of his trance. "I am NOT a dog," he assured her, his tone thick with repugnance. "Although some very good mates of mine are, and they don't seem to mind it."

"Then I was right. You must be a vamp." She resumed petting Mojo. "I'm not totally ignorant, you know. I've known you guys exist my entire life. Actually, I know quite a bit about your kind."

"Whatever is that for?"

"What?" she asked, confused.

"That...tone."

"There was no 'tone' in my voice." Was there? Maybe there was. She wouldn't be surprised if it had slipped out, though she hadn't meant it to.

He looked as if he was about to keep arguing with her, but then he sighed, shrugged, and shoved his hands into his pockets. "Honestly, I thought you would've figured it out sooner, what with my outrageous good looks and all." He gave her a wink. "Humans are not this pretty."

Grace rolled her eyes. "Yeah, yeah. You would think you all would have learned to be a little more modest by now." She ignored his gloating look when she didn't deny the fact that he was good-looking. "But it was the fangs that really gave you away."

"My fangs?" His tongue reached out and touched the tip of one. "Ah. Yes. I imagine that would do it. How very uncivilized of me. My apologies, love."

Eying up those canines of his, an unpleasant thought came to her. "You're not planning on eating me, are you?"

He scowled down at her, crossing his arms across his chest, letting loose another small poof of dust. "You know, you're the second female who's accused me of eating people recently."

"That doesn't answer my question," she responded.

He rolled his eyes. "Of course I'm not going to eat you."

An even worse fear came to her. "Are you going to eat Mojo?" she squeaked. "Like those vamps in all the teeny bopper stories these days?"

He dropped his head back in exasperation. "No! I don't eat rats!"

She threw the bag at him. "He's *not* a rat!"

Aiden waved away her protest. "All right, all right. I don't eat anything with prickles. Besides, I just fed shortly before I found you."

That didn't really make her feel better, and she kept Mojo close to her chest just in case. A mental image of him feeding on some poor, helpless person popped into her head. She wondered vaguely if he preferred men or women? Or if it even mattered to him? Maybe after living for so long, he'd want to mix it up a little.

Then she wondered what it would feel like to have him at *her* neck, pulling at her vein, taking her life force into his body; becoming a part of him.

Literally.

Her insides stirred at the thought, and not in a bad way. She quickly looked down and cleared her throat, trying to ignore the lust that was coursing through her. "Then why are your fangs all out and pointy?"

If he'd noticed her discomfort, he gave no sign of it. "They just do that if any emotions are running high." He shrugged, unconcerned. "Must be all of the excitement."

Without warning, he crouched down in front of her with a wicked smile. "Want to touch them?"

She drew back away from him. "Yeah. Not happening, dude."

His smile fell, disappointment taking its place. "You don't strike me as the wilting type, poppet."

Lifting her chin defiantly, she didn't bother to defend herself. Let him think what he wanted to.

He watched her pet Mojo. "Am I to take it you only like being jabbed by pointy things when they're attached to something that you think you can handle?"

"I don't like being 'jabbed' by anything."

"Don't knock it till you try it, love. You just might like it."

His grey eyes danced as he teased her, holding her own a little longer than necessary, and then he rose again to his full height.

She continued to soothe her pet as her face burned self-consciously. And it was not because she was worried that he was right. It wasn't.

Glancing at him sideways, she watched as he tilted his head to listen to the sounds around them. She studied his perfect profile, and barely caught herself before she let out a despondent sigh. It really wasn't fair. Why couldn't he be a normal guy? Even if he meant all the flirting he was doing, she knew better than to trust her heart to a vampire.

Vampires only looked out for themselves. As a human, she was nothing to him. He would betray her in the end, just like they all did.

Her mother had trusted a vampire, and he'd gotten her father killed.

Not to mention the whole eating people to survive thing.

Besides, she really, *really*, liked sex. Could vampires even have sex?

Seemingly satisfied that no one of any consequence was nearby, he pulled his hood up to cover his head just as a fat raindrop landed on her arm. Almost immediately, it turned into a steady drizzle.

He huddled over her, shielding her with his body. "Let's get us out of this rain, shall we? Before you catch a chill, and I turn from a pile of dust to a puddle of mud."

She opened her mouth to tell him that she was perfectly capable of making it home on her own, but before she could utter a sound, he'd scooped her up into his strong arms. She automatically threw an arm around his neck and supported Mojo with the other as he snuggled down into her ample cleavage.

"Lucky rat."

His wistful voice was so quiet she wasn't sure she had heard him correctly. She raised her eyes to find him watching the hedgehog burrow under her shirt as she protected him from the rain with her hand, an expression of such intense longing on his face she was a bit startled.

She smacked him lightly on the back of the head, just hard enough to get his attention. "In your dreams, dude."

He turned his head slightly, his grey eyes locking onto her green ones, his sensual mouth only a few inches from her own.

The raw intensity she saw there made her heart hitch in her chest, and her eyes were drawn to his lips of their own accord.

Her breaths grew shallow as she stared at that beautiful mouth, slightly worried that she'd gone too far. Although probably not as worried as she ought to be. Her tongue slid out to wet her bottom lip, and she felt his hands tighten on her.

But he only repeated, "Don't know what you're missing, poppet," and then gave her a devilish wink. Tossing her up a bit, presumably to get a better hold on her, he chuckled softly when she squealed, and gathered her even closer to him. With one last, lusty look at her breasts, he turned to leave.

"Wait! What about the bag?" she asked.

"What about it?" he responded without slowing down.

"I think we should bring it with us. Whatever's in there was awfully important to those Suits I was following, and they were obviously having a secret meet up with the scary dudes. Maybe having to do with whatever is in there?"

Aiden paused for all of half a second. "True." Spinning around, he walked back to where the bag was lying in the rain, switched her to one arm, and swiped it up.

"And who the hell were those other guys who came in?" she asked as they got moving again. "The ones who were calling you 'Waano'?"

"No idea," he answered quickly. Too quickly. "So, where do you live?"

She'd felt him stiffen slightly at her question. Squinting through the rain and the dark, she tried to get her bearings in the dim light of the street lamps. "Go that way." She pointed down the deserted street to the right.

He was lying about not knowing those other guys, she was sure of it. But why?

"What do you mean you don't know? You acted like you knew them, and they seemed to know you. Or know you as Waano, anyway. And you were calling the scary leader dude 'Steven'."

The rain came down harder and she shivered and cuddled closer to him as she waited for him to answer.

He hunched over her, shielding her as best as he could, and checked once behind him before he finally said, "I used to know them. They were good mates at one time, a long time ago. But I don't know who they are anymore."

He sounded so sad that her heart ached for him. Looking down at Mojo, snug inside her shirt, she frowned. She didn't need to be getting all mushy over a guy right now, especially a non-human one.

"Are they vampires too?"

He glanced down at her, a funny look in his eyes. "More or less."

What was that supposed to mean?

Maybe she should tell him that tonight wasn't the first time she'd seen those dudes around the city, and that every time she had, they'd totally freaked her out. There was something "wrong" about them, and she had a feeling Aiden knew more about it than he was telling her, because it was that same sense of wrongness that she got about *him*.

But as the rain continued to fall harder, she was distracted with trying to keep Mojo dry, and decided to save her other questions for when they got somewhere with a roof.

Speaking of which. "Do you have somewhere to stay today?" she asked. "Out of the sun?"

His cocky grin returned in full force. "I was hoping you would offer. Thank you, poppet. I'd love to stay at your place."

She scowled up at him. "I didn't offer anything. And you're not staying at my apartment! I was thinking more along the lines of an abandoned building you could break into or something."

His eyes filled with hurt. "But the sun will be coming up in less than two hours. You're going to kick me out to perish and burn after I saved you...and your silly rat? After I've carried you all the way home?" His features tightened suddenly. "I've seen vampires exposed to the sun before. Trust me, it's not pretty."

She opened her mouth to tell him that, yes, that was exactly what she was planning to do, but it didn't come out quite the way she'd intended. "Fine. You can stay at my place. I have a windowless closet you'll fit in, I think. But this offer is only for today!"

"Of course," he agreed in all seriousness.

She glanced up at him warily, but he was staring straight ahead, his expression impassive.

"Take a left up here," she grumbled.

This was going to rank right up there at the top of her current list of "Worst Ideas Ever". She just knew it.

6

His heavy boots made no sound as he navigated the narrow, damp tunnels through the underground labyrinth that he now called home. His long strides ate up the distance effortlessly, and at a speed not normally achieved by anyone other than vampires or werewolves, of which he was neither.

The old-fashioned torches lining the walls flickered as he passed, half of them blowing out completely, but he didn't need the light. He knew this route by heart. Reaching up, he pushed the black hood of his cloak off his head and ran his hands through his short, dark hair.

He had other things he should be doing, but he was eager to get back to his lair, and to the female waiting for him there.

At the thought of her, a feeling of possessiveness hit him so hard he nearly growled out loud. The moment he'd set eyes on the lovely, green-eyed vampire, something had clicked inside of him. No. Not clicked.

Exploded.

Luckily, he was a phenomenal actor. He'd had to be to get where he was now. Nothing he was feeling ever showed on the outside, not unless he wanted it to. He could even control his internal reactions, thanks to years of mind over matter techniques. It was the only way he could infiltrate this world of nocturnal beings where the slightest quickening of your pulse would give you away, and could mean the difference between living and dying.

He was also lucky that Leeha didn't trust his loyalty to her, so when he'd insisted that the female in his room was not going to be used for their last possession, she hadn't argued.

Much.

In the end, she'd broken down and used her beloved Aiden. Personally, he hadn't given a rat's ass which vampires they'd used, until now.

He'd had little time to talk to the female since he'd rushed her to his room and unchained her, giving her leave to help herself to his clothes and books. For her own safety, he'd barred her inside with a spell. She couldn't leave, but nor could anyone get in.

He heard her before he saw her.

"Stay on your own side of the room, bird."

Her words were followed by a great, suffering sigh, and his lips curved up into a smile as he imagined the look on her face as his raven edged closer and closer to her, as she was wont to do. The bird was as fascinated by her as he was.

His raven tittered companionably.

"She'd like to remind you that her name is Cruthú."

The vampire, Shea, hissed as he appeared in the doorway to his room, jumping up lightening fast from where she'd been sitting on the edge of his bed.

Her sea green eyes were enormous in her delicately boned face as she stared up at him, and only then did he remember that he hadn't pulled his hood back up. It was the first time she'd seen him without it.

"You're b-back," she stuttered.

She'd braided her long, dark hair, and the thick plait hung over her shoulder, the ends brushing the bottom of her breast. Loose strands curled around her face, accentuating her cheekbones. One of his T-shirts hung loosely on her small frame, hiding the swells and curves he knew were there.

He was happy to see she'd taken him up on his offer for clean clothes, at least partially. She still had her own jeans on, dusty from her ride in the back of the pickup truck that had brought her here.

Strolling over to her, he stopped just outside of her reach. He'd learned quickly that she didn't like anyone in her personal space. Every time he'd gotten too close to her, she would jump away. "I didn't mean to startle you."

Her eyes roved over his face, growing wider with each passing second.

He noticed her fangs were still out. He could see the tips of them when she talked. "Shea, right?" he asked.

She nodded warily.

"I'm sorry it's taken me so long to check in on you. Are you all right?" he asked.

She blinked, and then blinked again. "Uh, yeah, I'm good."

Cruthú gave up stalking the pretty girl and squawked out a happy hello to see him. Flying up to land on his shoulder, she rubbed her beak on his cheek. The fact that she stayed down here with him, rather than soaring the open skies where she belonged, was a testament to their bond. He took a moment to greet his only friend before shifting his gaze back to his guest.

She was still gawking at him.

He lifted a brow. "What?" The word came out a bit harsher than he'd intended, and he frowned at himself.

Recoiling from his harsh tone, she seemed to snap herself out of it. In a protective gesture, she wrapped her arms around herself, briefly closing her eyes as she gave him a small shake of her head. "I'm sorry. I don't mean to stare. I've just never seen you without..." She raised a hand and made a miming motion of something being pulled low over her eyes. "Your hood always covered most of your face before." She dropped her hand back to her waist. "I was just a little taken aback."

"Because I am so completely repulsive to look at?" he asked sardonically.

A horrified expression crossed her face. "No! No. Not at all. Just the opposite, in fact."

His brows lifted as he waited for her to elaborate.

She didn't. More's the pity.

She cleared her throat, and she suddenly looked so lost that he decided to take pity on her. With a last scratch under his friend's soft feathers, he stepped away to set Cruthú on her perch at the head of his bed.

"Is there anything you need to make your stay here more comfortable?" he asked Shea.

She shook her head. "What are you going to do with me?"

"I don't know," he answered honestly.

"You could just let me go," she suggested.

He heard the hopeful tone in her voice and sighed heavily, wishing that was so, but it just wasn't possible. He faced her square on so there would be no question as to the sincerity of his response.

"No, Shea. I can't."

Setting her jaw in a stubborn line, she watched the raven preening her feathers, but he knew she wasn't really seeing her. He could feel her frustration, and wished he could tell her something that would ease it. But he had told her the truth. He honestly didn't know.

And he couldn't allow her to leave him.

Undoing the fastening of his cloak, he shrugged it off of his broad shoulders and hung it on the hook by the doorway, leaving him in dark jeans and a long-sleeved cotton shirt. It was warmer here than it was in the altar room, or anywhere else within the mountain actually. A natural hot spring ran underneath the floor, and kept the room at a comfortable temperature, as well as providing a bathing room just down the tunnel to the left where it bubbled to the surface, creating a natural pool.

He was glad this room had survived the encounter between himself and the Master vampire. It was far away from the center of the mountain, the part that had taken the most damage, and accessed only by a maze of underground tunnels as far as everyone knew. It was why he had chosen this area.

As he rolled up the sleeves, exposing the tan skin on his strong forearms, he inquired over his shoulder, "Are you thirsty?"

A preternatural silence answered his question, and he turned to find that she'd gone eerily still, her heated eyes flickering from his exposed throat to his wrists.

It made him instantly hard.

She ran her tongue over her bottom lip, and shook her head again. "No. I'm fine."

The trembling of her husky voice belied the firmness of her words.

He clenched and unclenched his fists, fighting the urge to tilt his head to the side and offer himself to her. He held no love for vampires, but for some reason, this slight female affected him as no other woman ever had, and that included humans.

"I can get you some bagged blood if you need it, Shea. Please don't be afraid to ask."

Her eyes flew to his in surprise. "Oh. Um. Ok. I will. But really, I'm fine."

Grabbing a wooden chair from the small table in the corner, he pulled it over to the bed and turned it around to face him. Straddling the seat, he indicated for her to sit on the bed near him, then crossed his arms casually on top of the back rest. "Please. I'm sure you have questions. I'll answer what I can. I don't want you to be upset."

Swallowing visibly, she sidled over to him and sat down on the edge of the mattress, just out of his reach.

He studied her a moment: Her palms were on the bed to either side of her, her feet together, her spine rigid. She was ready to jump and run at the slightest provocation. "Are you frightened of me, Shea?"

Shaking her head, she said, "Not in the way you think."

He waited, but again, she didn't seem willing or able to elaborate.

"What's your name?" she asked suddenly.

He saw no reason not to tell her. "Jesse."

"Jesse what?"

"Just Jesse, for now."

As the silence lingered, he opened his mind to hers just a bit.

She wanted to ask him something, but was uncertain as to whether or not she should.

"Go ahead," he told her.

Startled green eyes flashed up to his.

"Go ahead," he repeated. "Ask me what it is you want to know."

The wariness returned, but she did as he requested. "You're the one who kept Luukas here. The one who helped Leeha. She wouldn't be able to hold him without a witch...or warlock." It wasn't a question.

He responded as though it were anyway. "No. It wasn't me. I've only recently come here."

"Then who...?"

"Keira Moss is the witch that made your Master's life hell." He neglected to mention the part he had played when Luukas came back after his witch was taken from him. "He appears to have forgiven her, however." He shrugged.

That got her attention. "Forgiven her? What do you mean?"

"Yeah, I guess you wouldn't have heard, having been waylaid yourself. Keira is Luukas' mate."

And Jesse had made Luukas believe he had killed her. He still wasn't sure how the witch had pulled the vampire out of that fun little nightmare before his mind had shattered into insanity.

It took Shea a moment to digest that little piece of information.

"His mate? Like as in a fated mate? Like the old stories the elders passed down that no one believes anymore?

"That would be correct."

"But, I thought they were just stories. I've never heard of that actually happening. None of us have. We all believed it was just folklore."

He smiled. "It's not just folklore. Actually, it used to happen quite often between witches and vampires, until about six hundred and forty years ago, when a certain High Priest lost his ladylove to a vamp. In his grief, he immediately created a dark spell to keep any matings from ever happening again."

"So, why is it happening again now?"

He'd been thinking about that himself since seeing the Moss sisters both mated. "I believe Keira did it. I think that, while doing a curse of her own that Leeha demanded of her, she found a loophole within the original curse. She's reversed it somehow."

"Moss," she repeated thoughtfully. "They were part of the coven that's in Seattle. We had an alliance with them, until the recent High Priest took over, and some of the families broke their connection with the coven and went into hiding."

"Yes. Keira is a member of one of those families."

Shea's forehead creased in confusion. "I don't understand. If they left the coven to get away from the new, less than admirable leaders, why would she get into cahoots with an insane wannabe like Leeha?"

His golden eyes crinkled in amusement at her choice of words. "If I remember correctly, she only did it to protect her younger sister. Leeha threatened to kill her if Keira didn't do as she asked."

Her mouth tightened into a thin line. "That sounds like Leeha."

Spearing him with those seductive eyes, she turned the conversation back to him. "So. If you're not here because of the whole Luukas fiasco, why exactly are you here? And why am *I* here?"

He took a deep breath and straightened his spine, rubbing his suddenly damp palms on his jean-clad thighs. How much to tell her?

Her eyes flicked down and caught the nervous gesture before he even realized he was doing it.

He nearly smiled. Didn't miss a thing, did she?

"Where is Aiden?" she continued before he could answer her first question.

Forcing himself to relax, he re-crossed his arms on the chair back again. He couldn't tell her anything. Not yet. And for some reason, that bothered him. He found he didn't like keeping things from her.

But she was safer not knowing. "I can't tell you that. I'm sorry," he told her sincerely. "But suffice it to say, that I saved your life."

His words didn't have the effect he was hoping for.

She glared at him. "If you cared enough to save my life, then why keep me here? Why won't you let me go?"

He had to steel himself against her displeasure. Returning her look glare for glare, he grudgingly admitted, "I just can't."

With a sound of frustration, she shoved herself up off the bed and was at the doorway before he could stop her. She hit the barrier spell hard and was thrown back into the room. With a curse, she tried again, running at it faster this time. But the spell held, as he knew it would, and again, she was propelled back into the room.

Kicking his chair away, he reached out a hand to stop her from trying again, but she jerked away from him in panic.

"No! Don't touch me! Please don't touch me!"

He reached for her anyway, determined to stop this foolishness, but she whirled away and went back to the doorway.

Raising her fist, she pounded at the invisible barrier. "Let me out!" she screamed. "Dammit! If you're not going to kill me, then let me out!"

He came up behind her and went to grab her fist, but once again, she spun away from him. Pressing her back to the corner, she threw one hand up, palm out, warning him away.

"Stay. Away. Don't touch me," she hissed.

Jesse tilted his head, observing her reaction. Her lips were pulled back, exposing her fangs. Her eyes shifted around nervously, looking for a way to escape.

This was more than anger. This reaction was from fear. Yet, she'd sworn earlier that she wasn't afraid of him.

Not in the way you think.

Something else was definitely going on here. But he could be patient. He didn't need many things in his life. As a matter of fact, he could count the things that were important to him on one hand.

But he needed this vampire to trust him, because he had the strongest feeling that she was someday going to become *the* most important thing to him.

Shea was cornered.

Please don't touch me. Please don't touch me.

She repeated the words over and over in her head like a mantra, hoping against hope that somehow they would keep him away from her.

If he touched her, he would see the chink in her armor.

If he touched her, she'd be on the floor, writhing in pain.

Yet, there was a part of her that wanted him to touch her...everywhere.

Lowering his arm, he stepped back.

She nearly sobbed with relief. Or was it disappointment?

Holding up his hands in surrender, he backed away a little more. "All right. I won't touch you. It's ok."

She watched him warily until he'd retreated a safe distance and sat back down in his chair. She felt like a fool.

Dropping her eyes, she slid down the wall until she was sitting on the warm stone floor. She couldn't look at him. He would know she was hiding something if she did. He would know she was a freak.

But what really bothered her was: Why the hell did she even care?

She didn't know why, but she did.

Pulling her knees up to her chest, she wrapped her arms around them and rested her forehead on her hands.

"Shea, why don't like to be touched?"

Well, hell. He certainly wasn't stupid, was he? But how was she supposed to explain it, when she didn't even understand herself? All she knew was, after Luukas had been taken, she suddenly convulsed in pain whenever a male touched her. It didn't matter if that male was vampire, human, wolf, or anything in between.

Males = Pain.

"You can talk to me, you know."

He was soft spoken, but his voice had a masculine timbre to it that raised goose bumps all over her flesh. She longed to respond to it.

But she wasn't stupid either.

Raising her head to look into those amazing amber eyes, she barked out a laugh. "Talk to *you*? Seriously? Why the fuck would I trust you?"

He looked away, but not before she saw his eyes darken with hurt. A derogatory half smile lifted one side of his sensual mouth.

"You're right, of course. I wouldn't trust me either."

A stab of guilt hit her at the tone of his voice.

Wait. What the hell am I feeling bad about?

"Don't try to guilt trip me," she told him. "*You're* the reason I was brought here. However, you decided I wasn't good enough for whatever sick thing you were planning on doing with me. And now...now you won't even let me go!"

"I never said you weren't good enough..." he rebuffed her accusation angrily.

She threw her head back into the wall, gritting her teeth against the temporary pain. "That's not my point!" she yelled. "Why am I still here? What are you planning to do with me? Just let me go! Let me leave!"

He thrust his hands into his dark hair at her outburst. He was angry, and distraught, but no more upset and confused than she was.

This place gave her the creeps.

"I can't!" he bellowed. "You know too much. You were in the room when Leeha, the idiot, couldn't resist telling Aiden all about the altar room and what we do there."

"Where *is* Aiden?"

He just stared at her.

She searched his ruggedly handsome face, not wanting to believe what she was thinking his stony silence meant.

"You didn't," she whispered. "Please, *please*, tell me you didn't do that to him."

His voice was like ice when he admitted, "Someone had to be the host. If it hadn't been him, it would've been you."

The air left her lungs in a whoosh, and she found it hard to breathe.

"I couldn't let her do that to you," he admitted.

Shea took an unsteady breath. "That's what you meant by 'saving my life'. Leeha was going to possess me with one of those things." It wasn't a question.

"With a demon, yes. And not just any demon, but with Waano, the biggest badass demon in hell. I don't know that you would have survived it, in any form."

Her eyes flew over his features, searching for the truth she was afraid to know. "Did Aiden survive it?"

He gave her a stony stare.

"Did he?" Her voice was rising hysterically. "Answer me!"

"He did. Physically."

Physically. She felt like she'd been punched in the gut.

"Where is he now?"

"I don't know," he admitted. "He, Waano, wasn't very happy about me dragging him out of his dimension. As a matter of fact, he'd straight out ordered Leeha not to bring him here. But in typical selfish Leeha fashion, she'd completely ignored his wishes and brought him here anyway. He nearly killed her, but I stopped him, and then he took off. We don't know where he went."

"In Aiden's body?"

He nodded once.

He sounded so calm about it all. Didn't he even care? Didn't it bother him at all that he was ruining lives? Taking loved ones away from their colony? Their families?

She felt ill for wanting his hands on her earlier. "What kind of a monster are you?" she breathed.

He stiffened, the muscles of his jaw clenching in anger at her judgment of him. "I'm not like Leeha. I have my reasons for doing what I do."

Her mouth twisted in disgust. "No reason is worth messing with those things, possessing living beings with demons. Are you mad?"

Standing up, he pushed the chair back under the table, and then dropped down onto his haunches directly in front of her.

He was so close, she could feel the warmth coming off of his skin. She immediately recoiled from him and shrunk back into the corner as far as she could, afraid he would touch her and the excruciating pain would come.

And even more afraid that he wouldn't, in spite of everything he'd just told her.

He ran his eyes over her cowering form, making her skin heat everywhere they touched. Then he glanced away and clenched his teeth. He didn't speak, or try to touch her.

Her hand started to reach towards him of its own accord, but she caught herself and clenched her fingers into a fist before he noticed.

Giving her one last searching look, he rose and left the room, grabbing his cloak from the hook on his way out.

The raven gave her a disapproving look from one beady eye, then left her perch to fly after him, swooping low to get through the doorway.

Everyone and everything can leave this fucking room except me.

7

"I have the key." Grace told him as they arrived at her high-rise apartment. "Put me down a sec."

Aiden set her carefully down on her good foot and waited until she'd fished the key out of her front pocket and unlocked and opened the door.

But before she could hobble inside, and possibly injure her ankle more, he scooped her back up into his arms again and waited patiently for her to invite him in.

She heaved a long-suffering sigh. "Um, are you going to stand here in the hall all day?" she asked. "If so, put me back down so I can go in. 'Cause I really have to pee."

Surely, with her family knowing so much about vampires, she knew their limitations?

"Seriously, dude. The bathroom is like, right there. I think I can manage it."

Guess not. "You need to invite me in, poppet."

She snorted out loud. "Since when do you wait for an invitation to do anything?"

What was that supposed to mean? "Since...I can't enter your residence without you inviting me to do so."

An adorable crinkle appeared in the middle of her forehead. "Really? I thought that was just a myth made up by Hollywood."

"No, it's unfortunately true in real life also." He fought to keep his face serious, but didn't quite succeed. "I thought you knew all about vampires?"

"Obviously not as much as I thought I did." A rebellious gleam appeared in her eyes and she lifted her chin defiantly. "What if I don't want to invite you in?"

"Then we'll be standing in the hall all day."

"Your arms will get tired."

"No, poppet, they won't. You weigh about as much as that silly pet of yours to me. Luckily, you don't have as many prickles."

She looked longingly towards a door just inside her apartment, back at him, and then scowled. "Fine," she grumbled. "Come on in."

He gave her a cheeky grin. Perhaps she did have one or two prickles.

Enjoying her discomfiture maybe a bit more than necessary, he strode into her one room apartment and kicked the door shut behind him. Setting her down on the couch, he pushed his hood back off his head and planted his hands on his hips as he took a look around.

"Cozy." He nodded with approval. "I like it." He turned in a circle, taking it all in. "Very en vogue."

She looked at him sideways as she fished Mojo out of her shirt and set him on a pillow, smiling at the little bastard with warm eyes when he yawned, showing his little rat teeth.

He wished she'd smile at him like that.

"In vogue?" she asked.

He turned away before she could see the longing on his face. "Yes, you know, doing the whole minimalist thing," he swept his arm in an arc, indicating her complete lack of stuff.

Her place was definitely small, yet modern: just one main room and a galley kitchen. The cabinets were fronted with clear glass, the appliances were small, and a large island with a granite countertop divided the two spaces.

The living area contained what he presumed to be a pullout couch (as he didn't see a bed anywhere, mores the shame), a T.V., and a small bookshelf. Bamboo floors and large windows behind the couch completed the contemporary look.

The entire place was clean and uncluttered, giving it a less than lived-in look. The only homey spot was a sitting space in the corner by the windows that contained a small desk with a lamp. A book lay face down on its surface next to an empty teacup, and a fuzzy blanket was thrown over the chair.

Surprisingly, the place smelled like fresh-baked bread - warm and yeasty - but in a good way.

He went into the kitchen and found the fresh bread wrapped in cloth to keep it warm. Pulling open drawers, he found the one containing more towels on his third try. Filling it with ice from the freezer, he turned to find she had taken off her sandals and was slowly hobbling her way back towards the front door to the loo. Dropping the makeshift ice pack in the sink, he rushed over to assist her.

She jumped when he suddenly appeared at her side.

"Jesus, Aiden! Don't do that!"

He wrapped an arm around her waist and ducked a bit so he could lift her arm up over his shoulders, taking some of her weight off of her bad ankle.

"Sorry, love. Didn't mean to startle you."

She glared at him out of the corner of her eye. "I can walk on my own, you know."

He smiled down into her rebellious expression. "I know, but my mum would box my ears if she saw me standing around like an oaf when there is a lady in need."

She gave him a funny look, but didn't protest any more as he helped her across the room and through a large walk-in closet, leaving her in the loo on the other side of it. Propping her by the sink, he closed the door behind him when he left to give her some privacy.

As he waited for her to finish, he wandered over to the small bookshelf by the window and glanced at the titles. He whistled softly as he read some of them: *A Practical Approach to Cardiac Anesthesia, 4th edition, Cardiovascular Physiology Concepts, 2nd Edition,* and *Cardiopulmonary Bypass (Cambridge Clinical Guides)* were there among others, all pertaining to the heart.

Was his spunky little female a cardio doctor? Somehow, it didn't surprise him in the least.

The bathroom door opened behind him and he rushed over to help her, moving at human speed this time...sort of.

"Like to do a little light reading at night?" he asked as got her settled on the couch again.

She frowned up at him, and his heart sank. He wished she would smile again.

"Your books." He waved a hand in their general direction. "Not one for easy reading, I see."

"Oh. That. Those are my books from school. I graduated a few years ago."

He went to sit down next to her, but changed his mind when she looked pointedly at his dusty clothes. He wandered into the kitchen instead. "Are you a doctor then?"

"I'm a Cardiovascular Perfusionist. I work at a hospital off of Zhongshan Rd. by the People's Square."

He raised his eyebrows in silent question.

"Basically, I operate the circulation equipment during heart surgeries, when the heart needs to be artificially supported."

"So, you're not a squeamish girl." If she was in the operating room during surgeries, it meant she wasn't grossed out easily by let's say, oh...blood, for instance. He knew there was something he'd liked about her the moment he'd seen her sweet tush sticking out of that doorway.

Other than her sweet tush, of course.

"No. I'm not squeamish at all. And it's a good job. There's only about two thousand of us here in China, and more than twenty thousand hospitals, so we're in high demand. Hey, would you mind getting me a drink of water, please?"

He blinked at the change of subject. "Water...yes."

Which reminded him, he'd left her homemade ice pack in the sink. Getting her drink and putting fresh ice in the towel, he took both over to her. Handing her the glass, he ordered her to put her ankle up on the couch.

She did so, wincing slightly, and careful not to dislodge Mojo from his cushion.

Aiden rolled up her pant leg and took a look. There was some swelling on the delicate curve of her inner ankle, and a small bruise was promising to be quite colorful, but with some ice it should be fine. Provided he could keep her off of it for a few days.

And he knew just the way to do that.

"So does this thing pull out into a bed?" he asked innocently as he propped the ice on her ankle.

She squinted her eyes at him warily. "I'm fine sleeping on it like this."

Was that a challenge he heard in her tone? Getting into this one's knickers may prove to be a bit harder for him than normal, unless he "persuaded" her to come around to his way of thinking. However, he rarely found the need to do that with females. He preferred to bed them only if they were willing.

And he wanted Grace willing. Her stubbornness would only make it that much sweeter when he succeeded.

"Aiden?"

Thoughts of exactly what kind of knickers she was wearing drifted away, and he reluctantly came back to the present. "Hmm?"

Grace looked down at her fingers, which were tangled in her lap. "Can I ask you a question?"

"Of course."

"What made you decide to be a vampire?"

What indeed?

Careful not to create too much dust, he perched himself on the arm of the couch by her feet.

"I didn't 'decide' to become a vampire, per se. Well," he scratched his head, rethinking that statement. "I guess I rather did. I *was* given the choice. However, I was dying, so it really wasn't much of a choice. Not for me."

"You were dying?" she asked. "What happened?"

"I somehow managed to get in the way of a particularly nasty sword being wielded by a rather angry man. It was during the war."

Her hands lay forgotten in her lap. He had her full attention now. "A sword? What war was this?"

"The Great Northern War, in 1712. I found it quite by accident, while on a walk."

"The sword?" she asked.

He barked out a laugh. "No, love. The war."

She scrunched her forehead up in that adorable way she had. "How the hell do you find a war by accident? Didn't you hear the fighting? Or the screaming? See the uniforms?"

"Well, it was a rather lengthy walk. My father and I had gotten into a row, and I went outside for some air. I ended up at the local pub until they kicked me out, and then decided to walk it off before I went home. However, I was *so* pissed...drunk," he clarified for her. "That by the time I had sobered up I was on the other side of the English Channel. I was also quite famished, due to my walk being rather spur of the moment, as they say. So I wandered up to a group of gentlemen to see if they had any food they could spare."

"And you didn't notice that they were soldiers?"

"They were sitting outside their tent, carrying on around their fire. I just assumed they were enjoying the outdoors, having a gentleman's outing."

"That must've been before strip bars." Grace grinned at him.

Staring at her lovely face, lit up as it was by a genuine smile, he completely lost track of what he was saying.

"Sooo, they fed you..." she prompted after a moment.

"Yes! Right." He cleared his throat. "They were quite generous. And all they asked was that I repay them by helping them with their little spat." He shrugged. "So, I did. A few days later, Luukas and Nikulas found me on the battlefield, lying amongst my deceased companions. I'll spare you the gory details."

She stared at him a moment. "That's some heavy stuff, dude. Who're Luukas and Nikulas?"

He picked up her ice pack and rearranged it on her ankle, saying distractedly, "Luukas is the Master Vampire that turned me, and Nikulas is his younger brother. Also a vampire." The swelling was already going down, he was happy to see.

She snapped her fingers. "Oh, hey! Nikulas...that's the friend that you called, right?"

"Correct," he confirmed. "He's my best mate. I'm his Guardian, and a Hunter for Luukas."

She shook her head slightly. "You lost me again."

"Ah, yes. Sorry." Rubbing his temple, he tried to explain. "Luukas is the Master Vampire, as I said, which means he is like the leader of our colonies in the States. He created all of us, and protects us, and Nik..."

She interrupted him. "Created *all of you*? How many of you are there?"

"At last count there were five hundred and thirty-one of us throughout the country, with a large portion of them living and working in the Pacific Northwest."

Her mouth dropped open in surprise. "Luukas created five hundred vampires?"

"Yes. He's one of the more conservative Master Vampires, unlike some of those over here in the East."

Leaning forward, he took the tip of his index finger and gently closed her jaw.

She stared at him mutely, and he could see her trying to wrap her mind around the fact that humans have been going around all this time with no idea that they shared the night with that many vampires.

After a few minutes, she asked, "So, what did you and your father fight about? It must have been a doozy to cause you to react the way you did."

He thought back to that day. It seemed so long ago, yet he remembered everything as clearly as if it had just happened. But as he usually did whenever someone asked about his family, he blew it off like it was no big deal.

"Oh, something about him being a cheating bastard, I'm certain, or maybe his bloated sense of self-importance. My father tended to take on airs. He thought himself to be much more noble than he was. And," he added. "He *was* a cheating bastard."

"What did he do? Like, for a living?"

"He was part of what they used to call the 'landed gentry'. My family had money, but only because my father was particularly good at cheating at cards. He won most of it, rather than earning it honestly. Then he bought land with it, and we rented out the land. Our family's position was high in society, only immediately below the nobility. But to hear my father brag about it, one would think we were part of the royal family. He was eventually killed in a duel, and my younger brother took over the lands."

Because I wasn't there to do so.

He didn't like speaking of his father. It left a rather horrid taste in his mouth. His father was a liar, and a cheat, and a mean son of a bitch. And he didn't care about anyone but himself. Everything he did was for his own benefit. The only sound decision he'd ever made was using his ill-gotten gains to buy land instead of gambling it all away again. At least his family had gotten something out of that.

However, in the end, all he'd managed to accomplish was to get his entire family killed.

All of them except for me. Because I'd thrown a hissy fit and left home. Leaving my younger brother to try to clean up our father's mess on his own.

Maybe if he had stayed...or come back to check on his Mum sooner...he could have protected them. Could have been there to appease the tenants. But the responsibility had fallen on his younger brother, and they'd been beaten down for too long to think the son would be any different than the father.

Their father had consistently raised their rent to fund his addictions, until the people on his land had become so poor and hostile that his mum had been afraid to leave the house. Whether it was because she was afraid of being attacked or afraid of seeing the proof of his father's ways, Aiden wasn't certain.

His father's tenants couldn't afford the ungodly amounts of money and goods he charged them. But they were afraid to make a stand against him. Afraid that he would make them leave their homes and they'd starve on the road. They were barely feeding themselves as it was. So they didn't protest the high rents, however, they did talk amongst themselves. And then the talking turned to anger, and the anger turned to rebellion.

When his father had died, and his inexperienced brother had taken over, the tenants had seized their chance. They'd formed a mob, and marched to the house to take out the family that had caused them so much misery.

His entire family had been killed that night. He wasn't certain exactly what had happened, only that the house had been burned to the ground with his mum, brother and sister inside. He only knew it had been the tenants at all because he'd already been reborn as a vampire when he'd come back, and he'd used mind control on the nearest pretty wife to find out what had happened.

If only he hadn't let his father get to him. If only he'd been thinking about someone other than himself...

You're a selfish man, Aiden. Just like your father!

His mum's voice echoed in his head. She'd told him that exact thing many a time. But she was wrong. He was nothing like that bastard.

The empty hole in his chest, the one that never went away no matter how much time had passed since that fateful day, throbbed painfully.

The night he'd found the burned remains of his family, Aiden had sworn to the gods that never again would he not be there to protect those he loved. And his impressive head collection was evidence of the fact that he had kept that promise. Every single one of those heads had been taken protecting his new vampire family.

He pushed away the memories. "Let's speak of something else, all right?"

"Okay," she agreed.

Glancing down at Mojo, who was lying on his back on the pillow, he asked, "Is this where he sleeps?"

"No. Mojo will need to go back into his home." She pointed to an extravagant cage set up against the one wall. It didn't have a top, but it did have multi-levels with little ramps going up to each one, toys, a litter box, and even a little house for him to hide in.

Aiden looked over at the little ball of prickles lying serenely on the other pillow by her foot. It stared back with one beady, black eye, keeping the other one closed.

With a great sigh, he rose, picked up the little rodent, pillow and all, and gingerly slid Mojo off of it and into his cage. The little guy huffed a few times, then waddled off into his house.

A muffled noise behind him had him turning to find Grace giggling behind her hand.

He struck an indignant pose. "Are you laughing at me, poppet?"

At that, she burst out into full-fledged guffaws, telling him, "It's just...so funny...to see a grown man -and a vampire at that! - afraid of...a few little spines!"

"I'm not afraid!" he insisted, tossing the pillow back onto the couch. "Just because I dislike being stabbed for no good reason."

And besides, I prefer being the one doing the poking, he thought to himself.

She started giggling all over again. "Which is why you just happened to wander into a war..."

He didn't know what was so bloody amusing. Leaving her to her cackling, he wandered over to the walk-in closet. "Any chance you have some men's clothes in here that might fit me?" As she wiped at the tears on her face, he took it upon himself to start rummaging through her stuff.

He was elbow deep in a particularly interesting section of silky things that still smelled faintly of her skin when she said, "Sorry. I didn't mean to laugh at you. I think I'm just overtired. Look in the dresser on the right, against the wall under the hanging clothes. Third drawer down. There may be something in there that will fit."

Dropping his handful of silkies with regret, he yanked open the indicated drawer. It was full of her workout clothes, and, at the very bottom, a few pairs of men's black nylon running pants and T-shirts.

As he sorted through them, he asked her, "How *did* the rat get into that bag anyway?"

When nothing but stony silence answered his question, he poked his head out to find her staring at him stonily at him from the couch.

Rolling his eyes, he corrected himself. "How did *the bloody hedgehog* get into that bag anyway?" Hands full of clothes, he pointed with his chin to the bag in question, sitting on the floor at the end of the couch where it'd been dropped.

Narrowing her eyes at him in warning, she replied, "*Mojo* was in my little tote bag I have for him when I stopped at a restaurant to get something to eat. I set him on the floor, and when I was finished and stood up to leave, I picked up his bag only to notice he wasn't in it anymore. There weren't that many people there that late, just a couple on a date and that group of Suits I followed. When I couldn't find him anywhere, I saw them leaving and thought I saw the bag move. So I followed them to that empty building."

"And you left your tote bag at the restaurant?"

Her eyes widened as realization hit her. "Shit! I did. Dammit, that was my last one. I'll have to go pick up more."

Aiden quirked an eyebrow. "I'm just going to rinse off, if that's all right?" He didn't wait for her okay, but left her groaning to herself on the couch and took his new clothes into the loo.

Leaving the door cracked open an inch in case she needed him, he stripped off his dusty clothes and stepped gratefully under the hot spray. Rolling his head around on his neck, he let the water rinse off the dust and sludge, groaning aloud as it ran down the grooves of his muscular body.

Spotting the various bottles on the built-in shower shelves, he grabbed one, opened it, and smelled the contents. It smelled like her hair, and the constant burning of his gums, an unexpected and ever-present problem since he'd first found her, worsened, his fangs even sliding down a bit.

Pouring some of the herbal shampoo in his hand, he scrubbed his head and rinsed. Finding the body wash, he started scouring himself quickly, trying not to think of how the scent of the soap he was using smelled when it was warmed from her lovely peaches-n-cream skin. He'd bet his right fang that skin was as smooth and soft as it looked. It would be like warm silk under his hands and mouth.

He smothered a different kind of groan as his blood heated and his cock twitched, but he resisted the urge to take the hard length in his hand and ease some of this tension. Somehow, he knew that it would only make it all worse. Gritting his teeth, he quickly rinsed off his now throbbing cock and moved on.

What the bloody hell was he doing here anyway? He could be showering in a hotel right now while he waited on a plane ride home to Seattle.

He should already be on his way back to his family, doing his job, not running around rescuing silly boot brushes.

He should be trying to figure out what happened to him and how he got here, not how to shag the crumpet in the next room, intriguing as she was.

She didn't need him anymore. He'd helped her get her Mojo back and had gotten them both home safe and sound.

He should be on the phone with Nikulas, arranging his ride home. There were plenty of other, more willing, females in the world. This...pull he felt towards her would go away as soon as there was some distance between them.

He scowled at the shower wall. She made him FEEL things. He didn't like it.

He would call Nik first thing tonight, as soon as he woke up.

Mind made up, he turned off the water, grabbed her towel off the rack and dried off, then threw on his newly acquired shirt and trousers. He'd have to ask about washing his stuff. He couldn't spend the rest of his time here "going commando" as they say, at least not comfortably, and he hated shopping. Besides, he wasn't going to be here long enough to warrant doing so.

Be that as it may, as long as he *was* here, he needed to take a look into that bag tonight after he made that phone call.

Grace watched from under lowered lids, pretending to be asleep, as Aiden came out of the bathroom and headed towards her. Even through her lashes, she could see that her ex-boyfriend's clothes looked way hotter on him then they ever had on her ex.

Whereas Jim, her Swedish-born, computer geek ex-boyfriend, had those clothes here only to impress her by working out with her when he'd stayed over (which hadn't been often), Aiden already had the physique to make them look good.

She squeezed her eyes shut and snored lightly for effect as he treaded soundlessly over to her in his bare feet.

He lifted the ice from her ankle, and she cracked her eyes open again, watching him as he leaned closer and touched her bruise with light fingers.

A concerned frown creased his brow as he took the towel to the kitchen, put more ice in it, then placed it gently back on her swollen ankle.

He made no sound at all as he walked over to the window and peeked through the shades. If she hadn't been watching, she would never know he was even in the room. After a long moment, he turned away from the window, picked up the crocheted blanket from the rocking chair, and covered her with it. He tucked it around her, kissed her lightly on the forehead, and then he stole Mojo's pillow.

She managed to keep her breathing steady through it all. Her eyes followed him as he took his pillow into the closet, dug around for another blanket on one of the shelves, and then shut the closet door behind him against the oncoming sunlight.

Maybe she should've used the bathroom again before he went in there. She rolled over and pulled the blanket up around her while she thought about tiptoeing around a sleeping vampire in the middle of the day. The image made her shiver under her blanket.

What if he woke up? Would he know that it was her? Would he be hungry? Or thirsty? Or whatever? She had to admit, with her luck, it was more likely that the worst thing that would happen is that she'd forget he was there and fall over him.

She wondered if he looked dead when he slept, which he pretty much was, right?

She'd just have to hold it until sundown, that's all.

Her ankle throbbed and she sat up to adjust the ice. The thought crossed her mind that she could use her insignificant magic to heal it, which was pretty much all it was good for, but then decided against it for now. Magic took a lot out of her. And if Aiden happened to come out again and surprised her while she was in the middle of a healing spell, she might end up breaking her bones instead of healing them.

Besides, she wasn't ready for him to find out what a freak she was.

When all had been quiet for a good thirty minutes or so, she got up as quietly as she could. Hobbling over to the kitchen, she found the large container of salt where she kept it hidden in one of the lower cabinets.

Beginning in the corner at the far end of the kitchen, she limped her way around the entire apartment, pouring salt along the edge of the floor where it hit the wall. When she was finished, there was a complete circle enclosing the room she was in.

She glanced at the closed closet door, but she couldn't risk waking him up to contain him inside the circle. Not without exposing herself.

Besides, if what her mother had told her was true, she couldn't depend on him to help her. She'd have to take care of herself. And he was a vampire. He was perfectly capable of defending himself. Those things never came out during the day anyway.

This would just have to do.

8

Luukas watched his brother run his hand through his blond hair in frustration as he watched the video footage from their security cameras around the building. They'd been sitting there in the office for hours, pouring over the tapes, phone records, and statements from the security team at their apartments, trying to figure out what the hell had happened to the other Hunters.

They'd come up with absolutely nothing. They'd disappeared into thin air.

"Three Hunters," Nik gritted out. "Just fucking gone. All within a few hours of each other, and all without a trace. They just vanished off the face of the earth. How is that possible?"

"Let's go over everything again," Luukas told him. He didn't know what good it would do, but he had to do something. Maybe they'd missed some small clue somewhere.

As Nik straightened out the notes he'd been taking that were strewn haphazardly across the desk, he glanced out the glass wall towards the living room, where he could see his Keira and her sister. She and Emma were "practicing", and their magic filled the air of the apartment as one of the lamps floated across the room. Clapping her hands with excitement, Keira urged her sister on as she managed to gently set it on the opposite table.

His heart swelled and his soul quieted as he watched his witch, even as his body tensed in fear.

After all he'd gone through, and all he'd suffered because of her sorcery, it still set him on edge. He couldn't help it. The only time he felt in control was when he had her flat on her back on the bed, or against the wall, or in the shower...

His body hardened immediately at the thought, and his gums burned as his fangs slid down a fraction, anticipating the taste of her.

"Luuk? Did you hear me?"

He tore his eyes reluctantly from the voluptuous curves of his raven-haired mate, giving his brother his full attention. "I'm sorry. What did you say?"

Nikulas repeated what he'd just said. "I just found something."

Joining his brother on the other side of the desk, Luukas stood next to him and leaned onto the desk to watch the computer monitor.

"That's Dante," he stated. "Is that our garage? Here?"

"Yes. I've been studying the footage from the hallways, the foyer, and the street entrance so much I almost missed this one. Now watch."

Luukas watched as a black van came to a screeching halt just as it passed the leather-clad Dante. Two men spilled out of the side door and approached him on either side. As Dante turned to confront the one, the other snuck up behind him and jabbed something into his neck. The massive Hunter went down like a toppling building.

Another human jumped out of the driver's side, and together, they managed to get the vampire into the back. They all got back in and the van took off out of the garage.

It had all gone down in less than two minutes.

Luukas straightened up.

"Where was the security guard?"

"I don't know, but I'm sure as hell going to find out," Nik seethed.

"Back up the tape again. Let's see if we can get a plate number," he ordered.

"You got it, bro."

Luukas wandered over to the window while his brother rewound the tape.

One Hunter found, two more to go.

And he had no doubt they would find Dante. That little clue was all he needed. Luukas would search every nook and cranny of this earth relentlessly until he found him.

He knew his Hunters were still alive. Dante, Shea, and Christian. He was their creator, he would know if anything had happened to them. He could feel their essence, and he would feel it if they left him.

"Got it," Nik exclaimed.

"Ok. Let's find our Hunter."

Nik paused his fingers on the keyboard. "What about the others, Luuk? We still haven't found a damn thing on them. We've only got the video of them leaving their apartments. Alone."

"Although," he added as an afterthought, "It did look like Shea was looking for the guys. But that only tells us that she was the last one to be taken, if that's what happened."

"They're still alive. Let's focus on finding Dante and then maybe we'll have an idea of what happened to Shea and Christian."

"Yeah, ok." Nik's fingers started flying over the keyboard again, searching for info on the plate number. "I'm not as good at this as Aiden," he told Luuk. "But I can find out who owns this van, and we'll go from there."

Luukas held his hands behind his back and gazed out at his city, his mind racing ahead. It wouldn't surprise him in the least if Leeha were the one behind the abductions.

He really should have burned her along with her father.

9

Dante sat in one of the troop seats towards the back of the aircraft, keeping a close eye on the three human men holding him at gunpoint. The way he figured it, only two out of the three were a real threat: The bald one who'd been driving the van they'd kidnapped him in, and the pilot of the V-22 Osprey they'd brought him to.

However, somebody had to fly the fucking thing. Which would bring the threat down to one.

"Don't bother strapping yourself in," Baldy sneered at him. "You ain't gonna be with us when we land."

Ignoring him, Dante focused on the one he was going to take out first - the chicken shit who'd pissed himself in the van when he'd broken free of the chains.

Or maybe he should take out Baldy first? But then he would be taking the chance that Chicken Shit would shoot him with one of those exploding bullets they claimed to have. He doubted his aim was very good, especially with the way he was shaking, but he might get lucky.

Decisions, decisions.

The pilot he would definitely save for last. By the time he figured out what was going on, it would be too late. He could smell another human in the aircraft, probably the co-pilot waiting in the cockpit.

Dante rubbed a hand over his shaved head as he contemplated his choices.

A loud "click" echoed in the silence, and he dropped it onto his lap again.

Baldy smacked Chicken Shit in the back of his greasy head. "What the fuck are you doin'? Trying to blow up the fuckin' plane? Jesus fucking Christ."

Chicken Shit turned on him. "You gave me an empty gun?" he yelled incredulously. He pulled the trigger again and again. The empty chamber clicked loudly.

He finally gave up and threw his arms in the air. "No bullets? You gave me a gun with no bullets? What the fuck?"

"Calm the fuck down," Baldy told him. "Of course I didn't give you any bullets. Look at you! He barely moves and you're trying to blow a hole in the plane just now!"

Well, that decided things. Baldy needed to go first, as he was the only one that was armed other than the pilot.

"Holy shit." Chicken Shit dropped his gun to the floor where it landed with a clank and ran his hands nervously through his hair. His eyes flew wildly around the plane.

"Relax," Baldy told him without taking his eyes off of Dante. "Nothin's gonna happen."

"Do you need me to leave this with you?" the pilot asked, indicating his own weapon. "Don has another one up front."

Don. The co-pilot.

Dante smiled. The more the merrier.

"Nah," Baldy told the pilot. "I got this. Let's go."

Chicken Shit sank into one of the front seats and dropped his head into his hands as the pilot disappeared into the cockpit.

"I'm gonna fuckin' die. I'm gonna fuckin' die," he mumbled.

Baldy sat down next to him and leaned back. Placing his ankle on his opposite knee, he rested his forearm on his leg and steadied the gun on Dante.

"Might as well get comfy," he told him. "We got about a two-hour flight ahead of us."

Dante felt his first inkling of nervousness as the aircraft taxied onto the runway and lifted into the air. He figured a two-hour flight could mean one of two things: They were either taking him to Vegas, or they were going to dump him in the middle of the Pacific Ocean. Neither of which would end well for him.

And he doubted Baldy was looking for a new gambling partner.

"Don't talk much, do ya?" he asked Dante.

Chicken Shit had cinched himself in and was now bouncing one leg nervously while he chewed on a thumbnail.

Dante narrowed his eyes on him while keeping Baldy within view out of the corner of his eye. All he needed was a half a second. A half a second when Baldy thought he wasn't paying attention to him and his guard would slip.

They traveled in silence for a good hour or more before Baldy got bored again.

"So what's it like? Being a parasite? Living off the blood of innocent people like a fuckin' mosquito?"

Dante nearly smiled. Did he truly think his childish taunts were going to get a rise out of someone such as him? Besides, right now he was too busy trying to gauge where they were to react to the human's jabs. He needed to exit this aircraft while they were still flying over land. His chances of surviving were much better on land than in water.

"I'm talkin' to you, asshole."

Chicken Shit glanced up briefly as the rear-loading ramp opened, then did a double take when he noticed Dante's complete attention was still on him. His eyes grew as large as saucers in his thin face and he began to visibly sweat, large drops running down his temples to drip off of his chin.

Dante smiled at his increasing fear, exposing his fangs, and hissed at him.

Unbuckling his restraints, Chicken Shit jumped up and pounded on the cockpit door. "Let me in! Let me the fuck in! He's gonna fuckin' kill me!"

"Sit the fuck down!" Baldy yelled. "He ain't gonna do nothin'."

But Chicken Shit was in a full out panic and beyond following orders. He continued to bang on the cockpit door, screaming for them to let him in, to lower the aircraft...anything to get him the fuck out of there. When that didn't work, he stumbled over to the side door, falling into Baldy when they hit an air pocket.

That was all the distraction Dante needed. Moving faster than human eyes could see, he took a running start and launched himself out of the back opening of the aircraft.

In the time it took Baldy to push the skinny one off of him and raise his gun, his prisoner was gone. He started to laugh.

"Well, that was easier than I thought it was gonna be."

10

Grace's eyes popped open, her heart pounding a mile a minute. She'd been sleeping soundly - surprisingly, with the first actual vampire she'd ever encountered passed out right in the next room and all - but something had startled her awake.

A quick glance around showed her it was barely twilight, and still raining. It was too early for the vampire to be up, or Mojo either for that matter, but she craned her neck around and checked his cage anyway.

Nope. She didn't see him. He must still be snoozing in his house.

She stretched, rotating her still-sore ankle around a little to test it, and wondered what had awoken her. But all was quiet. Maybe it had just been a neighbor. Soundproof as her place usually was, she did hear them coming and going occasionally.

Or maybe she'd just been dreaming.

With a mental shrug, she rolled over and closed her eyes again. She'd just convinced herself that it must've been the guy across the hall when she heard it again: A bump at the window next to her head.

She reacted immediately and without thought, thanks to her mother's training.

Quickly and quietly, she rolled off the couch and onto the floor, then took off at a fast crawl towards the kitchen. She kept her head down, silently praying that she wouldn't be seen through the blinds that covered the windows. Even though they were blackout blinds, and the chances were slim to none that they'd be able to see her, she still began to sweat as fear clenched her insides. It dripped down her temple, and she blinked her eyes rapidly.

Somehow she managed to make it to the kitchen without being spotted. Her heart pounded in her ears as she huddled on the floor behind the island and peered around the corner back towards the window. The setting sun outlined the distinct shadow of a person through the faux wood blinds.

Eyes wide, she drew her head back again and leaned back against the cabinet, breathing hard.

Shit. Shit. Shit. Was the window even locked? Probably not. She lived on the 9th floor, and there weren't any balconies. Locking her windows just in case a bad guy decided to scale the building like Spiderman and sneak into her apartment had never really occurred to her. How the hell had they gotten up here?

Her mind raced ahead. Unless it *was* a Spiderman-like something or another. But no, it had to be a human. It couldn't be those things Aiden had been talking to when they rescued Mojo. They couldn't come out during the day.

At least she'd never seen them during the day before.

But even if they could, if they were what she suspected they were, the salt circle would keep them out.

Maybe she should've warned Aiden about them, and told him what she knew. Then again, they seemed to know *him*. For all she knew, he was one of them, and this whole amnesia thing was just an act.

The distinct sound of a switchblade spurred her into action. Scooting across the floor backwards with her bad ankle dragging uselessly in front of her, she opened the corner pantry door just wide enough to stick her hand in.

Inside, her palm closed around the handle of her father's Glock 9mm. She pulled it out, then stuck her hand back in to find the clip, slamming it into place as quietly as she could. Reaching in one more time, she found the silencer.

Her hands shook as she attached it to the barrel, and she nearly dropped it once, but amazingly she managed to get it on without alerting her intruder of her presence.

Inching the door closed again, but not latching it, she scooted over to the shadowy corner on the other side where she could see the window clearly. Gripping the gun firmly in her trembling hands, she steadied her arms on her knees, and waited.

She was still hidden partially by the island, and the sun was rapidly sinking behind the horizon. Along with the clouds and rain, she hoped it would be dark enough that they wouldn't notice her right away.

At least not until she could take a shot. And by then it would be too late.

She cursed softly to herself as she heard them cutting through the screen. Couldn't they just pull it off and stick it inside? Nicely? Against the wall where it wouldn't get damaged? Now she'd have to buy a new one.

Uninvited intruders were so damned inconsiderate.

As the window slowly slid open, a smug laugh floated softly inside on the cool, damp breeze.

Grace gave herself a mental kick in the ass. Dammit. Dammit! Why the hell didn't she ever lock those things? She knew better, but she'd gotten soft in the years since her Mom had been gone.

The blinds pushed out from the window and she saw a black-clad leg with a climbing shoe attached to it appear from the bottom. It felt around blindly with its toe until it made contact with the floor, stepping right over the salt circle. A compact male body followed it a moment later, curling in backwards behind the blinds like an acrobat about to do a back somersault, and finally the other leg and shoe.

Once completely inside, he dropped down into a crouch, and his head poked out from behind the faux wooden slabs as he took a quick look around.

Wait. Wait. Not yet. Don't waste your shot.

Her mother's voice echoed in her head as she bided her time. She couldn't mess this up. If she missed her mark, or worse, didn't hit him at all, she'd give away her location. And then it would be a standoff as he went for cover either on the other side of the kitchen island or into the closet.

Where Aiden was sleeping.

She spared a quick glance in the direction of the closed door, fighting to keep her breathing soundless and even, refusing to panic needlessly at the thought of him being in danger. Would he even wake up? Or would he be helpless as he slept until the sun went down?

It was only because he'd helped her, she told herself. Anybody who helped her rescue her Mojo deserved a soft spot in her heart.

A sudden movement in front of her had her eyes darting away from Aiden's hiding place and back to her intruder. He'd come out from behind the blinds now and was cautiously scanning the rest of the room. Staying low in a half-crouch position, he snuck along the length of the couch, and was soon out of her sight on the other side of the island.

She listened to the light scuff of his shoes on the bamboo floor, trying to track his movements. Any moment now, she would see him when he got closer to the front door.

Any moment now...

She frowned when the scuffing stopped and he never reappeared. Long seconds ticked by as she waited for his next move.

What the hell is he doing? Taking a nap?

And then she realized what it was that he had come after. The bag! It was on the floor by the other end of the couch. He must've found it.

They hadn't even checked inside of it yet, but apparently, she'd been right. There must be something valuable in there if the Suits had gone through the trouble of tracking her down and sending someone after it.

Maybe he would just take the stupid bag and leave, and she wouldn't have to shoot anybody. If he believed no one was here, he'd just go right back out that window.

And she'd sure as all hell be locking it behind him this time - with goddamned titanium bars.

Time crawled as she waited for him to leave, but he stayed where he was. Was he searching through it? She held her breath and listened, but it was no use, she couldn't hear anything. Glancing towards the top of the closet door again, she saw that it was still closed.

He wasn't *seriously* taking a nap? Was he? Her couch was comfy and all, but napping in the middle of a heist? That was a far stretch, even for these idiots.

As stealthily as she could, she started scooting forward on her behind, holding her bad ankle up off of the floor and pushing with one hand while the other kept the pistol aimed steadily in front of her.

Just a little more, just a little more...

As she came around the side of the island, more of the couch came into view. She scooted up inch by inch until she could see the entire thing.

No one was there.

Dammit. Where the hell was he? Had he snuck back out the window? No, he couldn't possibly have gotten out without her seeing him.

Maybe he'd gone out the other one? But no, there was no breeze. It was still closed.

Well...what the hell?

She slouched back out of sight. She needed to get back to her corner where she couldn't be caught unaware. Guiding herself with one hand on the floor, she pushed with her good foot to slide her butt back.

Before she could make any progress, a sudden, blunt pain shot up her fingers and she whipped her head around with a stifled cry to find a climbing shoe digging into the delicate bones of her hand. Before she could react and try to pull her hand away, he lifted his foot and stomped down hard again with his heel, breaking the bones in her hand and wrist this time.

She screamed in agony even as she swung her pistol around with her other arm and took aim. Instinctively, she fired, and the pressure immediately eased off her hand as the bullet went completely through his left hip and into the wood behind him.

Her intruder staggered back on his useless leg, falling into the cabinets with a loud crash. Shattered glass rained around him as he collapsed with a yelp, landing on his torn up hip. Rolling to the other side, he reached around with both hands and slapped them over the entrance and exit wounds the bullet had left in an attempt to stop the bleeding.

Grace sat stunned, her hand and wrist throbbing in pain. She'd actually shot somebody. Fuckin' A.

He tore his eyes from his bloodied hip to glare at her, and she instinctively recoiled from the pure hatred she saw there. With an evil twist of his lips, he cursed her in Mandarin, promising revenge on her and all she cared about. Keeping one hand on the hole in his backside, he rolled onto his stomach. He started pulling himself towards her on his elbow, sliding along the floor, dragging his useless leg behind him. He looked like something out of a bad horror movie.

Grace scuttled awkwardly back away from him as fast as she could with her one good arm and leg, the gun clunking on the floor with her movements.

When her back hit the sofa, she lifted the pistol, taking shaky aim at his head just as the closet door flew open, slamming into the wall behind it with a bang.

Aiden took in the situation with one quick glance. "Poppet, you should really wait for me to get up before you start shooting people. It takes all the fun out of it for me."

Grateful tears welled up and ran down her cheeks as she watched Aiden stride calmly over to the kitchen to see who it was she had shot, but she kept the gun trained on her target's head, just in case.

"I know this bloke," he told her. "He was one of the humans you were following earlier."

His next question was directed to the guy who was still inching his way towards her. "All of this for a silly boot brush? He's really not worth it. He's no good at cleaning the muck off your shoes. He scurries around too much. You can't keep him under foot."

Was he was going to stand around and chat all day, or was going to do something to help her? Did he not notice that the bad guy was still coming after her?

Leaning over the island, his grey eyes were ablaze with excitement when they shot back over to where she still sat on the floor, wondering if she was going to have to shoot the guy after all. They were a direct contrast to the pained expression on his face. "I hate to tell you this, love, but he's bleeding all over your pretty floor."

His voice had changed. It sounded thicker, deeper, and...scarier...and completely unlike the teasing Brit she'd spent the last twenty-four hours with.

Grace's eyes flew from her target to Aiden, almost afraid of what she'd see.

She had to blink a few times at the sight of him, thinking at first it was just the water in her eyes contorting his features, but then she swallowed hard as she realized it wasn't the tears at all.

For the first time, she was seeing him for what he truly was.

His entire essence had changed. He'd become...more. His muscles were larger, his fangs longer than she'd ever seen them. And his face! His features had grown sharper, leaner, more menacing, and his eyes glowed from their sockets like they were lit from behind with an icy fire.

Frozen to the spot, she was unable to move or speak. True terror crawled up her spine for the first time since she'd met him. As he cocked his head to the side, the hair on the back of her neck and arms rose eerily.

He sneered, showing off his fangs as he honed in on her victim with a predator's stare. "How about I move him to the loo? Yes?"

She somehow managed to nod, but he was already yanking him up off of the floor with one hand.

A trail of blood smeared across her floor as he headed into the bathroom with his prize, dragging the terrified man behind him.

The slam of the door had her nearly jumping out of her skin. A moment later, a blood-curdling scream came from the bathroom and echoed off the walls around her, fading immediately into a wet gurgle.

She squeezed her eyes shut and threw her good arm over her head to cover her ears. The abrupt silence that followed was even worse than the screams. Grace's entire body began to shake.

She was still sitting like that, gun held tightly in her unbroken hand, when Aiden found her a few minutes later.

"Grace? love? It's all right now. It's over. He won't be bothering you anymore."

Aiden's hands were as gentle as his voice as he stroked her long hair down her back, and then carefully removed the pistol from her grasp. "I'm just going to set this over here."

She lifted her head cautiously as he placed the gun on the counter and turned back towards her. Other than a few drops of blood on his T-shirt, she could see no evidence of his latest meal. Thank the gods. His fangs had retracted, his warmth had returned, and he looked like, well...he looked like him again.

But that warmth rapidly disappeared as she uncurled her body and sat up, and she followed his eyes down to her broken hand where she held it cradled protectively against her chest.

Chills slithered over her skin as an animalistic growl rumbled low in his throat. Her eyes shot back up to his face just in time to see his fangs shoot down as his lips pull back into a snarl. Impossibly, his grey eyes grew even brighter than they were before, until they were so incandescent they were almost white.

He prowled towards her, and she watched him come, her heart thudding in her chest, unable to speak, unable to flee.

She was completely enraptured by his otherness.

He was an awesomely beautiful creature to watch when he was like this, even as he terrified her. His strong body flexed as he moved, so fluid, like a dancer, or a large feline. His handsome features appeared leaner, sharper. His attention on her was so focused and intense, she felt the rest of the world fall away until there was nothing left but the two of them and this moment.

Grace bit back a cry when he abruptly dropped down directly in front of her. She couldn't help but feel like a wounded animal, about to be ripped apart by a predator. Which, she supposed, was exactly what she was.

Unable to take her eyes from him, she started babbling nervously. "Aiden, you're scaring me. Please..." She choked back a sob, her words sticking in her throat as his glowing eyes flew to hers, capturing her gaze and hypnotizing her into silence as she waited for him to attack.

But instead of pouncing, he reached out and took her elbow with the most tender of touches. Catching her injured hand in his, he released her from his gaze as he gently probed her injury with his fingers.

She took a much-needed breath, and then cried out as he hit a particularly tender spot, and his eyes flew back to her face.

Fresh tears flooded her eyes. "It hurts..."

He sat so still for so long that her bones began to ache from sitting in the same position. Just as she was debating whether or not she should try to pull her arm back, he ground out between clenched teeth, "He did this."

It wasn't a question.

"Yes," she whispered anyway.

He growled low in his throat again, and then gently released her arm back to her. After a few deep breaths, he appeared to have calmed a bit, and when he raised his eyes to hers again, the glowing was gone, and they were only slightly brighter than normal. The lines around them crinkled attractively as he murmured with a sadistic smile, "If only I could kill him again. Humans are entirely too fragile."

"Yes," she said again, a little louder this time, then sniffed. She wasn't quite sure why she was agreeing with him.

He wiped a tear from her cheek with his thumb. "I suppose we should take you to the hospital."

She flinched slightly at his touch, and then gritted her teeth for being such a girl and almost told him there was no need, but just nodded instead.

"All right. Let me take care of him first."

He reached out to help her up, lifting her effortlessly from the floor. As she balanced on her one good ankle, holding her broken hand carefully against her stomach, he shook his head at her.

"You're just a mess, aren't you, poppet? Let's get you to the couch and I'll clean up my mess right quick, then we'll go get you fixed up, yes?"

"Okay." Fresh tears gathered and fell, and she wiped at her face with the sleeve of her shirt. She wasn't sure why she was still crying, but she couldn't seem to stop.

Wrapping an arm around her waist, he assisted her back to the couch.

Night had fallen, and after making sure she was settled comfortably, he raised the blinds to close her window, locking it firmly. Walking around to the other side of the couch, he locked that window also.

Her tears finally began to subside as she watched him, her mind unusually quiet. She was in pain, and in shock, she supposed, and for the moment was happy to let him take care of things.

He picked the black bag up off the floor and tossed it onto the couch beside her, along with her gun.

"Why don't you rummage around in there and see what you can find while I clean up the mess in the loo? There's definitely something in there that they want. I don't really think he came here to try to get Mojo back, I was just having some fun with him. Silly of them, really, to only send one person after it. And an unarmed human, at that! By the way, do you happen to have some extra shoes that belonged to this bloke?" He pulled at his shirt to indicate the "bloke" in question.

She blinked at him blankly, unable to comprehend his rambling in her current state of mind.

He cocked his head at her. "Grace? All right, love?"

The sound of her name on his lips jolted her out of her stupor. She blinked a few more times, her thoughts finally catching up with his words. "What? Oh. Yeah...yes. I'm fine. I'll look through the bag."

He looked at her a bit oddly, so she pulled the bag closer to her and started rummaging through it with her good hand. Satisfied, he turned towards her bathroom, calling over his shoulder, "By the way, you're going to need a new shower curtain...and plunger."

Plunger?

She opened her mouth to ask, and then snapped it shut again. No. She didn't even want to know.

11

Aiden rushed back to Grace's apartment after dumping the body, or at least what was left of it when he'd gotten through with it.

He was still quite astonished at the unusual level of rage that had filled him when he'd woken to the sound of a silenced gunshot and ran out to find an intruder bleeding in her kitchen. The reaction he'd had was a bit much, especially for him, yet he hadn't been able to help himself.

If the human had come just a few hours sooner, before he'd awakened...Ugh. No. He didn't even want to think of it.

Fear gripped his heart at the mere thought of his Grace out there all alone while he dozed away peacefully in the closet. Although, he had to admit, she'd proven herself quite capable of handling the situation without him for the most part...but still.

His blood boiled at the memory of her delicate, broken hand, but he firmly tamped it down. He needed to keep his wits about him. And besides, she'd been traumatized enough for the moment without him showing back up at her place all in a tizzy. He could analyze this strange occurrence he was having of *feeling things* later.

The real question was: Why would a female like her possess a weapon like that to begin with? With a silencer, no less? Who had she been expecting to use it against? She was obviously well trained with its use, but he had the distinct feeling that tonight was the first time she'd actually fired that impressive pistol of hers at anything other than a target at a gun range.

And the mystery that is Grace thickens.

He nearly clapped his hands together in glee. There was nothing he loved more than a good riddle. How could he possibly leave before solving it?

Aiden smiled as he leaped over the moving vehicles to the other side of the road, traveling so fast he was nothing but a passing blur to the humans going about their night in the city. He wasn't concerned about them seeing him. They'd look twice as he passed, unsure if they'd really seen anything, then shrug it off as a trick of the lights and continue on.

A few short minutes later he was back at her door. Letting himself in, he found her perched on the edge of the couch. Her hand, wrist, and ankle were wrapped with Ace bandages, her hair was pulled back in a low ponytail, trainers were on her feet, and a stuffed rucksack was sitting on the floor next to her.

Mojo's little rat head poked through the top zipper of her bag as he closed the door behind him. He wrinkled his nose at

Aiden, and stared at him with his beady little eyes when he came in, as though saying: *Finally! We've been waiting for hours!*

Aiden scratched his head and wrinkled his nose back at him. He hadn't been gone more than thirty minutes, for heaven's sake.

Dismissing the rat, he asked, "Going somewhere, love?"

She stood up at his question and swayed a bit, her face paling at the sudden movement.

He stepped forward to catch her, but she held out her hand, stopping him where he was. He noticed she barely favored her bad ankle at all. He also noticed she had changed her clothes while he was gone, and was now wearing hunter-green cargo pants and a beige long-sleeved cotton shirt with a white T-shirt poking out from underneath. An all-weather jacket was lying on the couch, and the black bag was sitting on top of it.

She'd done quite a lot in the short time he'd been gone. Interesting, considering she could barely hobble about the place when he'd left. He made a mental note of it, but didn't say anything. This female apparently had more than one secret. And he decided right then and there that there was no way he was leaving until he'd sorted them all out.

"I think it would be a good idea for us to get out of here, Aiden."

He looked down at his borrowed clothes. "But, I don't have a thing to wear."

She rolled her eyes. "I'm serious!"

"So am I," he retorted. "I chafe easily you know."

Her mouth dropped open, her forehead crinkling up at him in that adorable way she had when she was looking at him like he'd lost his mind.

"What does that have to do with anything?" she finally sputtered out.

"I chafe. My skin is very tender," he waved a hand in front of his hips. "And I'm not wearing any..."

She chopped her good hand through the air, effectively cutting off his answer before he could explain his lack of drawers and the issue it presented. "I don't want to know!"

"But you asked," he retorted.

"Aiden!"

"You did," he insisted. "What did you find in the bag?" he asked, pointing with his chin at the item in question on top of her coat.

"That's what I'm trying to tell you if you would just shut up and listen for a minute!" she hissed at him.

Her face was now turning a number of interesting colors, but as amusing as it was, he decided to give her a break. Mustering up a properly chastised look, he crossed his arms over his chest. "Go on then."

She opened her mouth, glanced down at the bulge of his nether regions, closed it again, and then finally took a deep breath and gave her head a quick shake before proceeding in a calmer tone.

"I didn't find anything in the bag."

She was lying. But what he found even more interesting was that she was very good at it.

"I don't know what it was they were after," she continued. "There's just some files, a few other things...nothing of any importance that I can tell."

Picking up the bag, he opened it up and started shuffling through the contents. She was correct. He didn't see anything of importance. Some manila files with what looked like charts written in Chinese, pens, tissues, and some type of wooden jewelry box.

He pulled the box out, thinking it was a rather odd item to have with business items, but didn't see anything unusual about it. There was nothing in it, and no unusual markings other than a strange symbol on the lid, probably decorative. He put it back in the bag.

Grace swallowed nervously, but otherwise gave no indication of being bothered by him looking for himself.

"I still think we should take the bag with us though," she told him. "There's something in there those Suits wanted, and they wanted it badly enough to send that dude to break into my apartment to steal it back."

"And," she continued. "They were obviously meeting with your old friends." She gave him a look, like it was *his* fault. "Maybe it was some kind of deal they were making? And that's why he came here in broad daylight, to try to get it back before the other ones could."

He picked up where she left off. "Which means both parties will be after it."

"Exactly."

Stepping closer to set the bag back on the couch, he caught a whiff of her tantalizing scent.

Ah, gods.

His mouth immediately watered at the thought of tasting her, and his gums burned as his fangs itched to be released. Of all the females he'd enjoyed in his long life, he'd never come across one quite as enticing as this little firecracker standing in front of him.

What was it exactly about this female in particular, he wondered? He ran his eyes slowly from the top of her cinnamon head to the tips of her trainers, trying to figure it out.

She was just his thing, sure: Curvy in all the right places. Skin like porcelain with a light scattering of cute freckles across her nose. Large, expressive eyes of clear green. A wide smile. And thick, gorgeous hair that he couldn't wait to feel tickling his bare skin.

But it was her scent, he decided, that really drew him in. He'd never in all of his years smelled anything quite like it.

His fangs finally broke through, sliding down into his mouth as he eyed up the graceful curve of her throat. Muscles tightened and flexed as his entire body hardened; images of her deliciously naked and writhing beneath him flashing through his mind.

She shifted her weight from foot to foot, uncomfortable with his intense scrutiny. As his eyes made their way back up to her face, she lifted her chin defiantly and met his gaze with a bold one of her own.

He smiled a slow, sexy smile, and lowered his head towards hers. Touching her cheek with his own, he closed his eyes and breathed her deep into his lungs, memorizing her scent.

She leaned away and cleared her throat, rudely interrupting his little fantasy.

Again.

Ah yes, they were talking about the bag, and the things that would be coming after it. He returned to their conversation. "And you waited for me to return? Why not just go off on your own? You haven't exactly seemed fond of having my company since I caught you attempting your rat's rescue on your own."

She backed away a step and cleared her throat again, dusting imaginary lint off of her shirt as she stalled before answering him.

He obviously made her nervous. But was it fear or desire that had her putting distance between them?

Finally, she looked up at him, and gave a shrug. "Honestly, I just figured I'd be safer with my very own vampire bodyguard, with those thugs chasing me and all. That is," she quickly added, "If you want the job. If not, that's cool too. Mojo and I have been on our own for a while now. We'll be fine doing it again."

"What about your life here? Your job?" he asked.

She looked away. "I'm already on a leave of absence from work, and I don't really have a life other than that, so...there you go."

Hmmm. She must really need his help. She hadn't even fussed at him for calling her pet a rat. And the way her eyes kept shifting around...

Ah, yes. His damsel in distress was definitely hiding something. Maybe it wasn't just his irresistible masculinity that was making her so twitchy.

"I'm in!" he exclaimed so suddenly that she jumped. "Let's just get out of here, shall we? You're not going to get your deposit back as it is. A little blood on the floor will just give your landlords a little something extra for their story about what a horrible renter you were." He walked to the door, not waiting for her to follow him. "I just need to make a stop for some clothes...I was serious about the chafing...and these shoes! Don't even get me started on these shoes..."

Holding the door open, he was mildly surprised to find her right behind him, backpack on her shoulder and jacket and bag in hand. As she passed him without a word, he exchanged looks with Mojo, and gave him a wink.

Locking the door behind him, he followed her to the elevator, ignoring the guilty little voice in his head.

I thought we were going home? To our family? To our job?

He wasn't being selfish. He was helping a damsel in distress.

He would call Nikulas and go back to his duties just as soon as he got her somewhere safe.

12

Grace waited anxiously outside the dressing room for Aiden. He'd been trying on clothes for the past hour, and she was seriously about to walk out of there, with or without him.

Picking up her backpack from the floor, she tickled Mojo on the snout and gave him a snack from her pocket before sliding the strap over her shoulder.

"Aiden? I'm leaving. The store is about to close. If you're coming with me, you'd better hurry it the hell up!"

His head popped up over the top of the door. "Do the males here seriously fit themselves into these trousers? How, I ask you? I can't even get them zipped!"

Her face burned as she looked around, hoping beyond hope no one had heard him. "Maybe you just need a bigger size," she mumbled.

"Rubbish. I've been wearing the same size for over three hundred years, love." He disappeared again. "And the colors! As if I don't stand out enough."

She rolled her eyes.

"But this shirt though, this shirt is brilliant! I'm going to take it."

The door opened and Grace gasped, then quickly averted her eyes as he casually strolled out wearing nothing but bright red boxer briefs and a body-hugging black T-shirt with a striking green and silver dragon on the front.

But not before noticing why it was, exactly, that he was having trouble fitting into the pants.

She watched him inconspicuously as he hung up the clothes he didn't want on the return rack and wandered over to a nearby display of dark jeans.

Her eyes roamed from his strong, perfectly formed legs to his muscular ass, and she bit her bottom lip to keep from moaning with sheer pleasure at the sight. It was just about the most perfect damn ass she'd ever seen on a guy. A long-dormant desire pooled in her belly as she watched the muscles flex while he walked.

Gods, she'd almost forgotten what that felt like.

She sighed in disappointment when he finally pulled down a few pairs of pants and held them in front of him as he came back her way, blocking her view. She averted her eyes again before he caught her ogling him.

Pausing so close to her she could feel the warmth of his skin and smell his clean, woodsy scent, he purred, "Staring at me like that, love...and in public, no less...is not going to help me fit into these trousers."

"I wasn't staring!" she hissed, mortified.

He leaned down and ran the tip of his nose along her jawline and up into her hair, breathing her in deeply.

"Yes, you were."

Then he abruptly turned away and entered the dressing room, slamming the door closed behind him.

Grace covered her face in her hands. He was right. What the hell was wrong with her? Lusting after him like this? And could she *be* any more obvious about it? Seriously?

She groaned softly. She'd sunk to an entirely new low. No matter how good-looking he was, she needed to keep her head on straight.

Besides, he was a frickin' *vampire*. She needed him right now, but not for that. She needed him for way more important things, so long as he was willing to stick around.

Maybe you should make it worth his while.

She guffawed at her own thought. "Yeah, right."

Slapping her hand over her errant mouth, she glanced around discreetly, but no one was paying her any mind.

Great. Now she was arguing with herself. Out loud.

Besides, could vampires even *do* that?

"Did you say something, poppet?"

"Um, no. Nothing," she responded innocently as the door to the dressing room opened.

Wow.

Her newly acquired vampire bodyguard looked like he'd just walked off the pages of a major fashion magazine. He'd added dark, acid-washed jeans to his black shirt. A pair of ankle-high, black, thick-soled boots covered his feet. And to top it off, he'd donned a men's sweater jacket, also black, complete with a hood that now covered his dark hair.

The clothes hugged his lean, muscular form perfectly. If he was hoping the dark colors were going to help him blend in, she had a feeling he was going to be severely disappointed.

His grey eyes glowed from underneath that signature hood as he watched her drink him in, a contemplative look on his face.

She stared back, wishing she knew what he was thinking. But then he blinked and looked away, and the moment was gone.

Shoving his hands into the front pockets of his new hoodie, he looked at her expectantly. "Ready, love?"

"Um. Yeah. I'm ready." She followed him as he headed towards the exit, bypassing the registers completely.

"Hey," she whispered, knowing he could hear her. "Aren't you going to pay for those clothes?"

He paused just inside the doors to wait for her. When she reached him, he looked down at her with an amused expression on his face. "And how do you propose I do that? I didn't exactly bring my wallet on this amnesia trip. Besides," he grumbled. "It was their bloody grain that ruined my other clothes to begin with."

"That wasn't the stores fault, " she began as he headed outside with her close on his heels, but she was drowned out by the sound of the alarms going off.

Aiden wrapped an arm around her waist and tugged her along with him at vamp speed when she made as if to stop.

"Sorry about that," he told her once they'd gotten far enough way. "I must've missed one of the anti-theft devices. Remind me to find it later."

They hit the street and quickly lost themselves in the crowd, heading east towards Zhongshan Square.

"You're seriously just going to steal those clothes?" she asked as he took the black bag from her and tucked her hand inside his elbow, making it appear as though they were out for nothing more than a romantic evening stroll.

He looked down at her, aghast. "*Borrow*, love. I would never steal."

"You just did! They have cameras, you know," she reminded him.

"Perhaps. But by the time they look up the footage, we'll be long gone."

He slowed down as they entered the Square. "Now, which way, poppet?"

She glanced around. The "Square" wasn't actually a square. It was more like the grassy center of a round wheel, with streets heading in every direction acting as the spokes. She guided him to one of those spokes coming up on their right and headed down Zhongshan Rd.

"I have a place that we can hide. It's not far."

"A secret rendezvous, you say? Why Grace, I didn't know you felt that way, love. It's the pants, isn't..."

He stopped speaking halfway through his sentence, and Grace felt him stiffen under her hand. She glanced over at him curiously.

"Aiden?"

He was scanning the street, his expression intent. "Poppet. I need you to do exactly as I say, all right?"

"Why? What's going on?" She looked around, even checking behind them, but didn't see anything but the usual street traffic of cars and people.

"I just need you to trust me, my lovely. We're being followed."

"How do you know?"

He gave her a strange look, hesitating a moment before telling her, "I'm not certain, I just know."

"Human?"

Her question seemed to catch him off guard, but only for a moment. "No."

To anyone passing by, they would look like any couple strolling down the street, but Grace could feel the tension radiating from his body and into hers like sound waves.

She pressed closer to him, whispering, "The place we're going, it's secure. We can hide there. We just need to get to it." She pointed ahead of them with her bad hand. "See that street up there? Jiefang Rd? We need to take a left there, and head to Labor Park. There's a soccer ball sculpture there..."

"I'm familiar," he interrupted. "What's at the soccer ball?"

"My families' emergency shelter."

"Smashing." He casually scanned the area around them again as they approached the corner. "Hand me your rucksack."

She did. Tucking Mojo into the top pocket, he zipped it up, then put his arms through the straps. Taking Grace by the hand, he pulled her close to his side. "Stay close. And be ready."

"Ready for what?" But no sooner had the words left her mouth then he pulled her tightly against him and lifted her into his arms as if she weighed no more than Mojo. Tucking her against his chest just as he turned the corner, he sped up to vamp speed, becoming nothing more than a passing blur to the people around them.

The speed made her dizzy, so Grace tucked her head into his neck and wrapped her arms around him.

In no time at all, he was setting her down amongst the trees surrounding the giant red and white soccer ball sculpture.

They waited until a small group of young tourists wandered away, but when Aiden made to leave the cover of the trees, she stopped him by stepping in front of him and placing her hands flat against his chest.

"Aiden," she said in a firm voice. "I need you to stay here for just a minute, and let me go over there alone."

"No," he immediately answered.

"Aiden, please!" she implored him. "I'll be fine. Just stay here for a few seconds, and please keep an eye on Mojo."

Reaching up, she unzipped the top pocket on her pack and let the little guy stick his head out. She looked directly at him. "Stay with Aiden. I'll be right back."

Aiden's displeasure was clearly written all over his face. He pushed his hood off of his head in exasperation. "Grace, I don't like this. Where are you going exactly?"

She held up her hand. "Just stay here and listen for me to call you. We don't have time to argue." Then, with a quick look around, she left the cover of the trees and jogged over to the sculpture.

She remembered halfway there that she was supposed to be limping, but there was nothing to do for it now. Maybe she could explain it away by the fact that her adrenaline was flowing and her ankle was wrapped, and therefore didn't hurt near as much.

Once she reached the ball, she cautiously circumvented it, keeping an eye out for witnesses. Crouching down, she checked the bottom white sections in front of her, brushing off the dirt here and there.

Finally, she found what she was looking for. A monogrammed "M" etched into the top of one of the sections. You wouldn't see it if you didn't know what to look for, but fortunately for them, she did.

Checking around one more time, and making sure she was out of view of Aiden, she closed her eyes, and began to chant quietly. A moment later, the section began to open, disconnecting from the rest of the ball and lowering like a ramp to the ground.

Once it was open, she called Aiden's name quietly, and jogged to the side until she could see the trees where he was hiding just in case he hadn't heard her, but he was already heading her way at an easy run.

Their pursuers must be close. Or he just wasn't good at following directions. Either way, it was time to go in. Throwing her legs over the edge of the opening, she flipped onto her belly and felt for the ladder.

Aiden arrived just as she found the top rungs, and she reached out for her backpack as he shucked it off his shoulders and handed it to her.

She threw it over her shoulder and headed down into the darkness.

13

Emma ran out into the hall outside of her and Nik's apartment, with Nikulas right on her heels.

"Em? Emma? Where the fuck are you going? What's wrong, sweetheart?"

She wrapped her arms protectively around her middle, looking frantically up and down the hall.

What the hell *was* that?

"Emma! Talk to me!" Nik planted himself in front of her and gripped her upper arms in his strong hands.

Her eyes flew to his as another shock wave rolled through her. He was completely vamped out, and if she didn't know him as well as she did, she'd be terrified.

A low growl rose up in his throat as he frantically searched her face, then twisted around searching for someone, or something, to fight for her.

"I don't know," she told him, bending over as another wave hit her. "I don't know, Nik! I just have this strange...pull inside of me. Like something is calling me. Like I need to go somewhere."

"You're not going fucking anywhere!" he bellowed. "Until you tell me what the fuck this is!"

"I don't know!" she yelled back.

Just then, the door to the stairwell flew open. Emma found herself thrown back against the wall as her overprotective mate shoved her behind him and spun around, dropping into a fighting crouch directly in front of her to guard her from this new threat.

Keira ran down the hall towards them, Luukas less than a second behind her.

"Emma!" she cried. "Are you all right?"

Emma ducked under Nikulas' arm and flew to her sister. They clasped hands when they reached each other, and then both fell to their knees with a cry as their mates roared with alarm.

Fangs bared and eyes glowing with anger, they paced around the girls like wild animals, their frustration at being unable to fight this invisible thing obvious.

Unable to release her sister's hands even if she wanted to, Emma had no choice but to let the vision roll through her like a freight train.

A girl appeared, with mahogany hair and light green eyes, and she was in trouble. Emma could feel her fear and determination, but could do nothing but watch helplessly as the girl ran towards a giant soccer ball sculpture. An athletic-looking man was following her, and she barely caught a glimpse of his face before they both disappeared through a door and down a ladder that led somewhere underneath the sculpture.

Aiden!

The vision faded away like fog, and Emma blinked her eyes to find her sister's face mere inches from her own. They were still on their knees, and their hands were still clasped.

"Do you know them?" her sister asked, ignoring the guys prowling around them, desperate by now to find something, anything, to kill.

Glancing up at them, Emma sincerely hoped no one wandered into this hallway until they could get the guys calmed down.

"Yes," Emma breathed. "The guy, it was Aiden. As we told you, he's been missing since we found you and Luukas. Leeha took him. He called Nik yesterday though, and told him he'd just...*woken up* in China, with no idea of how he'd gotten there. I don't know who the girl was though. Do you?"

Keira shook her head. "No. No idea."

Emma stared at her sister. "What the hell *was* that, Keira?"

"I'm not really sure."

Releasing her sister's hands, she reached back to touch Nik's leg as he passed behind her. Immediately, he dropped down and wrapped her into his arms as his brother pulled Keira up off of the floor to do the same.

"Are you ok?" he whispered in her ear.

She turned to look into his glowing blue eyes and gave him a small smile. "Yeah. I'm fine. It was some sort of vision, or something. I saw Aiden!"

He pulled back to search her face. "Aiden? Are you sure?"

She nodded.

"Where the fuck is he? What was he doing?"

"He was with a woman. A pretty woman."

Nik rolled his eyes, his fangs receding. "Of course."

"They were running towards a soccer ball," she continued.

Standing up, Nik planted his hands low on his hips and stared down at her in disbelief. "You mean to tell me that while we've been here losing our minds worrying about that damned Brit, he's been doing nothing but picking up chicks and playing games?" As an afterthought, he reached down and grabbed her under her arms and hoisted her easily to her feet. "Seriously?"

Keira and Luuk came over then. "Emma," her sister said. "That girl? I think she's in trouble."

"How do you know?" she asked.

Keira took Luukas' hand, as if preparing him. "I think that was a call for help. A magical call. I think she may be connected to us somehow. And I think we need to go find her..."

"NO," Luukas immediately intercepted.

"Luukas, please, hear me out," her sister pled softly.

He crossed his arms over his broad chest and clenched his jaw, but after a moment, gave her a nod to continue.

"What makes you think she's in trouble?" Nik asked before she could say anything more. "She's just playing soccer with Aiden."

"No, it was more than that," Emma said. "She was running towards a huge, soccer ball sculpture, in the middle of a park or something. Aiden was following her, and they both went through this secret hatch-like part of the ball and down into some kind of underground shelter or something."

Luukas and Nik exchanged looks.

"A soccer ball sculpture?" Luuk asked. When Keira nodded in confirmation, he added, "That's in China. In Dalian."

"Yes." Keira glanced up at him. "Aiden told Nik he was there when he called, but who is that he's with? And who are they hiding from? We need to help them!"

Emma watched as her sister and her mate locked eyes, both of their faces locked into a stubborn impasse, as they communicated silently with each other.

Luukas broke first, his face crumbling as his arms dropped to his sides and opened in supplication. "I can't go with you, Keira. I just...can't. And Nik needs to stay here to help me keep looking for the others. Please don't ask me to go by yourself. I don't..." He gritted his teeth and glanced at Emma and Nik, a look of embarrassment flashing across his face before he turned his back to them.

Knowing he didn't like to show his weaknesses in front of her, Emma grabbed Nik's arm and pulled him away a few paces.

Keira wrapped her arms around his waist and Emma heard him say, "I don't think I could do it. I would truly go mad. You can't leave me, witch. Not yet. I can't do it."

"Shhh," Keira told him. "It's all right. We'll think of something."

Out of earshot, Emma didn't hear anything more, and she was glad. She'd never known Luukas as he was before he'd been captured, but from what Nikulas had told her, he'd been lethal, logical, and confident. A total bad ass. And yet fair when it came to his colony.

Nothing like the broken male he was now.

However, here and there they saw flashes of the male he once was, and remained hopeful that, with time, he would become something resembling the vampire he had been once again.

But it still broke her heart. She didn't know how Keira remained so strong and optimistic with him.

Pulling Nik into their apartment, but leaving the door open for her sister and brother-in-law, she went to the kitchen to get a drink while he sat at the counter.

"Do you think that girl is in trouble?" Nik asked.

Taking a sip of her orange juice, she shrugged. "She was running from something, and it wasn't Aiden. And I trust Keira."

She watched Nik's brain go into vamp hyper speed, and knew he was thinking of possible plans to help them and discarding them just as fast.

His blue eyes locked onto hers a moment later, and he smiled.

He'd thought of a solution. "What?" she asked.

"The wolves," he told her.

"What about them?"

He narrowed his eyes, running them from the top of her strawberry-blonde head to her feet and back up again. "They owe me a fucking favor."

Emma smiled back, a look of understanding dawning across her face. "Yes, yes they do."

Smacking his palms on the counter, Nik got up and strode over to the door. "Luuk! Get in here! I know what we're gonna do."

He returned to the kitchen, and they waited for Luuk and Keira to join them.

As he strolled into the kitchen, the master vampire was considerably calmer now, although he still kept a firm grip on Keira's hand, keeping her close to his side. He cocked his head and raised an eyebrow at Nik in silent question.

Nik smiled. "We'll send in the wolves to help them."

Luukas nodded in agreement. "But will they agree to help?"

"They will," Nik told him confidently. "They owe me one hell of a fucking favor." He raised his hand, palm facing out, to Emma as she opened her mouth to speak. "And NO. You are NOT going with them. No way in hell. Don't even fucking ask."

She snapped her mouth closed and rolled her eyes at her sister, who tried to repress her grin.

Overbearing males, you had to love them.

14

Aiden followed Grace through the hatch and down into the ground below the ball sculpture, careful not to step on her fingers as he descended the ladder behind her.

He had a few questions he'd like answered, but first, they needed to close that door. His old friends from the night before were approaching fast. He couldn't quite put his finger on exactly how he knew that. He just...felt it, in every single cell of his body. It was a rather strange thing actually, but he didn't have time to chew over the reasoning behind it at the moment.

Right now, he just needed to get Grace out of harm's reach.

He peeked underneath his arm to find her already off of the ladder and standing motionless with her back to him, whispering so quietly even he had a hard time hearing her.

The door above him began to close, and he jumped down the last few feet as she came to life again and reached into a nearby cubbyhole in the wall.

Striking a match, she lit the candle in her hand and set it on the counter. Walking over to a metal box on the wall, she began flicking switches, and lights came on around the room.

Aiden set the black bag in one of the other cubbies and looked around. The entire shelter was no bigger than a large bedroom in the average American household.

A row of vertical cubbies was cut into the wall right next to the ladder. The top one contained matches and candles, a kerosene lamp, and boxes of extra ammo. The others contained towels, peroxide, alcohol, jugs of water, and a large first aid kit. The third had a food and water bowl, and some cat food.

Nowhere did he see a way to open or close the hatch door.

Interesting.

Hanging on the wall were the weapons for the ammo, including another 9mm and a shotgun, and right next to them, some wicked looking knives.

"Don't touch the knives." Grace's voice came from across the room. "The blades are silver."

He raised an eyebrow. "Silver?"

She made an affirmative noise. "Silver is bad for you, right?"

"It's not my metal of choice to be stabbed with, no." He wandered past some cabinets with doors, a steel counter with a propane camping-style cook stove on it, and over to the desk where Grace was now sitting at a state of the art computer.

Monitors came to life on the wall in front of her above the desk as he set her rucksack down next to her chair. Within a few seconds, they had views of the grounds in every direction around the sculpture above them.

Aiden leaned in closer. "Bloody hell," he growled.

The soccer ball sculpture above them was surrounded by demon hybrids, including the group that used to be his old friends.

Grace stopped breathing completely for a few seconds, and then she inhaled a shaky breath. "Jesus. They're everywhere."

"Can they get in?" he asked.

"No," she asserted confidently.

All right, then.

He kept a careful eye on the multiple screens, but it appeared as though she was correct. Their trail dead-ended at the sculpture, and they couldn't find their way in. Crawling the grounds above them like ants, they sometimes wandered off towards the streets, but would always come back to the soccer ball. Like hunting dogs on a scent.

How the hell did they know he and Grace were still there? There was no way they could smell them this far underground.

A sour feeling curled his insides. As much as he wanted to deny it, Aiden had a feeling he knew.

It was him. He was the one pulling them here. They sensed him somehow, just as he could sense *them* when they were anywhere near him.

As he watched them swarming above them, that strange sensation hit him again, like something, or someone, was stirring inside of him.

A forgotten memory of Leeha's red eyes suddenly flashed in front of him in bits and pieces. Tears streaming down her lovely, evil face as she told him goodbye. Her hands reaching out and catching him before his head had hit the ground and he'd passed out. Standing in the room full of her demon zombies - all vampires that Luukas had created yet had followed her to create their own colony. She'd possessed them all with the demons from the altar.

And he had been next, because the dark warlock had refused to use Shea.

His head started to spin, and he backed away from the monitors.

No! It couldn't be. Those things out there, they had no recollection of the vampires they used to be when they were under Luukas' rule. He, Aiden, was still himself. *His* body, *his* mind, *his* memories.

Yet, they had called him "Waano", and they could sense whenever he was near them. Like he was one of them.

He suddenly felt nauseous. Could it be possible?

But if Leeha had injected him full of one of those demon-ghost things, why was he still here? Why was he still him?

An unlikely scenario occurred to him: Unless, for whatever reason, it didn't *want* to be inside of him. Unless, unlike the others, who were eager to be corporeal again, his own demon didn't *want* to come out.

Poppycock.

However, he remembered how strange he'd felt when he'd first seen his old friends in that empty building. He remembered the violence that had risen inside of him when he'd seen the human male shot in Grace's kitchen.

It wasn't like him to get so overwrought with emotion. As a matter of fact, he couldn't remember ever reacting so intensely to anything since he'd gone home to find his entire family murdered.

Was that what this strange feeling was inside of him? That feeling like he was experiencing *someone else's* emotions? Could it be that that was exactly what he was doing?

No. NO. It couldn't be. He was going daft. More likely, Leeha had chickened out and found that she couldn't make him into one of her minions. She'd always had a soft spot for him, after all. She'd probably knocked him out and stuck him in that shipping container somehow to get him out of harms way.

"Aiden? Are you all right? What's wrong?" Grace's concerned voice came at him as if from outside a bubble. "Aiden, why are they still here? Why aren't they leaving?"

The slight tremble in her voice belied her calm appearance.

He stared into her exotic green eyes, and reached blindly for her good hand, too shaken up by his own thoughts to reassure her properly with words.

She gave it to him, squeezing his fingers and not letting go. Even that slightest of touches from her managed to ground him. And a few seconds later, he felt that presence inside of him begin to subside.

Her freckles stood out against her pale face as she waited for answers, but he couldn't tell her what he suspected. Not yet. Maybe not ever.

"I don't know," he told her instead. Without releasing her hand, he took stock of the room around them, trying to get his mind on to something else - like their survival. "How long can you stay here before you run out of supplies?"

"Um, about two weeks if we had to, maybe even longer since I'm the only one who'll be eating the food."

He waited for what she'd just said to sink into her human brain. And sure enough, after only a few seconds, her eyes flew to his. He knew exactly what she'd just thought of, and he gave her a tight smile. "I'm not a young vampire. I'll be good for a while, as far as feeding is concerned. Long enough for us to figure a way out of here, in any case."

She nodded, but her expression was grave.

If only she knew how gentle I can be, and how much she's going to enjoy it.

He may need to educate her on that sooner rather than later. But then he frowned a bit. What was he thinking? He would do no such thing. The only thing he'd be doing would be to get her out of this coffin and somewhere safe, and then he'd be on a plane back home.

He noticed her still staring at him, her face all screwed up with worry, and then suddenly she smiled.

He looked at her suspiciously. Did she read minds now? A bit affronted, he wondered if she was happy that he had no plans to seduce her.

Something tickled his ear, and he reached up to rub it, only to quickly pull his hand away.

"Bloody *hell*!" He rubbed his palm on his thigh. "How the hell did your boot brush get on my shoulder?" He reached up again to dislodge the bristling little guy.

Grace giggled as Mojo huffed and jerked away from Aiden's hand, raised his quills, and then promptly returned to Aiden's hood.

"He must've crawled out of the pack when you were holding it," she giggled.

"And into my *hood*? What if I'd needed to wear it? I'd have his bloody quills sticking out all over my skull. I'd look like Pinhead!"

"He likes you."

"Likes me? He won't even let me touch him."

"You just startled him is all."

He gave her such a look of exasperation that she laughed out loud. "Here. Sit down in the chair so I can get him."

Slowly, so as not to upset the grouchy beast in his hood, he took a seat and turned his back to her.

"Hey, baby," she murmured softly, her breath tickling the back of Aiden's neck. "It's ok. It's just me. We're all done running for now."

If he closed his eyes, he could almost imagine her soft lips moving against his skin as she whispered to him like that, but then he felt Mojo's slight weight get lifted from his clothes as Grace scooped him out and put him on the floor to run around. Once the little prickler was out of his clothing, he gave himself an internal shake, and swiveled around in the chair to check out her computer.

At least the little rat had distracted her from their previous conversation.

"What sort of system do you have on here?" He began surfing around the desktop, clicking on this and that, getting a feel for it.

"Nothing fancy," she told him. "Just the security cameras. No internet. No cell service in here either." She tossed her now useless phone onto the desk.

He clicked the mouse around a few more times. "No internet? How is that even possible these days?"

"I think it was something my Mom meant to get around to doing, but never got the chance."

She walked over to the adjacent wall, grabbed a handle that was sticking out of it, and partially pulled out a hidden bed to act as a couch. Plopping down on the mattress, she placed her elbow on her knee and rested her chin in her unwrapped hand. "So, what now?"

Aiden scratched his head and gave her a sheepish look. "To be completely honest, I'm not really sure. But give me just a bit, I'll think of something."

She yawned behind her hand. "Bet you're wishing you'd taken your friend up on that plane ride about now, huh?"

"And miss out on being all alone in this tin can with you?" he teased, giving her a wink. "Not for anything in the world, poppet."

She didn't need to know that he'd been thinking that exact same thing for a while now. He didn't want to hurt her feelings.

He turned back to the creatures on the monitors. They were examining the ball sculpture now, having honed in on him directly beneath it, and were searching for any telltale signs of where they could've gone.

"Grace?" he asked softly. "Are you quite certain there isn't any way those things would be able to find their way in here?"

She was silent for so long, he turned to look at her, but she was shaking her head. "No. I don't think so, not unless..."

She didn't finish her thought.

"Unless what?" he encouraged her.

"Nothing," she insisted.

He narrowed his eyes at her suspiciously. "Come to think of it, how did *we* get in here? How did you get it to open?"

She answered his question with a cool, level stare.

"Why is it exactly that your family has this shelter?" he continued. "And for that matter, where is your family, if I may ask?"

Apparently he couldn't, for again, all he received was that cool look that told him he wasn't going to be told anything she didn't want him to know.

"Ah. It's like that, is it?" He swiveled the chair around to give her his full attention, and gave her his most trusty look. "C'mon, love. There's no need for all of this secrecy between friends. You can tell me."

But she wouldn't break, just looked down at her hands as they twisted in her lap.

More secrets. Seems this female was stocked full of them. Having to watch what you say and do so much couldn't be healthy. It would really behoove her to share her burdens.

He joined her on the makeshift couch and sat right next to her. They weren't touching, but he was close enough to make her bristle.

Kind of like Mojo.

"Grace, love, if we're going to be risking our lives together, you're going to have to indulge me and let me in on some of your little secrets. I may be nothing but a lowly vampire, but you can trust me. I promise. I only want to get us all out of here alive."

She gave him a sideways look.

He scooted a bit closer, and heat ran down his thigh where it was touching hers. "Where is your family? At least tell me that. Are they nearby? Are they in danger? Do I need to go get them?"

Her teeth chewed her bottom lip as she shook her head, finally telling him, "No. My family is gone."

"Gone?"

"Yeah, it's just me."

She looked so lost for a moment that he almost hated to ask. "What happened to your family?"

"My parents are both dead."

"Do you have any siblings? Grandparents?"

She shook her head again. "No. No one else."

"May I ask how they died?"

"My father died in an...accident before we moved here. And my mom was in an accident a few years ago. A car accident."

"I'm very sorry," he told her sincerely.

She nodded, accepting his condolences as she watched Mojo explore the room.

A young woman alone, full of secrets, whose parents were killed in "accidents". This story was sounding vaguely familiar to him, and the more he thought about it, the more a nagging suspicion rose up in him. "Grace?"

"Hmm?"

"What's your last name?"

A steel rod slammed into her back at his question, and she looked him square in the eye as she told him, "Poland."

"Poland," he repeated in disbelief. "Grace *Poland*?"

"Yup."

This female was many things: Smart, compassionate, sexy, and an exceptional liar. But she couldn't fool him. However, he decided to play her game. For now.

"All right, Grace *Poland*, why do you think it is that our guests outside want that bag so badly?"

"I honestly have no idea."

The innocence in those green eyes pulled at his heartstrings, almost as strongly as the heat and scent of her pulled at certain other strings of his. Whenever she looked directly at him like that, he found himself hard pressed to look away. It was like she was staring directly into his soul, and he was suddenly more than willing to let her in there and allow her to rearrange until she felt at home.

"Why is it," he continued, "That just a few hours ago, you could barely walk and had broken bones in your hand, and yet now they are magically healed with nothing more than an Ace bandage? And why were you about to collapse when I got back to your apartment after hiding the body?" Her eyes darkened as he delved further into her secrets without restraint, and he noticed the strain around them for the first time. "Why did you have a gun, with a silencer, may I add, in your apartment? Why do you have this shelter?" When she broke eye contact and turned away against his barrage of questions, he took her chin gently in his hand and turned her face back to him. "I think I deserve to know. I'm risking my very life by helping you, after all."

She searched his face for a moment, and then closed her eyes and sighed heavily. "You're right. You deserve to know what you're getting into."

15

Grace stared into his clear grey eyes and knew she needed to tell him something. He was getting too suspicious. The question was, how much was safe to tell him?

"My family is...different. When I was born, my parents belonged to a community of sorts. Kind of an off the grid commune-type thing. We lived there until I was about four or five, I think?" Her brow furrowed as she tried to remember, then she shrugged. "I'm not really sure. Then suddenly one day my parents picked me up from my friends' house and rushed me home to start packing. My father...got held up, but Mom and I left town that same day, only taking what we could carry."

She fell into a thoughtful silence, remembering that day, and how scared she'd been when her parents had rushed into the house, screaming her name.

Her father had found her first, sitting outside in the midst of her friends' chickens. She'd been giggling as she'd watched them search for bugs in the yard, until she saw her dad. He'd run straight to her, scattering chickens every which way. Feathers had floated around in the air as he'd scooped her up and ran back into the house, yelling for her mother to take Grace in the car and go.

Aiden's voice snapped her back to the present.

"Where did she take you?"

"Um, we took a plane to Europe, and then we lived like vagabonds for a few months after we received word about my Dad. Now I know we were trying to stay under the radar. I couldn't even tell you where we were. We never stayed in the same place for very long, and my Mom would never let me go outside, never let me out of her sight, not even to use the bathroom." She took a breath, gathering her thoughts. "After...I don't know...weeks? months?...we finally landed here in China. She got a job teaching English, and I picked up Mandarin by sitting in on her classes. I was home-schooled there in other subjects as well. We always stayed together. I wasn't allowed to go to public school, or out with my friends when I finally made some, or even down the street to grab a soda. She never let me out of her sight. It was years before I could shower with the door completely closed, and I was never allowed to lock it. She always seemed terrified that I would just disappear into thin air." She gave a little cynical snort. "I had no idea what was happening back then. I was young, I just went with the flow. I thought everyone's Mom was that weird."

"But you know now." It wasn't really a question.

She stood up to pace to the other side of the room, needing some space. The warmth of his nearness, his clean smell, was entirely too distracting. She was too tired to keep her defenses up, and she needed to think through this next part.

He needed to know things, yes, but did he need to know *everything*? How much should she tell him? Her mom had never told her what to do if a handsome, virile, nosy male came to her rescue and demanded to know what he was getting himself involved in. Actually, she hadn't told her much of anything, except to keep their secret just that...secret.

And not to trust vampires. No matter what.

She stepped over Mojo as he scampered by and leaned back against the opposite wall, facing Aiden again. He sat patiently for once, elbows resting on his knees, giving her the time she needed to come to the correct conclusion.

That conclusion being, she was sure, to tell him everything.

She studied his posture. He seemed relaxed, not twitchy and impatient like someone would be if they were just trying to get information out of her.

Plus, her instincts were telling her that it was okay to trust him. And her instincts were usually spot on. Her mother's warnings echoed round and round in her head, but really, what other choice did she have? She needed his help. If not for him, she'd probably be dead twice over already. She could tell him this much at least.

"Yes," she admitted. "I know now."

He raised his eyebrows, silently urging her to continue.

Suddenly, she was nervous. What would he think of her when he found out what she really was? Who she really was? And then she laughed to herself. She was worried that a *vampire* wouldn't think she was normal.

Still, her voice came out stilted as she told him, "My parents weren't part of a hippie commune. They were part of a coven."

"Like a witch's coven?"

She took a deep breath. "Yes," she confirmed.

"Which means, *you* are a witch."

"Yes, if you can call it that."

"Grace?"

"Yes?"

"What is your last name?"

"France."

He grinned widely. "Grace France?"

"Yes," she confirmed seriously.

He nodded solemnly, but a trace of amusement lingered in his eyes. "Go on then with your story, Grace France," he told her, adding politely, "Please."

She clasped her hands nervously in front of her, seeing no sense in continuing the ruse that one of them was supposed to be injured. "So...my parents, from what they eventually told me, decided to leave so suddenly because a new High Priest had taken over. Our coven is old, and has had many leaders, but none were ever like this one. He was pure evil, and he brought his dark magic into the group by lying and pretending to be something he wasn't. He was so good at hiding what he truly was, the witches didn't catch on until it was too late. Many fled while they could, before he could 'convince' them that they should stay. And by 'convince' I mean threaten them with the deaths of their loved ones, those both in and out of the coven."

"He sounds lovely," Aiden told her sarcastically.

"Right? Anyway, we're one of the few families that got away."

"Where did the others go?"

She shrugged. "Don't know. They scattered, I guess."

"So, magic. That's how you fixed yourself." He indicated the bandages on her wrist and ankle.

Her face heated. "Um, yeah, guess I can go ahead and take these off now."

"May as well," he agreed with a slight twist of his lips.

She heard the amusement in his voice and knew that he was laughing at her. The bastard.

Joining him back on the makeshift couch, she took off her sneakers and unwrapped her ankle, then her wrist and hand. She bent her wrist back and forth, testing it.

Aiden reached a hand towards her. "May I?"

After a moment's hesitation, she placed her healed hand in his open palm. His skin felt warm against hers. She thought vamps would be cold to the touch, their skin smooth and hard, like in Anne Rice's novels. But it was nothing like that. He felt like the human he used to be.

He turned her hand over in his, probing the healed bones with his fingertips. "Amazing."

She tried to pull her hand from his, but he tightened his grip, refusing to release her.

Catching and holding her eyes with his, he slowly lifted it to his mouth, and pressed a soft, warm kiss to the delicate skin on the inside of her wrist. Running his nose lightly along the veins there, he inhaled deeply, smelling her skin. His eyes closed in pleasure as he scented her, for she knew that was exactly what he was doing.

Her breath caught at the simple, yet erotic gesture. She wondered what she smelled like to him. She wondered how he could be that close to the blood he craved and not bite her.

Adrenaline rushed into her veins at the thought, and her heart began to thud heavily in her chest as her body instinctively prepared for flight.

As if he could read her thoughts, his eyes flashed open again to catch hers, imprisoning her where she sat.

Somewhere in the back of her mind she knew that this was all just a part of his allure. It was how he ensnared his prey. At least the logical part of her knew this, but the not-so-logical parts of her couldn't care less. So she sat as still as a statue, unable to move if she wanted to (which she didn't).

He was pure, raw seduction. And she was completely and utterly captivated by him.

Opening her fingers with his, he slowly brushed his lips down her hand, his wet tongue snaking out here and there for a little taste.

A deep, pulsing ache began in her lower belly, increasing with every touch of his lips as he kissed each fingertip in turn. He sucked the last one into his mouth before pressing a final, firm kiss right in the center of her palm.

He closed her fingers into a fist, capturing the kiss he'd placed there.

"It's called a hand kiss," he told her softly. "Now, whenever you are lonely, all you have to do is press your palm to your cheek, and you'll feel my kiss, and know that you are not alone."

How did he know she felt lonely? That she often felt alone even in a room full of people? The loneliness was unavoidable. It had always been a part of her, living away from the coven. It was because she always had to be careful what she said, and what she did. She always had to hide her secret.

But I don't with him.

She gave him a small, tentative smile.

"You don't ever have to be alone again, Grace," he whispered.

Still holding her closed fist, he lifted his other hand and encircled her throat. Leaning in, he pressed a soft kiss on her forehead, and then her nose. With his thumb under her jaw, he gently tilted her lips up to meet his.

He paused for barely a moment, searching her face, asking permission and giving her time to say no.

She didn't try to pull away again, and his eyes glowed with triumph as he lowered his mouth to hers.

Grace moaned at the first touch of his kiss. His lips were warm and supple as they molded to hers, his tongue flicking out to tease her. As his hand moved to the back of her neck to pull her closer, she opened for him, and his kiss went from teasing to raw need in the span of a heartbeat.

Her free hand pressed against the hard muscles of his chest, then gripped the front of his tee shirt as she gave in to what she was feeling. She kissed him back with all the passion inside of her, and reveled in the moans she drew from him as he took it in and returned it to her.

Lost in the feel of his mouth on hers, she groaned unhappily when he suddenly drew away. She tried to resume their kiss, but he turned his face away and tucked her head against his chest and held her there.

"Just give me a moment, love," he rasped, bunching the back of her shirt in his hand.

They sat like that until their heartbeats returned to normal, and Grace's sanity returned.

Holy shit, what the hell was she doing?

She tried to sit up, and this time he let her do it. Embarrassed, she kept her head down, wishing her hair was unbound so she could hide behind it.

With a finger under her chin, he tilted her face up until she had no choice but to look at him.

"Don't hide from me, love," he said. "There's nothing to be ashamed of."

"I just...I don't know..."

He gave her a small smile. "It's all right. It was just a kiss."

Just a kiss.

"Is there anything else I need to know?" he asked abruptly, ruining the moment in typical Aiden fashion.

She blinked a few times, a little thrown by the sudden change in him. "Um..." she bit her lip, undecided.

"Poppet," he chided her. "I can tell you're still hiding something. Come now," he ordered. "Out with it."

"Well, I don't know if it has any relevance."

"Why don't you let me decide whether it does or not, all right?"

She twisted her hands in her lap until he covered them with his own, effectively stilling them. "Whatever it is, it can't be that bad. I've been around for a long time. There's little that would manage to surprise me these days. So, just tell me."

Still thrown from his kiss and not thinking properly, she decided he was probably right. Besides, it could have nothing at all to do with anything they were dealing with right now. But then again, it just might.

Pulling her hands out from underneath his, she slid her backpack over to her. Unzipping one of the larger sections, she reached in and unzipped a hidden pocket inside. Pulling out an old piece of parchment paper, she handed it to Aiden.

"Be careful," she cautioned him. "It's very old, and rips easily."

"I can see that." Handling the paper with a delicate touch, he opened it, and scanned the words inside. "Grace, what is this?"

"As far as I can tell, it's an old spell, but I'm not sure for what. However, it must be important. My parents practically came back from the dead to let me know where it was."

He studied the words, barely legible on the parchment. "It's written in a very old language. A language that was ancient before I was born."

"Do you know it?" she asked excitedly.

"Not well," he answered, "Just a few words here and there."

Her excitement fizzled out as fast as it had come on.

"I can't translate it either, but whatever this is, my parents needed me to have it, so it's got to be important. I mean, they *literally* came back from the dead to tell me where it was hidden in our house."

"*Literally?*" he teased. "Really?"

"Yes. *Literally*," she insisted. "They appeared to me in a dream, just a week or so after my mom's funeral, and they were like, *screaming* at me to knock a hole in the wall by our T.V. So I got out of bed and grabbed a hammer and started pounding on the wall. And lo and behold, there was this fireproof box in there, and it took me forever to find the keys. But I did find them, a full day later, taped underneath the windowsill in their room. When I opened the box, there it was. Just this one piece of paper with words written on it in a language I couldn't read. I searched online for days, trying to find a match so I could interpret the spell written there, but I didn't have any luck. And it's definitely a spell, I can tell by the way it's written."

She stopped babbling long enough to notice that Aiden had become unnaturally still as he stared down at the paper.

"Aiden?"

Nothing.

"Aiden, what's wrong? What is it?"

She touched his forearm to get his attention, and his head whipped towards her in surprise, only she had the strangest feeling that it wasn't Aiden looking back at her.

Dark shadows swirled through his normally bright grey eyes, and his expression was tense.

Grace felt a stab of the pain reflected in his eyes hit her right in the center of her chest. He looked like he'd just lost someone close to him.

He cocked his head, looking her over as if he'd never seen her before.

The hair stood up on the back of her neck. Slowly, she rose up off of the bed, not making any sudden moves, and backed away until she hit the desk chair. "Aiden? Why are you looking at me like that?"

He followed her movements, his head tilted at that strange angle, like she was some kind of new species of insect he was studying.

"Please talk to me," she whispered. "You're scaring me again, dude."

"Did you just call me 'dude'?"

His words were strange...rusty...like he hadn't spoken in a long time and was unused to forming the sounds. And his accent was gone.

"Aiden! Stop it!" she yelled, not knowing what else to do. "What the hell is wrong with you?"

He blinked rapidly a few times and looked down again at the paper in his hands. When he lifted his head again a few seconds later, he frowned at her in confusion.

Had she just imagined the weird shadows in his eyes? She moved closer, and leaned down for a closer look.

He cocked an eyebrow. "Grace? What's wrong, love? Why are you staring at me like that?" He set the paper down beside him, a crease forming between his brows. "Were you just shouting at me?"

As her heart returned to its normal speed, she shook her head slightly. "No. No. Not at you. I just thought I saw...something." Clearing her throat, she glanced over to the other side of the room where Mojo was sniffing around. "I'd better get him a litter box set up."

She could feel his eyes on her as she walked over to the cabinets and found a box with low sides that had cans of food in it. Putting the cans back on the shelf, she took the box over to the corner by the bathroom door and set it on the floor.

Glancing over at her backpack, which was sitting on the floor by his feet, she hesitated. A small bag of litter was in there, but she was still feeling too creeped out to go near him.

So instead, she just stood there, trying to get up the nerve and telling herself she was being silly.

"Why are you suddenly so afraid of me?" he asked.

She swallowed, and forced herself to look directly at him.

He sat where she'd left him, the paper folded in his hands, his expression concerned. She studied him closely, but saw no remnants of whatever that was she had seen before.

"I'm not," she insisted, striding over to her backpack. Yet she only got as close to him as she had to, and her hands shook as she reached for her pack, sliding it over to her and putting it up on the desk chair to find the bag of litter. Pulling it out, she filled Mojo's box. She scooped him up and placed him in it, and he immediately began digging around to do his business.

She smiled timidly at Aiden. "Close call."

"Mmm," he affirmed, still looking at her strangely.

16

"Whit can I do for ye, Nikulas?" Cedric Kincaid, pack master of the werewolves that inhabited the Pacific Northwest, set down his drink and picked up the remote to turn down the volume on the Rugby game he was watching.

"Hey, Ced," Nik greeted him cheerfully. "So, hey! Remember when you guys kidnapped my mate in the middle of the day and nearly got her killed?"

Cedric pulled his cell away from his ear and scrubbed a hand over his face. He was ne'er going tae be allowed tae forget that ill idea for a joke, was he? Although he didna see whit the big deal was. Emma was braw, 'n' it had ended up bein' a good thing that the wolves were there. Between them 'n' the vampires, they'd easily taken care o' Leeha's monsters 'n' gotten Luukas 'n' Marc out o' her lair safely.

He put the phone back by his ear. "Aye, Nik," he sighed. "I remember."

"And remember when I told you that you were going to owe me big time for that little stunt? And you agreed?"

"Aye," Cedric confirmed warily.

Nik's voice got serious. "I need you guys to come through on that promise, man. We heard from Aiden. And I think he's in trouble."

Cedric took his feet off of the coffee table and sat up straight in his chair. Aiden was a good male, one o' his favorite vampire friends. He would agree tae help him even if they didna owe Nikulas a favor.

"Whit dae ya need us tae do?"

"How long's it been since you guys have been to China?"

"China? Aiden is in China?"

"That's what he told me when he called," Nik said. "In Dalian, to be exact."

"Whit the hell is he doing in China?"

He could practically see Nikulas running his hand through his blonde locks like he did when he was anxious.

"We don't know. He called and said he woke up there, but doesn't remember how he got there. He was with a girl at the time..."

"Aye. That sounds like Aiden."

"Right? He said her name was Grace. And now Em and Keira just had some kind of weird witch-vision thing. They think he and the girl are in trouble. They saw them running to that big soccer ball sculpture. Know the one I mean?"

"Aye. I've seen it."

"Em says there's a shelter built underneath it, and they're hiding out in there. And get this. They think maybe this chick Aid's with is a witch, like them. They think she did some kind of magical call for help, and that's why they had the vision. That she's connected to them somehow."

"Do they have kin they're no' aware of? Do ya think she's a Moss witch?"

Nik sighed audibly. "I dunno, man. It's possible, I guess. The way they all scattered years ago. But right now, we need to get them out of there, and bring them both back home. I would go myself, but ya know, with Luuk the way he is..."

"I ken what yer sayin', Nik. Ya dinna need to say any more. Consider it taken care o'. We'll leave first thing."

"Thanks, Cedric. You guys are all right. For a bunch of mangy dogs."

Cedric guffawed.

"But if you ever pull a stunt that puts my female in danger again, I swear I'll..."

Cedric started to protest that comment when he heard Emma smack Nikulas, then her soft voice came across the line.

"Pay no attention to him, Cedric. And thank you so much for doing this."

The werewolf leader smiled warmly into the phone. "Anything for ye, my bonnie lass."

He chuckled at the sound of Nikulas' possessive growl, and ended the call before he could get the phone back from his mate.

"Tell me again why we're running off tae do a job that they should be doin' themselves," Lucian grumbled as the wolf pack left the plane.

Fed up with him and his bad attitude, Cedric whipped around to confront him, blocking traffic in the middle of the air bridge.

He stuck his finger in Lucian's face. "Haud yer wheesht!" he hissed. "You ken Nik has his hands full with his brother. A' this is Aiden...our friend. He would do the same for any one of us. And ye fooking ken it."

Lucian's stormy grey eyes darkened with anger just before he dropped them in submission to his alpha.

"I dinna want tae hear another word from ye, ye hear? No' unless it something that's going tae help us get our friend home safe."

Marc shoved past Lucian and shot him a glare as he followed Cedric into the airport.

Duncan stopped beside him and slapped him on the shoulder. "C'mon then. Let's get out of the way. We can fight when we get tae the hotel."

Shrugging off his hand, Lucian shot him a dirty look and walked away.

"Wha'? Wha' did I dae?" He watched Lucian stomp away for a few seconds before following the rest of the pack, mumbling to himself, "Better pull that stick out o' yer arse, afore Cedric shoves it up in tae yer throat."

They acquired a rental car and were at their hotel in less than an hour. When they got to their floor, Cedric said, "Lucian, yer with me."

"I'd rather bunk with Duncan."

"I dinna care." Holding the door open for him, Cedric nodded to the others and told them to meet him in the lobby in thirty minutes before following Lucian inside.

Tossing his overnight bag onto the bed by the window, he turned to Lucian. At six foot seven inches, he had a good few inches on the other male, and more importantly, he had physically proven himself the dominant male many times over; hence his position as leader of the pack.

"Whit's the matter wit' ye, Lucian?"

"Nothin' is the matter."

"Bullshite. You've had yer head up yer arse since Marc got taken by Leeha. And ye haven't pulled it back out, even though we got him out with wee harm done. So, whit's wrong?"

Lucian ran both hands through his auburn hair, yanking at the ends in frustration. "I said tis nothing! Why canna ye leave me alone?"

"Because yer in my pack, and I canna have a member of my pack running around half-cocked, ready tae explode at any moment. And I dinna have a clue as tae how come! So, you need tae tell me whit the hell is going on with ye, and ye need tae tell me now."

"Or else whit?"

"Or else I'm going tae stick ye right back on that plane 'n' send yer arse back home 'til we get this thing wi' Aiden taken care of. Then I will come home 'n' deal wi' ye."

"Yer kicking me out of th' pack?" Lucian asked in disbelief.

"Do I need tae?" Cedric retaliated. "Because I'm beginning tae wonder."

"I'm no' leaving the pack."

"You'll have no say aboot it if that's what I decide."

Cedric held his ground in the middle of the room, legs braced apart and arms at his sides, ready for Lucian to lose his temper and come at him. He almost hoped that he would. Maybe then they could work out whatever was wrong with the lad.

But Lucian didn't react as he expected. Instead of losing his cool and raising a hand towards his alpha, he turned on his heel and slammed out of the hotel room.

"Dammit," Cedric swore, and sank down onto the bed. Scrubbing his face with his hands, he pondered what he was going to do with that wolf pup.

He'd better tell the others what had happened. They'd have tae find Lucian now before they could do anything else. Much as he wanted tae let him go 'n' go find Aiden, pack came first.

Always.

17

Three Days Later

Grace's newfound fear of him had become quite obvious since the day she'd spilled her secrets. Was she worried that he was going to steal her spell? What good would it do *him*? He was a vampire for heaven's sake! He couldn't do all that hokey-pokey.

She had also proven to be quite brilliant at evasion tactics, somehow managing to avoid being anywhere within three feet of him for days, even as cramped as they were in this underground tin can. If he tried to so much as touch her hair, she flinched away from him and quickly found something else to do.

He only wished he could figure out why.

She was acting as though he was going to pounce on her at any moment, like a wild animal. And if he was going to be completely honest with himself, her fears weren't far off the mark. The thought had crossed his mind on more than one occasion. Just not in the way she seemed to fear.

It was definitely a test of his willpower, being holed up in here with her. Grace was everywhere: her voice, her scent...her tiny knickers hanging in the shower stall after she laundered them. He couldn't escape her.

They watched the monitors constantly, taking turns, of course. Despite her obvious nervousness around him, he would stay awake as long as he was able in the morning after she had risen, just to stand close to her as she sat in the desk chair studying the screens while he updated her on their friend's activities the night before.

He'd watch with her until he couldn't resist the lure of the sun any longer. Then he would slide one of the beds out of the wall and crash for the day. He'd usually wake up to find Grace already in the lower bed, reading or sleeping, her pet curled up in his makeshift house near his litter box.

Aiden had made the tiny house one night while she'd slept. Finding another box that had contained cans of lo mein, a favorite staple of Grace's, he'd folded in the top panels, and slid a T-shirt over the sides so that the neck formed the opening. Laying it sideways on the floor, it made the perfect little hedgehog home.

When Grace had awakened that morning, she'd found her beloved pet settling down to sleep for the day, curled up in his house on some nice, soft bedding of shredded toilet paper.

She'd gazed at the little house for a long moment, then got up to use the loo without a word. When she'd come out, her eyes had been suspiciously red, and she'd thanked him sincerely if not eloquently, then went over to make her breakfast.

They'd fallen into a routine. He slept during the day, and she would watch the monitors, read the books she'd had stashed there, eat, clean, shower, wash her clothes and play with Mojo when the little guy was awake. At night, she would sleep, Mojo would play, and he would watch over them both, climbing the ladder occasionally to make sure the door was securely shut.

Sitting at the desk, he would spend his time going back and forth between watching the live footage of what was happening aboveground to watching the video that recorded while he was sleeping.

He didn't really need the monitors. He could feel the demons above them, almost to the point of knowing how many were out there at any given time.

During the daylight hours, humans lingered around the square, and not just tourists. Aiden recognized a few of them as the Suits that had inadvertently taken Mojo the day he'd met Grace, and they'd brought friends.

They searched the grounds with metal detectors, poking at the grass with sticks, looking for any hidden spots he and Grace could've disappeared into. However, with each passing day, fewer and fewer of them would come, as they came to the conclusion that there was nowhere in the vicinity they could be hiding.

When darkness fell, Leeha's hybrids would come back. But unlike the humans, who'd given up so easily, they only seemed to become more and more obsessed with finding them.

They swarmed the grounds around the sculpture like insects, scaring off any humans who happened to wander by that late, seemingly unconcerned about keeping a low profile. And every night, there were more of them.

He didn't mention this to Grace, unwilling to add to her distress. If she noticed when she was studying the footage, she didn't speak of it. She hardly spoke to him at all, actually.

He wanted to smooth away the worry lines from her forehead. He wanted to pull her into his arms and tell her it was going to be all right. He wanted to tell her that she had no need to be afraid of him, that he wasn't capable of hurting her. He wanted to kiss her again, desperately.

But he stubbornly refused to acknowledge the reason why.

On the fourth day, Aiden awoke to find the room empty and the bathroom door wide open. He jerked up out of bed, landing gracefully on his feet. Mojo was snuffling around in his house, the backpack was on the floor against the wall, but there was no scent of Grace.

She was gone.

He was up the ladder and at the hatch in less than half a second, not caring that it was still daylight out. Throwing his shoulder into the door, he put all of his strength behind it, but the bloody thing wouldn't budge.

A sudden and unreasonable panic gathered inside of him. He started hurling himself violently into the door without thought, over and over, until the bones in his shoulder cracked and crumbled under the impact.

With a roar of rage, he jumped down off of the ladder, beyond caring if anyone above ground heard him. He barely missed the now awake hedgehog as he landed, and began to pace. His right arm hung useless at his side, but he didn't feel anything except the fear in his gut.

Suddenly, he stopped pacing. What the bloody hell was he doing? He was acting like Nikulas (the fool), when he'd attempted to turn himself into a bonfire after Emma had stepped outside of the cave they were hiding out in. She'd gone out in broad daylight to relieve herself, and only hadn't come back because the wolves had taken her.

The Kincaid werewolves, that is, who are actually good mates of theirs.

Of course, they hadn't known what had happened to her at the time, and Nikulas had repeatedly tossed himself from the opening of their hideout and out into the sun trying to follow her outside.

Aiden had finally had to tackle the loon and threaten to tear off his limbs to keep him inside until the sun had set, and even then, things had been touchy as he'd tried to keep him from going after Emma.

Emma Moss. The female, and witch, who'd turned out to be Nikulas's *mate*.

The revelation hit Aiden like a truck. He stumbled backwards until the backs of his knees collided with Grace's bed and then he sat down hard, automatically holding his right arm against his stomach to avoid jarring his busted shoulder.

No, it wasn't bloody possible! He was the babe magnet of the group, the philanderer, the fantasy granter, and he bloody liked it that way. No one got more action than him, (other than Christian, but that fanger would bang anything lately). He had no use for a clingy female. He lived for variety, for feeding and for shagging. He had no desire to be chained to one female.

Hold on, mate! Let's not panic just yet.

He hadn't even tasted her yet. And according to the stories, which Nikulas had, unfortunately, found to be true, he wouldn't know his mate until he tasted her blood. The tricky part was, once he'd fed from that mate, he would then have to keep her around, alive and well, as he'd need her blood to survive. No other blood would do after drinking hers, and he wouldn't be able to feed from anyone else. Ever. Without his mate and her blood, he would weaken day by day, and eventually die the true death.

Even worse, if his friend were any example, he wouldn't want to shag anyone else either. Ever.

That was fine for Nikulas. He enjoyed being monogamous. He'd practically been a monk before he'd met Emma anyway.

But that fairy tale was not for him. He wasn't made to be a one-girl kind of bloke. Never had been, never would be. To be dependent on one person for your every joy? For your very existence? No. That was just too bloody much.

He swallowed hard as the thing he was trying so hard not to admit crept to the surface. His biggest fear of all: Was she, at this very moment, in danger? Dead?

And where was he? He'd been in bed, napping away. Nowhere near her. Just like before. Even though he knew there was nothing he could've done about it, he couldn't stop from being wracked with guilt.

And if she were still alive, how would he be able to protect her? A vulnerable, fragile human who could wander around in full sun? He couldn't, not forever, and then she would die and he would be all alone with his heart feeling like it was being torn from his chest.

Again.

But isn't that exactly what you're doing now? he asked himself. *Isn't that why you're here in the first place? To protect her?*

Yes, he answered as he looked around at the empty room. *And a bloody fine job I'm doing, as you can see.*

He rolled his shoulder, testing it. The bones were already healing.

I just need to get a bloody grip. It's not feasible for me to be so attached to her already. It must be something else. The vampire in me reacting to my only food supply scampering off and leaving me here to starve, that's all.

Yes, that had to be it. She was a feisty, delectable source of what he knew would be the sweetest blood he'd ever tasted, and that was all.

He scowled. So, where the bloody hell was she?

He began to pace the room again at vamp speed, easily dodging Mojo as the silly thing ran around with his head stuck in an empty toilet paper roll. Reaching down as he passed, he repeatedly pulled it off of him and dropped it on the floor, but finally gave up when the daft thing just kept sticking his nose back in it.

Finally, a rush of fresh air came from above, bringing with it the last rays of afternoon sunlight. They streamed down from the open hatch to land directly onto Aiden's head. Before he could react, the skin on his bare head started to sizzle and smoke.

"Bloody hell!" he yelled, slapping at his hair with his good arm while he danced back out of the beam of light.

The circle of sunlight narrowed and then disappeared as Grace climbed down the ladder with a paper bag tucked securely under her arm, the hatch closed behind her.

"WHERE THE BLOODY HELL HAVE YOU BEEN?" he bellowed. "AND HOW THE FUCK DO YOU GET THAT FUCKING, BLOODY DOOR OPEN?"

She nearly jumped out of her skin, practically falling down the last few rungs. Her eyes flew to his, and he saw a momentary flash of guilt there. It was there and gone so fast that if he hadn't been watching for just such a thing, he would've completely missed it.

She stared at him like a deer caught in the headlights at the sight of his anger and smoking hair, and then tucked her chin down without a word and tried to scamper past him.

He headed her off, stepping in front of her as she made for the loo to hide, the only other room in the place with a door.

"Fucking *stop*," he growled. "And *tell* me what bloody possessed you to go outside alone, and unprotected, with those *things* about to show up for the night!"

Staring at his chest, she mumbled, "I just needed something. No one saw me."

She went to walk around him again then, but he crossed his arms across his chest and made like a wall. A sliding wall that stuck to her like glue as she tried to sidestep around him, until she finally gave up and stood still.

"You will tell me where you bloody went, and *why*," he ground out between clenched teeth. "And then you're going to tell me how you open that bloody door."

She muttered something under her breath.

"Girl stuff? You needed 'girl stuff'?" he mocked. "You risked your bloody life, for what? Nail polish? Makeup? Have you gone off your trolley?" he asked in amazement.

Clenching her jaw, she eyed him defiantly as she pulled a box out of the bag and held it up in front of his face.

He raised an eyebrow. "Tampons?"

"Yes, if you must know. I got my *bloody* period! Happy now?"

Speechless for once, he did nothing to stop her this time as she marched around him and into the loo, slamming the door behind her.

Taking the first deep breath since he'd awakened, he inhaled her sweet scent, and then frowned.

Funny. He didn't notice anything different. Of course, she was in the other room now, and he'd been slightly distracted by the feel of the sun *frying the skin off of his head* to notice a change in her smell. He rubbed his tender skull ruefully.

Luckily for her, he was quite used to being around human females, and therefore could control himself even with the stronger blood scent.

But other human females didn't smell as good as Grace.

He grimaced. There *was* that.

No, no. It would be fine.

Scratching his head, he glanced around aimlessly, not quite sure what to do with himself now that she'd effectively knocked the steam out of him.

A thought occurred to him then: Why did she bother to come back? If she had truly made it past the Suits and to a store, why ever would she have come back here?

Wandering over to the desk, he sprawled out in the chair and watched Mojo bounce off the walls as he waited for her to come out.

Thirty minutes later, she did, eyeing him warily as she sidled into the room. She'd twisted up her long mahogany hair, showered, and changed into some of the extra clothes that had been stored here. Cargo pants and a button-down shirt, similar to what she'd worn on the way there.

Feeling a bit foolish now, he immediately stood up at her appearance, eager to make amends. "I apologize for yelling at you," he told her sincerely. "I was only a bit worried."

Mojo finally lost his toy and waddled towards her. Scooping him up, she flipped him onto his back in her palm, rubbing his soft belly with her free hand and playing with his feet.

For the first time in days, she spoke. "Continue," she said. "I'm listening."

Will miracles never cease to exist, he thought sarcastically.

"I was upset that you put yourself in danger. You should have waited for me to awaken. I am not unaware of the natural cycle of human females, I could have gone out and gotten what you needed for you."

She shook her head. "No. No sense in you risking yourself either. It was much easier for me to get around the few humans that are left then it would have been for you to sneak past our nighttime friends. I just had to wait for them to wander away from the hatch, and get to the cover of the trees without them seeing me." She shrugged. "It was pretty easy actually."

She was lying again.

Aiden rubbed his forehead. He didn't have the patience for this right now.

"Speaking of which, will you *please* tell me how you open that door?" he asked. "It will save me many broken bones the next time you disappear like that."

Her eyes darkened with concern as they flicked over him, searching for injuries.

Ah, see? She did care.

"Are you done yelling at me?"

"Absolutely." For now.

She glanced up at him again, gauging whether or not to trust him, he could tell.

Finally she said, "It's just a spell. And there are wards to keep evil out. And," she pointed to a large container of salt sitting on the counter. "I've been blocking the entrance with that, just for good measure."

He nodded. "Good. Good thinking, that."

"My Mom had this place built before she died. She made sure no one would be getting in here. I think she knew something like this was going to go down." Her voice dropped to just above a whisper. "I just wish she'd filled me in on it."

Her sorrow washed over him, taking the edge off the last remnants of his anger with her. Unable to help himself, he moved to stand closer, standing by her side but not touching her.

To comfort her? For his own reassurance? It didn't really matter at this point.

He breathed her in, letting her now familiar scent wash over and into him, sinking all the way into his bones.

Relief flowed through him at having her near again, and then he furrowed his brow. She smelled exactly the same as she always had.

So she was lying about that also.

The little minx. Did she truly think she could fool *him*, a vampire, with her woman's excuse? Blood doesn't lie, and his nose was telling him that there was no evidence of her being on her menses. Which meant the emergency tampon run had just been a cover for something else entirely. And that couldn't be good.

What did you do, Grace?

Mojo, as if sensing the sudden tension in the air, started wiggling and huffing in her hand until she set him down on the floor.

"Ow. All right, all right," she told him as he bristled. "Calm down, little dude."

Aiden tried to catch her eye as she stood. But like the liar that she was, hers skittered around the room, looking anywhere but at him.

An irrational disappointment filled him.

"Where did you really go today, Grace?"

Picking imaginary lint off of her shirt, she said, "I told you."

His patience at an end, he took a firm hold of her chin and lifted her face to his.

She fastened her lovely, lying eyes somewhere in the vicinity of his left clavicle, and refused to look at him.

Aiden heaved a weary sigh. There was nothing he hated more than a liar. If she wasn't going to let him help her, why should he stay any longer? He should leave here and go home. Let her deal with all of this on her own.

But imagining her here by herself had his chest tightening with such panic, he suddenly found it hard to breathe.

Letting go of her chin, he slid his hand around to the back of her neck so she couldn't run away. With the other one, he untwisted her hair from its bun.

The silky strands tumbled over the back of his hand, and he sucked in a breath as the smell of her shampoo filled the air. He wanted to run his fingers through the mass of it and spread it out across his bare chest so he could feel all of that fragrant softness tickling his bare skin.

But one thing at a time.

Keeping a secure grip on her nape, he lowered his head ever so slowly towards hers.

The rhythm of her heart sped up more with every fraction of an inch, pounding louder and louder as he heard her blood rushing through her veins.

With fear? Or with excitement?

He stopped less than a hair's breadth from her lips.

She frowned when she realized he wasn't going to kiss her, and at long last, her wide eyes flew to his.

Now that he had her attention, he needed to make it clear to her that although he was good-natured and tended not to let the world get him down, he was no fool. If she thought she could pull the wool over his eyes that easily, she was sadly mistaken. "I don't know what it is that you're hiding, Grace *France*," he told her with a tight smile. "But you're hiding *something* from me, and I *will* find out what it is."

Closing the distance between them, he took her mouth in a possessive kiss. He wrapped his other arm around her waist and yanked her soft, feminine body flush against his hard one, moaning with pleasure at the feel of her against him.

She gasped at the sudden contact, and he deepened the kiss, his tongue delving into her mouth to taste her natural sweetness.

Her hands came up between them, halfheartedly pushing him away at first. But as he continued to plunder her mouth, she finally gave up the pretense and they slid up his chest to grip his shoulders as she finally kissed him back.

He moaned again as she touched his tongue with hers. She smelled absolutely divine, and tasted even better as she gave in to his kiss and returned it with a passion that surprised him.

Her body bowed into his, attempting to get closer still, and his arms tightened around her.

Releasing her lips, he moved his hand from her nape and tangled his fingers in all of that silky hair. Pulling her head back, he exposed her throat to his heated gaze. Her blood pulsed heavily just under the thin layer of her skin, and a feral growl rose from his throat, followed by the sudden rush of her desire permeating the air, tempting him nearly beyond reason.

"Why won't you trust me, love?" he whispered throatily, his voice thick with both his sorrow and his craving for her.

She whimpered as he ran the tip of his tongue along her throbbing artery, before kissing it tenderly, careful of his fangs. Working his way down to the sweet spot between her neck and her shoulder, he splayed his other hand across her luscious ass, pulling her up and into his arousal.

"I would never hurt you, Grace," he whispered against her smooth skin.

He lifted her up until she wrapped her legs around him. Rolling his hips, he ground his hard length against her, reveling in her soft sounds of pleasure until he could stand it no longer.

Tucking her face against his shoulder, not wanting to frighten her with the evidence of his excitement, he strode to the bed.

18

Grace shivered when she felt the cold sheets of her bed, but Aiden's heat immediately warmed her as he followed her down, chasing away the chill.

She knew she should stop him before he found out that she had lied to him about the reason she had left. She wasn't on her period. She'd just had it. She wasn't due for another three weeks.

Why won't you trust me, love?

His words echoed in her head as he kissed her throat, unbuttoning her cotton shirt with one hand while he held his weight off of her with the other. Guilt and shame rose within her for what she'd just done, and she opened her mouth to confess right then and there, but he spoke before she had the chance.

"Grace, don't be frightened, love. I'm a bit riled up, and I can't control it. But I swear I won't hurt you, all right?"

He must have sensed her distraction, and mistook it for anxiety.

Then he lifted his head from the curve of her neck, and she saw what he meant.

"I want to look at you, love."

As his burning eyes roamed over her face and down her torso, his hand followed, skimming her breast in her cotton bra to rest lightly on her ribcage beneath.

Goosebumps rose on her skin everywhere he touched.

He opened his mouth on a labored breath, and she could see his fangs were fully extended. A quick stab of fear went through her when he raised his glowing eyes back to hers, but it quickly dissipated. He was nothing like the vampire that had killed her intruder. His gaze was intense, but warm, reverent even, as he slowly lowered his mouth back to hers, giving her time to reject him.

Instead, she welcomed him eagerly, wrapping her arms around his neck and holding him close. She didn't think, she just kissed him back with everything she was feeling inside. Running her hands down his back, she slid them under the neckline of his T-shirt to feel the smooth, warm skin beneath.

He moaned in her mouth at her touch, deepening the kiss until she forgot everything but this moment. Reaching down, he slid a hand underneath the back of her knee and bent her leg up, allowing him to settle more fully between her thighs.

She lifted her hips to meet him, rubbing the core of her desire shamelessly against the hard ridge bulging beneath his pants.

He immediately picked up her rhythm, thrusting against her until they were both gasping for air.

"Aiden, please..." she begged breathlessly between kisses, completely beyond caring that he'd know she'd lied. She'd think of some excuse to tell him. Right now, she needed this ravenous vampire inside of her, and she needed it now.

She reached between them, closing her palm around his hardness.

Suddenly, she felt a cool breeze on her bare skin, and she opened her eyes to find him holding his weight on his arms while he glared down at her.

Dark shadows swam through the bright grey of his eyes.

"You're lying to him," he growled.

The British accent she found so endearing was gone again, and the words sounded strange, unpracticed. Like they had the other day. His entire demeanor had changed. Gone was the warm, teasing male she'd come to know.

She was looking at a stranger.

His lips pulled back from his fangs in an enraged snarl, "YOU'RE LYING TO HIM!"

Grace screamed and rolled out from underneath him, falling onto the floor in a heap.

Jumping to her feet, she nearly tripped over Mojo as she ran to the bathroom with her pet close on her heels.

She slammed the door, locking it behind them, then looked around frantically for a weapon as Aiden pounded on the door.

"Grace! Grace, what's wrong? Are you all right, love?" He knocked again. "Poppet, please open the door. I apologize for...whatever I did. I didn't mean to frighten you. Grace!"

He pounded on the door again.

With no weapon at hand, she resorted to backing as far away from the door as she could while Mojo rolled into a ball in the corner. Pressing her back against the wall by the shower stall, she weighed her options.

It was actually a pretty easy decision. She had none. She had no weapons, and she had no magic against a vampire. All she could do was heal herself, and move things around, if they weren't too large. And she had an unusual connection with animals, but she sincerely doubted Mojo would be able to do much against him by himself.

She had nothing. Nothing that would cause any damage to someone such as him.

"Grace!" He shouted. "Open this bloody door and talk to me!"

"No!"

"What do you mean 'No'"?

"No!" she repeated.

"Fine! I'm coming in!"

She shrieked as the door busted off its hinges and slammed into the opposite wall, crumbling the plaster. Aiden stood at the threshold, but didn't come in. He looked her over from head to toe, briefly closing his eyes and sighing when his inspection was finished.

She eyed him warily, pulling her shirt together. "Stay away from me!"

He scratched his head, confusion and hurt fighting for dominance on his face. "Poppet...whatever it was that I did, I didn't mean to frighten you. I told you I'd never hurt you, and I meant it. I can't help the way my body reacts to you, but that doesn't mean I can't control myself."

She rolled her eyes. "I'm not afraid of you vamping out. It's the other side of you that I don't like."

His face screwed up in confusion. "The other side?"

"You yelled at me, dude!"

"What? I didn't ye..."

"Yes, you did! Don't act like you don't know. You growled and you yelled at me! I was about to become your next kill!"

Spotting the hairbrush on the counter just as he took a step towards her, she sent it flying through the air at him. It bounced off of the door jam next to his head and clattered onto the floor.

Now it was his turn to eye her warily. He stopped where he was.

"Grace..."

The glass she used to rinse her mouth soon followed the brush, and would've hit him if he hadn't dodged it. It smashed on the floor behind him, the noise sending Mojo scampering around Aiden's legs and into his house to hide.

"Bloody hell, woman! Stop tossing things at me!" he bellowed.

"Stop pretending you weren't planning on eating me!"

Palms up in a peace making gesture, he gave her a quizzical look. "Define 'eat'."

She looked around for something else to hit him with.

"Grace, I honestly don't recall doing any such thing. Now please, stop this, and come out of the loo and tell me what happened."

Crossing her arms over her breasts, she stared at him with a mulish expression.

He backed away from the door, giving her plenty of space to get by him. "Please, love. This is just silly."

She chewed her lip as she studied him. He seemed so sincere, and honestly confused by her actions. And more importantly, he appeared to be back to his normal self again.

She had a sudden thought: Maybe he had a split personality! He *had* said she was lying to "him", and not "me". But, even if that were the case, would his other personality know something that the other one didn't?

It was just her luck that the one unequivocally panty-dropping worthy guy she'd met in her life would end up being a complete psycho case. Not to mention the whole not even human thing.

Still. She couldn't hide in the bathroom forever, and she had nowhere else to go.

Buttoning up her shirt, she never took her eyes off of him as she eased past him to go stand by the ladder. If he wacked out on her again, she'd take her chances with the things creeping around their hideout outside.

"All right," he breathed with relief. Sitting down on the edge of the bed, he scooted across the mattress until his back was against the wall. Stretching his long, muscular, jean clad legs out in front of him, he crossed his ankles and laced his fingers together on his lap.

She hesitated. He really did appear confused.

"I'm going to sit right here, and I won't move," he promised. "Please, just talk to me so we can get this sorted out."

"You really don't remember?" she asked.

"Yelling at you? No, poppet, I really don't."

"I'm not lying. You did. You yelled at me," she insisted defensively.

"Okay," he acquiesced. "What did I yell at you?"

Well, hell. She hadn't been prepared for that one.

She sighed and rubbed her nose, thinking she may as well fess up. She'd been about to anyway, earlier, when he was kissing her.

"You said, 'You're lying to him'."

One eyebrow lifted. "To whom?"

Now she was confused. "What?"

"You said, that I said, that you were lying to 'him'. Who is 'him'?"

"Um, I think it's you."

Rolling his eyes, he said, "Well that makes no sense at all, poppet. I am 'me'. Not 'him'."

"Yeah. That's kind of why I freaked out." At least he wasn't questioning what it was she was lying about. "And you bared your fangs at me. Not in a good way. And your voice was different."

That caught his attention. "Different how?"

She rubbed her arms as she remembered. "Well, your accent was gone, for one. And the words sounded strange." She thought for a minute. "I can only explain it like, when you talk like that, it always sounds like you're not used to pronouncing the words, or something. Like English is a new language to you."

His eyes locked onto her, his sharp mind not missing a thing. "Always?" he repeated. "What do you mean, always? Has this happened before?"

"Just once," she told him. "Right after we got here."

Comprehension dawned across his features. "And that's why you've been acting so wonky since we arrived here. I had no idea," he said, almost to himself.

He fell silent, but she could see the wheels turning in his head.

"Aiden?" she asked when he didn't seem inclined to explain.

"Hmm?"

"Do you have a split personality or something?"

He gave her a sad smile. "No, love."

"Do you know why this is happening?"

He studied her for a long moment. "Yes. I believe I do."

"Are you going to tell me?

He propped his laced fingers on top of his head, showing off his bulging arm muscles to her hungry gaze. "Yes, because unlike a certain other person in this room, I rarely feel the need to lie."

The blood rushed to her face and she guiltily dropped her eyes from those tantalizing muscles.

Why did it bother her so much that he knew she had lied to him? She lied to people all the time, to protect herself and her family. And sometimes she got caught, and would have to think up some other explanation. She didn't like doing it, but it had never bothered her this much before. And why wasn't he asking her what she'd lied about?

Because he's already figured it out. But how much has he figured out? That's the real question.

She was distracted from her inner dialogue when he said, "I have a bit of a wild tale to tell you, poppet."

19

Grace was staring at him like he was utterly bonkers. And after hearing himself say the words out loud, he was beginning to wonder if perhaps she was correct.

People had been telling him that for years, but he'd never taken them seriously. He'd only thought it was his unique sense of humor that threw them off.

Now that he thought of it, his head collection didn't seem to be a big selling point either. Not certain why not, it was quite the impressive collection.

She held her hand up, palm out. "Wait. So you're telling me those things above ground right now, they used to be vampires? Luukas' vampires?"

"Yes," he confirmed.

"And now they're what? Possessed? By demons?"

"Yes, you could say that."

"I knew it!" she exclaimed. "Well, not the vampire part."

"You knew they were demons? Since when?"

She shrugged. "I've seen them around town for a while now. They always gave me the creeps."

"Do I give you the creeps?"

She chewed her lip while she contemplated him. "At first you did...sometimes you still do."

"I see." He wasn't sure what to think about that.

"And this other vampire bitch, what's her name again?"

"Leeha."

"Leeha, yes, this Leeha bitch is creating an entire army of these things?"

"Yes."

"And you know this because she told you, right before she did the same thing to you? But for some unknown reason, your demon hasn't taken you over completely."

"That would be correct." He paused. "At least, from what you've told me, that's what I'm beginning to believe."

She rose gracefully from the floor where she'd been sitting during his story to pace back and forth in front of him.

He sat patiently and let her go. It was a lot to take in.

While she wore a path in the floor, he wondered again what all she was hiding from him. Part of him wanted to make her tell him, and with a little mind manipulation, he easily could. But a much larger part of him wanted her to trust him enough to fess up on her own. He didn't know why it was so important to him for her to tell him of her own free will, it just was.

That wasn't quite true. He knew why it was important to him. Just like he knew why he was finding it so hard to resist her.

He was deep in thought about the little mole on her belly just to the left of her navel when she stopped and faced him again. Her eyes searched his, but he couldn't quite read what she was thinking.

She had to clear her throat a few times before she could get the words out. "You really have one of those things inside of you?"

He sighed sadly. "I didn't want to believe so at first. Leeha and I have always rather fancied each other."

He didn't miss the stiffening of her spine and the angry flash in Grace's eyes at that comment, and he had to stop himself from smiling with pleasure at the thought of her being jealous of Leeha. "And I was quite certain that she hadn't gone through with it. But with all that's happened to get me here, and from what you're telling me happened earlier, it appears that I was nothing to her but a sacrifice that had to be made. I'm rather gutted about the entire thing, actually."

"Was she like, your girlfriend or something?" Grace bit out.

Aiden tilted his head, letting the warmth he felt for her shine from his eyes. "No, poppet. I've never even shagged her."

This seemed to appease her. A little. She continued her line of questioning. "So, how do we get it out? This...thing in you?"

"I have no idea," he told her honestly. Then an unpleasant thought occurred to him. "I don't know that we can, really, unless it wants to come out."

Her shoulders drooped and she kind of fell back against the wall as she absorbed that.

"You seem to be taking this all in stride," she commented offhandedly.

But he only shrugged a bit. "What else am I to do?"

"I don't know," she sighed and rubbed her temples, then changed the subject. "So, what is she planning on doing with this army?"

He laughed. "What else? Use them as her soldiers to take over the world. Just as all the evil villains do. She believes our kind are superior to humans, and she wants to create enough of these things that she'll be able to take over Luukas' territory, and eventually, the world."

"Luukas is the vampire that created you?"

"Yes."

Her forehead wrinkled in confusion. "But, didn't he create her also? How can she turn on him like this? Isn't there some kind of code, or something?"

"No." Aiden shook his head. "Leeha was adopted into our colony and turned by one of Luukas' vampires, who has since been destroyed. That's against the rules, you see," he answered her unspoken question. "She was invited to accept Luukas as her Master, but he's not her master other than by her choice, or not. And apparently," he snorted. "She chose 'not'."

Grace didn't seem to share his humor about the situation.

"Don't look so gloomy, love. She won't get away with it in the long run. There are too many flaws in her plan," he continued.

"Such as?"

"For one, she *has* to use Luukas' vampires to create those things. If she attempts to use her own vampires, ones she turns herself, they deteriorate into these disgusting grey monsters within days. Her blood isn't strong enough inside of them to handle the possession. They begin to rot almost as soon as they are taken over, and don't last very long. Second, I've learned since arriving here that her hybrids seem to have a plan of their own. I think *they* are using *her*, and not the other way around. Those blokes up there," he pointed towards the ceiling. "They're up to something."

She didn't bother hiding her suspicion as she asked, "How do you know?"

"I can sense it," he told her honestly. "Just like I can sense when they're near, and they can sense me."

It didn't take her long to put two and two together. "They know you're here."

It wasn't a question.

"I'm so sorry, love," he told her earnestly. "I think they're sticking around because they can feel me here. I didn't realize. Not until we were already trapped down here."

"Can you feel it?" she asked after a moment. "The thing inside of you?"

"Sometimes," he answered honestly. "Although I didn't recognize what it was at first."

"What does it feel like?" She wrapped her arms around her middle.

He tried to find the words to describe it. "It was quite subtle at first. Just a strange fluttering in my belly. But then, when we were at that new building rescuing your pet, that's when it really got bizarre."

"How so?"

How to explain it without her thinking he was off his rocker, or frightening her more than she already was? "I started feeling things after the others arrived. I was feeling emotions, and urges, but they weren't my own." He glanced up at her, uncertain of how much he should say, but he supposed it was only fair for her to know what it was exactly, that she was imprisoned with. "He's not nice, and I can't control him, poppet. It's like a wound, festering inside of me now. Unlike the others, however, he's decided to hide out for the most part. But apparently he has taken quite a fancy to *you*." He grinned at her, trying to lighten the mood. "I can't say that I blame him."

"Yeah, which is why he scared the crap out of me earlier."

"Well," Aiden told her coolly. "You shouldn't lie."

"I think we have bigger issues here than my little white lies."

"Such as?" he asked innocently.

She threw her arms up in exasperation. "Such as you have a demon inside of you, you loon, and we don't know when he's going to reappear. What if he decides to pop his ugly head up again while I'm sleeping, or in the shower, or if we're..." She trailed off, a blush creeping over her face and neck.

"If we're...what?" he teased with a sexy half-smile.

She glowered at him until he chuckled.

Mojo started making little noises, and she watched him bristle up at one of her shoes.

When she raised her eyes back to his, hers were large and worried. "What are we going to do, Aiden?"

He scratched his head. Good question, that.

Scooting off the bed, he sauntered across the small room to her. He waited for her to shy away from him like she had before, or to run back to the loo in fear. But though he heard her heart speed up with his every step, she raised her chin and held her ground.

His brave girl.

Tucking her hair behind one ear, he ducked his head until they were face to face. "I won't let anyone hurt you, poppet. Not even me," he told her fervently. "I swear it."

Now if only he knew how to keep that promise.

Grace wanted to believe him, she really did. But she was afraid that it wasn't something he could control.

And what if this was all a big ruse on his part? What if he really was one of those things, and it was just acting like the vampire Aiden used to be? What if it was all a big plot to get at the thing it wanted? The thing that she had in her possession?

Listen to me closely, Grace. This is important. If the time ever comes that you meet one, never, ever, trust a vampire. They're beautiful and charming and everything you want them to be, but believe me when I tell you that you can't trust them. They only use you for what they want. And they are loyal to no one but themselves and others like them. You'll be left with nothing but a broken heart. If you're left alive at all.

Her mother had trusted a vampire once; a vampire that had charmed his way right into her bed. She had told Grace the entire story shortly before she had died.

He had fed from her, and made love to her, and drove her insane with wanting him. She'd been on the verge of leaving her beloved husband and child when all hell had broken loose within the coven and they'd decided to flee. Her father had wanted to leave immediately, but her mother had been so obsessed with that vampire that she couldn't bear to leave without telling him. So, she'd made up an excuse, and while her husband was packing some of their things, she ran to her lover to say goodbye.

And he had betrayed her.

The vampire had gone straight to the new High Priest as soon as she'd left and made a deal with him. He'd ratted out her parents and the rest of the families who were going to make a run for it without a second thought for the woman he'd claimed to care about.

Her father had killed that vampire while she and her mom had escaped. But he'd received a fatal injury in the process. He hadn't remained alive long enough to join them.

Her eyes slid over to the black bag, still in the cubby where Aiden had put it. The box was inside of it. The one both the humans and the demons were after.

Grace knew the moment she'd seen the picture of the dagoba under the red felt bottom that the box was what they were after. She just didn't know why.

She'd spent the last few days trying to reason it out: A dagoba was a type of tombstone for monks. The largest group of them was in the Forest of the Dagobas of Shaolin Temple. They were all different, depending on the monk, and they all had different inscriptions on them. Each one was unique.

But why would a detailed etching of one be hidden under the felt padding of a wooden box? Unless it was some kind of sign? Maybe some kind of clue?

There were many rumors surrounding the Shaolin Monks, some were true, and some were not. And some were only speculation and hadn't been proven either way. However, she'd never heard anything of consequence concerning the dagobas. Nothing that a demon would want with them anyway.

But it had to be the box they were after. There was nothing else in the bag of any significance.

Unable to figure out why the box was such a hot property, she'd done the only other thing she could think of to get herself out of this mess.

She'd snuck out while Aiden was sleeping and made a deal with the Suits. She'd give them the box, and in exchange, they would allow her and Aiden to leave.

She smiled at Aiden. "I know you won't let anyone hurt me."

And neither will I.

20

Christian paced his hot cell, waiting for the girl to come back, the girl with hair like the last hushed rays of sunset.

He'd been here for weeks, stuck in this...display case or whatever the fuck it was, and it was the same thing day after day. No one ever came except for the girl.

Every day she walked through that door and into the empty room on the other side of his glass wall. The music would start up in a hypnotic rhythm as soon as she entered, and she'd strut over to the stripper pole and dance for him.

She never spoke. She never looked at him. She would dance her little striptease until she was wearing nothing but the tiniest G-string, then the music would stop and she would gather her things and leave out the same door she came in.

And every day, he paced like a caged animal, waiting for her. Even knowing that lusting after her sultry curves would bring him nothing but more agony.

He was going fucking insane in this steel box. No matter what he tried, he couldn't make so much as a dent in the steel walls and ceiling, or the one freaky glass wall that gave him his view of his own personal Calypso. No matter how hard he hit it, it would just bend out like rubber and snap back to its original shape.

He licked his dry lips. He was so thirsty; he hadn't fed in a long time. He needed blood, and a bath. However, that was really the least of his problems.

Christian stopped pacing when the door opened at the end of the room. His entire body began to tremble as the girl entered the room and ambled over to the pole.

She was wearing gold today. Instant pain wracked through his body at the mere sight of her, pulsing in time to the erotic beat of Nine Inch Nails that suddenly filled the room. He wanted to turn away, to just fucking ignore her, but he couldn't *not* look at her.

His fangs shot down into his mouth instantly, and his tongue flicked out to tease the tips, drawing blood. Licking his lips again, he tasted the salt of the sweat running down his face, and as she swayed to the music, he palmed the hard bulge pressing against the front of his pants.

He knew it wouldn't do any good. He couldn't make himself come. But it felt so fucking good, he couldn't help himself. At least until she left, and he was left rock hard with aching balls, while his muscles cramped with pain until he was screaming on the floor like a pussy.

Whatever it was that had happened to him after Luukas disappeared, these assholes knew exactly how to make his life hell with it. Stick a pretty girl in front of him to seduce him, but not let him touch her. Ever.

He needed to fuck, and he needed to feed, and he needed to do both as soon as possible, before he lost his fucking mind.

Before he'd been taken off the streets of Seattle and brought here, he was going through four to eight girls a night to keep the muscle cramps away. He'd never tried going this long without sex before. Two days had been his limit, and he'd nearly raped Shea at the end of it.

He vaguely wondered if Shea and Dante were going through similar tortures, or if he was the only one who'd been taken.

The girl suddenly stopped dancing in front of the pole and leaned back against it to face him. As always, he wished she would look up, but she didn't.

Ever so slowly, she pulled down the spaghetti straps of her silky crop top, then reached around to untie the back. The soft material slithered off of her, revealing the perfect mounds of her breasts with their large, dusky nipples.

Christian moaned aloud and slammed the glass with one hand, all thoughts of his friends completely forgotten. Leaning his forehead against it, he kept her in his sights while his other hand undid his pants and slid inside to fist his cock.

She dropped her top onto the floor and spread her legs wide. One of her hands slid across her thigh to disappear under her sheer skirt while the other one moved across her ribcage to cup her breast. It spilled out of her small hand as she fondled herself, pinching her nipple until it was hard, and then moving to the other side.

As the song Closer pulsed through his skull he watched, mesmerized. This was new. She'd never touched herself in front of him before.

Her head fell back against the pole, exposing her slender throat and the artery pulsing there, and his cock jumped in his hand. It took everything he had to remain upright and not to give in to his cramping muscles as his body tortured him for teasing it.

His breath was coming in heavy pants, matching the rhythm of her heaving chest as she became more and more excited. He squeezed himself tight, the pain nothing compared to the burning acid that was streaming through his limbs.

He was going to die like this.

The thought almost made him laugh. Death from lack of sex. What a way to go. But it was probably true. He felt like a drug addict going through withdrawals from hell. His heart was probably going to give out before he ever made it out of here.

Suddenly, she lifted her head and looked straight at him. Sapphire blue irises ringed with black stared into his own amber ones. The whites were bloodshot, and she had dark bruises under her eyes.

Her mouth went slack with desire, and her eyes closed again as she came, her body convulsing beneath her hands as her legs gave out and she slid down the pole.

Christian cried out with her, and smashed his head into the glass wall. His hand squeezed his cock until he thought it was gonna pop right off. His chest heaved, his legs and shoulders seized with pain, but he couldn't bring himself relief.

His palm streaked down the unbreakable glass as he collapsed to his knees. He lifted his head at the same time she did, and they stared at each other.

A single tear slid down her cheek as he pressed his forehead to the glass again.

21

Aiden let Grace's long hair trickle through his fingers as he watched her sleep, his inner demon happy to stay dormant again for the moment. He leaned back against the wall as he had earlier. Her head was in his lap, and her scent wrapped around him like a warm blanket as she slept.

He ached for her, physically and spiritually. It was bloody painful, this need he had to bury himself inside of her, to become a part of her.

His gums burned, his fangs ready to pop down at the slightest provocation, and he hissed softly as he pulled his lips back, seeking some relief. It didn't really help.

However, he was rather enjoying the anticipation of tasting her - in more ways than one.

Gazing down at her face, peaceful in sleep, he was again surprised at this trust she had in him after all he'd told her. She seemed to be taking him at his word that he wouldn't hurt her, and they'd picked up their normal routine again, only she was speaking to him now. Which was nice.

He'd discovered...by plying her with endless questions...that she often tried to use her healing powers to help patients undergoing heart surgery at the hospital where she worked, and that she had yet to succeed.

He could hear the frustration in her voice that she couldn't save them, and knew exactly how she was feeling. But she was wrong. Her powers weren't useless. Not at all. He could feel her power simmering beneath the surface, and believed that she only needed something to give it a boost before she would reach her full potential.

She'd asked him to tell her about his life, and he had. Fascinated with all he had seen and experienced, she'd sat quietly while he told her a number of outrageous stories. Most were true, some he'd embellished just a bit. But it was worth it to keep her mind off of the elephant in the room.

Or in this case, the demon.

It hadn't worked. She'd insisted on talking about it, and so they had. After coming at it from every possible angle and having no new ideas, she'd eventually succumbed to her exhaustion and curled up on his lap to sleep.

His chest tightened. He needed to get them out of there, and soon. He could feel his craving to keep this quirky, secretive female intensify by the moment, and if he didn't get away from her soon, he was afraid he might never want to. In spite of her horrible habit of calling him "dude".

Would that really be such a terrible thing?

Yes! Yes, it would.

He scowled at the mere idea. For one, he had his own problems right now, the greatest of which being this bugger of a demon hitching a ride inside his body. Two, he didn't want to be tied down like stodgy ole Nikulas.

But then he sighed in resignation a second later, knowing that he wasn't fooling anyone, least of all himself.

As he absent-mindedly played with the soft strands of her hair, he set to figuring out a plan to escape this coffin they'd inadvertently trapped themselves in. She should have never come back here once she'd gotten out.

Except that her Mojo was here. He wondered why she hadn't just taken him with her and escaped? If she'd made it to a store to buy something for her ruse, why not run off? Could it be she did care for him? Just a little?

Another good hour of brainstorming later, he arrived at the only possible conclusion. He would just have to fight his way out, hopefully distracting the demon hybrids away from Grace so she could escape. He would tell her to call Nik at the number on her phone. Nik would get her off of this continent safely.

As for him, well, maybe his bloody demon would finally come out to play. It was the only way he'd have a chance against the bastards outside.

But if he did, what would happen to *him*? Aiden? Would he ever be himself again?

The thought sobered him. He needed to get Grace away from him sooner rather than later, for he'd promised her that he wouldn't hurt her. And he always kept his promises.

His inner clock told him the sun would be coming up soon. They'd leave at sundown the following night, just as soon as he could safely risk being outside.

Suddenly, the wall shuddered against his back.

Aiden's hand stilled in Grace's hair as he listened. He heard Mojo scratching in his litter box, and the slight hum of the cameras on the monitors, but nothing else.

A frown creased his brow as he cupped his hand under Grace's head and slid out from underneath her, gently settling her back down on the bed. Walking over to the desk, he checked out the live feed.

There was not one demon on the screen.

One eyebrow went up, but otherwise his face remained passive. This didn't bode well at all. Where the bloody hell were they all?

Then he heard it. A scratching sound like nails on a chalkboard, so faint human ears wouldn't have noticed it. It came directly from the wall behind Grace.

The dimwits had finally figured it out. They were digging down to them.

Sure enough, the sound came again, louder this time, followed by a clank as they hit the outside of the shelter with something hard.

Everything went quiet and still for the span of a few heartbeats, and then everything happened at once.

Aiden burst into action as the things outside started slamming something against the outer side of the wall.

Grace's eyes fluttered open, and she jumped from the bed to stand in the middle of the floor, disoriented from being woken so suddenly.

Mojo ran into his house to hide.

Her head whipped around towards the noises coming from the wall. "They found us." Her voice wasn't quite steady.

She looked around frantically, but he already had her rucksack and was throwing things into it. Throwing it over his shoulder, he shoved Grace towards the ladder.

"We've got to go, poppet. NOW."

She didn't stop to ask questions. Grabbing her shoes out of the cubby by the bag, she started up the ladder without even putting them on. At the top, she started chanting, but paused suddenly. Looking back at Aiden on the rungs below her, she yelled over the noise.

"Mojo! Aiden, you have to get him!"

He jumped down off the ladder, shook the little guy out of his house and into his palm, and then, with a myriad of curses, stuck the prickly little bugger into his hood. When he got back to the ladder, Grace was just finishing up the spell and the hatch door was opening.

Leaning to the side, Aiden grabbed a knife and a 9mm off of the wall that he'd loaded after they'd arrived, and followed her up and out into the early morning darkness.

Stepping out onto the grass, he stayed down, gun at the ready. The moon was low in the sky, and he could sense the dawn wasn't far off. They'd have to find shelter, and quickly.

He scanned the area around him. They must all be on the other side digging. He could hear them, banging against the wall of it, trying to bust their way inside.

Funny they'd left no one to guard the rest of the area.

Keeping low to the ground, he crept around the side of the sculpture. The densest area of trees was on this side, and so he assumed Grace had gone this way. All they'd have to do is make it across the garden without being seen.

But when he got around to that side, she was nowhere to be seen.

His heart stopped as his eyes pierced through the dark, searching for but not finding her. He wanted to call out, but couldn't risk those things hearing him. Even Mojo was quiet in his hood, like he knew the danger they were in.

Had she already run across that quickly? Gone to the other side? Why hadn't she waited for him?

He hesitated, undecided on which way to go now, when he heard a noise behind him: the ominous and unmistakable sound of a number of pump action shotguns loading a shell into their chambers.

Slowly, he straightened out of his crouch position and looked back over his shoulder, holding his hands up in the air.

Grace stood in the center of a group of the human Suits, all armed to the teeth, the wooden box in her hands.

He hadn't even noticed her grab it from the bag.

But what he did notice was that she wasn't being physically detained. He also noticed that none of them were watching her, as if they had no fear of her running away.

And what he noticed most of all, was the defiant tilt of her chin, in direct contrast to the guilty tears streaking down her cheeks. Her lovely forest green eyes pleaded with him to understand.

A stab of betrayal pierced his heart, and he closed his eyes, suddenly unable to stand the sight of her. His breath whooshed from his lungs as pain clenched in his chest.

He'd been a bloody fool.

"Drop your weapon," the Chinese leader said in broken English. "The bullets in guns are silver. No wrong moves, or we kill you."

Aiden opened his glowing eyes and dropped the pistol and the knife. He didn't need the weapons to annihilate these wankers.

Baring his fangs, he leaned towards them with a feral hiss. Silly humans thought they were going to keep him from his lying female with a few little guns? He would rip them apart before the last one could manage to aim and fire, and add their heads to his collection.

Well, maybe not the horrid looking one on the left.

At his show of aggression, the humans took a step back almost as one, and the smell of piss filled the air as one in the back revealed himself to be the weakest link of the group.

Just as he gathered himself for the attack, something hard and cold jabbed Aiden in the back of the head.

"Hello again, Waano." The thing that used to be Steven crowed happily.

Aiden's guts churned at the name. Ignoring them, he leveled his glare on Grace and she recoiled visibly, turning her face away.

"Don't turn from me now, love," he growled at her. "Don't you want to watch? Enjoy the show you orchestrated all by yourself? I only wish you had let me know what my bloody lines were." He gave a derisive laugh. "I'm finding myself a bit at a loss here. Am I the one who lives? Or the one who dies a horrible death in front of your eyes?"

"Aiden, stop!" she begged. "Just do as they say. They promised to let you go if I gave them the box. I offered it to them. There was no other choice!"

He threw his head back and laughed out loud. He laughed for so long the Suits began to exchange worried glances with each other. "And you believed them?" Clutching his stomach to try to relieve the searing ache there, his smile turned into a sneer. "Come now, poppet. I know even you are not that naive."

"I had no choice," she insisted quietly.

"There is always a choice," he snarled harshly. "And I choose not to believe your bloody lies anymore." He smiled. "And also, I don't want to be in your bloody show."

Without looking he twisted to the side, knocking the gun at his head aside with one hand and throwing an elbow back into Steven's face. Blood spattered everywhere as the crunching sound of bone blended with the thing's scream of rage.

But before he could follow through with anything else, two others rushed forward and grabbed him by the arms, wrenching them up and to the sides behind him.

He tensed to throw them off, and then felt Mojo in his hood. It gave him just enough pause for Steven to recover.

Grabbing him by the hair, he yanked Aiden's head back until his blood-covered mouth was right next to his ear.

"Oh, you're going to be in the show, Waano. But we're not going to kill you. Not just yet."

22

Grace hugged the box protectively to her chest as she shoved her way through the group of Suits until she was next to the leader.

"You swore you would let him go," she admonished him in Mandarin. "You swore it!"

"I did," he agreed with a shallow nod of his head. "I gave you my word, and I will honor it."

She closed her eyes, exhaling in relief.

"However," he continued, "I cannot be held accountable for what *they* will do." He jerked his head in the direction of the things holding Aiden.

Her eyes snapped open. "What? What do you mean? We had a deal!"

"You and I had a deal. And *we* have a deal with them," again he indicated the things holding Aiden. "The two deals have nothing to do with each other."

Aiden grunted and she whipped her head around, pushing her hair out of her face. The one called Steven had him by the hair on the crown of his head as he eyed up the box in her hands. As she watched, he pulled Aiden's head back until she thought his neck would snap, and two others had his arms outstretched painfully to either side. Fresh tears filled her eyes.

He looked like a sacrifice.

The leader of the Suits bowed to the hybrids. "We will meet you at the appointed place for the exchange."

Steven wiped the blood from his face with the back of his free arm and gave them a gruesome smile. "Agreed."

"Come," the Chinese man told her. "There's nothing we can do here. You can come with us to the meeting place, away from here. Give us the box there, and you will leave unharmed as we agreed."

"What about him?" She indicated Aiden.

The leader didn't even bother to look his way. "He is no longer your concern, or ours. There is nothing we can do for him. They will bring him...or they won't."

Grace locked eyes with Aiden, and his look of complete betrayal nearly knocked the air from her lungs.

Her mind spun as she frantically tried to come up with a way out of this. She couldn't just leave him here with those things.

She had no weapon, and what little magic she possessed was useless in situations like this. Still, there had to be a way. Something she could offer them, something she could do...

"Go along then," Aiden growled at her. "Get out of my sight, you bloody bitch, before I kill you myself."

His words hit her like a slap of cold air, and she reared back with a gasp.

"Aiden..." she nearly sobbed.

He surged forward with bared fangs, fighting his captors to get to her.

Pain and fear ripped through her. She spun away before he could see and automatically put one foot in front of the other, walking away in the midst of the humans.

What had she done?

He doesn't mean it, she told herself. *He's just pissed off. Really pissed off.*

Uncontrollable tears ran down her face, but she refused to look back. She couldn't. She couldn't stand to see the way he was looking at her anymore.

I didn't betray you! I was trying to save us! She screamed the words in her head hoping that somehow he would hear them, but knowing he wouldn't.

She'd been stupid. Stupid!

Why won't you trust me, love?

She fought back a sob as Aiden's husky voice came back to her. Why hadn't she trusted him? He would've gotten them out of there somehow.

But more and more of those things had kept coming every night, and he couldn't leave during the day, and she'd been running low on supplies. She thought she'd come up with such a great idea: the perfect solution. Play nice with the less dangerous humans by giving them what they wanted, and work out a way to get Aiden out of there.

She'd believed her Mom, believed he couldn't be trusted, and in turn, *she* had become the treacherous one.

Way to play hero, Grace.

The group picked up their pace as they got farther away from the sculpture, all of them except Grace looking back over their shoulders every few steps. Seems they didn't quite trust their business partners.

Couldn't say that she blamed them.

They got to one of the roads and hurried towards a line of vehicles parked on the one side. She was herded to the front car and she climbed into the back seat gratefully, wiping the tears from her cheeks. Her back was on fire from holding herself so stiffly upright, when all she wanted to do was curl up in a ball around the ice in her chest until it either melted, or hardened enough so that she didn't care anymore.

None of them noticed the soft sounds of padded footfalls following them to the cars within the shadows of the tree line.

23

Aiden watched Grace walk away until she was out of sight.

She didn't look back. Not once.

Good. That's good. At least that's what he told himself.

He hadn't meant to shriek at her like that. The look on her face...he felt like a total bastard.

With his next breath, he stubbornly pushed aside the feelings of remorse. He'd needed her to go away: Far, far away from these things.

He was hurt. Yes.

He was disappointed in her. Yes.

She had lied and completely and utterly betrayed him. Yes.

Yet the thought of her being at the mercy of these evil things around him turned his bowels to water.

His mouth twisted up into a tight smile. He was being a fool. A fool for a wisp of a girl who had only used him as a means to an end. She didn't care what happened to him. And there was absolutely no reason he should think otherwise. Not after what she'd so blatantly done.

A ghastly thought suddenly occurred to him.

Was that what the last few hours had been about? Distracting him with her feminine wiles so he wouldn't figure out her plan? Had that been her strategy all along?

Yet she'd seemed as completely panicked as he when she'd realized they were busting through the wall.

A hard yank on his hair brought his mind back to his own rather sketchy predicament.

"Mmm, mmm, mmmm," Steven murmured behind him as he watched Grace rush away with the Suits. "Check out that juicy ass. I'm going to enjoy seeing all that pale skin turn red and raw from my palm. Right before I fuck her until she screams. Or maybe while she screams."

Anger, hard and hot, rose up in Aiden at Steven's words. He gritted his teeth against it, biding his time.

There was no bloody way he would let this thing get anywhere near her.

"You won't be able to keep me away from that little piece. You can't protect her," He-Who-Used-To-Be-Steven gloated in his ear. "And she has no powers that are strong enough to be used against us. Oh, yes," he said when Aiden stiffened at his words. "I know exactly who she is. As soon as I'm done with you, I'll be going after that sweet ass. And you won't be around to stop me. Just like you weren't around to stop the ones that killed your family."

Aiden breathed deeply, in and out. This thing was a demon. A demon in his friends' body. It was only fucking with him, playing on his insecurities. He needed to remember that and not rise to the bait.

For that's what it wanted.

Steven shoved Aiden's head forward and let go of his hair, coming around to stand in front of him. The other two tightened their grips on his arms. They were freakishly strong.

Without a word, Steven stared into his eyes for so long that Aiden finally arched a disdainful brow, "Don't be staring at *me* like that," he gritted out. "I'm sorry to say I don't swing that way, and your ogling is making me rather uncomfortable, to be completely honest."

Steven's nostrils flared as he breathed in through his nose and exhaled heavily, his face the picture of waning patience. "I'll ask you again, what game are you playing, Waano?"

"And I will tell you again, *Steven*, that I have no bloody idea who this Waano character is..."

Steven's fist came up faster than even Aiden could track, connecting hard with a bone-shattering uppercut. If he'd been human, his jaw would've been pulverized.

"See, the thing is, I *know* you're in there, Waano. I can feel you. Although..." He cocked his head to the side and smirked as Aiden spit out a mouthful of blood and glared at him. "Hold on. Don't tell me you're hiding behind this vampire?" He made a sound somewhere between a snort and a laugh.

"I would shut up now if I were you," Aiden suggested. "And clear off, while you still can."

"Don't tell me that the big, bad demon feared by all is really nothing but a fucking spineless coward?" Steven continued as if he hadn't spoken. "A recluse who's afraid to leave your safe, little world. Afraid your inferiors will rise up against you and you won't be able to do a fucking thing about it."

He spit on the ground between them in disgust. "I always knew you were nothing but a fucking pussy."

Aiden felt a nauseous stirring inside of him, and fought to tamp down the spike of fear that accompanied it before it showed on his face.

Leaning towards Steven as far as he could without pulling his shoulders from their sockets, he glanced from side to side and whispered confidentially, "I wouldn't call him that if I were you. I don't think he likes it."

Steven leaned in also, his hot breath heating Aiden's face as he spit out, "I don't fucking care. *Pussy*."

Aiden wrinkled his nose and pulled back. "I wasn't yanking your chain earlier, mate. A little mouthwash, at the very least..."

Pain exploded in his cheek and his head whipped to the side as Steven backhanded him. The strength in that casual strike was staggering, even for a vampire.

Of course, he wasn't just a vampire anymore, was he?

Much as he didn't want to admit it, Aiden knew what was going to have to happen if he had any hope of gaining the upper hand on these twats.

Working his jaw from side to side, Aiden frowned. "I apologize if the truth hurts, but it's not like I didn't make the suggestion to you before."

Another crushing uppercut nearly separated his head from his neck.

A low growl began from somewhere within the innermost depths of his being, part him and part something else. It rose up until it vibrated deep in his throat. Raising his head, he gave Steven a bloody smile as he felt a roiling heat swell up inside of him.

"Well, now you've gone and done it."

His head dropped down onto his chest and his body sagged between the guards.

Steven chuckled, glancing around at the group. "Come on. We'll take him back alive to show 'our mistress'." He made air quotes. "Leeha likes this vampire. Wait until I tell her he's still residing in his body with her pussy ass demon lord." He nodded, almost to himself. "We can hold him over the stupid bitch's head; use him as collateral when we need something from her." Gripping Aiden's hair, he lifted his head. "Hear that, Waano? You're nothing but a pawn in our game now."

Dark shadows swirled in the grey eyes. "Take your filthy fucking hands off of me, Mammot."

Instead of complying, Steven moved his face in closer. "Ah, so you *are* in there. I was beginning to worry that you really *had* turned into a complete pussy. And it's 'Steven', you fucker."

Aiden could feel the demon's anger rising fully within him, and he didn't fight it. He was quite convinced now. Letting him loose was the only way for him to get his body out of here in one piece. These demon hybrids were freakily strong, even more so than Dante, the oldest vampire Aiden knew.

Once the demon took him over completely, he would just have to trust that his mates would find him and get it out again somehow. Then maybe they could help the others, now that he knew from experience that they were still there inside of their bodies.

Somewhere.

The foulness of the entity that possessed him rose up then, drifting around like smoke inside of his body. It oozed through his cells, infesting his muscles and polluting his bloodstream until he felt vile and filthy throughout. Bile filled his throat, and he fought the urge to vomit.

Hello, Aiden.

The voice in his head was rusty with disuse. It's English heavily accented.

Waano, I presume?

His physical form was feeling a bit crowded. It was the strangest feeling. He was still aware of himself and everything that was going on, but the demon, Waano, was there also. Sharing what little space there was.

He felt transcendental within his own body for the first time, and idly wondered if this was how it was with the others.

Were they inside their bodies, aware of everything that was happening? Screaming for help, knowing no one could hear them?

He started in surprise as a menacing smile lifted the corners of his own mouth, and his head tilted to the side of its own accord, stretching his neck. His fangs shot down and he felt his muscles harden, tensing for the fight.

Aiden wasn't controlling his body anymore, yet he was aware of everything that was happening. It was rather disconcerting.

No. It was utterly frightening.

Steven's groupies were still holding out his arms to either side. Not bothering to fight their hold, Waano dropped his head back and closed his eyes.

Short bolts of lightening flashed around him as the static electricity in the air collided together. It massed together, swirling in the air, gaining strength, crackling and sparking.

As the power of it wrapped around him, he roared aloud. His body convulsed once as it broke through his skin and shot through him: The voltage feeding him, empowering him, juicing him up.

At the same time, the demon within him completely unfurled itself, like a sail billowing open in a strong wind. It completely filled his physical body, infusing every cell, until he became...more: More than a supernatural being, more than a vampire, more than any organic entity in this realm.

Aiden felt all of that energy coil into a tight ball within his core, and then without warning, Waano let it loose in one hard shot. Any demon within ten feet of him went flying violently through the air as if a dynamite blast had just gone off, landing hard no less than thirty feet away.

Free of their hold, Waano turned him to face the others behind him. They immediately packed together, standing against him as one, their expressions determined and rebellious. They were not going to back down.

Aiden immediately noticed that there appeared to be power in numbers. The more of them there were, the stronger their connection. They seemed to feed off of each other, sharing their energies. He could feel the vibration of their combined strengths cross the distance between them.

But Waano only chuckled.

"You think to intimidate me with your meager show of force?" he sneered, his words sharp with displeasure. He narrowed his eyes, and Aiden could feel Waano's feelings of disgust for these others. "Are you forgetting who it is that you are dealing with?"

The demons stood where they were, waiting.

For what, he didn't know.

Aiden heard Steven coming up behind them, the others who'd been thrown from the energy blast staggering to their feet to join him.

Waano took a step back and turned to the side so he could keep an eye on all of them. Through the shadows of the demon's eyes, Aiden could see he was tracking Steven as he came around to stand in front of him again, apart from the rest.

Waano crossed Aiden's arms in front of his chest, and spoke to Steven as if to an errant child. There was absolutely no fear within him that he could feel. "You wanted to challenge me? Well, here I am, Mammot. Here is your chance."

"My *name* is Steven, and I am not your lowly servant boy anymore. *I* am the boss here. *I* am the one with all of the power. The others," He swept his arm around to indicate the group standing off to the side. "They do as *I* say, as *I* order."

Aiden felt his eyebrow lift. Apparently, Waano was unimpressed.

Steven paced back and forth, suppressed anger rippling off of him in waves. He began to roll up the sleeves of the white, button down shirt he was wearing. "I've been waiting a long, long time to take you down a notch. You may be lord in our realm, but here? Here I am the king."

He drew up in front of Aiden and they stood eye to eye. Aiden could feel Waano's rising irritation, although he didn't show it.

"I challenge you, Waano. Winner takes all, including the other's soul."

Aiden's head was thrown back as Waano laughed loudly and arrogantly. "I knew you were resentful of your rightful place, but I never thought you were an idiot."

Steven bared his fangs and hissed, his chest bowing out in a show of intimidation.

Waano stepped up until they stood toe to toe. "You are not worth the effort," he spit out. With one hand on his chest, he drove Steven into his group of buddies effortlessly.

The force of the shove sent him sprawling into the middle of them, but he instantly untangled himself with a bellow of frustration. Launching himself forward, he came at Waano with clenched fists.

An eerie howl sounded in the distance, followed quickly by another, closer this time.

Steven stopped halfway across the distance separating them. Everyone froze to listen.

Another howl sounded less than a mile away.

What is that? Waano asked Aiden silently.

Aiden felt the dread rising within him: His own emotion this time. He knew those howls.

Sure enough, a large, rangy wolf burst from the trees and headed straight for the group at a steady lope.

They're on our side. They won't hurt you! Aiden told Waano, but there was no need.

As soon as the largest wolf ripped into the nearest creature, distracting the group, the demon pulled out.

Aiden cried out in agony as it retreated. He felt like his insides were being turned inside out as the entity detached itself from his physical form to settle somewhere deep within his soul. Once it was gone, he would've never known it had been there at all if it wasn't for the lingering need to scour himself inside and out with bleach to get rid of the persistent feeling of filth.

As the remaining three wolves joined in the fight, he fell to his hands and knees and vomited blood, feeling like a tree that had just been crushed into pulp.

His last thought before he passed out amidst the carnage was to wonder if Grace had made it out all right.

24

"Whit are we? Yer rescue gang? Seems to me we do nothing but bail out yer silly vampire arses."

Duncan's teasing voice came to Aiden as if through a fog. Lying completely still, he took stock of his body as the werewolves, once again in human form, bantered playfully with each other around him.

He felt like a freight train had punched its way through him. Which, he supposed, it had. And it went by the name of Waano.

"Ye know, if it was nae for us, they'd be an extinct race by now," Marc commented.

"What would ya ken aboot it? Ye've been holed up with Leeha 'n her lot for weeks," Duncan teased.

"Aye. No thanks tae Lucian," Marc bit out.

Lucian shot him a hostile glance. "Shut yer filthy hole!"

"Haud yer wheesht!" Cedric barked out. "He's comin' round." As the pack master of the group, and the largest wolf in the room, his voice rang with the alpha timbre of authority. With a few more looks and shoves, the others settled down.

Aiden opened his eyes to find four concerned male faces gazing down at him. "Hallo, mates," he managed to rasp. "Fancy meeting you here."

Cedric grinned, his startling ice blue eyes filled with such warmth for his friend, they were more blue than white. Reaching out, he clamped his hand down on Aiden's shoulder. "Good tae see ye, Aiden lad. Sorry we took so long tae get tae ye."

"I think you all just like to make an entrance," Aiden told him suspiciously. "Show up at the last possible moment and save the day."

Cedric laughed, and gave him a once over. "We didna think ya were gonna make it, but ye look good." He nodded in agreement with himself, looking around at the others for them to back him up.

"Oh, aye, ye dae," Marc agreed.

"Aye. Ye look downright bonnie," Duncan teased.

"Och, 'ave seen him look better."

They all turned to glare at Lucian.

He just shrugged. "Wha'? I'm only bein' honest."

"Yes, well, I feel positively horrible," Aiden responded as he attempted to sit up. Four pairs of hands reached out to help him, yanking him up from the couch he'd been napping on.

His stomach rolled and he threw his arms out to stop them from pulling him all the way to his feet.

"Give me a moment," he gasped as he bent over, swallowing down the bile rising in his throat.

"Aye. Ye look a wee bit green," Duncan wrinkled his nose and backed away, leaving the others to deal with any repercussions they may have brought on from moving him too soon.

Cedric tossed his long, dark ponytail back over his shoulder as he indicated for the others to give Aiden some space.

"I'll be all right," he reassured them. Just as soon as he scrubbed himself with a scouring pad and drank a gallon of strong whiskey. He felt disgusting, like he'd just rolled around in manure, and swallowed some while he was at it. And now it was roiling through his bloodstream. Maybe the alcohol would decontaminate things.

The wolves watched him from afar as he tried to keep from heaving.

"Is there a shower here?" he managed to choke out to Lucian, the closest one to him.

He nodded and pointed to a door down the hall. "Aye, over there."

One arm wrapped around his middle and the other held out to the side for balance, Aiden stumbled in that direction. He barely took any notice of the antique furniture as he passed.

When he reached the loo, he quickly shut the door and turned the water on as hot as it would go. Ripping off his clothes, he made it into the shower just as the first heaves hit him.

By the time he was finished he was on the floor of the shower stall, naked and exhausted. He felt like he'd vomited up his insides along with all the blood in his system, and was slightly surprised that he didn't see any of his organs trying to squeeze down the drain.

He heard the soft knock on the door, but didn't have the energy to answer it. The door cracked open anyway and he heard Cedric's deep brogue.

"I dinna mean tae disturb ye, just wanna make sure yer all right."

Aiden groaned pathetically in response.

The door opened wider, and he saw Cedric's dark head duck under the doorframe through the blurriness of the shower curtain. Or maybe it was just his vision that was blurry.

The wolf quietly closed and locked the door behind him. Squatting down onto his haunches, he pulled the curtain back just enough to peek in at Aiden's face.

Aiden rolled his bloodshot eyes towards him. "I can't get clean," he rasped. "I need to get clean."

With a nod, Cedric dropped the curtain closed again and rolled up his sleeves. Folding a towel, he placed it on the floor to catch the spray of water. Next, he grabbed the soap and a cloth, and knelt down outside the shower next to Aiden. Sitting back on his heels, he pulled the curtain aside and soaped up the wet cloth.

He paused with the cloth midway between them. "This dinnae mean we're datin'," he told Aiden in all seriousness.

Aiden grinned weakly. "No worries, mate. You're not my type."

Cedric frowned. "How come nae? I'm vera bonnie. Thick, dark locks...sparkling eyes...big muscles. I dinna know how ye cannae be attracted to me."

Aiden shrugged weakly. "It's my loss, mate."

Cedric smirked. "Aye. That it is." He aimed for his face with the cloth, but Aiden stopped him again with a hand on his arm.

"I realize this would be brilliant new material for the pups out there to ride me about for years to come, but I'd appreciate it if you didn't tell the others the details. I believe I'll be all right in a bit. I just need to get clean, and rest."

"Ye 'ave my word," his friend vowed.

"Thank you. I do have a reputation, you know."

"Aye," Cedric smirked. "I know."

Quickly and efficiently, the pack master scrubbed his friend clean, even washing his hair.

Although he knew the wolves were quite comfortable with seeing each other naked (they had to be as there were no clothes made stretchy enough to survive the change they went through), Aiden would've been highly embarrassed if he'd had the energy.

Fortunately, he didn't.

As he rinsed the soap out of the cloth, Cedric asked him if he needed anything else before he got him out.

"You wouldn't happen to have some strong whiskey?" Aiden asked.

Cedric grinned. "We may 'ave a wee bit o' somethin'." Opening the bathroom door, he bellowed for Lucian to bring a bottle to him, interrupting the continuous arguing between him and Marc. Bottle in hand, he slammed the door in his pack mate's face and turned back to Aiden. "Do ye want tae get out first?"

"That would probably be good, yes. I'm beginning to prune." Lurching to his feet, he steadied himself on the walls of the shower stall while Cedric turned off the water and wrapped a large, fluffy towel around his bare arse.

A huge arm wrapped around his waist as the alpha wolf supported him so he could step out. Sitting him on the closed lid of the loo, he handed him the bottle. "Drink up, lad. I'll go find ye some clothes."

Aiden tipped the bottle up to his mouth and took a few large swallows, rubbing the large scar on his flat stomach. The whiskey burned going down, but it felt rather good. He waited for it to settle, and then took another hefty swig. He didn't have to worry about getting sloshed. Unfortunately, liquor didn't affect vampires any more than a nice cup of tea.

The alcohol started working its way through his bloodstream, burning away the filth inside of him, and he began to feel slightly less contaminated.

Cedric knocked softly and came in with some clean clothes. "These are Marc's, but I think they'll fit ye."

"Thank you." Aiden took the clothes from him and laid them on his lap before taking another swig of the whiskey.

The immense wolf stuck his hands in his jean pockets and shifted his weight from one foot to the other. He cleared his throat a few times, opened his mouth once or twice, smoothed his hair back with one hand, turned to leave, and then turned back.

Aiden arched an eyebrow in question, although he was pretty sure he knew what his friend was going to ask.

Cedric cleared his throat again. "I dinna ken how tae ask..."

"I have a demon inside of me." Aiden tilted the bottle up again, swallowing down the remaining liquor. Wiping his mouth with the back of his arm, he handed the empty bottle back to the wolf, who reached out for it automatically. "I'll get you another bottle," he promised.

The master of the toughest pack of werewolves in North America paled as he stared at his friend. "Ye 'ave a..."

"Demon. Yes."

Cedric stared at him blankly for a minute, then shook his head in denial. "Dinna be daft. If ye had a demon inside ye, I would ken."

Aiden stood up on shaky legs and dropped his towel. There was really no sense in being modest now, was there? He started pulling on the borrowed clothes.

"Oh, it's there. Trust me on this one, mate. Although it took me a bit to figure it out myself, as he's only just recently come out to play."

"Wha's he been doin' the rest o' the time?"

Aiden paused with his hands on the button of his jeans and frowned. "I really don't know." With a shrug, he stuck his arm through the sleeve of the grey T-shirt and pulled it over his head.

"But, ye dinna 'ave grey skin 'n ye still 'ave all yer locks. Ye dinna look like those things we fought when we went for Luukas. How can ye 'ave a demon inside of ye?"

"Those ones are different," he told him as he sat back down, exhausted from the effort it took him to get himself dressed. "Those things that attacked Emma when you sent her off by herself to 'check for guards'?"

Cedric looked away guiltily.

"They're the failed result of Leeha's little experiment. She has a secret room deep in that mountain, and there's this ancient stone altar in the middle of it. Demons are tied to the altar somehow, put there by someone much more intelligent than she is, obviously. But somehow, she found a way to release them."

"Aye. But if their no' but rottin' idiots, I dinna think we 'ave much to worry aboot."

Aiden rubbed his eyes tiredly. "If only the rotting ones *were* all we had to worry about."

Cedric crossed his arms across his massive chest and glowered down at him. "Spit it out. Whit exactly are ye trying tae tell me, vampire?"

"Those grey ones, they're only used for guard duty and such. The real ones we need to worry about are the ones she's creating from Luukas' vampires. Apparently, her blood doesn't make vampires that are strong enough to handle it, so she has to use vampires created by a Master vamp." His eyes were grave as looked up at his friend. "She's possessing them with those demons. She's building an army."

"And how do you ken this?"

"Because she took me there, and she told me what she was doing, and then she did it to me. Only my demon has gone rogue. I woke up over here in a grain container with no recollection of what happened to me or how I got here."

Cedric's massive chest rose and fell with the deep breath he took. "Och. The bitch is beyond daft. How does she think she's aff tae control th' things?"

"That's the thing. She can't. She's losing control of them. Which is why she conjured out the bad boy inside of me I guess. From the reaction of the others I've run across here, I think he may have been the boss man in their own dimension. Their knickers get all in a twist whenever I'm around."

Cedric scrubbed his face with his hand. "So, the vamps we just chewed up an' left fir th' sun...they were possessed? No' just gone rogue?"

"Yes." Aiden smiled suddenly. "However the joke's on her, for this bloke," he slapped the center of his chest. "Doesn't seem to want anything to do with her, or her desire for world domination, or whatever it is she's after. He's only popped up a few times, and only partially. Tonight was the first time he took over my body completely. And he ran off again as soon as you blokes arrived."

Cedric nodded in understanding. "And he left you feelin' less than braw."

"He left me feeling absolutely disgusting," Aiden agreed. "Like my body was turned inside out, soaked in sewage, squeezed through a clothes wringer, and thrown over a rack. Would you give me a hand, mate?"

Lifting him to his feet, Cedric helped him to the other room and onto the couch.

"Oh, you didn't happen to find a little ball of prickly things in the hood of my coat, by chance?" Aiden asked.

"Th' boot brush? Aye. Duncan cried like a bairn, but he managed tae put it in that box." He pointed to the table. "It jumpt around 'n' huffed at us, bit seems tae hae settled down now. I gave it some water and some of the food in your bag."

"Thank you. I was worried that he hadn't survived Waano's ball of energy trick back there. Would you make sure nothing happens to him? He's important to someone, and I need to get him back to her." Grabbing both pillows, he put them both on one end for his head.

"Aye," Cedric assured him. "I'll do that." He glanced towards the window. "The sun is coming up. Get some rest. I'll close up the curtains and catch up th' pack. Then, we'll figure out what tae do." As he turned to walk away, he paused.

Catching Aiden's eye, he warned, "If th' thing comes out, we'll do what we 'ave tae tae protect ourselves."

Aiden returned his somber look. "I wouldn't expect you to do anything less."

With a solemn nod, Cedric ushered the others into the other room to get some food and rest themselves.

25

Grace got out of the car to follow the Chinese men into the same building she and Aiden had retrieved Mojo from, back when all of this started. As they got closer and closer to the heavy door, her fingers tightened around the wooden box she held in her hands.

What had she done? She'd just left Aiden there with those things. Abandoned him. What if they were hurting him? Or worse?

Then she thought: What if she was right? What if he wasn't Aiden at all, but the demon, and had been all along? What if he'd just been playing with her?

Grace thought back to the days she'd spent with him. No. There was no doubt in her mind when it was Aiden she was talking to, and when it was the demon. Even when he was angry, he didn't strike fear in her like the shadows that swirled in his eyes when that thing decided to come out.

She should have tried to do something, should have tried harder to get those things to let him come with her. She could've explained to him why she'd done what she'd done, after they were somewhere safe.

Her hands began to hurt from gripping the wood so hard. Duh! The box! How could she have been so stupid? Maybe she could've traded the box for Aiden! The head demon dude was certainly keeping his eyes on it. And the humans wouldn't have dared to do anything about it. Not surrounded by those things.

It just might have worked.

She held back a sob. Now she may never get that chance. It had all gone so horribly, horribly wrong. It wasn't supposed to have gone down that way. Aiden was supposed to be here with her.

And even worse than that, she'd lost her Mojo again.

No. There had to be something she could do. She slowed her steps, letting the men pass, and made herself think.

She glanced down at the box gripped in her hands: The one thing of value she had in her possession to barter with.

Would it be enough to get Aiden back? It had to be. Both the humans and the demons seemed to have major hard-ons for it. If she could get away, maybe she could still barter the box for her vampire.

She glanced around discreetly. No one was paying her mind. The idiots. They just expected her to meekly follow them, as women were supposed to do.

As they passed by the next alleyway, she veered away and ducked behind a large trash bin. Peeking around the side, she checked to make sure the coast was clear, and then climbed up and dropped down inside of it, quietly pulling the lid closed above her.

Ick. Disgusting.

Breathing as shallowly as she could, she waited.

Sure enough, one of them eventually noticed she was no longer there. Footsteps pounded past her putrid hiding place as they ran down the alley searching for her. She heard them come back and go out to the street, taking off in the opposite direction.

Guess they thought that no one in their right mind would ever hide in a trash bin full of rotting food from the restaurant next door. Luckily, she'd never been accused of being in her right mind.

Inch by inch, she lifted the lid and then scrambled out with the box. Keeping to the shadows, she ran.

Glowing eyes watched her from the shadows, and then followed her at a discreet distance.

Grace had barely gotten one knock in on her friend's apartment door before it was swung open and she was yanked inside, the door slamming closed behind her.

"Where the fuck have you been? And why do you smell like you just crawled out of a garbage disposal?"

Heather Knight was not one to mince her words. A few inches taller than Grace, with chestnut hair, cognac-colored eyes, and some seriously dangerous curves, she stuck out worse than Grace in this country. She was also her best and only friend.

A transplant like Grace, they'd met in college, and had gotten jobs at the same hospital after graduation. Heather was originally from Pennsylvania; having moved to China with her parents when she was twelve, when her mother's company transferred them there.

"I'm an idiot," she told her.

"Yeah. And?" Heather waited for her to elaborate.

Grace groaned aloud and headed into the living room, which was almost exactly like her own, even though it was in a different building. "Holy shit. You're never going to believe..."

"Hold it right there. I can't talk to you while you're stinking up my place." Holding her nose with one hand, she used the other to shoo Grace towards her bedroom. "Shower. Use soap. Or maybe Comet. Borrow whatever clothes you want."

Grace giggled at the nasally sound of her voice, but went off to do as she was ordered.

Twenty minutes later, she emerged. Her hair was wet, and the drawstring was barely holding up her borrowed sweat pants, but she had to admit, she felt better.

"What did you do with your old clothes?" Heather asked from the kitchen where she was sipping on the coffee she'd made.

"I threw them down the garbage shoot."

"Awesome." Handing Grace a cup of hot coffee, she patted the stool next to her. "Sit. Talk."

Gathering her thoughts, Grace took a sip of the bitter liquid and smiled. Heather sucked at making coffee. Everyone knew it but her.

Maybe she should get her one of those single cup machines? Even *she* couldn't mess that up.

"Grace!" Heather slapped her hand on the counter.

Startled from her musings on her friend's lack of culinary skills, she jumped, and her coffee sloshed all over the clean counter. "Now look what you made me do!"

Heather got up and tossed a dishtowel at her. "If you don't start talking, I'm gonna do a lot worse. Now, come on! I haven't seen or heard from you in days. AND, you didn't warn me beforehand that I would be neither seeing you nor hearing from you. Which tells me that I *should* have seen or heard from you, and I didn't. So, spill."

How much to tell her? Though she'd been her best friend for years, Grace had managed to keep her family secrets safe. Mostly through the art of distraction. If Heather ever started prying too much, Grace would just ask her something about whatever current gossip was making the rounds at work, and she'd be off on another subject. Usually forgetting all about what she'd been nagging her about.

However, she had the oddest feeling that ploy wasn't going to work this time.

"Well," She took a deep breath. "It all started when Mojo snuck out of his carry bag and into someone else's..."

Leaving out the words "witch", "vampire", and "demon", she gave her the complete low down of what had been going on for the last few days. When she finished her story, she discovered that she'd managed to do the impossible.

Heather was struck mute.

But not for long.

"Why did you have Mojo with you at a restaurant? I've told you that that was going to happen. You can't just leave him on the floor like that, he's a curious little dude."

Grace blinked dumbly. "Of everything I just told you, that's the part you choose to focus on? Telling me 'I told you so'?"

Heather shrugged and took a sip of coffee. "I did tell you so."

Grace busted out laughing.

"So how are we going to save your hot, British friend?" Heather asked innocently.

Taking her empty cup to the sink, Grace shook her head. "Oh no. You're not getting involved. These are dangerous Suits I'm dealing with." (Not to mention the one's who have Aiden are actually vampires possessed by demons.) "I'm not dragging you into it."

"Who's dragging? I'm volunteering!"

"No way, chickie. You're not coming."

Heather gave her a disbelieving look. "You can't tell me 'no', Gracie. You're not the boss of me. I'm coming with..."

A steady knock on the door had both of their heads pivoting in that direction.

Grace waved her hands frantically as Heather got up to open the door, but she just shushed her and mouthed, "I've got this."

Heart pounding, she half hid behind the counter as Heather opened the door. For the second time in so many hours, she actually saw her friend struck mute, and it wasn't hard to see why.

The guy at the door had to be the most perfect specimen of a male she'd ever seen, if you were into the outdoorsy type. Or even if you weren't actually.

Standing at least six foot seven and dressed casually in jeans and a tee shirt, he had long, brown hair shot throughout with golden highlights. It hung past his broad shoulders in soft waves that made a girl itch to bury her hands in it. Clear blue eyes sparkled underneath heavy, dark brows, and a close cut beard covered his strong jaw. His upper arms were nearly the size of her thighs, and his heavy jeans did nothing to hide the defined muscles of his legs. He practically oozed masculinity and confidence.

Her statuesque friend barely came up to his shoulder.

"Excuse me for interrupting." His voice was deep, as one would expect from a man his size, but his words were intelligent and cultured.

Definitely not what one would expect from a mountain man.

Grace came around the counter as Heather finally realized her mouth was hanging open and snapped it closed.

"My name is Brock," he continued. "Brock Hume. I don't mean either of you any harm. I'm, uh, actually here to offer you my help."

Heather smiled like the cat that had just stolen all the cream. Stepping back to allow him entrance, she swung the door open wide in invitation. "Please, come in," she purred. "Please," she repeated when he didn't move fast enough to suit her.

Running up to block him, Grace muttered a quick "excuse me" and slammed the door in his face.

"What are you doing?" she whispered.

"What are *you* doing?" Heather asked in disbelief. "Did you *see* him?" Fanning her face with her hands, she mouthed, "Oh. My. God."

"Seriously?" She lowered her voice again. "He could be a serial killer, or a kidnapper, or both. He could be working for the Suits!"

"I'm not working for the Suits," he called through the closed door. "Or anyone else for that matter. I just thought you ladies could use a hand, is all."

"*Ladies*," Heather emphasized, before pushing Grace out of the way and opening the door again.

"I'm so sorry. Please, come in," she told him again.

Running his eyes up and down her voluptuous form, perfectly displayed in her yoga pants and tank top, he barely glanced at Grace before ducking his head and coming inside.

Heather stuck out her hand. "I'm Heather Knight."

His large hand engulfed hers as he raised it to his lips to press a firm kiss on the back.

"Heather," he acknowledged.

Grace thought her friend was going to get an old fashioned case of the vapors when his deep voice rumbled out her name.

Clearing her throat loudly, she managed to pull his attention away from Heather's cleavage long enough to introduce herself. "I'm Grace."

With a slight shake of his head, he tore his eyes from Heather and pierced her with honest blue eyes. "Nice to meet you, Grace."

"Can I get you anything to drink? Some coffee?" Heather offered.

Grace tried to catch his eye to warn him, but he was too mesmerized by her friend to notice.

"Coffee would be great. Thank you."

His head tilted to the side and his eyes wandered down to watch Heather's plump behind strut over to the kitchen to get him a cup.

Really, dude?

As Heather disappeared around the counter, blocking off his view, he bit his lip and caught Grace watching him.

She lifted her eyebrows, and he had the good grace to look sheepish.

"Your friend is stunning," he told her low enough so Heather didn't overhear.

"Yeah, I know. So, who the hell are you and what do you want? Besides my best friend, that is? And by the way," She snapped her fingers at him to make sure she had his attention. "You can't have her."

"Does she have a boyfriend? Oh man, is she married? Please tell me she's not married."

The 'she' in question sashayed back into the room and handed him a mug full of hot, steaming coffee.

"What are you guys whispering about?" She shot a questioning look at Grace before smiling at their guest.

"I was just asking him what the hell he was doing here," Grace announced loudly.

Instead of berating her for being rude, Heather cocked her head and looked at him curiously, waiting for him to answer her friend's question.

Thank the gods, I was starting to worry I'd completely lost her for a minute there.

He looked back and forth between the two women a bit nervously, and took a sip of his coffee.

Grace waited for the inevitable wince and painful swallow that always happened when people first tasted Heather's coffee, but he surprised her by nodding appreciatively.

"Mmmm. Finally! A good cup of coffee. Everything here is so damn weak."

Grace rolled her eyes as Heather beamed with pride.

Brock froze with his cup halfway to his mouth and stared at her friend's smiling face like he'd been buried in a mine for his entire life and was seeing the sunrise for the first time.

Grace couldn't take any more. "All right you two, cool it before I douse you both in ice water."

"Sorry, I just..." he mumbled.

"Whaat?" Heather said at the same time to Grace.

"How about we all sit down and you," she pointed a finger at Brock. "Can tell us why you're here."

"Of course," he agreed. "Sorry."

As they made their way over to the couch, Grace pushed her way to the middle and sat smack between the two of them. With the sexual tension between them this hot and heavy, they'd never get around to talking about anything if she didn't keep them separated.

Brock smiled at Grace with a look that said he knew exactly what she was trying to do, and it wasn't going to work. Then he shot Heather a lusty wink.

Angling himself so he could face both the girls, he settled back into the corner of the couch cushions and stretched out his long legs, crossing his ankles.

"Comfy?" Grace asked with a sardonic lift to her eyebrow.

Heather smacked her on the arm for her rudeness, but he just grinned and took a sip of his coffee. "Very. Thanks."

Crossing her legs and arms defensively, Grace asked, "So, why are you here, Brock?"

"I followed you here."

"You've been following me?" Grace asked their visitor. "Why?"

Brock's eyes skipped over to where Heather was sitting on the other side of Grace. "Would you mind getting me another cup of this fine coffee, sunshine?" He gave her another wink and a roguish grin.

"Sure, no problem." Heather smiled back, then took his cup and went over to the kitchen to get him another cup.

As soon as she was out of earshot, he leaned in closer to Grace, saying quickly and quietly, "I don't know how much she knows, so I wasn't sure if I should say anything in front of her. But I know you've been hanging out with that vampire, and I know you guys were hiding from the demons. I also overheard the deal you made with the humans, and I was there when you guys were forced out of your hole like moles and it all went to hell."

"How do you know all this?" she asked quietly.

He looked directly at her. "I have good hearing. I'm a wolf."

"A wolf?" she whispered.

"A werewolf."

Grace stiffened and jerked away from him as Heather came back and handed him his coffee.

"What did I miss?" she asked as she plopped back down on the couch next to Grace.

"Nothing," Grace said too quickly. Standing up, she grabbed Heather's hand. "Excuse us a moment," she said to Brock.

Dragging her best friend into the bedroom, she closed the door behind them and leaned back against it. "You need to stay away from that guy."

"What? Why?"

"Just trust me on this one."

Heather planted her hands on her generous hips. "This is the first good-looking guy that's paid any attention to me in years, and you're cock-blocking me? What the hell, Grace? I'm not exactly the type guys go for around here."

Grace grabbed both her friends' hands and held them in hers. "Heather, please. Just listen to me on this one. *Please.*"

Suspicion darkened her eyes to more of a russet color. "What aren't you telling me, Grace?"

She stared at her friend, wanting so badly to tell her, but after a lifetime of keeping secrets, it was hard to change her ways in the spur of the moment.

And, whether her friend realized it or not, she was doing her a great service by not dragging her into all of this craziness. It was better if she went on believing that the things that went bump in the night were nothing but the result of her watching too many cheesy horror movies.

Her chin dropped down to rest on her chest, and when she looked up again, her green eyes were full of remorse. "I wish I could tell you, I really do. But I can't. I'm so sorry. Please, Heather, just believe me when I say that this guy is dangerous."

Heather shook her head in denial. "I'm not getting that vibe from him, Gracie. I think you're overreacting."

"I'm not. I swear. Please, believe me. I would *never* cock-block you for no good reason. You know me better than that."

They stared at each other for long moments. Then Heather finally heaved a great sigh, squeezed her hands, and nodded.

"Okay. Okay. You're my best friend. I guess I'll have to trust you. For now."

Grace breathed a sigh of relief. "Thank you."

Releasing her hands, Heather took a step back and laughed derisively. "Don't be thanking me. You're the one who's going to have to put up with my moody ass because I'm not getting any."

"I thought that's why you went to kickboxing class?"

"It is. But beating on a bag can only do so much."

"I hear ya," she agreed, thinking of her own lack of a sex life up until now. "Ok. Let's get back out there. And Heather?"

"Yeah?"

"I swear I wouldn't ask this of you if I didn't honestly know the guy was bad news."

Heather gave her an affectionate smile. "I know. Don't worry. I'll behave."

"Thank you," she told her earnestly.

Brock was standing at the window when they came back out. Turning around, his eyes went directly to Heather, but his smile faded when she averted her eyes and took a seat across the room on the barstool at the kitchen counter.

His eyes skipped over to Grace, but she just returned his stare with a cold one of her own, daring him to say something. With a sigh of resignation and a last longing glance Heather's way, he went back over to the couch to join Grace.

With no further ado, she demanded, "Tell me how you can help me get Aiden away from those thugs." She hoped that her saying "thugs" rather than "demons" would indicate to him that he'd been correct. Heather knew nothing about the supernatural beings they were dealing with.

"Well, I don't know that Aiden is with them anymore," he admitted.

"What do you mean? Did he escape?"

"Not exactly. I think he may have gotten some help from some...acquaintances...of mine," he told her, with an emphasis on *acquaintances*.

Acquaintances? Ohhh. Did he mean other werewolves?

"Do you know this for sure?" she asked hopefully.

He shook his head. "No. I don't. But I was...with them, when I came across you and your friend and saw what was going on. I followed you, and they stayed there to help."

"Well, can't you just, like, call them or something, and ask?" Heather asked.

"Uh. No. I don't have a phone." He held up his hand before she could suggest that he use hers. "And I don't know any of their numbers off the top of my head."

"How many of your 'friends' were there with you when you found us?"

He returned his attention to Grace. "There were four others besides me."

"Would that have been enough to take them out?"

"I don't know."

"It doesn't sound like enough guys to me," Heather interjected, turning to Grace. "You said there were at least ten of those ugly guys, plus the Suits that you snuck away from. Right?"

Grace nodded.

"What if they went back to help their friends? Four guys wouldn't do much damage." Her face lit up as a thought suddenly occurred to her. "Unless they were packing some serious firepower! Did they have guns?" she asked Brock.

"Uh, no," he told her, smirking a bit when her face fell.

Grace flopped back onto the cushions, thinking furiously. This dude seemed to be on the up and up about everything supernatural that was happening around here. She wondered if he would know why they were all after the box.

Jumping up, she retrieved it from the bedroom where she'd left it and brought it out to Brock. "Do you happen to know anything about this?"

His eyes widened as he reached for it with a tentative hand. "Where did you get that?"

"I kind of accidentally stole it," she told him with no remorse whatsoever.

Opening the lid, he reached in and removed the red felt material to reveal the engraved picture of the dagoba underneath.

"No fucking way," he breathed. His eyes remained riveted to the box as he asked her, "Do you even realize what you have here?"

"Well, obviously not, or I wouldn't be asking you."

Snapping the lid shut, he grabbed Grace by the upper arm and stood up, pulling her along with him.

"Hey! Let go!" she yelled.

Heather hopped down off of her stool to help her friend, but stopped where she was when Brock told them both, "We need to get out of here. NOW. Both of you are coming with me. Get ready." Letting go of Grace's arm, he slapped his hands together. "Come on, ladies! Let's go! Let's GO!"

Jarred from their shock, Grace exchanged an anxious look with Heather, and then they both ran to get their shoes and coats. The alarm in his voice was all the encouragement they needed.

As soon as they had their stuff, he shooed them towards the fire escape.

Dammit. Looks like she may need to enlighten Heather after all, but she was determined to hold off on that as long as possible.

26

Josiah watched as Leeha paced the floor within their temporary home. Her white, ethereal gown billowed out behind her like a silken cloud with every stride of her long, shapely legs. Her deep red hair was piled high on her head in careless disarray, exposing the graceful curve of her neck. The skin revealed on the back of her neck flushed and damp from her fretfulness.

He longed to sink his fangs into that sweet skin there while he sank his dick into her tight cunt from behind, but knew he would not be welcomed right now. She had much on her mind, and so he bided his time.

Nonetheless, he couldn't stop his hungry eyes from following her near-nude form as she swept across the room. They darted back and forth from the back of her neck to the perfect curve of her ass, unable to decide which view was his favorite.

When she turned and headed his way again, he had to resist the urge to moan aloud. The white gown did nothing to hide the dusky pink of her areolas, or her nipples, hardened from scraping against the fabric. In contrast to the bodice, the skirt of the dress slithered in and out of her legs as she walked, only teasing him with brief glimpses of the soft red curls between her thighs.

The ache to have her naked and breathless beneath him was so strong that it was nearly painful, but this feeling was nothing new. He wanted her, always. Ever since she'd made him a vampire, and had made him hers. His desire for her body and her blood was a constant longing that never went away.

His eyes crawled back up to her neck and along her striking jaw to worship the flawlessness of her face, then narrowed at what he saw there. Her timeless features lined with worry and fatigue. Seeing his mistress like this infuriated him. Her blood red eyes, so unique and chilling in their wickedness, fluttered around the room without landing on anything in particular. She'd barely fed or slept for weeks.

All over that fucking vampire - Aiden.

He thought they'd be done with that douchebag Brit once he'd been used for a possession, but noooo. She was even more obsessed with him now than she had been before, if that was even possible.

Between her affection for Aiden and her fixation with being Luukas' queen, Josiah was beginning to wonder why she even bothered to keep him around. Other than to have someone to slake her lust on, he was nothing but her whipping boy.

He lifted his chin. He needed to be patient. The roles were going to change, and he just needed to chill until the time came.

She didn't realize what an asset he was to her right now, but someday she would. Someday she would pay more attention to him and understand all the things he did for her, see all the ways in which he protected her. Someday she would realize how much he meant to her.

Someday.

"I have to get him back, Josiah," she said.

His anger flashed instant and hot at her words. Gritting his teeth, he tried to mask his temper from her. He needn't have bothered. She was too preoccupied to notice.

She shot an agitated look his way as she continued to pace, her movements jerky and unstable, like her psyche.

"I have to," she repeated. "I must try to talk to him again."

"Why? He nearly killed you before," he reminded her, but she only smiled.

"Aiden would never harm me."

Losing the tentative grip he had on his emotions, Josiah jumped out of his seat and moved to stand directly in her path, halting her endless pacing. He'd been listening to this shit for weeks. He'd had enough.

"He's not Aiden anymore, dammit! He's that fucking demon! The demon that did NOT want to come here, but that you brought out anyway. The demon that explicitly told you not to bring him here. The demon that could put an end to our world as we know it with nothing more than a wave of his hand. What the HELL were you thinking?"

His blood ran cold the moment the words were out of his mouth.

Ah, fuck.

He really needed to learn to keep his goddamned mouth shut. But then again...

Cocking her head jerkily to the side like a bird, those disturbing eyes of hers swept over him like he was no more than a bug about to be squashed under the stiletto heel of her shoe.

Which was exactly what he was to her, he knew. For now.

"You would do well to remember your place, Josiah," she said, her voice deceptively quiet.

He bowed his head and dropped his eyes. "I didn't mean any disrespect. I just worry about you is all."

His heart pounded while he waited to see what she would do. It was always a gamble with her. You never knew how she was going to react. Which was just one of the things that made her so dangerous, and so exciting.

It turned him on.

Though he was a few inches taller and many pounds heavier than she, he was completely at her mercy, and he liked it.

For his mistress was no normal vampire.

His fangs shot down and his engorged dick strained against his pants, the zipper cutting painfully into his flesh as he waited to see what punishment she would dole out for his insolence.

Something soft touched his cheek, and he raised his head to find her gazing at him with a tender expression. "You always look out for me, my love. How can I be angry at you for that?"

The breath he hadn't realized he was holding rushed out of his lungs as his dick withered in disappointment. But he dared not voice such things. If she knew how much he enjoyed her punishments, she would stop doling them out, just to be spiteful.

Instead, he took her pale hand in both of his darker ones, and kissed the back of it reverently. Falling to his knees in front of her, he bunched her gown in his hands and stuck his face in the folds, breathing deep to draw in her scent. "Forgive me, mistress. I had no right to speak to you like that. I do worry for you though."

Her fingers slid through the tight curls on the top of his head, rubbing against his scalp with affection, at first.

A gasp of surprise escaped his throat when she suddenly tightened her fingers in the strands in an unyielding grip. He smiled at the sudden pain.

Ah, fuck yes.

Yanking his face out of her dress, she sneered down at him, "I forgive you, Josiah...this time...but speak to me like that again and I will have you whipped to within an inch of your immortal life."

"Yes, mistress," he breathed. His blood rushed to his groin at the threat, and he closed his eyes so she wouldn't see how desperately he desired her to do just that.

"Now get up," she snapped.

There was the evil bitch he knew and loved.

She resumed her erratic pacing as he took up his stance by the door again. It was all he could to resist the urge to palm himself to relieve the ache there, but he kept his hands at his sides. If she sensed his discomfort, she gave no sign.

She picked up the conversation where it had left off as if his little outburst had never occurred. "I need to speak to Waano again. He *will* see my side of things. He will help me, Josiah. You'll see. I just need to make him an offer he can't refuse."

"What would a demon want that he couldn't just take for himself?"

The red oceans of Leeha's eyes swirled and sparked, a self-satisfied smile curling up the corners of her lips. "Why, souls. Of course."

Josiah felt the hair stand up on the back of his neck.

"Souls?"

She nodded.

He wanted to ask her how the hell she thought she'd be able to harness a soul, and then be able to give it to a demon. But honestly, he was afraid to know. For as much as he scoffed at the idea, he had no doubt that she had discovered a way to do just that.

And it terrified the hell out of him.

"But how will you get him here?" Josiah asked. "If he doesn't want to come?"

She halted her pacing, her lips turning up into a devilish smile. "He'll have no choice. My blood brought Aiden's body back to life. It runs through his veins. He is a part of me now, and I of him." She looked up at him, her eyes bright. "I'll just call him, and tell him to come to me."

Josiah shook his head. "It won't work. It never worked with the others."

Slithering across the floor to him, she placed her palms flat against his chest. "It will work."

He stiffened at her touch, jealousy eating away at his insides. "How do you know?"

"Because unlike the others, I can feel him. The blood I gave him calls to me. Aiden is still in there, and he is still vampire. The demon has not taken over his body, and therefore will not resist the blood call. He will come."

This was not playing out the way Josiah had imagined. Not at all. But he was having a hard time remembering that with her soft, full breasts pushing against his chest.

Her hand wandered down to the bulge in his pants and squeezed, hard.

27

Brock grabbed Heather's hand in his much larger one and pulled her along behind him, forcing her to pick up her pace as the three of them ran down the alley outside her apartment.

Grace reached the end of it first and hesitated. She looked left, then right, and then back over her shoulder at Brock with a panicked expression.

"Go right," he ordered as he caught up to her. Placing his free hand on the small of her back, he urged her to go ahead of him. Once Grace took off, he let go of Heather and sent her out behind her friend. A quick glance behind him confirmed what he'd been afraid would happen as soon as he saw that box.

They were being followed by demons. A LOT of demons. And the fuckers were currently bottlenecking at the opposite end of the alley.

Their only hope was to outrun them until the sun came up. Luckily for them the bodies the demons possessed were still vampire bodies, and would burst into flames within minutes of being exposed to the sunlight.

If he could keep the girls alive until sunrise, they would have a good chance of getting away without being tracked.

Jogging behind the girls as they weaved in and out of the people on the street, he racked his brain for a plan that would put some distance between them and those things on their tails. Failing to protect the witch...yes, he knew she was a witch...and her clueless but incredibly sexy friend certainly wouldn't earn him any brownie points with the new wolf pack, or the vampire they'd obviously come here to help.

The same vampire he could smell all over Grace.

Earlier that night, Brock had been hot on the trail of a group of demons. He'd hunted them to the park with the silly ball sculpture, but had stayed hidden, curious as to what they were up to.

Staying just inside the tree line, he'd seen the entire thing go down: The demons chasing off the people at the park, then digging underneath the sculpture. He'd seen the humans in the fancy suits arriving, and Grace and the vamp appear from a secret hatch when they'd gotten rousted out of what had to be an underground hideaway. They'd had a fight, and then she'd left with the humans while the demons physically detained the vampire.

Then the other wolves had arrived. He'd scented them just a few seconds before they'd shown themselves, and knew right away that they were foreign to the city that had become his home. Staying to the trees, he'd watched as they'd quickly shifted and attacked the demons.

Unwilling to reveal himself to a strange pack in the middle of a fight, he'd decided to follow the female that had gotten into the car with the humans.

Shifting into his own wolf form, he'd kept to the shadows and loped along behind the cars, moving fast and keeping out of sight of the few humans who were still out and about.

The entire time he was chasing the cars, he'd been wondering what the hell he was thinking, getting involved with something that was obviously none of his business. He was risking a lot by doing this, and he had no pack to protect him if anything went wrong.

Brock was a lone wolf, exiled from his pack three years before. Something that was practically unheard of. He'd wandered aimlessly for a while until he came upon this city and its unusual population of possessed vampires. It had taken him a while to figure out what they were, but once he had, he began to do what he did best.

He started to hunt them.

That was what he'd been doing when he'd followed that group to the park and saw what was going down. Instinct alone had made him follow the witch.

He had no reason to help this girl, but something was telling him it was what he needed to do.

When they'd arrived downtown and she'd given the humans the slip, he was glad he'd listened. Her actions showed him beyond a doubt that she was just as much a victim as the vampire she'd left behind.

And now that he knew that she had possession of that box, and the clue inside of it, he really had no choice but to get her somewhere safe, and to keep that box out of the hands of the things that were following them. Hopefully not getting himself killed by demons or an unfamiliar wolf pack in the process.

On the other hand, if he'd known he was going to get the added bonus of meeting her exquisite friend, he wouldn't have thought twice about it.

Heather.

Just her name alone brought to mind the rolling pink and purple hills that were native to his Scottish homeland, and the sweet childhood kisses that were stolen there from the neighbor's daughter. In contrast to his innocent memories of his first love, the reality of Heather's voluptuous curves and honey-musk scent was all woman, and made him think dirty, dirty thoughts.

He wanted to sink his teeth into her soft flesh, and then kiss her wounds until she was whimpering like a bitch in heat underneath him. And that was just for starters.

But he'd never be able to do that or anything else if he didn't get her and Grace somewhere far, far away.

Up ahead at the intersection, he saw a taxi stop at the red light. Perfect timing.

Easily catching up to the girls and passing them, he ran to the driver's side and yanked open the door. "Sorry, man. But we need your car." While the driver protested loudly in Chinese, he reached in and unbuckled his seatbelt, then yanked him out of the car and tossed him out of the way. Scooting the seat back to make room for his long legs, he got in just as Grace and Heather arrived.

Following his lead, they eagerly got into the taxi.

With a quick glance in the rearview mirror, he accelerated through the light, barely avoiding a collision with another car coming up fast on his left.

Grinning widely, he asked, "I take it you ladies have no issues with me borrowing this car?"

Grace snapped her seatbelt on then pushed her long hair out of her face. "Nope. None at all."

"I'm good with this also," Heather chimed in from the backseat.

"Awesome," Brock told them. "Let's get the hell out of here."

They drove for about thirty minutes before anyone spoke.

"Thank you," Grace told Brock earnestly. "You saved us back there."

He reached over and rubbed her leg reassuringly. "Don't worry about it. I couldn't let such pretty ladies get hurt by those things."

"Who were those guys anyway?" Heather asked from the back.

Grace widened her eyes in warning, and he gave her a reassuring wink in return.

Brock told Heather simply, "They're after this box that Grace has."

"Why?" Grace asked, curious to know what he knew about it. "What's so important about this box?"

Turning on his turn signal, Brock headed north on the toll road. "That etching in the bottom of the box, it's of a dagoba."

"Yes, I know."

But what I need to know, Grace thought, *is why demons are so hot after a box with a picture in it?*

With a quick glance in the rearview mirror, Brock pressed his lips together. "I don't really know why they're after it. Maybe it's worth a lot of money or something."

He was lying, she could tell. But she decided to hold her tongue for now. She'd question him again when Heather wasn't around.

Heather leaned forward and rested her arms on the backs of their seats. "Well, something's got them all hot and bothered about it. Which tells me that we need to hang on to it, especially if we can use it to get Grace's hot, British friend back."

Brock's hands tightened on the steering wheel at Heather's choice of words. Actually, he looked like he wanted to rip it right out of the dashboard.

She scowled with disapproval. She didn't like him being so aware of her best friend, and as soon as she could get him alone, she was going to order him to keep it in his pants.

Heather was the most important person in the world to her. She was smart, and funny, and innocent of all the fucked-up-ness Grace had been experiencing recently. And she wanted to keep her that way.

"I think we should just get somewhere far, far away from here," Grace told her.

"What? But what about what's-his-face? Aiden? You're just gonna leave him with those mafia guys, or whatever the hell they are?"

She looked over at Brock for backup, but he just stared straight ahead at the road. So much for getting any help there.

She chewed her bottom lip, questioning her decision. But he'd told her that friends of his had helped Aiden. He was probably fine, slurping down a human somewhere.

"I'm sure he's fine," she said. "Brock said he saw some friends of his show up and help him, remember?"

"Well, don't you want to call him or something?"

"No."

"Grace..."

"I said no! Now please, Heather, just leave it alone."

With a huff, Heather plopped back in the seat. "Fine. Whatever."

"And put your seatbelt on," Brock ordered, then softened it a bit by adding, "Please."

The "click" of her belt seemed loud in the suddenly quiet car.

Brock glanced over at Grace. "I was thinking we should head to the Shenyang Taoxian International Airport. It's a few hours away, but they won't expect us to go there. They'll think we went to a closer one if we planned on leaving the city."

"I don't have any money. I don't even have my ID."

"Let me worry about that," he smiled. "Now where do you ladies want to go?"

Grace looked back at Heather, but she just shrugged, still in a snit about Grace snapping at her.

Turning back to the front, Grace watched the taillights of the car in front of them.

"Seattle," she finally said.

"Seattle?" Brock repeated. "Like in the state of Washington?"

"Yeah," Grace nodded, feeling more and more sure of her decision with every passing moment. "Aiden lives there. That's where he'll go back to. And he has friends there."

"Okay then. Seattle it is."

They arrived at the airport a few hours later. Grace didn't know how Brock managed it, but he bought their tickets and somehow got all three of them bypassed through security.

As they headed to their gate, Grace dropped back to walk alongside Heather. Linking her arm through her friend's, she told her sincerely, "I'm sorry, chickie."

"For what?"

"For snapping at you in the car, and for getting you involved in all of this. I never should have come to your apartment. I just didn't know where else to go."

Heather stopped in the middle of the aisle, eliciting dirty looks and a few rude comments from the people rushing around them trying to make their planes.

"Are you fucking kidding me?" She looked at Grace incredulously. "This is the most excitement I've had in years! And, I get an unscheduled vacation from work. And," she emphasized, "I get to look at *that*." She sighed aloud as she watched Brock walking off, not realizing that the girls had stopped. "Even if I can't touch him. Which I still think is totally unfair, Grace."

Grace squeezed her hand. "I'm only trying to protect you."

Heather squeezed back. "I know, and I love you for it. Even though you really don't have to."

Brock finally noticed they weren't behind him and stopped to wait for them.

Heather pulled Grace close and they both looked at him, standing head and shoulders above every other male in the airport. "Just look at that hunk of manliness, Grace."

"That man is trouble, Heather."

"Yeah, I know. I have to have him."

"We'll fight about this later."

"Deal." Heather started walking again.

Grace grinned and followed her. Their plane didn't leave until late this afternoon, so they had plenty of time.

28

Aiden came awake slowly, an unusual occurrence for a vampire that normally went from asleep to alert within the space of a heartbeat. For a few seconds, he had no idea where he was or why he was there, and then it all came flooding back to him. The possession, how disgusting he'd felt afterwards...Grace's betrayal.

Pushing himself up into a sitting position, he waited for his stomach to revolt, but it never did. Actually, he felt rather good.

Hearing the rumblings of deep voices coming from the other room, he got up and headed towards them. They stopped talking as he sauntered into the room, all four heads swiveling his way.

"Hallo, mates," he greeted the wolves. "You wouldn't happen to have any of that disgusting bagged blood, do you? I'm bloody starving."

Marc was the first to react. "Aye. Just so happens we dae! Duncan and I ran out while ye were sleeping. I'll get it for ye." Jumping up from the kitchen table where they were gathered with their coffees, he yanked open the door to the fridge and grabbed two bags. Tossing them across the table to Aiden, he sat back down.

"Thanks."

Cedric pulled out the empty chair next to him and patted the seat. "Come! Sit! How're ye feelin'?"

"Much better." He looked askance at the alpha of the pack, slightly embarrassed now that he wasn't heaving in the loo. "Um. Thank you for...you know...everything...last night."

Cedric lowered his brows in confusion at first, and then his face lit up with understanding. "Dinna mention it, my brother." Nodding at the blood bags lying on the table, he said, "Drink up. Ye look a bit pale. Even for a vampire."

Aiden grimaced, but dutifully picked up a bag and ripped off a corner with his teeth. This stuff was bloody horrible. He didn't know how Nik had lived on it for so long.

Speaking of which... He paused with the bag lifted halfway to his mouth and glared at each of the wolves in turn. "Any one of you ever mention this to Nikulas, I'll add your head to my collection. Understand? I'll never hear the end of it if he ever finds out I was drinking this stuff."

They all shook their heads adamantly.

"Would no' say a word."

"Dinna worry about that."

"I'm no' daft," Lucian pointed out.

"Well, that isna any fun."

This last from Duncan as he sat back in his chair and crossed his arms over his chest, his laughing, blue-green eyes downcast with disappointment.

"Not a bloody word, Duncan. I mean it."

"Aye. I heard ye the first time," he mumbled unconvincingly.

"Duncan," Cedric speared him with those eerie eyes of his, such a light blue they appeared white, and a low growl sounded deep in his throat.

Duncan held up his hands in surrender of his alpha's unspoken order. "I will nae say a word," he promised. "I swear."

Once he was convinced his order would be obeyed, Cedric turned to Aiden. "Whit are ye going tae do aboot that lassie of yers?"

Aiden slurped down the last of the second bag as he thought about that. Balling it up with the empty remains of the first one, he got up to toss them in the trash.

"How do you know about her?" he asked. "Actually, how did you even know where to find me?"

"The witches," Cedric said.

Aiden cocked an eyebrow. "The witches?"

"Emma and her sister. The lasses had some type 'o' dream. Saw you and yer lassie runnin' in that park."

"You don't say?" Aiden slam-dunked the wadded up bags into the trash.

"So?" Duncan asked. "Whit are ye going tae do about her?"

"I don't know," he finally admitted.

Lucian scoffed at him in disgust. "Yer just going tae let her get away wi' whit she did? Leavin' ye there like that? Why am I no' surprised?"

Aiden was behind him before anyone could track his movements, the knife he'd just swiped off the counter at Lucian's throat. "Are you trying to say something about vampires in general? Or just me in particular?"

"Oh, I was thinkin' ye in particular," Lucian ground out. His hands gripped the table as Aiden pressed the blade closer until it indented his skin.

"ENOUGH!" Cedric roared. "Aiden, kindly take yer blade from his throat. And Lucian," he gritted out. "Ye will haud yer wheesht, or I will reconsider letting Aiden at ye wi' that knife."

Aiden grinned as he dropped the knife into the sink.

One of these days, he was going to have to find out what the deal was with Lucian. He'd been a right angry bastard ever since last night. But right now, he had other things on his mind. Or rather, one other thing in particular - that disloyal female of his.

"I apologize for Lucian," Cedric told him. "He had nae right to speak tae ye like that."

But Aiden just shook his head. "No. Actually, Lucian is right. I need to go after her."

All four werewolves stood up so fast, a couple of their chairs fell over with a clatter.

"We'll go with ye," Cedric told him. "And dinna argue wit' me aboot it."

Aiden smiled at his friends. "I wouldn't think of it. Let me just grab Prickles out of his box and we can be on our way."

They arrived at the soccer ball sculpture a few minutes later, having mutually agreed that that was the best place to start looking. Hopefully, out of the five supernatural noses, one of them would be able to pick up her scent and follow it to wherever she was.

Strolling around casually amongst the humans, Duncan was the first one to find it. Heading off in the direction she'd gone, he whistled over his shoulder for the others to follow and they fell in behind him.

With Mojo snuggled up in his hood again and his rucksack over his shoulder, Aiden glanced around at the area where it all had gone down the night before, and his stomach clenched at the memory.

What a brilliant mess he now found himself in.

At least the demon, Waano, had been quiet ever since the wolves had appeared, and he could only hope he'd stay that way. At least until they found Grace and could get back to Seattle.

Falling in line behind the werewolves, he wondered (and not for the first time) why the hell he was going after her. After what she'd done, she deserved whatever situation she now found herself in.

If only he didn't feel this undeniable urge to find her and kiss her senseless.

After he severely scolded her for mucking everything up, of course.

They reached the road and stopped. Duncan walked in small circles searching for the scent, much like a bloodhound. After a few moments, he shook his head.

"It's gone. I cannae find it anymore."

"She must've gotten into a car." His hands on his narrow hips, Aiden looked around for a clue...anything...that would give them some idea of where she'd gone.

Lucian looked around at the others. "Do ye no' smell that?"

All of them, including Aiden, scented the air again.

"Who is that?" he asked. "Is that...?"

"A wolf," Cedric confirmed.

"Someone you blokes know?" Aiden asked.

Marc shook his head. "No."

"So there's a strange wolf following Grace?" Aiden looked at each of them in turn, seeing his own feelings of concern reflected on their faces.

Cedric cleared his throat.

Looking up at him, Aiden cocked an eyebrow impatiently. "Yes? Spit it out."

"I was only wonderin', kin you no' feel her? She is yer mate, isnae she? Ye should be able to track her."

Three more pairs of eyes turned to him in surprise.

"She's yer mate?" Marc asked. "Why didnae ye just say so?"

Aiden held his hands out in front of him, holding off any more questions. "I never said she was mine."

"Och, the lass is yers," Cedric told him confidently.

"Poppycock," Aiden insisted, for some reason unwilling to voice what he pretty much knew. "I have no evidence that she is anything but a lovely lady in distress, and I decided to lend her a hand while I was here."

"Ye can tell yerself that all ye like," Cedric said. "But in all the years I've known ye, ye've never once...no' once...ever bothered this much with a lass. Yer a love 'em and leave 'em kind o' lad. I bet ye ne'er sae much as spent a whole night wi' a lassie until now."

"What's your point?"

"Ye 'ave her boot brush in yer hood," Lucian stated, as if that was the only evidence he needed.

Aiden scratched his head. He opened his mouth to protest, but what was the use? "I've never fed from her, so no, I can't feel her."

Duncan smacked him on the shoulder, upsetting Mojo. Aiden heard his little huffs and smiled as he wiggled around a bit before settling back down.

"Dinna worry, my friend," he told him. "We'll find yer lassie."

A thought suddenly occurred to Aiden, and his head snapped up. "I think I know where she went."

"Where?" Cedric asked.

Aiden nodded, feeling daft for not thinking of it before. "She was with those Suits. The same humans she was following when I met her."

"Aye?" Marc asked. "And?"

"And they probably went back to the same empty building we broke into to get Mojo back after they stole him. That must be where she is." Without waiting for the others, he took off in that direction.

Duncan looked over at Marc. "Why in the world would anybody want tae steal the boot brush? He's no' very friendly."

But Marc just shrugged and pulled him along behind the others.

29

Aiden came back from the ticket counter at the airport and rejoined his group. The human woman who had "helped" him was quite the crumpet, and she'd smelled wonderful, though nowhere near as good as his Grace.

He'd turned on the natural charm that came so easy for him, and managed to get absolutely no information whatsoever from her. With a bit of a bruised ego, he'd resorted to mind manipulation without a speck of guilt.

No one who fit Grace's description had bought a ticket today that the woman had seen, and her name wasn't anywhere in the system as a passenger.

Aiden didn't know what else to do or where else to look.

Before coming to the airport, they'd gone back to the abandoned building where he'd first met her. Almost immediately, the wolves had picked up Grace's scent again and followed it into a trash bin.

Aiden's heart had been in his throat as he'd thrown open the lid, terrified that he was about to find her cold, beaten body lying amongst the rubbish. He dug around a bit, just to be sure, but she wasn't in there. Thank the gods.

Slamming the lid closed, he'd turned back to his friends in relief, but that relief was quickly followed by frustration.

She'd obviously given the humans the slip. Why? And more importantly, where the bloody hell had she gone?

Surprisingly, or maybe not, they'd found it was actually rather easy to track her from there. All they had to do was follow the aromatic stench of rotten food.

They'd followed her to an apartment. An acquaintance of hers? Someone else she'd made a deal with? Aiden's mind had spun in circles, trying to stay a step ahead of her.

At the apartment, Marc picked up the scent of the strange wolf again.

Once more, panic flooded through Aiden. Ignoring the advice of the wolves that they should scope it out first, he busted into the apartment.

What he'd found there did not sit well with him at all.

The place had been completely turned inside out. Even the furniture had been shredded.

"Demons?" Cedric had asked.

"It appears so," Aiden agreed. "And I think I know just what they were looking for."

Again, there was no sign of Grace, or the box she'd taken with her.

Back outside, they'd circled the building, and found her scent again (clean this time) in the alley alongside the building. There was another female with her, and the strange wolf was there too.

Aiden had struggled to remain calm when they'd lost her scent again a few blocks away at the stoplight. The other trails disappeared also, which meant they all must've gotten into another vehicle, and he had no more ideas as to where they'd taken her.

His Grace was gone.

At an utter loss, they'd stood around like a bunch of tourists until Aiden happened to overhear a human male across the street ringing someone up on his phone just as a couple of policemen walked away. He couldn't understand much, as the bloke was speaking Chinese, but he did pick out a few words including "giant", "taxi", and "airport".

A giant stole his taxi and it was found at the airport?

Sounded about right. And in any case, it was the only clue he had at the moment, so he was willing to check it out.

Now here they were at the closest international airport. His hope was that Grace and the others had come here, although he didn't know how she would manage to get on a plane with no money and no ID.

Or did she actually have those things? All part of her evil plan?

Since they'd arrived, he'd used his vampire influence to read the minds of over ten people so far, too impatient to try to charm them, and no one remembered seeing his Grace.

Again, he didn't know what else to do, where else to look.

Why the bloody hell had he not fed from her when he'd had the chance? But he knew why. It was because he'd been afraid of finding out the truth. Of finding out that he was going to be a one female kind of vampire from now on.

What's so bloody wrong with that? he asked himself. Other than the fact that his fated mate to be was a lying, scheming minx?

"We could stay with ye here, help ye look for yer lassie," Cedric offered. "But my opinion, 'n' ye can take it or leave it, is for ye to get back home 'n' tell Nikulas whit's going on whit ye. Maybe his Emma 'n' her sister will know how tae get out th' demon."

"And what about Grace?" Aiden asked. "I can't leave here without her."

Cedric looked down at him and put a reassuring hand on his shoulder. "She seems tae be a fiesty lass, I'm willin' to bet she's on a plane 'erself, 'n' we missed her somehow."

Just then, Lucian walked briskly towards them.

"I found her," he announced to the group.

Aiden's heart resumed beating for the first time since they'd lost her trail. "Where?"

Lucian pointed back the way he had come, where a sign notified travelers as to the location of the restrooms. "Over there. She's 'ere...somewhere."

Aiden grabbed him by the face and planted a solid kiss right on his lips. "You've always been my favorite bloke, Lucian," he grinned happily at the grumpy werewolf, and kissed him again.

"Och, stop it, ye crazy creature." Lucian shoved him away, then turned and stalked away again.

"We still dinna know where she went," Cedric pointed out.

"But at least she's safe," Aiden finished. "Alright, then. Let's go home. Once I get to my computer, there's nowhere in the world she can hide. I *will* find her."

Bypassing security thanks to a subtle suggestion given to the security guards, Aiden and the wolves received more than a few interested looks from the female travelers especially, but he ignored them all. There was only one female he was eager to get his hands on, and when he did, he wasn't wasting any more time. She may be a lying, scheming minx, but she was *his* lying, scheming minx.

And at least he'd never be bored.

Duncan, on the other hand, was having a hard time keeping up with the group while flirting with every cute skirt that walked by.

Cedric rolled his eyes and finally told him, "Just catch up w' us at gate fourteen at nine-thirty, ye horny jimmy."

"Aye!" Duncan agreed, and pulled an about-face to catch up to one of the girls.

"You shouldn't encourage him like that," Aiden told Cedric with a grin.

But Cedric just shrugged. "He gets right grouchy if I dinna let him go once in a while, in case ye haven't noticed."

Aiden hadn't noticed any such thing. Duncan was, as always, a ray of bloody sunshine. No matter what was going on or what they were doing, he always had that rakish smile on his face and his eyes practically glittered with good cheer.

They arrived at their gate and found seats as far away from the windows as they could get.

Marc and Lucian sat to either side of Cedric and Aiden. They didn't speak, but would occasionally glare at each other around the heads of the others.

"Are ye going tae call Nikulas? Let him know yer comin'?" Marc asked Aiden.

He grinned at him. "What would be the fun in that?"

"So, yer just going tae surprise him?"

"Absolutely. I can't wait to see the look on his face."

"He's goin' tae be surprised all right." Lucian's tone was downright surly. "When he finds out it's no' only ye coming home to him."

"You mean Grace? Why would Nik have a problem with Grace?"

"No' Grace, ye eejit. Ye and yer demon."

Ah, yes. He'd nearly forgotten about that unfortunate bit. Nikulas, especially, was going to be gutted when he found out.

Maybe the witches would be able to help him? There had to be something they could do. Some hoax. Some spell...

A spell.

Pulling the rucksack between his legs, Aiden searched for that ancient piece of paper Grace had shown him. He found it at the bottom of the bag under Mojo's cat food.

He tossed a few pieces into his hood for Prickles, then carefully opened the paper, keeping it partially hidden from prying eyes within the bag.

He jabbed Cedric with an elbow. "Have you ever seen anything like this, mate?"

Cedric glanced over and surveyed the paper. His eyes were nearly completely white with excitement when he looked up. "Where did ye get that?"

"It belonged to Grace's family. Her parents made sure she knew where it was when they died. She showed it to me at the shelter."

"That has tae be ancient," Cedric's voice was filled with awe. He reached out a hand to touch it, but then pulled it back again. "I'm feart tae touch it."

"Can you read what it says?" Aiden asked hopefully.

"No. I cannae. But it looks like a spell o' some kind."

"Grace said the demon came out when she showed it to me the first time."

"No shite?" Cedric's eyes were wide under his heavy brows. "Well, whit did it say?"

"I don't know. Nothing of importance at any rate. At least nothing she told me."

Rubbing his chin, Cedric voiced what Aiden had been wondering. "Do ye think, if it appeared when she showed it to him, that maybe the spell can affect him some way? Maybe even send him back?"

"There's only one way to find out," Aiden said. "I happen to have two witches at my disposal. Three if I can find that flighty female of mine. We'll have the spell interpreted, and, well, have them do their witchy thing."

"What if it's no' the right spell?"

Aiden glanced over at his friend, then back at the spell. He listened for the demon inside of him to see if he had any ideas, but all was quiet. Hopefully he wouldn't choose to make an appearance stuck on an airplane halfway to Seattle.

Maybe he should've called Nik for that private jet.

"Well, mate," he finally said. "I don't really see that I have a lot of options here. I'll just have to 'put all of my chickens in one basket', as they say."

Cedric took a deep breath and patted Aiden on the knee. "Aye," he agreed solemnly.

The announcement that it was time to begin boarding came through the speakers just as Duncan came jogging up to the gate.

"I dae love traveling," he told the guys breathlessly. "The lasses cannae resist a man wi' an accent."

Aiden pointed at his own jaw just below the corner of his mouth. "You've got a bit of lipstick there...no, over a little...yes, right there."

Wiping at his mouth with his sleeve, Duncan grinned.

Aiden put the spell away and stood up, reaching back to check on Mojo. "Stay very still, Prickles, and I'll give you some more of that nasty cat food once we're on the plane. Ow! Stay still, I said." Scowling, he rubbed his hand on his jeans and tossed his rucksack over his shoulder.

"So, whose ready to go home and exorcise my demon?" he asked.

Lucian shot him a look, and then got in line to board the plane. The others followed, leaving Aiden standing by himself.

"You know, you guys need to lighten up a bit. See the bright side of things," he told them as he caught up.

"There is no' a bright side to your situation," Lucian insisted.

"Sure there is!" Aiden told him. "Imagine the look on Nik's face when I let the demon loose for the first time around him." He turned to Cedric. "You must promise that you will take a video so I can watch it later. Please. Please? Promise me," he pleaded.

Cedric waved him ahead of him in line. "Och. Alright. I promise, fer th' gods sake. Now get yer arse on the plane."

They handed their boarding passes to the attendant. "You're in seat 1A," she told Aiden with a fake smile.

"Really? First class? Smashing. Thank you, mate," he told Cedric over his shoulder.

"No need tae thank me," he said. "Ye try sitting in coach in that tin can when yer six foot seven. They dinnae have any legroom. I'm nae goin' tae fly all that way wit' my knees in my chest."

"Still, thank you." Puckering up his lips, Aiden reached up for a kiss, but Cedric face palmed him, literally, and shoved him towards the air bridge.

"Get on th' plane, ye loony Brit." His tone was harsh, but he smiled back when Aiden grinned at him.

30

Grace shuffled off of the plane in Seattle with Heather and Brock. It was ten o'clock at night here. She was stiff from sitting for so long, and worried about Aiden.

"I need to stop by the restroom," she told her traveling companions.

"I'll come with you," Heather said. "Meet you back here," she told Brock with a smile.

His face lit up as he smiled back. "I'll be waiting."

Grace had tried, and finally given up, attempting to keep those two from getting too wrapped up in each other during the long flight. She should've insisted on sitting in the middle, but the plane was so crowded that she'd gone to the window seat and quickly sat down so everyone else could board. Heather sat next to her, leaving Brock the aisle seat so he could stretch his long legs.

She tried to keep Heather engaged in conversation, but no matter what she'd talked about, they'd kept turning back to each other, like moths to a flame. And just like the stupid moth, they were going to get burned, she just knew it.

It just made her even more determined to protect her friend.

Letting Heather go into the restroom first, she watched until she was locked in a stall, then bee lined it back out to the waiting werewolf. Sticking a finger in his surprised face, she told him, "You stay the hell away from my friend. She deserves better than something like you."

Recovering quickly, he narrowed his eyes at her. "You know nothing about me, Grace. Other than the fact that I just saved both your asses."

"I'm warning you for the last time," she ground out. "Leave her alone." Turning on her heel, she stormed back into the restroom and into a stall before Heather noticed she wasn't in there.

By the time they came back out, talking and laughing, Brock was leaning casually against the wall. Following Grace's lead, he greeted them both as if nothing at all had happened.

Heather linked her arm back through his, and leaned her head on his large bicep as they headed towards the baggage claim area.

Grace heaved a sigh. This was going to be much more difficult than she'd first thought.

However, she decided to leave it alone for now. They were all exhausted, and she needed to find a phone so she could call Aiden's friend.

Reaching into her pants pocket, she pulled out the piece of paper she'd stuck in there, glad she'd had the foresight to grab it out of her other pants before she'd thrown them down the trash chute. On it was Nikulas' number, Aiden's friend that he'd called when she'd first met him. She'd written it down before her cell had died at the shelter, just in case.

She was looking around for a phone while Brock and Heather cuddled in a corner when a lovely girl with bright strawberry-blond hair walked right up to her. She was wearing yoga pants and a short-sleeved shirt.

Grace noticed that she had scars on her arms, and a nasty looking one just under her collarbone.

By her side was a girl with similar features, though darker-haired and curvier. She had the same large hazel eyes as the first girl.

"Hi," the blond girl said. "Wow. You're even prettier in person!"

Grace was at a loss. "I'm sorry?"

"Oh! Sorry. Um, you don't know us, but we're friends of Aiden's."

She narrowed her eyes at the two gorgeous women. Friends of Aiden's, huh? Why the hell would "friends" of his be waiting for her at the airport? Jealousy burned instant and white hot inside of her, only to fade away as quickly as it had come about at the girl's next words.

"I'm Emma Moss. I belong to Nikulas. He's Aiden's best friend. And this is my sister, Keira. She's Luukas' mate. Luukas is Nik's brother."

"Ohhh," Grace recognized the names immediately. Had Aiden gotten away? Maybe called them and told them she was coming? But how would he know? "Okay. Yeah, I've heard about you two. How did you know I was here?" she asked.

Keira grabbed her hand and pulled her away from listening ears, Emma following right behind them. "We saw you in a vision," she told her quietly. "Emma and I, we're witches, and I believe you are too." She gave her an apologetic look. "Not sure if you were aware of that or not, but we don't have time to tiptoe around the subject."

Grace laughed a little and shook her head. "No, it's ok. I know what I am."

Keira gave her a dazzling smile. "Great! That saves us lots of trouble."

"So, yeah," Emma continued. "The first time we had one of those weird visions, we saw you and Aiden running towards a giant soccer ball, and we could tell you were in trouble. We sent some friends of ours to help you guys. Did they get there in time?"

"Uh...the wolves? Yeah, they did."

"Great! So, we've been getting them sporadically ever since. The visions, that is." She indicated her sister and Grace with her hand. "We think maybe the three of us are connected somehow? The visions are always of you. Other people are only in them if they happen to be with you at the time. Like Aiden if he's with you, or whoever." She looked around. "But he's not with you now. Where is he?"

Grace looked down. How to tell them what she'd done? "Um, I don't know. We were...separated when we left the shelter."

Emma's face fell. "Dammit."

"Who are the others that are with you?" Keira asked.

Grace looked over to find Heather and Brock watching her with curiosity as she talked to the two girls. She waved them over.

"Emma, Keira, this is my best friend, Heather," she introduced the girls and they smiled hello to each other. "We met in school, and we work together," she told them, hoping the girls would get the hint that Heather was clueless about all of this this stuff. "She was sort of pulled into all of this without any say so. I went to her for help after Aiden and I got split up, and then Brock here showed up," she touched his arm as he nodded at the witches. "And thank the gods he did. He got us out of there in the nick of time, and onto a plane." She shrugged. "It's a long story."

Keira looked from Brock to Grace. "You do know he's a werewolf? Right?"

Maybe she should've made that hint a bit more obvious. Avoiding Heather's eyes, she mumbled, "Um, yeah. I knew that."

Heather laughed nervously. "You guys are messing with me, aren't you?" But as she looked from one straightforward expression to the other, her smile faded. She gazed up at Brock last, and he gave her a small apologetic smile and a little shrug, as if to say, "I would've told you, but it didn't really come up."

She backed away from him so fast she almost knocked Emma over.

Grace glanced back and forth between the two of them. Hmmm, this may work out the way she wanted after all. Heather wasn't very picky when it came to whom she dated, but it was looking like she drew the line at her potential lover being a supernatural creature, unlike herself.

Grace blushed as she remembered how Aiden's fangs had turned her on. She was always getting on Heather about her choice in men, but it appeared her friend actually had higher standards than she did.

"So, come on," Emma grabbed Heather's arm to steady her while Keira took Grace's. "The guys are waiting outside. I take it you don't have any luggage?" She laughed merrily at her own joke. Over her shoulder, she told Brock, "Don't worry. They know you're here, and what you are. You'll be safe with us."

"Thank you," he told her earnestly. "I appreciate that."

They walked out the automatic doors and up to a black as night SUV that was idling at the curb. A tall, lean, powerful-looking, gorgeous man with longish dirty-blonde hair was leaning against the side of it with his arms crossed over his muscular chest.

Grace looked around for camera crews. There was no way this guy hadn't just walked straight off of a Hollywood screen. Not with those movie-star good looks and the sizzling charisma she could feel from twenty feet away.

He pushed away from the car as they approached, his bright blue eyes going straight to Emma. They surveyed her from head to toe before his features relaxed and he turned to greet the rest of them with a roguish grin.

The driver's side door opened and another man got out. The complete opposite of his companion, this guy was all dark and brooding...and just as riveting to look at.

Keira let go of her arm and went to greet him. Obviously not caring who was watching, he wrapped her in his arms and kissed her reverently on the forehead, his eyes closing in relief as he breathed her in. When he looked up again, the stressful lines around his stormy grey eyes were gone.

Wow.

"Grace," Emma tapped her on the arm to get her attention. "This is Nikulas Kreek. Aiden is his best friend."

"Nice to meet you," Grace told him as she shook his hand. "I'm sorry to just show up like this, I didn't know where else to go."

"Don't worry about it." He grinned at her, all white teeth and sparkling blue eyes. "Any friend of Aiden's is a friend of mine. Besides," He ruffled the top of Emma's curls. "My Em here didn't really give me a choice."

Emma looked at Grace and said without shame, "It's true."

Remembering her friends, Grace introduced them. Heather still looked a bit shell-shocked, but otherwise seemed to be taking the revelation about Brock pretty well.

Keira walked over then with Luukas and they did the introductions all over again. Grace noticed that whereas Nikulas was quick to smile and easy to talk to, his brother only spoke when necessary and kept his emotions tightly reined in.

Unless he was interacting with Keira, then it was easy to see everything he felt for her in every touch or nuance of his voice. He came alive when he was with her.

Nik clapped his hands together, "Cool. If we're done with the how-do-you-do's, let's get the hell out of here. We can talk more once we get home."

"Brock, I'd like you to come to our place when we get there," Luukas told him. It wasn't really a request. "I need to know more about you before I'm completely comfortable having you here with us."

"Join the club," Grace mumbled.

Heather smacked her on the arm and rolled her eyes.

Great. She was still defending him. Apparently, she wasn't weirded out as much as Grace had hoped.

But Brock just nodded once. "Of course."

"All right, let's go," Emma said.

The ride to their apartment building in Seattle was silent except for Nik and Emma, who pointed out landmarks and told them some of the history of the city.

"Have you ever been here?" Emma asked Grace and Heather.

"I'm from here originally," Grace told her. "But I was young when we left. I don't really remember it."

"And I'm from Pennsylvania originally," Heather said.

Keira turned around in the passenger's seat. "No way! That's where Emma and I grew up."

Heather smiled at her. "Small world. I knew I recognized those accents."

They arrived at the apartments, and Luukas pulled into the underground garage. The guys helped them all out of the car and then Nik led them to the elevator and up to the top floor.

As they followed Luukas and Keira into their apartment, Keira pointed out the restrooms and the kitchen. "Help yourselves to anything you'd like."

"I'll pull out some stuff for sandwiches," Emma said. "That ok?"

Brock told her, "That would be awesome. Thank you."

And then the three of them stood awkwardly in the middle of the large apartment while she got the food ready.

After they'd eaten and washed up a bit, Luukas called Brock into his office to talk while Grace and Heather sank down onto the couch across from Nik and Emma. Keira took the last chair.

"Is there anything else I can get for you guys?" she asked her guests.

They both shook their heads and thanked her.

Nik scooted forward to the edge of his seat and rested his elbows on his knees. "So Grace, why don't you fill us in on what's going on?"

"Don't you want to wait for Luukas?" she asked.

"Nah. I can tell him everything when he's done interrogating the wolf." He grinned widely as he said this. "I almost feel bad for the guy."

Heather raised her hand. "Yeah, can we get back to that part? About the guy I had every intention of putting out for being a werewolf? Seriously?"

Grace turned to her friend. "Do you want the quick version or the long one?"

"Quick is fine for now, since Nik is waiting for your story, and you can enlighten me more later."

"Okay." Grace took a deep breath. "So, I'm a witch, and so are Emma and Keira. Brock is a werewolf. Nikulas and Luukas are vampires, and so is Aiden. Aiden is also possessed by a demon."

"Wait, *what?*" Nikulas asked.

Emma gasped beside him, while Keira closed her eyes and dropped her head.

"Good God," Heather said. She sank back against her chair cushion, visibly deflated.

"Yeah," Grace responded, knowing exactly how she felt.

Nik stood up and flashed over to the window. When he came back, his voice was tightly controlled. "Aiden isn't Aiden anymore?"

"Oh, no, he is," Grace was quick to reassure him, patting Heather on the back. Her friend's eyes were about to pop out of her head at Nik's burst of speed. "But he's sharing his body with a demon named Waano. He doesn't come out very much though."

Nik sank back down onto the couch, and took Emma's hand.

Keira leaned forward. "You mean to tell me that Aiden survived one of Leeha's possessions, while still aware and fully functional in his body?"

Grace nodded, "Yes. It seems so."

"I think you'd better tell us the whole story," Nik suggested.

And so she did. She told them everything Aiden had told her, and everything that had happened since she'd met him.

When she was done, you could've heard a pin drop.

Finally, Nik raised his head. His eyes were glowing and his features were sharp. "You just left him over there?" he gritted out.

Grace's heart pounded in sudden fear. "I told you, I didn't mean to! I was trying to get us both out of there alive, but those things showed up..."

His lips pulled back, revealing his fangs, and Grace heard Heather's sharp intake of breath.

Emma laid a hand over his, and murmured something to him under her breath.

"She did the best she could," Keira told him. "Sometimes that's all you can do." Her eyes were sad and filled with compassion when she looked back at Grace. "So, we don't know where Aiden is now?"

Grace shook her head. "No. But Brock said that 'friends' of his had shown up to help him after I left. I assumed he meant other werewolves?"

"That would be the guys Nik sent to find Aiden," Emma said. "The ones I asked you about earlier."

"But where are they now?" Nik asked the room in general. "I haven't heard anything since they arrived in China."

"I wish I knew," Grace told him.

Luukas and Brock came out of the office. "When the others get back, we won't be able to interfere, but I'll put in a good word for you."

"Thanks," Brock told him. "I appreciate that."

Luukas gave him a nod.

Nik and Emma exchanged a glance, and then Emma said, "It's nearly 2am. Why don't the three of you come down to our place with us. We have plenty of room. You can get cleaned up and get some rest." She looked over the girls. "Between me and my sister, we can find some clean clothes for you guys."

"Thanks." Grace and Heather said in unison.

Nik stood up and looked at his brother. Luukas nodded once, and Nik did the same.

He eyed Brock's six foot seven inch frame. "I may have something large enough for you left at my place from Cedric. Emma can get it for you."

"That would be great," Brock told him.

Leaving Nikulas to fill Luukas in on what Grace had told them, Emma took the three of them down to their place.

"You guys can stay in Aiden's room," Emma told Grace and Heather as they entered the apartment. "Brock, we have a pullout in the office you can crash on."

"Sounds perfect," he told her. "Thank you."

"Help yourselves to anything you want. There are clean towels in the closet there if you'd like to shower, and lots of food in the fridge. I'm going to go back upstairs. Keira's been helping me with my magic."

"Your magic?" Heather asked.

"Yup," she answered. "I had no idea I had any 'witchy powers' until just recently. But I'm learning. Oh, and Grace..."

Grace turned from the window to face her.

"If you're not too tired, maybe you can come up in a little while and we can compare tricks?"

"Sure," Grace grimaced. "But I'm warning you now, I don't have very many. My 'witchy powers' are pretty useless, honestly."

But Emma just smiled. "Well, we'll just have to see about that." With a wave, she left them to their own devices.

"I got first dibs on that shower, and I'm going to need every drop of the hot water," Heather announced, then headed to the bedroom she and Grace were staying in, her arms full of the clothes Keira had shoved at her as they were leaving her place.

The bedroom door slammed shut, leaving Grace and Brock alone.

He cleared his throat. "I'm just gonna go into the office and crash. I'll shower later, when the water has had time to heat up again."

"Brock, wait." Grace grabbed his arm as he walked by. "I know I already thanked you for getting us out of there, but I want you to know that I truly mean it. Everything else aside, I really do appreciate what you did." Feeling rather like an ungrateful child for how she'd been behaving towards him, she glanced up at him a bit sheepishly. "I still don't know what it was exactly that made you follow me, but I'm very glad you did." She shrugged one shoulder. "I owe you one."

Brock was silent as he looked down at the floor, but only for a moment. "You can always repay me by letting me kiss your friend," he teased.

Grace barked out a laugh. "Good try."

He suddenly got serious. "I would never hurt her, Grace."

The smile dropped from her face, and she narrowed her eyes.

He sighed heavily. "I know you don't know me. You don't know where I came from or what kind of male I am, but please believe me when I say that I am not a guy who would do anything to hurt a sweet girl like Heather. Not on purpose." That sexy grin of his came back full force. "And believe it or not, I'm glad that she has a friend like you. A friend that cares about her so much that she would threaten a *werewolf* if he so much as looked at her the wrong away."

Grace scowled up at him. She didn't want to like this guy, she really didn't. But he was making it kinda hard not to.

"Flattery will get you nowhere with me."

"I know. I respect that about you."

They were quiet a moment, and then he said, "So, what do you say? Just one little kiss. It doesn't even have to involve tongue..."

"Eww. No. Forget it."

He gave up all pretense of kidding around. "You know, I don't really need your permission. Heather is a grown woman, and I know you're her friend and you're just trying to watch out for her, and I respect that. But come on, Grace. You're being a bit hypocritical here, don't you think?"

Grace looked away. He was right. Who was she to tell her friend she couldn't hook up with a manly werewolf when she'd been getting all hot and heavy with a vampire that practically made her orgasm just by looking at him?

She studied him, trying to get past...whatever it was that was making her so against him being with her friend. But she couldn't. There was just something about him...something that made her wary. And it wasn't just that he was a werewolf. If that were the case, she'd have run far, far away from Aiden the moment she'd figured out that he was no longer completely human.

"No. I'm not being hypocritical. I'm not acting this way because of what you are. I'm acting this way because I don't trust you. I couldn't even tell you why. I just don't."

"Grace..."

"Stay away from my friend," she told him emphatically.

They were standing less than a foot apart, eyes locked in a silent battle of wills, when suddenly Brock disappeared.

One minute he was there, large and brawny in front of her, and the next he was just...gone.

Stunned, Grace blinked and looked around. Then a small noise to her left caught her attention. She turned to find Brock on the floor. An infuriated Aiden was straddling him, and he had his hands around his throat. One look told her he was in full "kill-the-wolf" mode.

"Aiden! Stop! Dude, what are you doing?"

His response to her question was to tighten his grip around Brock's throat. A spine tingling hiss followed. It made her hair stand up on end, and she wrapped her arms around herself and shivered.

Brock's face was bright red as he struggled to breathe, and his large hands were around Aiden's wrists, but he wasn't fighting back. Why wasn't he fighting back?

"Aiden!" Grace knelt on the floor directly in front of him, sending up a silent prayer to the gods that she'd get through to him without having all of that anger turned on her.

"Aiden," she said more calmly. "Please, let him go. He hasn't done anything wrong." When he didn't respond, she reached out and touched his face with tentative fingertips.

Without releasing his grip on the wolf's throat, he closed his eyes and turned his face into her palm. A few seconds later, she heard Brock wheeze in a breath as Aiden's grip loosened just enough for him to get some air.

"Aiden..."

Bright grey eyes, glowing with need and anger, flashed up to hers.

"You are MINE," he growled.

Grace dropped her hand from his face, taken aback.

"Um..." She wasn't quite sure how to respond to that declaration.

Leaning down until his face was barely an inch from Brock's, he pulled his lips back and bared his fangs. Another eerie hiss filled the room.

"She is MINE," he growled at the other male.

Brock's mouth moved as he tried to speak. After a few tries, he finally managed to rasp out, "Understood."

Grace looked from Aiden to Brock and back again. Finally, she reached out and tugged at Aiden's arm. "Aiden, please. He saved me. He saved me and you're hurting him."

Grey eyes locked onto hers and he cocked his head to the side.

"Yes, he saved me." She answered his unspoken question. "I probably wouldn't be here right now if it wasn't for him. He even got me safely to Seattle. Let him go."

She breathed a sigh of relief as his features lost some of their feral sharpness and his glowing eyes dimmed a bit. He was listening. Thank the gods.

Grace watched anxiously as he released his grip from Brock's throat and stood up. She bent down over the werewolf, "Are you okay?"

Keeping a wary eye on Aiden, he nodded.

She helped Brock to his feet, or at least she tried to. He was a big guy, and she wasn't sure how much help she actually was. His neck was already bruising from the death grip Aiden had on him.

Brock immediately pulled away from her when Aiden flashed his fangs at him and took a seat at the kitchen counter.

She spun around to Aiden. "What the hell is wrong with you?"

He scowled down at her. "What's wrong with me? There was a bloody werewolf threatening you!"

"He wasn't threatening me! Well, he kind of was, but not the way you think."

Aiden suddenly stilled. Leaning closer, he took a deep breath, and his lip turned up in a snarl. "I can smell him all over you."

"What?"

"Hey, man," Brock started, putting his palms out in a gesture of peace. "Nothing is going on here, I swear."

Aiden's stare nailed him to the chair. "Sod off, dog," he gritted out.

Brock lowered his hands slowly to his lap.

"You know, love," Aiden told Grace. "If you'd wanted me to clear off, you could've just said so."

"Aiden, I didn't..."

But she never got the chance to finish her sentence. He was gone just as suddenly as he'd shown up.

31

Leeha paused mid-stroke, her hand tightening on her hairbrush.

He's back.

Her Aiden was back, and he was close by.

Dropping the brush onto her vanity, she stared at her reflection. Her pale skin was flushed, her blood-red eyes roiling with emotion.

He was back. She threw her head back and ran her hands down her neck and her collarbone, over the mounds of her breasts and her flat stomach, until they came together again between her thighs.

Gods, she could *feel* him. Everywhere.

A maniacal smile lit her features. She knew he wouldn't have left her forever. Not her Aiden. Her Aiden was special. He cared about her. He would never leave her.

And now she could invite him to come to her.

She could feel his blood calling to hers like a siren's song. She could feel his mood, his emotions, and his angst.

A frown marred her smooth features. Why was he upset?

Unused to the privileges attained by becoming a creator, she forced herself to still and concentrate on the foreign emotions flowing through her, emotions that were not her own. Gradually, she learned to filter through them, separating the different feelings, picking out the bits and pieces.

She felt anger, yes. But she also felt sadness, frustration, protectiveness and...possessiveness. The type of consuming possessiveness one would only feel for a mate.

Her heart withered in her chest. No! It could not be!

Aiden would never succumb to that fate. He would always be available to her. Always searching but never finding one that would replace his lust for her. That was his part of the curse she'd had Keira place on all of Luukas' Hunters, and she'd even managed to weaken the Master vampire himself.

Luukas would be mad the rest of his unnatural life, unable to tell nightmares from reality.

Nikulas would kill any female he loved the moment he fed from her.

Shea would never be able to enjoy the touch of a male without excruciating pain.

Christian would spend his nights seeking carnal relief with female after female, enduring the never ending urge for sex, or suffer the agony of his decision.

Dante would always be in darkness, like the monster that he was.

And Aiden. Aiden would never be able to truly love another. Would never lust after another more than he did her. Though he may enjoy others, just as she did, he would always be hers in the end.

Rising from her stool, she wandered over to the window. Looking out over the pine-covered valley from her temporary mountain home, she tried to think of how these feelings he was having could be possible.

Her jaw suddenly clenched and her fingers tightened on the windowsill.

That *bitch*.

Keira had told her, but once Leeha left the cell that day, she became convinced the witch had only been trying to distract her. She should have seen it the moment Luukas had overcome his fears, to come back to the place where he'd been beaten and starved for seven years to save the one who had allowed it to take place.

And Nikulas, his brother, showing up with the witch's sister to save him. Leeha had known right away that he had mated with her...

Without killing her.

And now Aiden. Her Aiden. Having mate-like feelings for another female?

The witch had found a way to add a caveat to the curse. That was the only answer. She'd snuck something in there, unbeknownst to Leeha, something that would enable them to be...happy.

Turning away from the window, she went to call Josiah.

Aiden may have those feelings for another female, but he hadn't completed the mating ritual yet.

And if she had her way about it, he never would.

32

Bloody fucking werewolves. Leave them alone with your female for one second, and they're running off with them.

Aiden flung the door open and strode into Luukas' apartment. He could see Luukas and Nikulas through the glass walls of Luuk's office, deep in conversation.

"Lucy! I'm home!" he called.

Two heads swiveled his way.

"Aid?" Nikulas ran out to greet him, grinning ear to ear. "It's about fucking time you got here, Princess." Pulling Aiden into a giant bear hug, his voice was overcome with emotion. "It's good to see you, man."

"You too, you bloody Estonian bastard," Aiden choked out, hugging him back.

Their reunion was interrupted by a deep growl coming from the vicinity of the office doorway. Aiden let go of Nik to look around his shoulder.

His eyes went wide. "Bloody hell..."

"Whoa..." Nik said at the same time.

Luukas was standing just outside his office, breathing hard. His fists were clenched at his sides, his fangs were fully extended, and his burning gaze was zeroed in on Aiden.

Nikulas pushed Aiden behind him and held his hands up in a calming gesture.

"Luuk? Bro, it's ok. It's just Aiden. You know Aiden. You turned him yourself way back when, remember?"

Aiden peeked over his shoulder. Luukas' eyes seemed to blaze right through Nik and straight into him, and the message he saw there chilled him to the bone.

"That's not Aiden," Luukas snarled.

Aiden slowly stepped out from behind Nikulas.

"Aid, man..."

"It's all right, Nik," he whispered. He felt Mojo turning around in his hood, and held his breath until the little rodent settled down again.

Now was not the time for one of his hissy fits.

He contemplated the vampire who had saved his life by giving him a new one, shocked at the changes in him. This male before him had little similarity to the one who had found him that day in the muck of the battlefield.

Aiden tried to reach through his bond to Luukas to reassure him, but...funny...he couldn't seem to find it. Actually, he didn't feel the blood bond at all anymore.

Because of what Luukas had gone through? Or himself?

Maybe if he explained. "Luukas, mate, it *is* me. I swear it. I've just got a bit of a pest problem going on."

Luukas lowered his chin and his upper lip lifted into a snarl.

Nikulas grabbed Aiden's arm, stopping him from saying anymore and called, "Keira!"

The bedroom door opened and Keira and Emma came out.

"Aiden!" Emma exclaimed happily.

"Hey, poppet," he greeted her quietly without taking his eyes from Luukas.

"Keira," she said. "This is Aiden!"

Keira's answering smile was cut off when a loud hiss filled the room. Only then did she notice Luukas.

"Oh, shit," she breathed. "I've got him!" She went towards Luukas, calling over her shoulder. "I've got him. Get Aiden the hell out of here, Nik."

Nikulas reached for Emma's hand. "Come on, sweetheart. Come with us."

They started backing away as Keira lifted a hand and touched Luukas' cheek, murmuring to him soothingly. After a moment, his crazed eyes found her face, and he blinked.

Aiden wasted no time, but took advantage of his distraction to hightail it out of there, Nikulas and Emma close on his heels.

"Come on, let's go down to our place," Nik said.

"Already been there, mate. I'd prefer to go *anywhere* else."

"Um...ok." Nik and Emma exchanged looks. "The bar down the street?" he asked.

Aiden headed to the elevator. "Smashing idea."

While they waited for it to open, he ran his eyes up and down Emma. "Emma, love, you're still just as scrumptious as the first time I saw you."

She started to roll her eyes but stopped just in time, glancing up at him awkwardly. "Um. Thanks."

He chuckled to himself as a low growl came from Nikulas. The elevator door opened, and they all stepped inside. Nikulas pulled Emma behind him and stood between her and Aiden, keeping a close eye on his friend.

"Ah, Nikulas, mate. This will never stop being fun for me."

Emma giggled as Nik attempted to look like he did not just act like an overbearing, possessive male. "And you're still a pain in the ass Brit, but I'm very glad you're back."

Once they were settled at a table at the bar and had drinks all around, Aiden finally allowed himself to take a deep breath. He eyed his glass of whiskey. "What I wouldn't give right now to have the ability to get bloody pissed." Picking up the glass, he downed it in one swallow and called for another.

Swallowing that one down as quickly as the first, he looked up to find Nik and Emma watching him warily.

He cocked an eyebrow, and they both looked away uncomfortably.

"I see you know about my demon," he stated blandly. "And obviously, so does Luukas." Reaching into his hood, he cursed as he pulled Mojo out and set him in the middle of the table.

Nikulas sat back in his seat and Emma giggled as the little rodent huffed and jumped around, threatening each one of them in turn.

"What the fuck is that thing?" Nikulas asked.

"It's a hedgehog," Emma told him, putting her hand down for him to investigate. "Haven't you ever seen a hedgehog?"

He looked up at Aiden. "Why the fuck is it in your hood?"

Aiden gave a long-suffering sigh and took a sip of his new drink. "I have no bloody idea."

Nikulas watched Mojo for a minute and then closed his eyes and shook his head. Opening them, he leaned forward again. "So, Grace filled us in on everything that's happened, including what Leeha told you."

"Did she tell you about the spell?"

Emma stopped tickling Mojo's nose. "What spell?"

Unzipping the rucksack, he pulled some food out for Prickles and tossed it on the table, and then handed Emma the parchment.

She took it from him gently, excitement shining from her eyes, but her smile turned to a frown when she looked it over. "Can you read this?" she asked Aiden.

"Nope," he told her. "I was hoping you could."

"Let me see," Nik reached for the paper. "Wow. This is some ancient sorcery happening on here. Where did you get it?"

"Grace's parents had it. They passed it on to her when they died."

"Does she know what the spell is?" Emma asked.

Aiden shook his head.

"Speaking of Grace..." Nik began.

"No," Aiden cut him off. "We're not having that discussion."

"I just find it pretty damn interesting that you ran straight to her when you got here, instead of coming to Luukas' first."

Aiden took another sip of his drink and lied through his teeth. "I figured you would be there, being that you live there and whatnot."

Emma pushed Mojo's scattered food back into a pile for him. "I think she has a thing for crazy Brits."

Aiden paused with his glass halfway to his mouth. "What makes you say that?" he asked a little too casually before taking a sip.

She looked over at Nikulas. "What were her exact words when you asked her to describe the guy she was with? Oh, yeah. Something along the lines of 'dude, the guy was so hot he nearly made my clothes spontaneously combust from ten feet away, so I let him use my phone'...something like that."

Aiden scratched his head. "She said that?" It certainly sounded like something she would say.

"Among other things," Emma teased with a grin.

Nikulas narrowed his eyes at her and wrapped his arm around her waist to slide her closer to him. "Stop teasing him. I'm the only male you should be teasing," he grumbled.

Aiden left them to their bickering and ordered another drink. What he wouldn't do to feel the effects of all the alcohol he was consuming so he wouldn't have to feel this hollow ache in his gut.

How was he ever going to face Grace again after the way he had acted? But he hadn't been able to help himself. When he'd followed her scent to his apartment and saw that huge male looming over her, he'd just...lost it.

He'd better be careful. People were going to start to think he was a tad off his rocker.

While Nikulas whispered something to Emma that had her entire face turning red and her breathing pick up, Aiden sighed and watched a couple of blokes hitting a cue ball around the pool table. He was just about to tell his friends that he would be fine if they needed to go get that out of their system when the door opened.

His eyes were immediately drawn to the exquisite female standing just inside. A frown marred her smooth forehead as she unzipped her light jacket and her green eyes searched the room.

She found him just as Nikulas said, "So, about this demon..."

"Later," Aiden told him.

Grace made her way over to the table. "Hey, you guys," she said to Nik and Emma. "Would you give us a minute? Please?" A smile lit up her face and her eyes filled with tears when she noticed Mojo. "Hey, little dude," she greeted him as she rubbed his cheek with a finger.

"We'll just go hang out at the bar," Nik said, grabbing Emma's hand and pulling her out of her seat.

"Be nice," she told Aiden, looking at Grace pointedly.

"I'm always nice," he responded. When was he not nice?

"Mm hmm." With a last look of warning, she let Nikulas lead her over to the barstools.

Aiden indicated the chair across the small table from him. "Sit. Please. Would you like a drink?"

"No, thanks. I'm good." She sat and twisted her hands together on the table, the nervous gesture belying her words.

"How'd you know I was here?" he asked.

She grabbed his glass and took a sip of his whiskey, setting the glass back down in front of him. "Keira told me she thought you all may have come here when you didn't show back up at Nik and Emma's."

Before he could ask her anything else, she blurted out, "You were supposed to come with me...when we left the shelter," she clarified. "You were supposed to come with me."

Downing the last of his whiskey, he slammed the glass down onto the table, startling Mojo. He ignored the little beast. "So tell me, poppet. Would that be before or after I was ripped apart by the hoard of possessed vampires that was waiting for me?"

"They weren't supposed to be there," she insisted. "The deal I made with the box wasn't supposed to go down until dusk the following night. We couldn't foresee that they would come up with the idea to start digging."

"The deal you made with the humans when you snuck out while I was sleeping?"

"Yes."

"When you snuck out, scaring me half out of my wits, and then lied to me about the reason why when you returned?"

"Yes," she whispered.

"A secret you kept from me, just like all the other things you've kept from me?

She had the decency to look ashamed. "Yes."

Huh. He hadn't really expected her to admit it. His sharp mind stashed away that comment for a later date. Possibly to blackmail her into giving him more kisses.

"Tell me again why I should believe you now?"

She gazed up at him with large, sad, watery eyes, and he had to grip the bottom of his chair to keep from pulling her into his arms and comforting her.

"Aiden, I'm so sorry. I didn't know what else to do. We needed to get out of there. So I snuck out and made a deal with the Suits. I would give them the box, and they would allow us to leave unharmed. They were going to come up with something to keep the demons away for a few minutes just as the sun went down." She rubbed her temples with her fingers. "I didn't know what else to do!" she emphasized again.

"You could have trusted me to help you."

She gave him a sad smile. "Yeah, well, I just wanted to say I was sorry. And I'm glad you made it back home in one piece."

"I did. Thanks to some friends of mine showing up."

She nodded, and then stood up to leave. "I'll take Mojo up to the apartment. Thank you for taking care of him."

He grabbed her wrist as she scooped him up off of the table. "Don't go."

She looked at him with surprise.

He should be angry with her, and he was. He should want nothing at all to do with the little liar, and he didn't.

Besides, he'd make a horrible husband.

His mind told him to cut his ties with her now, before it was too late. Before he took that step that would make her bound to him, and he to her, forever. And if she was anywhere near him, he would take that step, and very soon.

Aiden let go of her. He didn't want a mate. He had a demon. It was way more predictable and far less dangerous than a female.

Yet he couldn't seem to convince his heart and soul of that. They craved her like nothing else he'd felt before, or, he somehow knew, ever would again.

Truth was, she hadn't done anything that he hadn't done in the past, abandoning him to his fate like that. Wasn't that exactly what he had done to his family? She at least had had a better reason.

And he was happy when she was with him. Life was short. He only had another few hundred, or thousand years or something. Why waste it?

"Or better yet," he stood and threw the rucksack over his shoulder. "I'll come with you."

Getting Nik's attention at the bar, no easy feat when he was caught up in his mate, Aiden indicated for him to pay for the drinks and gave a wave.

Nik lifted his chin and winked and smiled once he saw why Aiden was leaving.

Bloody Estonian bastard.

Aiden sighed. He was never going to hear the end of this.

33

Once back in Nik and Emma's apartment, Grace got Mojo settled while Aiden went to reclaim his room from Heather.

"She's not here," he told Grace when he came back out.

"What?"

He handed her a piece of paper.

Don't freak out, Gracie. I took off. I'll be fine. I'm a big girl.
Call me when you get a new cell.

Love ya,
Heather

. . .

Grace turned the paper over, but there was nothing else written on it. "That's it? That's all I get? Where's Brock?"

"The wolf? Not anywhere near here if he knows what's bloody good for him."

She rolled her eyes.

"This is your fault," she told Aiden, waving the note at him.

"My fault? How is it my fault? And how do you know this Heather?"

"She's my best friend. I went to her place after...well, she came with me. She had to..."

"Come shower with me," he interrupted her.

Thrown off guard by his suggestion, Grace could only blink owlishly at him. She cleared her throat. "I'm sorry? What?"

"Come along, poppet. I need a shower after that flight. And so do you. You reek like that wolf."

"I do?" Grace smelled her forearm. She didn't smell anything. "I'm not showering with you."

"Why ever not?" he asked as he walked towards the bedroom, pulling off his shirt on the way.

Why ever not indeed? Grace eyed the expanse of pure muscle rippling across his back and could not think of one single reason why this was a bad idea. "Uh...umm...okay, I'm coming."

Following the sound of the water, she found him in the bathroom. He laid out two towels and closed the door behind her.

"Come here," he ordered huskily.

She stepped closer, vaguely wondering but not really caring where the hell her sanity had gone.

His grey eyes were bright as he grabbed the hem of her shirt and he yanked it up and off.

Whoa. Wait. Just wait. "Aiden, what if he comes back?"

"Who?"

"Waano."

His hands stilled in the process of untying her pants.

She watched his face, but he gave no indication of what he was thinking.

Finally, he lifted his head. "I can't promise that he won't appear, love. Does that frighten you?"

She wasn't going to lie to him. "Yes."

He pressed his palm to the side of her face and then ran his hand through her hair. Sighing, he kissed the top of her head. "Let's just clean up, yes? And then we'll talk some more." Tilting her chin up until her eyes met his, he confessed, "I want to shag you in the worst possible way. If we can't do that, at least give me the honor of seeing how lovely you are."

Wow. That was possibly one of the most romantic things anyone had ever said to her. "Okay," she whispered, and closed her eyes as he pressed a kiss to the tip of her freckled nose.

"Okay," he whispered back.

She stood in her bra as he finished untying her pants and let them fall from her hips. Kicking off her shoes, she held onto his shoulders while she lifted one leg and then the other as he knelt in front of her to pull off each pant leg.

Next, he hooked his fingers in her panties and slid them down too. She stepped out of them and he tossed them into the corner with her pants.

His palms were warm as he slid them up the backs of her legs and grasped her by the hips. He held her still and leaned in to place a kiss just above the line of soft curls that covered her.

Her hips lurched forward and she gasped, a surge of desire slamming through her.

"So lovely..." he murmured against her skin. With a soft moan, he kissed her there again, inhaling deeply. "I want to taste you here," he said huskily, running the tip of his nose down to her slit.

Grace's knees nearly buckled, but his hands on her hips kept her from sinking to the floor.

Rising smoothly to his feet, he reached behind her and unsnapped her bra. As he pulled the straps down, he stepped back, taking the bra with him and tossing it into the pile of clothes.

She fought the urge to cover herself as he ran his eyes over every single inch of her, taking his time, pausing hungrily at her breasts and the V between her legs.

Her skin began to burn everywhere they touched, and her blood rushed through her veins in anticipation.

His eyes grew brighter still as he continued to gaze at her, and a low growl rumbled in his throat. She caught a glimpse of his fangs as he declared: "MINE."

"What does that mean?" she asked.

But he only smiled, and quickly stripped off the rest of his clothes.

Grace watched him, forgetting her shyness as he unwrapped his body like a gift that had been created just for her.

She'd seen him in nothing but a tee shirt and boxer briefs, but the magnificence of him completely naked was not something she was ever going to forget.

He stood still, allowing her time to look her fill as he had done to her.

Lean, powerful muscle covered latte colored skin from head to toe. His shoulders were just broad enough, his arms and chest powerful. Lean, sculpted abs, marred only with a nasty looking diagonal scar, led down to narrow hips where his manhood jutted out thick and proud from a nest of dark curls.

Her mouth actually began to water just from looking at him. She hadn't had sex in so long.

"Let's get clean, shall we?" he indicated for her to get in first.

She pouted a little but did as he suggested, stepping underneath the cascading water. As the water hit her, she gasped, every drop a caress to her sensitized skin. The shower door closed, and she felt Aiden standing behind her. Turning around to face him, she closed her eyes and tilted her head back. She could feel the heat of his stare on her breasts as she lifted her arms to wet her hair.

"Spin around, love," he rasped when she lifted her head again.

She did so, and he began to work shampoo through her long hair. Guiding her by the shoulders, he turned her around again to rinse it out.

When that was done, he picked up the body wash. "May I?" he asked.

Grace could only nod. But he didn't pour the soap into a cloth as she expected, he poured it directly into his hand.

Her breath caught, desire pooling between her legs before he even touched her.

Rubbing his hands together, he lathered them up and then reached for her arm.

Disappointment flooded through her, and she thought she saw him smirk right before he dropped his chin to his chest.

As he washed one arm and then the next, she waited breathlessly, anticipation building inside of her as she waited for him to get to the more intimate parts of her.

Running his hands up both arms, he paused only for a second before running them over her shoulders and down around her breasts. He cupped their fullness in each hand, skimming his thumbs across her nipples.

He wasn't playing fair. Grace swayed towards him, unable to deny her longing for him anymore. "Aiden..." she breathed.

"Yes, love?" he answered quietly.

Looking directly into his eyes, she told him, "I want to be yours."

His hands stilled for a moment, then glided down her stomach and around her hips, where he grasped her hard.

Running her palms up over the ridges of his stomach to his chest, she stepped closer until barely an inch separated them, and wrapped her arms around his neck.

Sliding his arms around her bare back, he pulled her up against him until she was on her toes. His moan joined hers as her soft breasts were crushed against his chest and his hardness pulsed against her belly.

Gripping him tight, she pressed her lips to his collarbone, and then she kissed her way to his neck, biting him gently.

He shuddered in her arms. "Grace, love," he moaned. "I feel I've waited forever for you."

He ran his hands up her back and into her wet hair. Pulling her head back, he captured her lips with his, kissing her gently, reverently. Leaving her mouth, he pressed hungry kisses down her chin to her throat.

Grace moaned and tried to lift herself higher on her toes so he could reach more of her.

Loosening his tight hold, he stepped back into the water, pulling her with him to rinse her off fully. He ran his hands over her breasts and stomach to help the water while she clutched at his upper arms. When she was clean, he stepped back out of the spray.

Grace went to follow him but he suddenly stopped her with a hand around her arm.

"Wait," he snarled.

The hair at the nape of her neck rose at the tone of his voice. She stopped where she was. "Aiden? What's wrong?"

He glanced down at her, breathing heavily, and a jolt of fear shot straight through to her bones.

Shadows were darkening his eyes.

Aiden closed his eyes, fighting the now familiar feeling of his demon attempting to rise.

Not now, you bloody twat. Not now!

It must have heard him, for a moment later it was gone. Surprised, he waited a few more seconds, just to be sure, before he opened his eyes again.

His lovely Grace trembled before him, her face white with terror as she watched him. His heart ached to see her like that.

"It's all right, he's gone," he assured her.

"Are you sure?"

"Yes. Come here. Hurry," he urged.

She did, and he wrapped her up in his arms, groaning aloud at the feel of all of her delicious softness pressed against him.

Lowering his mouth to hers, he kissed her over and over, overcome with a sense of urgency in the wake of what had just happened. Gradually, he felt her become pliant in his arms again, and she hugged him to her as her blood rushed through her veins and he again scented her desire.

Turning her until her back was against the wall, he lifted her with one arm under her luscious derriere. "Wrap your legs around me, love," he ordered against her swollen lips.

As she did, he skimmed along her slick softness and found her entrance. With one quick thrust, he impaled her on his throbbing cock.

She cried out, and he tore his mouth from hers, worried that he had hurt her.

"Don't stop," she breathed urgently.

The scent of her blood and her desire wafted in the air, and he threw his head back with a hiss as he began to move within her. He ached to sink his fangs through her supple flesh, but knew if he did, there would be no going back for them.

But gods, she felt so good. He'd never been so wound up by a female.

Bracing his legs apart, he gripped her hips and lifted her up, then slid her back down hard. He did it again, and again, until she was clutching at his shoulders, begging him for relief. With a growl, he maneuvered one arm behind her back and palmed the back of her head to protect it. The other he wrapped around her bottom.

"Hang on to me, love," he ordered, then began to thrust into her hard and fast.

She fit around him like a glove, tight and wet, and he felt her start to tremble as he moved within her.

"Aiden!" she cried, throwing her head back against his hand.

He hissed again at the sight of her exposed throat, crazy with thirst and desire for her. Slowing his thrusts, he growled, "I want to taste you, Grace."

Her eyes opened and saw where he was looking, saw his elongated fangs. "Do it," she groaned, tilting her head away again. "Aiden, please..."

Aiden began to shake as he fought the blood lust. The power of it was all consuming and very nearly overwhelming. Her artery pulsed before him, but he couldn't bring himself to do it. He was overcome with an unusual sense of decency. He couldn't bring her into his world without her understanding what she was getting into.

With a roar of frustration, he quickened his thrusts, losing himself in her body until his sexual hunger pushed back the thirst.

Pressing his forehead to hers, he tried to hold back to extend the pleasure. But when she cried out and began to convulse in his arms, squeezing every inch of him with each pulse of her orgasm, he lost his control.

Slamming into her over and over, he exploded with a roar.

"MINE!"

The power of his orgasm shook him to his core.

He held her close, moving slowly in and out of her as they caught their breath.

"I think we need another shower," she said when their hearts had both calmed and their breathing had returned to normal.

With a roguish grin, he agreed enthusiastically, and grabbed the body wash.

34

Brock checked the address Luukas had written down for him and lifted his hand to knock on the door. It swung open before his fist had the chance to connect.

The male in front of him was about his height, with eyes such an icy blue they were nearly white. His long, dark hair was pulled back and clasped at the nape of his neck, accentuating the harsh angles of his face.

He was also the alpha of the pack. Brock would've known from his aura, even if he hadn't already known. As a sign of respect, he fell to his knees in front of him and tilted his head to the side, exposing his throat in a sign of submission.

"Och. Get up, ye wee pup. There isna any need for that." Stepping back, he opened the door wide in invitation.

Unsure of what to expect, Brock stood and sidestepped past the alpha, keeping his eyes averted.

"My name is Cedric Kincaid, 'n' I can see ye ken that I'm the alpha 'o' this territory." He stuck his hand out.

Brock took the proffered hand and shook it firmly. "Brock Hume."

"Aye. I ken who ye are." Closing the door, Cedric led the way into his home and offered Brock a seat at the kitchen table.

After offering his guest a drink, Cedric got straight to the crux of the matter. "Luukas tells me that ye helped Grace, Aiden's lass, 'n' her friend. That ye saved their lives."

Brock nodded. "I guess you could say that."

"Whit were ye doin' there in China?"

Annnnd, here goes the hard part. He'd been trying to think of a good way to explain his situation the entire way over here, but in the end, he figured the truth would be his best chance of surviving. At least what they needed to know. "I was traveling around a bit, when I came across Dalian and I noticed something strange about the city."

Cedric hefted a brow, waiting expectantly.

Brock glanced up at him. "It has a large population of possessed vampires."

"And what do ye ken aboot that?"

"Not much," he lied. "Except that they're up to no good, and they were killing humans left and right with no regard for staying under the radar. So, I began to hunt them."

"Ye hunted them? No shite? And yer still alive?"

Brock laughed. "I am."

Cedric narrowed his eyes and studied him. "Whit are ye hopin' to gain by coming here, wee pup?"

His direct question took Brock slightly by surprise. "Um, well, I really hadn't thought beyond getting the girls to safety." One girl in particular kept weaseling her way into his thoughts, much as he tried to keep her out. Surprising himself, he said, "However, now that I'm here, I'd like to respectfully ask your permission to stay for a while."

"How long is 'a while'?"

"Until I can win over the girl, at the very least." Brock grinned.

"The friend?" Cedric asked.

"Yes, Heather Knight is her name."

The alpha leaned back in his chair and crossed his arms over his massive chest. "Ye 'ave my permission tae stay. On one condition."

Brock's "thank you" stuck in his throat. "What condition is that?"

Leaning forward in his chair, Cedric speared him with those eerie eyes of his. "Ye see, I ken that yer no' telling me the entire truth. There's more tae yer story, wee pup. But I'm willin' to let ye get more comfortable here 'n' with me. I ken it's hard to trust when ye 'ave been on yer own for awhile."

"Aye, I ken that yer without pack," Cedric answered his look of surprise. "And until I ken more aboot ye, I'm no' inclined to bring ye into mine. Ye ken?"

"Sure. I understand. And thank you, for letting me stay."

"Och. Aye. Now git yer arse out of here before the other lads show up and give ye a hard time. They will nae harm ye. Ye 'ave my word."

The two wolves stood and shook hands again.

"Thank you again. I really appreciate it," Brock told him again at the door.

"Take this just in case I need ye." He handed Brock a cell phone. " Now, go get yer lass," Cedric answered.

Back on the streets of downtown Seattle, Brock couldn't suppress a surge of excitement. He couldn't wait to get back up to Nikulas and Emma's place and start winning over the woman who hadn't left his thoughts since she'd first opened her door to him. He realized he'd have his work cut out for him, now that she knew what he was, but he was confident he'd be able to win her over.

He picked up his stride when he saw the building just ahead. He was so anxious to get back there that he almost missed it.

Almost.

Just two buildings away, he caught an intriguing scent, a scent that he knew well. What was Heather doing out here? Following the path she'd taken, he discovered that she was heading towards the bus tunnels under Nordstrom's.

She was running? From a werewolf?

His smile widened.

And the hunt was on.

35

Grace propped herself up on one elbow. Following several "showers" Aiden had finally deemed her clean enough, and after a quick snack for her, they'd retired to his bed.

"Aiden?"

"Yes, poppet?"

"What exactly do you mean when you refer to me as being 'MINE' in that way you do?"

Rolling over, he traced his fingers lightly over her exposed nipple, plucking at the hard pebble when it strained towards him.

She shivered, a now familiar ache settling low in her belly. Slapping his hand away, she scolded him. "Stop trying to distract me, and tell me."

"Why ever would you think it means anything?"

She arched a delicate eyebrow. He was stalling again. The question was, why? What was he trying to hide from her?

When she didn't answer him, he tore his gaze from her breast to peek up at her. Upon seeing her mulish expression, he sighed in surrender and mimicked her pose so they were eye to eye.

"Do you want the long story, or do you want me to get straight to it?"

"Straight to it, for now. Long story maybe later."

"All right." He took a deep breath. "I say that you're 'mine' because you are. Literally."

She wrinkled her forehead in confusion. "Like a girlfriend?"

"Like my fated mate for life."

"I don't understand," she said.

Sitting up and leaning back against the headboard, he pulled her up with him, lifting her leg around until she was straddling his lap.

Grace felt him hardening beneath her bottom and her eyes widened in surprise. Again? Seriously? Dating a vampire sure did have its perks. But she was digressing.

Grabbing his wandering hands and holding them flat on her thighs, she ordered, "Explain."

He finally gave in. "I'm just going to lay it on you, all right?"

"All right."

"As I believe you know, I'm a vampire."

She nodded.

"And there are times when vampires run across a human that the gods have deemed to be their perfect match and they decide to make that person their fated mate. And no matter how he fights it, he's destined to be with that person for the rest of their unnatural lives."

"But, how does that work? A vampire lives much longer than a human, right?"

"Correct. But the vampire would feed their human some of their magic vampire blood, and that person will stay young and healthy until death do they part. The vampire's death, usually."

"And what happens to the human after the vampire dies?"

"The human will no longer have access to the magic blood and they will begin to age again as they naturally would."

"And how does a vampire know who their mate is?"

"The vampire knows as soon as they taste their humans blood." He cocked his head at her.

Grace's mind was spinning. "So, you won't know that I am, in fact, your fated mate until you drink from me."

"Technically, yes," he said.

"And my blood will tell you that I am 'yours'?"

"Yes, well, that will just confirm it actually. I was relatively certain the moment I met you."

"So, why didn't you take me up on my offer when I told you to go ahead and do it?"

He lifted a lock of her hair from where it lay on her breast and rubbed it between his fingers. "I didn't feel right doing that to you without you knowing what all it would entail between us."

She was Aiden's fated mate? That was why she'd been so attracted to him?

At first she'd just assumed it was because there weren't many other guys around that measured up to him. But being here, around all of these other beautiful vampires, had disproven that theory. Even meeting Brock, the single, hot, but annoyingly single-minded werewolf, hadn't rocked her boat.

Only Aiden did it for her since he'd scared the hell out of her that day and almost made her lose her Mojo. Even having a demon inside of him didn't deter her attraction, though if she had any sense at all, she would've ran for the hills the first chance she'd gotten.

"There's one other thing," he said.

"What?" she asked curiously.

"Once I've had your blood, I'll be unable to drink from anyone else."

Her mouth dropped open. "Ever?"

"Not ever," he confirmed.

"What would happen to you?" she wondered aloud. "If you didn't have access to me?"

"I would weaken day by day until I died the true death."

Grace stared at him in disbelief.

"But if you never drink from me, that can be avoided?"

But he just shook his head. "It will happen, eventually. There's no sense at all in fighting it. I watched Nikulas try. It nearly drove him mad." He shrugged. "Our paths are fated, love."

"So, there's no way to get out of this?"

"Not that I'm aware of, no."

How could he be so calm about all of this?

"You're telling me that your very life is all in my hands now?"

"Once I've had your blood, yes."

"Your LIFE?" She pushed herself off of his lap and his bed and started yanking open drawers, searching for something to cover herself with. She couldn't have this conversation naked. She just couldn't.

"Grace, love..."

"What am I supposed to do with that, Aiden?" she yelled as she yanked one of his tee shirts over her head. She covered her face with her hands. "Gods."

He was standing in front of her before she realized he had moved. Pulling her hands gently away from her face, he forced her to look up at him. "I am *truly* sorry. I've known for some time that this was how it was with us, but I hesitated to say anything because I wanted to protect you."

He scratched his head and then rubbed his hair hard with his both hands until it was sticking up all over. "Thing is, poppet, I have a bloody demon inside of me. How can I ask you to be with me?" His features hardened with determination. "I'll fight it until I can't anymore. For you."

Grace saw the pain in his eyes and took a breath. If she was going to be honest with herself, she knew she wanted to be with him. She'd known since that night at the shelter when she'd come back from making the deal with the Suits, the guilt at what she'd done eating her alive inside. Maybe even sooner than that.

"Please trust me, Grace. I'll find a way to get us through this."

Trust me, Grace.

Listen to me, Grace! You can't trust a vampire. Ever!

"I need some time," she whispered.

He opened his mouth to say more, then seemed to change his mind. Instead he just nodded.

Picking up the pile of clean clothes Emma had lent her from the dresser, she said, "I'll just go sleep on the pullout since Brock is gone."

"There's no need for that. Stay here with me," he pleaded.

But she shook her head. "I need some time alone, Aiden. Please. I won't be far."

He rubbed his forehead. "No, love. You stay in here. I'll sleep out there."

Pulling on a pair of running pants, he strode out of the room, pausing at the doorway to tell her, "Just call if you need anything. Or when you come to your senses and realize that you love me and cannot go a second longer without sacrificing yourself to my lusty vampire needs."

She giggled as he closed the door, but her laughter faded fast as she sank onto the edge of the bed, and the full impact of what he'd just told her hit her full force.

"Wow," she said aloud to the empty room. "Gives a whole new meaning to the words "safe sex, doesn't it?"

Aiden smiled as he heard Grace giggling, and pulled the door closed behind him. She would come around, he told himself; she just needed some time to digest it all. Barging back in there now would just muck everything up again, no matter how he ached to be near her.

At least she hadn't kicked him out completely. Or left the apartment.

He glanced out the window on his way to the office and the location of his temporary lodgings. The sun would be coming up soon.

Maybe the wolf would come back and pick a fight when he found him in his bed.

Ah, see? There was a bright side to everything. He briefly wondered if Grace would be upset if he added his head to his collection?

Somehow, he didn't think she'd be fond of that idea. He sighed. Well, he'd better get used to having the old "ball and chain". His life was about to change forever. No longer will he be able to run off whenever he wishes and wander into a fight somewhere or shag a pretty female.

Retract that last part. He'd still be shagging a pretty female. The loveliest female he'd ever had the honor of being with.

He smiled, wondering how long she would need to think about things.

Suddenly, his blood began to hum in his veins. The smile left his face and he rubbed the center of his chest, his brows drawn together in confusion. What was this strange feeling? It seemed vaguely familiar...

Then it came to him, and he realized what it was he was listening to, but it wasn't a song he wanted to hear. It had been so long since anyone had evoked this power over him, he was a bit taken aback at first.

He was being summoned, and it wasn't by Luukas.

Bloody hell. It couldn't be!

The humming grew stronger and more painful. Stumbling over to the phone, he hit the fast dial.

"What's up, man? We were just heading back up that way," Nikulas answered.

"Nik..." he rasped, then groaned as the pain became more severe. The demon, Waano, stirred unhappily inside of him.

"Aid? Aiden? What's wrong?"

Aiden could hear Nik's pounding footsteps as he began to run.

Unable to hang onto it anymore, Aiden dropped the phone just as the front door slammed open.

"Aiden!"

Grace ran from the bedroom just as Nik got to him.

"Keep her away!" he hissed.

"Grace, stay there!" Nik ordered.

His eyes rolled back in his head and he jerked backwards, his spine nearly twisting in half as the agony of his blood flowing through his veins hit him with a whole new level of pain.

Waano roared with displeasure within him, his presence rising from whatever depths he'd hidden away in.

Aiden gripped the front of Nik's shirt.

"He's coming, mate," he rasped. "I can't stop him. She's calling me, and him...I can't stop him."

"Who's calling you?" Nik asked just as Emma arrived at a run.

"Leeha...the bloody bitch."

"Leeha?" Emma exclaimed.

"Emma, take Grace and get the hell out of here. Go! Now!" Nik yelled when she didn't move fast enough.

"I'm not going anywhere," Grace insisted.

Aiden begged Nik with his eyes as he writhed in pain on the floor, no longer able to speak without crying out like a girl.

"Grace..." Emma started towards her.

"No! No! I'm not leaving him!"

"Just take her to the other room," Nik told Emma. "And call Keira. Keep Luukas away from here. No matter what."

Aiden saw Grace dig in her heels from the corner of his eyes. There was no help for it. He was going to have to kill her, just as soon as he was finished dying.

Another pulse of burning pain pounded through him, and Waano began to unfold, stretching into Aiden's limbs, polluting his cells.

What is this?

It's Leeha. She's calling us to her.

An angry breath blew through him. *I'm growing weary of her.*

"Nikulas," he managed to choke out. "Get away from me."

36

Nik's couldn't believe what he was seeing. He was looking at his best friend, but it wasn't his friend at all, not anymore.

Aiden, or whoever it was inside of Aiden, pushed his hands away.

"Get off of me," it growled.

Nik backed off immediately.

"Oh my gods." Emma's voice came from somewhere in the vicinity behind him. "His accent is gone completely."

"Because that's not him," Grace said quietly.

Nikulas glanced behind him, his instinct to protect his mate kicking into high gear. "I told you to take her into the other room!"

Emma never took her eyes from Aiden as he came to his feet. "I tried."

Nik stood in the middle of the group, trying to divide his attention evenly between the girls and Aiden.

Damn stubborn witches.

Grace walked up to stand beside Nikulas. "Give him back to me," she gritted out.

Waano brushed off his sleeves, tilting his head at her strangely. "No."

Nik's arm shot out as she went after him, her hands curled into claws.

Emma took a step forward to help him. Or her. He wasn't sure. He pointed at her. "You! Stay right where you are. Or so help me, Em..."

The thing in Aiden's body began to laugh. "I'm not going to hurt your precious female, though she does smell delicious."

Nik's head whipped back around to Aiden, or the thing inside of Aiden. A feral growl rose up as his fangs shot down and his body prepared to fight for his female, to the death if necessary.

Shadowy grey eyes focused back on Grace. "I can smell your fear." He smiled a sick smile. "It excites me."

Nik stepped in front of her. "Grace, back away, and you two get out of here. NOW."

"I'm not leaving you here with that," Emma insisted.

"Emma! Do not fucking argue with me on this!"

"I'm not leaving either," Grace said quietly.

"Are you *fucking* kidding me?" Nik asked, at his wit's end with the both of them. He weighed his options. If it came down to it, he would save Emma. He had no choice. She was his.

But how was he supposed to tell his best friend that he didn't protect his Grace? He eyed up the entity in front of him. If he ever saw his best friend again.

The thing inside of Aiden chuckled. "You won't be able to save either of them, vampire."

Nik narrowed his eyes. The fucker was reading his mind now? "Try me, you son of a bitch."

But it just scoffed. "All of this quarreling. There is no need. Let me pass, and you will all survive another day."

"Let you pass?" Grace repeated in disbelief. "No! You're not going anywhere with him!"

He heaved an impatient sigh. With a flick of his wrist, he sent them all flying through the air to different sides of the room, where they stuck to the walls three feet off the floor.

"Where are you going?" Nik shouted as the thing strode by. Fear shot through him as he fought against the invisible hold the thing had on him so effortlessly.

"To finish this," Waano told him, slamming the door closed behind him.

A few seconds later, they all dropped to the floor.

Nik rushed to Emma's side but she yelled out, "Go get him!"

Giving her a quick once over anyway, he flew out of the apartments, moving faster than any human could track, but he was too late.

Aiden's body was gone.

Back at the apartment, he found Emma still on the floor consoling Grace. She looked up questioningly when he came in, but he shook his head. "He's fucking gone. Again."

Chewing on the inside of his cheek, he came up with multiple ideas and discarded them just as quickly. He went round and round in his head, but he kept coming back to the same thing.

They needed Luukas.

As a Master vampire, he was the only one who had any hope at all of competing with that thing.

Emma looked up at him as she pulled Grace to her feet. "What is it? Nik? What is it?"

"I think I know where he went."

"To Leeha," Emma said.

He nodded.

Grace looked up at him hopefully. "You know where she is?"

"Not exactly. But we can find her."

"Oh, thank the gods," she breathed. "But, he said he wasn't giving Aiden back." She glanced between him and Emma. "Do you really think he's not going to give him back this time?"

Nikulas shared a look with Emma. He wasn't giving up. Not yet. "Oh, he'll give him back, don't you worry. I'm not losing my best friend again."

"How are we going to accomplish that if he doesn't want to leave?" Emma asked.

"We need Luukas. Why don't you get dressed," he said to Grace. "And we'll go upstairs."

"I'll stay with her," Emma told him. "And we can meet you up there."

Nik's heart stopped in his chest, imagining all of the things that could happen to her. Besides, she tended to have a knack for getting herself into trouble.

"No way in hell, sweetheart. You're not leaving my sight until I know for a fact that that thing is far, far away."

She rolled her eyes and he lifted his eyebrows, daring her to challenge him.

Grace murmured, "I'll just go get dressed."

Luukas listened to Nik's account of what happened, Keira at his side. When his brother was finished, he reached over and took Keira's small hand in his.

"I'll go."

"Luukas..." Keira began.

But he cut her off. "It's all right, witch. I can handle this."

"But what if you can't?" she asked worriedly. "You freaked out when he was in the room as Aiden."

He smiled at her. "But he's not Aiden now, is he?"

"You can't kill him, bro," Nikulas insisted. "He's my best friend. I won't let you kill him."

Luukas turned to his brother. Would he be able to control himself enough to not kill him? Possibly. In any case, the demon had to be dealt with.

"Is there any way to get the demon out?" Grace asked Keira.

"I don't know. I only ever saw them after the vampires were possessed. I never saw how Leeha did it, and if she ever reversed the process, I never heard of it."

"Keira was kept in a cell also, not far from me," Luukas told her. His bowels clenched thinking of that wretched place he'd spent seven years of his life in, but he pushed it from his mind. He needed to concentrate on what was going on now. It was bad enough that they all watched him so closely, just waiting for him to break.

"Oh, I didn't know," Grace said. "I'm so sorry."

Keira smiled at her. "Don't look so horrified. It's all over now. And it all worked out for the best."

She squeezed Luukas' hand, and his heart swelled with love for her. She had saved him in the end. She saved him still, every day.

"Grace," Emma said. "Aiden showed us something that you have. An old spell?"

"What? Oh! I'd forgotten all about that with everything that's been going on." She rubbed her temples. "Yeah, it's old. Ancient. My parents made sure I found it after they died, but I don't know why."

"You have no idea what it is? Or what it's for?"

"No. I'm sorry, but I don't. I had no idea it even existed until after they were both gone. I tried to ask them, but they never came to me again."

"We'll look at it when we get Aiden back here. Maybe between all of us, we can figure it out. So, what are your powers?" Keira asked.

Grace gave a self-depreciating laugh. "Nothing that will help us. Or Aiden."

"Tell us anyway," Emma said encouragingly.

"I can sort of communicate with animals."

"Like talk to them?" Luukas asked.

"Um...not really? More like, if I concentrate, they can get the gist of what I'm telling them. Like, I'll tell Mojo that I'm going to work, or whatever."

"Her hedgehog," Emma told Luukas and Keira when they looked at her questioningly. "He's up in our apartment in the office."

"It's running loose in my office?" Nik shouted.

"Don't worry, he has a litter box," Grace said.

"Anything else?" Keira asked. "Can you do anything else?"

"I can move objects. That's pretty easy. And I can heal, but only myself."

"Have you ever tried to heal someone else?" Nik asked.

"All the time, dude. I work in a hospital, in the operating room. I've never been able to save anyone. Ever."

Luukas heard the sadness in her voice. "That's all right, Grace. Healing yourself is a very useful power to have. I wish I were able to do that." He smirked a little. "It would've come in handy in recent years."

Everyone stared at him strangely, except for Grace.

He scowled. "What?"

"Look at you," Nik said. "Cracking jokes."

He frowned at his brother, not understanding what the big deal was.

"What about you and Emma?" Grace asked. "What can you do?"

"Well, other than moving things without touching them...that seems to be pretty much the norm with us witches...Emma can immobilize people. Even vampires and werewolves."

"Especially when she's pissed off," Nik chimed in, and Emma smacked him on the arm.

"You bring it on yourself," she told him.

"And you?" Grace asked Keira.

She glanced up at Luukas and he nodded once. "Go on, witch. Tell her what you can do."

She hesitated a moment, and then said quickly, "I can take the powers away from vampires."

"Even a Master vampire," Luukas added, smiling at her. He held no ill will against what she had down to him. She'd been trying to protect her sister, and she had suffered as greatly as he had. He could feel her suffering still, just as he did.

"Does that work on anyone besides vampires?" Grace asked. "Like a demon, for instance?"

"No," Luukas said instantly. He knew where this was going.

"Luukas. I could try..."

But he didn't let her finish. He flashed his fangs at her, the thought of her in any sort of dangerous situation making his blood run cold. "I said no, witch. I need you here, where you're safe, if I'm going to be in any condition to help Aiden."

His beautiful angel narrowed her eyes at him in challenge, and he met her look for look. She didn't like to be told no, although she gave in to him quite often to protect his sanity. However, he had a feeling this time was not going to be one of those times.

But he could not give in to her. He would tie her down if he had to. He'd done it before.

"The dawn is coming," Nikulas said.

"We'll head out at dusk," Luukas told him. "Do we know where she is?"

"Leeha? We have a general idea. She didn't go far from the mountain prison you destroyed. I'll call our scouts. See if they can nail her down." He stood up to leave, Emma and

Grace following suit. "Should we ask the wolves if they want in on this?"

"It wouldn't hurt."

Luukas noticed the three witches exchange looks, and he sighed.

They were going to have to tie them ALL down.

37

Aiden awoke at dusk the following night. The scene was hauntingly familiar. Only instead of waking up covered in grain with no idea of where he was, he was covered in dirt.

With no idea of where he was.

Luckily, the dirt was much less condensed than the grain had been, and as such he had a much easier time unearthing himself from the ground. Lifting himself out of his shallow grave, he sat beside it and shook the dirt from his hair. He'd never been buried alive so much in his life, and was *this* close to becoming seriously claustrophobic. Not a good syndrome for a vampire with severe sun allergies to have.

Looking down at himself, he was happy to see that the thing had at least acquired some trainers for his feet, and even a grey hoodie to cover his bare chest.

Waano stirred inside of him. He hadn't completely retreated this time, but had only settled down to doze after getting them within a few miles of Leeha's call; and apparently burying them in the dirt under a large rock overhang to protect him from the sun.

"At least you don't leave me out in the elements to burn."

He looked around at the pines, foliage, and mountains of Western Canada, and he was afraid he'd been mistaken earlier. He knew *exactly* where he was.

He sighed heavily. "This is really getting old, mate. If you want me to go somewhere, you need only to ask nicely."

No sooner had the words left his mouth than his blood began to boil in his veins, or at least that's what it felt like. It seemed Leeha was getting impatient.

Aiden pulled his knees up and hunched over himself in agony. "Ahhh! Stop it! You bloody bitch! How the hell do you expect me to get there if you have me writhing around in pain like a snake with its head cut off?"

Another burst of acid wracked him with white-hot fire, and Aiden cried out incoherently. He knew the longer he went without going to her, the worse it would become.

He was almost grateful to feel the demon coming to life. At least it would take the pain away. It slithered around inside of him and stretched its tentacles, invading his muscles, his nerves, even his blood.

The pain began to ease to a point where he could bear it, but in return, Aiden had lost control of his body. He again was sharing space with the demon. Aware, but unable to speak or have any say in how his physical body behaved.

Waano got up, dusted the dirt off, and took off at vamp speed, following the call of Leeha's blood. His wrath and determination flowed through Aiden.

Right. So, I guess we're doing this now.

The demon didn't bother to respond.

A sixth sense told him he was either going to leave here without the demon inside of him anymore, or he wouldn't be leaving here at all.

The call got louder and louder, pulsing through him until it made his very bones ache. Right when Aiden thought he couldn't stand it anymore, Waano came to an abrupt stop in a clearing in front of a large, stone home. He fell to his knees and pulled back a bit, allowing Aiden control again.

He waited, too weakened from her hellish summoning to do anything else.

Snow capped mountains surrounded them, even in the middle of summer, with thick groves of pine trees along their base. When he looked over his shoulder, a turquoise blue lake was spread out before him. At least, he imagined it would be turquoise in the sunshine. The night air was crisp and cool, and he breathed it in gratefully.

The burning in his blood began to ease, and he looked up to see a female with dark red hair prowling towards him across the moonlit grass. Her sheer white gown billowed in the cool evening breeze, teasing him with glimpses of the slender nude form underneath.

He watched her come towards him, expecting to feel the familiar surge of lust that he always felt around her, but this time, there was nothing. Not even a twinge.

"My Aiden," she purred in her thickly accented voice. "At last you have come to me. Did you not hear me calling you, my love?"

Aiden didn't bother to answer her. Silly question, really. He wouldn't be kneeling there getting grass stains on his knees if he hadn't heard her.

She came closer, until Aiden could see the terrifying, blood red depths of her eyes. "It's really you, is it not?" Her voice was full of awe. "You have proven yourself stronger than the others. You've learned to control the monster inside of you! I always knew you were special, my Aiden."

Not wanting to be at a disadvantage, he stumbled to his feet and smiled down at her, content to let her lead the conversation for now.

An answering smile began to curl up the corners of her red lips, but it froze on her face before reaching its full potential. Leaning forward, she sniffed him daintily. When she was done, her eyes were alive with fury.

Before he knew what she was about, she slapped him hard. His head whipped to the side, and he felt the bones fracture in his jaw.

"You filthy bastard! You have betrayed me! I can smell that human woman all over you!" She lifted her hand to hit him again, but hesitated this time. Gripping her fingers into a fist, she pulled it back down to her side, and took a calming breath. Her smile was downright disturbing. "No matter. You haven't mated with her yet, or I would smell her blood in you. You will forget about her soon enough."

"I sincerely doubt that," he told her.

"Ah, he speaks at last," she teased. "My Aiden, you doubt me? You should know better than that by now."

"What is it that you want, Leeha?" he demanded, tired of her games. "You went through all of this trouble to get me here, why beat around the bush?" Another thought occurred to him. "By the way, how did you do that?"

She seemed disinclined to answer him at first, but then shrugged a shoulder. "You are mine now, Aiden. My blood flows in you."

"Yours? That's not possible. Luukas is the one that turned me."

"No longer, my love. It was my blood that resurrected you after your...initiation...into my army."

"You mean when you possessed me with this bloody demon?" He slammed his palm into the middle of his chest.

"When I made you mine in the truest form, finally, after all of this time," she corrected him.

He was hers now? *She* was his Master? No, no, no. This was not going to work for him. No, not at all. For one, he highly doubted that Grace would be very understanding about him running off to another female whenever that female crooked her finger. And for two...well, he was simply too aghast to think of a second reason at the moment, but he imagined the first reason was enough in any case.

"Yes, you see, that's not going to work for me," he told her when he could manage to make his throat work again. "I have obligations. I can't be running amok all over the Pacific Northwest every time you need someone to hold the hem of your gown up out of the mud."

Clasping her hands behind her back, the action thrusting her full breasts out against the thin material of her gown, she walked in a tight circle around him. Her hardened nipple scraped his arm when she passed, purposefully, he was certain.

"I think you will change your mind when you hear what I have to offer."

"Oh, I don't know about that, poppet."

Stopping in front of him again, she leaned into him and ran her hands lightly down his arms until she was holding his hands. "What would you say if I told you that I could give you the chance to go back and change the one thing that's haunted you for your entire immortal life?"

He tilted his head, trying to figure out what she was about. "I don't have any regrets, Leeha. You should know me better than that by now."

One hand reached up to caress his cheek. "You don't have to keep up that brave front for me, my love. I know you better than you think."

She jerked back, pacing away from him. "For instance, I know that you have a collection of heads hidden in the underground of the city. And more importantly, I know why you feel the need to keep such mementos." She turned to look at him with pity in her fiery eyes. "I know that you feel that you failed your family, running away the way you did. I know that you fear that you are exactly like your father, only thinking of yourself. And as a result, you weren't there to save your mother, or your siblings."

She paused a moment. "Am I wrong?"

He studied her closely, not bothering to answer her.

"Nothing to say?"

"I don't really see the need," he told her quietly. He felt naked in front of her, all of his innermost guilt exposed for the world to see. It was not the type of intimacy he'd always imagined they'd have between them. How did she know all of this?

"Well, let me continue then. Stop me if anything I am saying is incorrect." She smiled, knowing damned good and well that she had hit it right on the button. "You keep the heads to prove something to yourself and to those you care about. You keep them to prove that you are nothing like your father. Every one of them shows that you were there to protect those you love. That you do not only think of yourself."

Tired of her dramatics, he waved a hand in front of his face. "What is the bloody point of all of this? Anyone who'd taken a psych class could figure that out. Don't tell me you called me here just to dance around my shame."

"No, no, my Aiden. I would never be so cruel."

He almost snorted aloud, but caught himself just in time. She forgot that he also knows her much better than that.

"As I said, I have something to offer you. But," she held up one finger, "I expect something in return for giving you this gift."

He shouldn't ask. He really shouldn't. He knew better. "What gift would that be?"

Coming so close they were nearly touching, she paused again for effect, and then exclaimed, "I can give you the chance to go back in time, my love! To save your family!"

Aiden took a step back, putting some space between them. "What are you blathering on about?"

She clapped her hands. "It's true! I can do this for you. You can change history. Save your mother and siblings."

"And my father?" he asked.

Some of the excitement left her face. "I am afraid there is nothing that can save him. He will die no matter what you do, either from illness or his own hand. It is what he deserves. I didn't think it would bother you overmuch."

"No. Not particularly," he agreed.

Go back in time? The female was daft! All the magic in the world wouldn't be able to accomplish such a thing.

She had truly lost her mind. He nearly felt sorry for her.

Out of some sense of morbid curiosity, he asked, "And what would I have to give you in return? For such a thoughtful gift?"

She lifted her chin proudly. "You would agree to stay with me, and be my lover, as we've always been meant to be. And when needed, your demon would help me control the others so I can bring a halt to this silly uprising that is taking place against me."

Aiden laughed out loud, and Waano seemed to join him as he drifted around inside, listening. "You are truly off your rocker this time. Leeha, I can't control this thing you've put inside of me. He comes and goes as he jolly well pleases, sometimes at the most inopportune moments, may I add."

Her face tightened as she watched him. "You dare to laugh at me? After everything I've done for you?"

He laughed even harder. "Done for me?" It took him a full minute to be able to speak coherently. "What, exactly, have you done for me? Well, you haven't killed me. Yet. I guess I should be grateful for that."

She clenched her jaw. "Let me speak with Waano."

He scratched his head. "Yes, about that. I don't think he wants to talk to you, poppet."

Her head tilted jerkily to the side and her eyes narrowed. "Well, make him speak to me. Order him to do so."

Did the twit not hear a single word he'd said? "As I said, I have no control of him. If I could, I would not be nearly as upset with you as I am for putting him in there."

She whipped around and paced away again.

He knew she didn't like what she was hearing, but there was nothing for it. As he watched her, some lingering sense of affection for her had him throwing her a bone.

"Besides, I don't think your demons are planning to rise up against you. I think they have a wholly different agenda."

She was back in front of him in the space of a heartbeat. "What do you mean by that?"

He put his hands in his pockets and shrugged. "I spoke with some of them when I awoke overseas. I assume I ended up there because Waano woke up in this body he'd never wanted, and when he discovered what you'd done, he took off on you?" He didn't wait for confirmation. "I honestly have no idea what it is they are up to, but I *can* tell you that your name was not brought up once, other than to threaten to bring me back to you. I imagine so that you would be distracted with me and would stay out of their business."

She looked away, and he could practically see the smoke coming out of her ears as she tried to figure out what her little pets were up to.

"Leeha, take this demon out of me."

She ignored him.

You'll need to be more convincing than that, vampire.

He took her hand, the gentle touch finally gaining her attention. He knew from experience with this one that you definitely got more flies with honey.

"Take him out of me. He's unclean, uncooperative, and honestly he's just horridly rude. His lack of manners is taking a real toll on my delicate British sensibilities."

Sadly, she smiled at him. "If what you say about him being uncontrollable is true, I would release you from him if I could, my love. But alas, it is not possible."

The demon growled with displeasure inside of him.

"What do you mean it's not possible? You put him in there, just take him out again." He smiled encouragingly.

"I was told the magic to bring out the demons quite accidentally, but that's all. I'm sorry, but taking them out again was never an option. His soul is tied to your body, forever, even if the physical you is naught but ashes in the wind. There is no escape for him now."

Aiden stared into the nightmare of her eyes and knew she was telling him the truth.

That's impossible. She cannot hold me here if there is no life in this body.

Aiden's heart froze in his chest.

Whoa, whoa, whoa. Just hold on a minute, mate! Let's not do anything rash!

I will not be a prisoner to this stupid woman!

The demon's filth roiled around inside of him angrily, his wrath filling every cell of his being.

Aiden began to shake, fear and frustration freezing him where he stood. He could do nothing to stop it as the demon took over inside of him.

Leeha leaned forward and stared hard at his eyes. Her head twitched to the side as a self-satisfied smile turned up the corners of her red lips. "I see you in there, Waano. Come out, come out, wherever you are...." she sang.

The demon snarled back at her.

So, this was it then.

This is how I am going to die.

He wondered if Grace would mourn him.

38

Nikulas and Luukas had left early with the help of the wolves, worried that if they waited until nightfall, they would arrive too late to help Aiden. Traveling in a blacked-out van, they'd slept in the back while Cedric, Marc and Lucian had watched over them. Duncan drove, getting them as far into the mountains as the vehicle would take them. As soon as the sun dipped below the horizon, they'd set out on foot.

When they arrived at the clearing, they stayed concealed, and came up along the side of the two people standing at the center. The sight before them played out like a scene from their worst nightmare.

Nikulas heard Aiden taunting Leeha, "You're bloody insane! Who in their right mind would choose to be with you? Who would want your maker's leavings?"

"Oh, yes," he continued when she drew back in horror. "I know exactly how you whored yourself out to him. Tell me, love. Did his touch excite you? Were you jealous when he brought the human girls up to your room? Feeding from them? Fucking them right in front of you?"

"Shut up!" she screamed at him.

"No wonder everyone rejects you. You're nothing, Leeha. Nothing but a lowly, jealous whore trying desperately to be a queen. I never wanted you. I only used you to find out what I needed to know. Everyone can see through you. Everyone knows what you *really* are."

Out of nowhere, her arm rose, the knife in her hand flashing in the moonlight. She brought it down in a wide arc, neatly slicing Aiden's throat.

He smiled as blood spurted from his neck to soil the front of her gown.

With a scream, she swung her arm back and sliced him again.

His head tilted precariously off to the side as he dropped to his knees.

"NOOOOOOO!!" Nikulas roared. Without a thought for his own safety he charged out into the clearing.

"Guards!" Leeha called shrilly when she saw him coming.

Nik arrived at his best friend's side and fell down beside him. He heard Luukas let loose a war cry, and looked up to see him in close hand to hand combat with Josiah, both of them completely vamped out. The look on his brother's face plainly spoke of the history between the two of them.

He looked past them. The disgusting creatures Josiah had brought out, the decaying monsters that had almost killed his Emma, were heading straight towards him. They hissed loudly through mouths filled with razor-sharp fangs and dripping with bloody saliva. Their emaciated arms hung past their knees, yellow claws nearly scraping the ground as they clambered towards the intruders, their uncovered organs swinging obscenely.

Howls filled the air as the wolves transitioned from their human forms. Before the creatures could reach Nikulas and Aiden, the wolves were there. Their powerful jaws ripped off pieces of the things, flinging blood and gore every which way as they delightfully tore them apart.

He caught Leeha's eyes as she stood motionless, looking down at what she'd done. Tears ran down her porcelain cheeks.

While the battle raged around him, Nikulas looked down at the knife in her hand. It was silver. His fangs shot down and he threw his head back, bellowing with a rage that shook him to his core.

Pain lanced through him and he turned his back to her, uncaring of what she may do. He waited to feel the cold blade come down against the back of his neck as he hovered over his friend, desperately searching for a sign of life.

But it never came, so he ignored her.

"Aiden?" he said. "Aid? You can't do this to me, man. You can't leave me. Come on!" he yelled when he didn't respond.

Aiden lay on the grass in a puddle of his own blood. He eyes staring off into the distance.

Nikulas growled deep in his throat and turned towards the one who had done this. Fangs flashing, his eyes glowing nearly white in his grief and anger, he attacked.

Leeha saw him coming and slashed out with her knife, catching him across the abdomen.

He ignored the burning pain, wrapping his hands around her throat as he tackled her to the ground.

She choked with rage and stabbed at him crazily, catching him in the arm and shoulder, the silver weakening the muscles until that arm was nearly useless.

One thrust caught him in the side of the neck, and he loosened his hands in surprise just for a second, but it was enough for her to turn the tables.

With a surge of strength and speed, she flipped them both over until she was on top. Before Nik knew what was happening, she drew back her knife. His eyes widened, Emma's ethereal face appearing before him as he watched it descend towards the middle his chest.

But instead of feeling the blade sink into his heart, he only felt a brush of fur as Lucian caught her around the throat with his teeth, knocking her off of Nikulas. He shook her violently in his powerful jaws, her own blood joining Aiden's to soak her gown, her arms hanging useless at her sides. The knife fell from her hand to lie in the grass as her head went flying through the air. It landed with a thud next to where Josiah and Luukas were still fighting.

Josiah blocked a punch from Luukas and glanced over at the thing, his eyes growing wide when he realized whose head was now lying at his feet. He bellowed with grief and struck at Luukas with a strength belying his age as a vampire.

At the same time, Luukas was attacked from either side by two of the rotting, grey creatures; Leeha's failed attempts at demon possession. With a roar, he turned to his new opponents, sending them flying away from him with a wave of his hand. He turned back to Josiah to continue their fight, but it was too late. He was gone.

Nik rolled over in the grass and crawled back over to Aiden, protecting his friend's body from the creatures battling around him. Whenever anyone came too close, friend or foe, he shoved them away and back out into the fight.

Aiden blinked up at him, and tried to speak through the blood filling his mouth.

Nik leaned closer. "It's all right, man." He gave him a pathetic attempt of his normal cocky grin. "Don't try to talk. We'll get you out of here."

Squeezing his eyes closed hard, Aiden opened them again and tried to speak anyway, but only a cough came out.

Again, Nik saw his mouth moving. He frowned, but leaned down to listen.

"Wasn't me..." Aiden gasped out. "It...wanted her to...kill me."

Understanding dawned across Nik's face. "That thing inside of you was goading her until she cut you? But, it sounded just like you..."

Aiden's eyes widened, begging Nikulas to get the warning.

Oh, shit. That thing was imitating Aiden. "Okay. I hear ya, man," he assured him. "We'll get you through this, and we'll be careful." It was a lie. Aiden wasn't going to come through this. The wound was made with silver. It wasn't going to heal.

Now that Josiah was gone, Luukas stalked through the clearing. He sent what remained of Leeha's creatures flying through the air with nothing but a look as he made his way over to his brother.

Squatting down next to him, his lips pulled back from his fangs as he surveyed the damage Leeha had done. "Oh fuck."

Nikulas bit back a sob and felt his brother's hand on his shoulder. He knew what it was costing his brother to be so close to the thing that was inside of Aiden, but the scene became surreal to him. He and Luukas kneeling next to Aiden while he lay dying on the battlefield. Only this time, Luukas' blood wouldn't save him.

Cedric was suddenly beside him, naked, dirty, and covered in blood. "Aiden, lad?" He looked up at Nikulas and Luukas in disbelief.

"Silver?" he asked.

Luukas pointed with his chin towards the knife lying in the grass near them.

Cedric threw his head back and howled with rage.

Around them, the other three wolves finished off the last of their creatures and turned toward the group huddled on the ground. Their howls joined their leader's, ringing sad and eerie through the trees.

39

A howl rang hauntingly through the trees, causing chills to run down her spine as Grace jogged alongside Keira and Emma. A feeling of foreboding overcame her as more howls followed, just as full of pain as the first.

The sisters exchanged a worried glance with Grace and picked up their pace.

Not the best at obeying orders, the girls had left shortly after the guys, borrowing one of Luukas' cars.

Emma had overheard Nik telling the wolves where to go, and had had the foresight to write down the directions. Once they'd found their abandoned vehicle, the two mated witches had followed their instincts as to which way to go, hoping that they weren't leading them astray. Turns out they didn't need to guess.

Following the sound of the grieving wolves, the three girls burst into the clearing.

Grace immediately zeroed in on the group huddled around someone on the ground. A quick glance around proved her worst fear was correct.

All were accounted for except for Aiden.

"No," she breathed. "No!" she yelled, louder this time.

Running up to the group, she heaved the huge males away from the body lying on the ground with a strength she didn't know she possessed.

Nik growled at her and tried to go back to his position beside his friend, but Emma wrapped her arms around him and he turned to her automatically. Tears were running down her face and she covered her mouth on a sob as she turned to look back at Aiden lying lifeless on the ground.

Grace collapsed beside him, staring at Aiden in disbelief. Two large slash wounds, like from a knife, wrapped around his throat. His head lay in a pool of blood. Her body felt numb as she picked up his hand and held it in hers.

He squeezed it weakly.

With wild eyes, she searched for Luukas. "You're a Master vampire, right? You can help him. Why aren't you helping him?" She sounded hysterical, even to her own ears, but she couldn't help it. "Help him!" she screamed when he just stood there.

But he just ground his jaws together and shook his head. "I'm sorry, I cannot. The knife was silver. It's beyond my powers."

Gradually, what she was seeing in front of her began to penetrate through the protective shield her mind had thrown up to protect her. Pain cracked through the center of her chest, knocking the breath from her. A keening cry rose from the center, gradually gaining volume, until it was a scream of grief and pain.

One of the wolves crept up to her and Aiden, its head lowered in deference.

She saw it advancing out of the corner of her eye and her head whipped around. An animalistic growl rose from her and without thinking, she crawled over Aiden's body to protect him from this new threat.

The wolf backed off, whining, and eyed her with a new respect.

Tears fell to drip onto Aiden's face as she bent over him to kiss his face. Her heart was ripping in two, and she'd never felt so powerless.

Lowering her weight down, she laid her head on his chest and listened to his weak heartbeat. Fresh tears filled her eyes as she stared through the grass. She could picture his heart muscle moving inside of his chest as the blood pumped through it. Could picture the blood moving through his veins and arteries to nourish his cells.

She could picture his body healed.

Grace sat up, straddling his body. He blinked up at her, and she tried to give him an encouraging smile.

Placing her hands over his wound, she closed her eyes, drawing on the powers within her. She could heal herself, and he was meant to be a part of her. Somehow, she would heal him too.

The others watched as the wind whipped around them, blowing pine needles from the trees to lash at their skin. Grace's magic shimmered around her in the night, giving her an almost ghostly appearance.

She vaguely heard Nikulas' gasp of hope as the wolves whined and backed away.

Concentrating with everything she had, she let the warmth within her flow through her body. It took her a moment, but eventually she felt it converge into one solid mass, and she pushed it down to her hands.

Now to get it to leave her and go into him.

She began to imagine his body healing itself, and the more she imagined it, the clearer it became until she could feel her power reaching out towards him. Although she'd never had to heal such a severe injury on herself, with her medical background she could picture the interior of his body perfectly.

Her fingers ran along the cut on his throat, and everywhere they touched she willed his bones to fuse back together, his arteries and tendons to reattach. When she felt the blood start to flow, a surge of excitement went through her, but she tamped it down. She couldn't risk losing her focus now.

She reattached the muscle, and then moved on to his nerves.

He flinched beneath her as the nerves took hold, bringing feeling back. His airway was next, his esophagus, his voice...

The skin under her fingertips began to close and heal.

"Holy shit," Emma breathed.

Luukas bent down cautiously beside her, his eyes lit with amazement. He watched with Grace as Aiden drew a shallow breath. "Amazing..." His voice was filled with awe.

The wolves crept closer again and they all waited as Aiden fought to breathe.

Grace raised panic filled eyes to Luukas as she fought not to pass out. The effort of using her magic to such an extent had her seeing spots.

"Can you help him now?" she asked weakly.

He looked from her to Aiden, his upper lip twitching with disdain.

Nikulas grabbed his arm and turned him to face him. "Brother, please. It's *Aiden*, man. It's Aiden! Not that thing inside of him. *Aiden* is still there."

Luukas shook his brother off. Taking a deep breath, he raised his arm and sank his fangs into his wrist, opening a wound. When the blood was flowing freely, he pressed it to Aiden's mouth, pausing only for a moment.

She watched with bated breath as the blood flowed from his wrist into Aiden's mouth.

Why wasn't he swallowing?

Luukas pressed his wrist harder to his lips, and Nik inched closer. "Come on, you pain in the ass Brit. Drink."

"Try to help him work it down," Luukas told her, and she moved her fingers where they still rested, massaging his throat. After what seemed an eternity, Aiden swallowed, and a loud sob of relief escaped her.

Reopening his wound, Luukas again pressed his wrist to his mouth, and this time, Aiden swallowed on his own.

Grace removed her hands and laid them flat on his chest as she watched him drink. Her heart thumped so loud in her chest she was sure that everyone could hear it. Even Emma and Keira.

When he moaned and his beautiful grey eyes flickered open, Grace began to cry all over again.

He watched her as he drank a few last swallows, lifting a hand to wipe away her tears. Pushing Luukas' arm away, he tilted his head back, his fangs bared as he inhaled the night air deeply and fully.

In a flash, he sat up. Wrapping his arms around Grace, he flipped her over, protecting her head from the ground with his hands.

She wrapped her legs around him as he settled his hips between her thighs and hugged him as tight as her meager strength would allow.

"Hallo, love," he mumbled in her ear. "Did you miss me?"

Crying through her laughter, she held him close until Nikulas pulled them both to their feet to give them his own bear hug. Wiggling her way out from between the middle of them, Grace stumbled away, still unable to believe what she had done. One of the wolves slid up beside her, still in wolf form, and offered his back to lean on.

For the first time, she realized they weren't all still changed. One of the wolves was human again, and stark naked. She averted her eyes as he kissed Aiden soundly, and then trotted off to get his clothes from the shelter of the trees.

"Alright, alright," Aiden laughed as they all surrounded him. Wiping his mouth off with his sleeve, he searched for and found her, and his eyes immediately filled with concern. But then he noticed for the first time that she was leaning against a wolf. He scowled and was suddenly in front of her. With a hiss at the wolf, he lifted her into his arms.

"Sod off, Duncan," he grumbled to the wolf, gathering her close. "What's wrong with you, poppet? Why do you need a wolf to hold you up?"

Tired as she was, her eyes lit up with the amazement she was feeling. "I healed you," she told him. "I did it, Aiden. I healed you!"

He arched a brow. "Well, no wonder you look so bloody knackered. Let's go home, love. Yes?"

"Yes," she agreed.

Not waiting for the others, he turned on his heel and carried her back to the waiting vehicles. But they caught up soon enough.

"You brought the BMW?" Luukas accused Keira. "My favorite car?"

She frowned up at him. "I disobeyed your direct order and all you're worried about is which car I stole?"

He narrowed his eyes at her. "No, witch. That's not all I'm worried about. However, we'll have that discussion when we get Aiden and Grace home."

She noticed Grace watching her worriedly and smiled reassuringly. "He's gonna tie me to the bed again."

Looking at the handsome Master vampire, and how he gazed at his mate adoringly even as he scolded her, Grace thought she could understand why Keira didn't seem overly concerned.

Aiden climbed into the back of the van, still holding her. Nik and Emma and the wolves piled in around them as Luukas and Keira got into the BMW.

Exhausted, she snuggled down into his arms for the ride home.

40

Grace had slept in his arms all the way back to Seattle. Unwilling to wake her, he'd laid her in his bed and left her to sleep while he took a shower.

When he headed out to the kitchen in his pajama pants to find some food for when she woke up, he found Nikulas pacing outside the door like a concerned mother hen.

"Nikulas, how long is this going to last?"

"What?" Nik asked innocently as he followed him to the kitchen.

"This hovering."

Nik shrugged and with all seriousness told him, "Couldn't tell ya. A week? A month? I dunno."

"Well, I suggest you clear off and go busy yourself with Emma or something, for when Grace wakes up, I fully intend on making her mine. In every way, shape and form, if she'll have me."

"No shit?" Nik asked with a wide grin.

"Yes, no shit," Aiden repeated. He eyed up Nik's bloody shirt. "And do go clean yourself up, mate."

Nik looked down at himself. "Yeah, I kind of lost it when I saw that bitch go after you with that knife. She got me a few times before Lucian ripped off her head."

"Ah, so it was Lucian." Something strange was going on with that wolf. There being no love lost between him and Aiden, or him and Nikulas for that matter, he highly doubted it was loyalty to them that made him jump at the chance to kill Leeha.

Nikulas nodded at Aiden's unspoken thoughts. "I know, something's up with him." He lifted up his shirt with his uninjured arm. "But look, man! Matching scars!"

Sure enough, Nikulas had a diagonal wound across his gut nearly identical to Aiden's scar.

"I can't believe you copied me," he said.

Nik laughed out loud. "Yeah. Cuz I aimed my stomach at the silver knife just so I could be like you."

"I wouldn't put it past you, mate. You know you've always been jealous of me."

Nikulas laughed again, and to his surprise, engulfed him in another hug.

"Stop, stop. Really, Nik. What is it with you and the hugging?"

Nik gave him one more good squeeze and then released him with a smile. "Goodnight, man. I'll talk to you...whenever you're done in there."

"Night, mate."

Aiden watched Nik stumble off to his room before he smiled, his heart filled with affection for his friend.

Even if he was nothing but a bloody Estonian bastard.

But that was neither here nor there. Right now he had other things on his mind.

Gathering up his bounty of orange juice, grapes, crackers, and cheese, he sauntered back to his bedroom. Closing the door behind him, he had a moment of panic when Grace wasn't in the bed, but a moment later, she came out of the loo.

"Hey, poppet," he said softly as his eyes roamed over her.

"Hey," she answered rather timidly.

"Are you hungry?" he asked. "I brought you some snacks."

She shook her head, and he frowned. "Poppet, you really need to eat something."

"Aiden?"

He looked at her standing in the soft light across the room from him. She was wearing nothing but the large T-shirt she'd had on earlier, as he'd removed her pants when he'd put her to bed. Her long, shapely legs were smooth and strong, and her breasts pushed against the material. "Yes, love?"

"Am I dreaming? Are you really here?"

He was across the room in a heartbeat. Cradling her face in his hands, he kissed her softly. "Does that feel like you're dreaming?"

Her green eyes smiled into his. "No."

Running his hands through her gorgeous, auburn hair and down her back, he breathed in her luscious scent as she touched the scar on his neck with her fingertips.

"Thank you for saving me, love."

She shook her head in wonder. "I can't believe I did that. I still don't know how I managed it."

"Well, you'll have to pay more attention next time," he teased.

That steel rod slammed into her back. "You'd better not ever give me need to do that again." Her lip began to tremble. "When I saw you lying there, with your *head* nearly cut off..."

"Hey, now. None of that. I'm fine, thanks to you." He tilted his head down until he caught her eyes. "I do have something of great importance to ask you, however."

She sniffed delicately. "What?"

He couldn't believe how nervous he felt, like a young bloke about to have his first shag. "Have you thought at all about what we discussed before you kicked me out of my own room? And before Leeha so rudely pulled me away?"

Stepping back out of his arms, she said, "Yeah. I've thought about it." She cleared her throat. "See, the thing is, it wouldn't just be you I'd be agreeing to be with. You've got a demon inside of you, Aiden."

His heart plummeted in his chest. Was she truly going to refuse him? Whatever would he do?

"And you know," She looked up at him from under her lashes. "I *have* had some better offers from guys I was with before I met you."

"From whom?" he snarled. The idea of her with anyone else was unthinkable.

"Well, there was Gary, the marketing guy. He wanted me to quit my job and travel with him."

"I'll kill him!"

"And then there was Jim, the guy who's clothes you borrowed..."

"I'll kill him also! And burn his clothes!"

She laughed. "What are you gonna do? Time travel into the past and kill anyone I've ever been with?"

"Quite possibly, yes!"

"Go for it, dude."

"Stop calling me 'dude'!"

"Stop calling me 'poppet'!"

He cocked his head at her, his jealousy forgotten. "What's wrong with 'poppet'? It's a term of endearment."

She crossed her arms in front of her. "It's a term of endearment you use for every female you see."

Distracted as he was by the sight of her lovely breasts spilling over her arms, it took him a moment to notice the note of possessiveness in her tone. He closed the distance between them again, wanting to ease her insecurities. "Grace, love. *You* are the only female I see."

"Do you mean that?"

"I do. With every fiber of my being. Please, love, say you'll be mine. For I fear it's entirely too late for me. I can't possibly live without you now."

"What about Mojo?"

"The boot brush?"

She smacked him in the arm, and he laughed. "I let him snuggle," He wrinkled his nose. "And other things...in my hood, did I not? All the way from China to Seattle, might I add."

"Yes, you did," she laughed. She touched his face, her eyes glowing with warmth. "All right."

He scarce dared to believe it. "All right?"

"Yes. Make me yours. I want to be with you. Only with you."

A low growl vibrated through his chest as his body hardened at her words. "I'll do my very best."

Scooping her up into his arms, he carried her to the bed. Laying her down gently, he crawled up alongside her and gazed down at her stunning face. He feared his eyes were already glowing as they wandered down her body and back up again. His blood rushed through him in anticipation.

"Ah, Grace, love. I'm afraid I won't be able to go slowly."

"Good," she answered, reaching up for him.

He groaned as she pulled his mouth down to hers and kissed her passionately, thrusting his tongue into her mouth, then biting her bottom lip. Small beads of blood gathered there, and he licked them off.

Even that measly taste of her slammed into him like a freight train.

MINE.

Waano stirred inside of him briefly at the surge of emotion, but then settled back down again. Perhaps he sensed there was no threat to his host?

Pushing the demon from his mind, he slid his hand under her shirt and up the warm skin of her side and cupped her breast. It overflowed his hand as he kneaded it, then pinched her nipple.

She arched her back with a cry, and pulling his hand out, he ripped that bloody shirt right down the middle.

Her hands were hot on his skin as he lowered his mouth to her and made his way down her body, nibbling on her skin as she writhed beneath him, careful not to break the skin. When he got to her breasts, he gazed at them in awe, never having seen such perfection in all of his long life.

"Aiden, please..."

Her hands moved to the back of his head and she pulled him down to her breast.

Greedy female.

With his tongue, he flicked her nipple, laving around it, and sucking it into his mouth. Moving to the other side, he pulled the hard bud into his mouth, and nipped it with his teeth.

She bucked beneath him with a cry, her hands gripping his short hair.

The scent of her desire wafted in the air around him, and he groaned aloud. Nipping and licking his way down her stomach, he moved between her legs, spreading her thighs wide with his hands. She opened in front of him, pink petals glistening with moisture.

His mouth watered at the sight of her. Sliding his arms under her legs, he gripped her hips to hold her still.

She whimpered when she realized what he was about, and as he watched, she became wetter still.

He pulled his lips back from his fangs with a hiss, pushing his hips into the bed in response. Closing his eyes a moment, he gathered some control, and lowered his mouth to her. She tasted sweeter than he ever could have imagined, like honeyed wine. His tongue ran up her cleft, finding the little bundle of nerves that was the center of her pleasure.

Flicking her with his tongue, he reveled in her cries and moans. Pulling one arm out, he pressed a hand to her lower belly, holding her down as he tasted her, thrusting his tongue in her opening, then sliding back up to tease her clit.

When he felt her body tensing, he moaned, and his tongue worked its magic until she was repeating his name over and over again. Pulling his other arm out, he slid two fingers inside of her.

Her body began to move in time to his thrusts as he worked her higher and higher until she came hard and loud, her body wetting his fingers even more.

With an animalistic growl, he surged up her body, and buried himself to the hilt with one thrust. He gave her no time to recover, but started moving inside of her, the feel of her wrapped so tightly around him making him shudder.

She wrapped her legs and arms around him as he thrust within her. His gums burned and his throat ached. The urge to sink his fangs in her nearly overwhelming, but he didn't want to frighten her, and his need for her was such that he was afraid he would be too rough.

However, he couldn't keep from expressing his need to her. "I want to taste you, Grace, so very badly." He kissed her hard, absorbing her cries of pleasure as he pulled out slowly and then pushed himself back inside of her. She was so tight, so wet...

With a growl, he did it again, and again, until she was digging her nails into his back. Breaking off the kiss, he moved his lips down her jaw to her throat. He could feel the blood pulsing beneath her skin.

She tilted her head away and dug her nails into his back. "Do it," she breathed. "Ah, gods, Aiden...do it. Please."

Tightening his arms around her to hold her still, he reared back and struck, his fangs sliding through her skin effortlessly. He roared as her blood gushed into his mouth, the taste of her like nothing he'd ever had before.

MINE.

The word pulsed through him, confirming what he had always known, and he delighted in it. A sense of rightness spread through him as he lost himself in the taste and feel of her.

Grace cried out as he pulled on her vein, increasing his thrusts again at the same time. He felt her blood quicken with her rising excitement, racing through her and into him, and he fought to control how much he took from her: Careful of her even in the throes of his lust.

Aiden's entire body began to shake as he tried to hold back his orgasm, but when she began to cry out incoherently and convulse in his arms, he couldn't wait any longer. With one last draw of her sweet blood, he slammed into her over and over until he exploded inside of her.

Withdrawing his fangs, he threw his head back. The tendons strained in his neck as he roared with pleasure and the domination of his mate.

When he could think again, he licked her wound closed and rolled off of her, gathering her up in his arms.

"No demon?" she asked breathlessly.

"No demon," he confirmed. "Just me, love."

As he rubbed her soft skin and their pulses returned to normal, he said, "When you feel up to doing so, you can drink from me."

She looked up at him hungrily with those large, lovely eyes. "I want it now."

He narrowed his eyes at her, then lifted his wrist to his mouth.

She took his arm in her hands and put it to her mouth, sucking hard. Her eyes rolled back in her head at her first taste of his life-giving blood.

His cock twitched and hardened with every pull of her mouth. A low growl of pleasure rumbled in his throat.

Bloody greedy female.

If putting up with a spitting boot brush was the price he had to pay to have *this*, then so be it.

The Series Continues with
A Vampire Betrayed.
Keep reading for a sneak peek!

CHAPTER ONE

He was dying. Literally.

Christian slammed his sweaty palm against the glass wall in front of him as his bloodshot eyes watched the woman on the other side. His silver cuff bracelet clanked against it so hard, the turquoise stones should have left chips in the glass. But they didn't, because this was no ordinary glass. It was some type of indestructible, vampire-proof glass.

Through eyes that burned with lust and sweat, he watched her: The woman who had been both his sweetest fantasy and his worst nightmare for as long as he could remember now. The girl with skin so pale and translucent he could see the delicate blue veins just underneath where her life's blood flowed. The girl with eyes just slightly darker in color than the ancient stones on his wrist. The girl whose full, up-tipped breasts made his mouth water to taste them and his hips rock to and fro uncontrollably, like a dog near a bitch in heat. The girl with the hair that had stolen all of the colors of the fiery sunset he missed so much.

CHAPTER ONE

He shoved his other hand down the front of his jeans, gripping himself tight at the head and then sliding up and down the swollen girth with short, hard pumps. The hypnotic beat of "Closer" by Nine Inch Nails thumped throughout the room, and his blood pulsed heavier through his veins with every beat. His fangs were bared on a hiss and his gut ached with a razor sharp hunger he had yet to experience in all of his long years — until now. But he knew it was his eyes that would surely give him away for what he truly was. From the feel of them, they would be glowing bright and eerie from under his heavy brows, the color a vivid topaz, as he tracked every move she made with an intensity that human men did not possess. Yet he couldn't bring himself to *not* watch her.

Besides, she never looked at him when she was dancing.

She was alone in the empty room of the club on the other side of the glass, her back up against a single silver pole that ran from floor to ceiling. Facing him, she writhed against that cold metal that she could work like nobody's business. But she wasn't dancing anymore. She'd stopped dancing a while ago.

Instead, one of her dainty hands was shoved up under her short, gold skirt, and although he couldn't see it, he knew that she was touching herself. Something she'd never done before; at least not for him. Her other hand was on her bare breast, manipulating the soft flesh and then pinching the dusky nipple. Her skimpy top had long since been removed as part of her striptease.

As the end of the song rose to a throbbing crescendo, she threw her head back and cried out, her body convulsing as

CHAPTER ONE

she made herself come while he watched. Her face contorted into an erotic mien, lost somewhere between pleasure and pain and made all the more beautiful for it.

He cried out with her, his forehead smashing into the glass as his body jacked towards her instinctively. But even though he was hard as a fucking rock and rubbing himself raw, he couldn't get off. And he knew he wouldn't be able to, not until he was inside of a woman's tight sheath, whether it be hers or another's.

She wobbled in her stiletto heels as her legs gave out and she slid down the stripper pole to sit on the floor. His hand was still fisted around his cock, and he squeezed it way too hard as he collapsed to his knees, wishing he could just rip the fucking thing off. But honestly he barely felt the pain he was causing himself. He couldn't feel anything over the burn of his screaming muscles as they cramped and twisted around the acid in his veins.

He lifted his head at the same time that she lifted hers, and they stared at each other through the glass for the first time. Her sapphire blue eyes were large in her pale face; the purplish circles underneath making them appear even brighter than normal. As she stared at him, a single fat tear slid down her flawless cheek, and he pressed his forehead to the glass again as he watched it fall.

He wanted to go to her. He wanted to gently wipe that tear from her delicate face. Then he wanted to rip that flimsy excuse of a skirt off of her and bury his aching cock in her warmth as he sank his fangs deep into that slender throat. He groaned aloud at the thought of feeding from her while he fucked her senseless. He swore he could almost taste her

CHAPTER ONE

from behind the glass. But he couldn't do any of those things, because he was trapped in this goddamned, vampire-proof viewing box with his jeans hanging open and his cock jutting out of his hand like some kind of animal.

Gritting his teeth against the pain that scorched through his body like hot acid, he slapped his palm against the glass. "Help me!" he snarled.

She blinked once, slowly, her eyelids appearing heavy. Lifting her hand from beneath her skirt, she stared at it for a moment with a frown marring her pretty features before it dropped onto her lap, like she didn't understand what it had just been doing.

Christian folded forward as the fire in his blood surged across his abdomen and down into his balls. Releasing his throbbing cock with a hiss of pain, his other hand joined the first to pound on the glass. "Open this fucking thing!"

Her bemused gaze wandered to the side, and then drifted over the entire wall of glass, as if she were searching for something but didn't quite know what it was. She closed her eyes again for so long that he began to wonder if she'd fallen asleep, but then she seemed to rouse, and slowly pushed herself to her feet. She teetered unsteadily for a moment in her ridiculous shoes. Gathering up her top that she'd taken off during her dance, she stumbled across the room and out the door in the back. The music shut off as soon as the door closed behind her.

She couldn't see him, he realized. She couldn't fucking see him.

CHAPTER ONE

Rearing back, he threw his head forward and smashed it into the glass wall so hard it should've shattered. But it only formed an outline of the shape of his head, and then snapped back into its former shape as soon as he pulled away.

"AHHHHHH!!!" He screamed until his voice gave out.

Collapsing onto his side, he curled up into a ball with his arms wrapped around his middle to ride out the pain. It would subside after a bit, enough so he could move about freely, though it never completely went away. And he knew that it wouldn't until his body had what it craved.

He needed blood. And he needed sex. Physically needed it. Thanks to whatever the hell had happened to him after his creator, Luukas, had been taken. Before he'd been swiped up off the street near his home in Seattle and locked in this hellhole, he'd been going through six to eight females a night — every night — for the past seven *years*. He'd fuck them, feed from them, and then send them home to their families. Safe and sound. And he'd discovered real quick that if he tried to change up that routine, he suffered the consequences. The urges would become more and more intense until he was a danger to anyone around him. Thank the gods Seattle was a large city with a rising population and had plenty of human females. And that vampires were immune to STD's.

And now, if he wasn't mistaken, he'd been locked in this place for weeks. Long enough that it wasn't only his body that was suffering. He was beginning to feel like he was losing his mind, losing what was left of his humanity, and turning into the mindless creature that the horror movies always depicted those like him to be.

CHAPTER ONE

Of course it was all because he'd lowered his guard and gotten himself captured because he was too busy thinking about his dick, rather than what he should've been doing.

Keeping to his usual nightly routine, he'd left his apartment building to hook up with a new girl at a nearby strip club instead of helping Dante and Shea prepare for Luukas' rescue mission. He and the other Hunters were supposed to join Nikulas and Aiden across the Canadian border. They'd only just discovered that the psycho who had taken their leader had returned to the area with Luukas in tow.

He'd let down his friends who'd been depending on him. And worse, he'd failed his creator. The male that had taken him under his wing and taught him what it was to be a male worthy of calling himself such.

He wasn't worthy of anything or anyone these days.

Christian groaned and flopped over onto his back, the pain in his body overriding everything else as it always did. God help the first female he came across when he finally got the fuck out of here. And he *would* get out of here, somehow. He only hoped the first woman he came across wasn't his dancing girl with the fiery hair, because the odds of her surviving that encounter were pretty much shit. At the thought of hurting her, a sharp, stabbing pain pierced through his heart and added to his agony.

He wouldn't mean to hurt her. He wouldn't. But in the state he was in, he didn't think he'd be able to avoid it.

And didn't that just suck balls.

Read **A Vampire Betrayed**

CHAPTER ONE

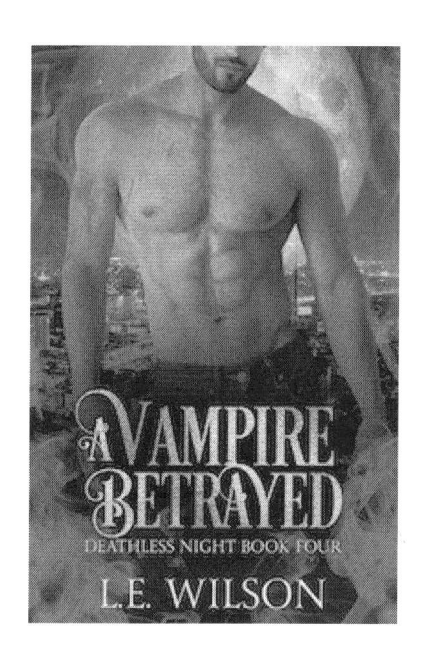

ABOUT THE AUTHOR

L.E. Wilson writes romance starring intense alpha males and the women who are fearless enough to love them just as they are. In her novels you'll find smoking hot scenes, a touch of suspense, some humor, a bit of gore, and multifaceted characters, all working together to combine her lifelong obsession with the paranormal and her love of romance.

Her writing career came about the usual way: on a dare from her loving husband. Little did she know just one casual suggestion would open a box of worms (or words as the case may be) that would forever change her life.

On a Personal Note:

"I love to hear from my readers! Contact me anytime at le@lewilsonauthor.com."